Mark and Julie,
 You Guys are so
us. Thank you so much for
your support, Prayers and most
of all friendship all these
years! Julie, I'm so Grateful
we Got to share in an
 Indonesian with you those

Java Wake

rich years. Thank you for
enriching our lives. Love and
Deep thanks —

Mike O'Quin Jr.

P.S. Also so grateful for
how your ministry
has impacted Ana!!

Cover design by Hilary Combs
www.HilaryCombsDesign.com

Copyright © 2015 Mike O'Quin Jr.
Mantap Publishing

Library of Congress Control Number: 2015902760
ISBN: 0692350136
ISBN-13: 978-0692350133

For Caleb
fellow adventurer and son of my youth

PART I

WEDNESDAY

CHAPTER ONE

It was the bright orange exclamation point that grabbed Stephen's attention. He was standing at the airport bookstore, head cocked sideways, perusing titles crammed into the tight shelves. The little book screamed out at him, *Fear Not and Live Hot!*, with the colorful intensity of a high school pep rally. He looked both ways and felt slightly guilty sliding the thin book all the way off the shelf, like he was about to pick up a terrorist manual or rifle through a dirty magazine.

After glancing through the chapter titles, he decided that this one would probably do. Placing the book face down on the counter, he tossed a yellow pack of chewing gum on top to further hide the fact that he was buying a self-help book. The bored African-American lady at the register gave him his change without any indication that she cared whether he helped himself or not. Dropping his purchase into his laptop bag, he clipped down the busy corridor toward gate C-23 of the international terminal.

The cross-Pacific flight was grueling and near sleepless, but at the Hong Kong airport he found a comfortable transit lounge where he was able to sprawl out and get a couple of hours of sleep. The final flight was a four-hour leg to Surabaya, Indonesia. Stephen was hoping to get some more rest to battle jet lag, which he imagined would be brutal with a fifteen-hour time difference.

He stuffed his stout, mid-thirties body into the window seat, and soon two more large men took their places in the middle and aisle seats. It was Stephen's bum luck that the larger of the two men took the middle seat. Even worse, soon after takeoff the middle seat man leaned back into a nap position and had the audacity to stretch out one of his legs into Stephen's precious legroom space. Having already lost the subtle tussle over who had control over the shared armrest, Stephen would now have to bear the additional trespassing on another long flight.

From his scrunched position, Stephen eyed his large sleeping seatmate, an outdoors type man. His outfit of dirt-dusted hiking boots and khaki cargo shorts suggested rugged adventure, while Stephen's casual business attire suggested indoor non-adventure. Stephen compared his plumper body and thinner hair with the adventurer's. His own light brown hair was already peppered with grey on the sides and the man's was jet black, accompanied by bushy unkempt sideburns. Drool trickled down the man's stubbly chin and every now and then he would twitch.

A half-hour into the journey, the in-flight entertainment fired up its offerings. Stephen could find nothing worth watching, although the other passengers had settled for any mind-numbing scrap of distraction they could endure. Instead he reached for his new book, hoping to transform his stagnant existence into some sort of *Fear Not and Live Hot* orange exclamation point. He couldn't remember ever in his unexamined life wanting to read a book like this...maybe this was a mid-life crisis a decade too early?

Carefully reaching into the seat pocket to retrieve his book, Stephen accidentally jostled his seatmate's elbow. The man shot up awake and looked around to get his bearings. Stephen apologized softly, "Oh, sorry."

"No worries, mate. Always ready to be woken up," the man said with a heavy Australian accent and without a hint of frustration.

"Oh, well, I, uh, hope it wasn't too soon."

"Never too soon for me. Always prepared, that's my motto."

He now regretted that he had woken up the confident-sounding Aussie. Stephen guessed from his pithy little sayings that the man probably loved to hear himself talk.

"Name's Chopper," the man said as he wrenched his curled arm around and stuck it out for an awkward but firm handshake. He pulled his boot back into his own legroom.

"I'm Stephen. Nice to meet you, Chopper."

2

A long pause hung between the two men as Chopper eyed his new conversation mate. Stephen was silently lamenting that his inner life couldn't just hide away under his reading light, undisturbed, and he felt uncomfortable under the blaze of Chopper's blue eyes. A flight attendant came by offering drinks. Stephen asked for a ginger ale and Chopper ordered a beer.

Finally, Chopper broke the uncomfortable silence. "So why don't we cut through all the bull and tell each other what kind of men we really are?"

"Excuse me?" Stephen caught himself as he was about to take his first sip.

"Well, the way I see it is that blokes are always sizing each other up. We ask what kind of work we do, where we're from and all that, but what we really want to know is whether this is a man I should be intimidated by or that I should intimidate."

Now Stephen really regretted getting the Chopper off the ground. He had no idea how to respond to this bizarre question, and the man's intense eyes kept boring into Stephen, waiting for an answer. So far Chopper was winning the intimidation contest.

As Chopper's leathery face leaned in slightly closer, Stephen could smell the man's strong breath and resented that his own personal space was being further encroached upon. He tried to think of a clever answer as he scooted himself back closer to the oval window.

"If you don't want to respond, mate, that's fine with me," Chopper shrugged. "But I'll say I'm the kind of guy that wants the gusto out of life, you know what I mean?"

"I know what you mean, but that's not the way I really look at life."

"Well, then, Mr. Stephen, mate, how do you really look at life?"

Stephen tried again in vain to think of some retort. He already felt trapped in this window seat, having to defend himself from a corner. Later he knew he would think of a really good comeback zinger in his hotel room, probably in the middle of the night, and he hated that he couldn't just get it now in advance.

3

Luckily for Stephen, an attractive Asian flight attendant came by, holding a large plastic bag. "Rubbish?" she asked with a cheerful British accent.

"Just my thoughts, darling," Chopper mischievously purred. She stared at both men with a professionally plastic face as if she either didn't understand or didn't plan on dignifying the remark. Stephen felt embarrassed and quickly downed the rest of his ginger ale and tossed in the plastic cup.

"Thank you," she said with a nod and a smile and turned to the next row of passengers.

"You didn't answer my question, mate." Chopper's focus was bearing back down on Stephen.

The small child seated behind him suddenly kicked the back of Stephen's seat as if to mock him too. That jolted him into starting to respond, but before he could, Chopper gave him a big disarming smile and said, "That's okay, mate. I'm a little strange. Don't answer that." He laughed a big manly laugh to himself. "I got a weird way of getting conversations started. I guess I've spent too much time in the outback doing adventure tours for guys just like you."

Stephen was starting to feel better now that Chopper was smiling but his last statement carried the aftertaste of a put-down. He knew this outlandish Aussie was challenging him with the "guys just like you" part. If he took the bait, Stephen thought, he would get roped into a defense of his own bland existence versus Chopper's exciting life of adventure. Chopper was a tanned and strong outdoorsman and Stephen looked like a pale American cubicle dweller. *Okay, I get it. You're the big adventure man.* He could understand why Chopper would size him up so quickly and put him in the "people to intimidate" column. *This guy doesn't know the first thing about me. He has never seen me in action.* Stephen only absorbed the backhanded rebuke and redirected the conversation toward more polite ground.

"I take it you are going to Indonesia for business, Chopper?"

"That's one way to look at it, I guess. My business is my pleasure. Always wanted to see a live volcano. I've heard Java's got some beauties. They call these islands 'The Ring of Fire' because of all the active volcanoes. You know, like that Johnny

Cash song." At that, Chopper's voice went two octaves lower and he started singing out, complete with an air karaoke microphone, "I fell into a burning ring of fire..."

Stephen tried to cut him off, especially when he saw the other passengers looking over. "Didn't know that. I take it you have been to Indonesia before."

"You take a lot of things, Stevey," Chopper said. Then he leaned forward a little more, squinted, pointed at Stephen's chest and asked, "But what do you give?"

"Pardon?" Stephen asked, leaning back again closer to the window. He wasn't sure if Chopper was just joking or insulting him.

"You take it that I am going to Indonesia for business. You take it that I have been to Indonesia before. Don't you think that's a lot of taking, mate? Ain't it time to start giving?"

Stephen tensed up, feeling defensive again, yet still couldn't think of any clever barb to fling back.

Chopper flashed a big grin. "Oh, I'm just kidding, mate. I know what you mean. Yeah, I've been to Indonesia but only to the island of Bali. I usually go there to try to drum up a little business from all my countrymen getting sloshed in the bars down there. But there's so much more exploring to be done across these islands. How 'bout you? Where are you heading to on Java?"

Stephen loosened his grip on his armrest and felt himself relaxing. They were now back on safe turf. "I'm heading to Surabaya to do a training presentation for International Courier Services, where I work. We're opening up an office in East Java and I'll be the first one to show the natives there our way."

"Hmm," Chopper said nodding his head slowly up and down. "Sounds interesting."

Stephen was smiling now. "You're not a very good liar, Chopper."

"No, I'm not, Stephen. I'll give you that. But you're okay. You're an honest sort too," he said while flashing an approving smile.

The conversation continued from there, mostly about the Aussie's adventures in life and play, and Stephen did find him a bit fascinating for a time. Chopper was on this flight from

Hong Kong to Surabaya after leading extreme adventure tours for middle-aged European businessmen who were trying to find themselves out in the winter wilderness of Mongolia. They all slept in yurt tents and ate yak fat for exorbitant prices, and Chopper mocked his overweight and high-paying clients. It was all at least more interesting than how new global supply chains were demanding more flexibility, speed and creative services from international couriers. Chopper went on and on, as Stephen had feared, seeming really to enjoy hearing himself talk. The other passenger in the aisle seat, pretending to be absorbed in the in-flight magazine, would crack a slight grin at some of Chopper's more outlandish and braggadocios statements. The aisle seat man never made eye contact with Stephen to help him co-tackle the larger-than-life mercenary of adventure, even though Stephen had tried plenty of times to make eye contact with him.

Finally, after about an hour of the rambling autobiography, Stephen excused himself and did the delicate hop dance over both his seatmates on the way to a lavatory break. As he waited in line, he decided that he had endured enough of Chopper's life story and philosophy. When he got back he would apologize and explain that he really needed to work on his presentation now, which was almost true.

When he got back to his row, Stephen was relieved to see that Chopper was already dozing. He deftly climbed back over the two men, careful not to wake up the sleeping adventurer, and settled back into his seat. Glancing over at the slightly snoring Aussie next to him, Stephen again reflected on their polar opposite differences. Chopper was relishing this trip to Java because he wanted to peer inside active volcanoes. Stephen wouldn't mind seeing live volcanoes, but preferably from a safe distance. Chopper would probably shake off the heat and hustle of a third-world country and easily navigate through unfamiliar cultural waters. Stephen would be based out of a five-star hotel, paid for by his company, and would only venture out to places likely to be visited by other foreigners. Simply put, the Aussie was living hot and Stephen was not. He felt like a wimp in the reflection of Chopper's brazen and bronzed glory. The guy was an orange exclamation point in life. Stephen considered himself as more of a semi-colon—he left people wanting more.

He definitely left Leah wanting more. She had once been attracted to him because he had a certain spark in life, with creative ideas brimming in his busy mind mixed with a good sense of humor to keep her amused over long conversations. Now after more than a decade of marriage, they had drifted from passionate soul mates to cordial roommates. Resignation had crusted over the hope of intimacy long ago. Recently she seemed even to be contemplating a violation of their decade-plus truce, launching threats of leaving him during their more heated arguments. He would counter that she was just being emotional, as if that were a character flaw.

Earlier that morning—or was it yesterday—he had kissed his sleeping wife on the top of her head and whispered that he would miss her. She mumbled a "Goodbye hon" as he silently closed the bedroom door behind him. Walking slowly down the darkened hall, he felt the familiar chill of loneliness. He peeked in the kids' rooms. Randall's pre-adolescent body looked so long and grown up still asleep in his bed, surrounded by muscle-car paraphernalia. He stepped down the hall and cracked open Tristan's door. She was conked out sideways on her princess bed, the covers tangled around her feet. He straightened out her pink bedspread and covered her little seven-year-old body back up. Closing the door quietly behind him, he felt both an intense love for his children and guilt over the lack of true fathering in their little lives. His work kept him busy as the provider, he told himself, but the gnawing on his soul continued unabated. He wasn't doing for them what they really needed deep down—offering an emotional and not just a physical presence. Leah definitely needed so much more. Why had she stayed with him so long?

Besides the ongoing cold war on his home front, a mild depression had been clouding over his mind the last couple of weeks. A funeral was the harbinger. Bill, a by-the-book co-worker, died suddenly of a heart attack, and the new widow asked around for someone to do the eulogy. An awkwardness hung in the office air when no one stepped forward with eagerness. People just didn't know Bill that well, or really at all, outside of work. The unspoken fact was that he didn't have a real friend, someone who would voluntarily want to spend free time with him. Bill showed up for work, kept his head down, and got through his daily to-do's with as little risk and passion as possible. He was more of a person that people were used to having around, like a plastic office plant in the corner that nobody notices until it's gone one day. Stephen finally stepped forward do the eulogy since he had known Bill the longest. As he stood in front of the sparse crowd in the funeral home, trying to apply a bright coat of paint over a drab life, it dawned on him that someday some valiant soul would be giving the same lifeless speech at his own funeral. Stephen's ten-minute speech included words like "dedicated," "dependable," and "always there for you." The polite eulogy was a sad tribute to a life half-lived. *That's me. The world will go on just exactly the same after I'm gone.*

Now armed with *Fear Not and Live Hot!,* all that was going to change. He committed to beating the funk by using this long stretch of travel time for a little emotional tune-up. Introspection wasn't exactly his forte, but he figured it couldn't hurt to take a look under the hood. He checked on Chopper, relieved to see the adventurer still snoring lightly. Stephen could study his little motivational book and not have to withstand the clichéd commentary from a man who was already larger than life. Stephen's life wasn't much compared to Chopper's, but it was his own, and only he could change it.

He placed the book on the tray table and breathed in deeply. First he checked the author's bio. Chaz Wilton had enough academic letters after his name along with life experience to seem to know what he was talking about. On the title page Stephen wrote his own full legal name in all caps, planting his emotional flag down on the rock of soul exploration.

Risk aversion was the subject of chapter one. It came with a self-awareness inventory at the end, asking him to number himself on a scale of one to ten on spectrums such as harmless to daring, and nice to consequential. Stephen finished the exercise and gave himself mostly fours.

The second activity was to create a Personalized Action Plan for how to live with more passion. Chaz insisted that the steps in the plan had to be measurable. You couldn't say, for example, be a better lover, without saying something more concrete, like write your wife a love poem before this Friday.

Stephen spent about ten minutes outlining the broad categories of his Personalized Action Plan first:

Action Items for CHANGE:
1) Do something spontaneous
2) Take a risk
3) Fight a good fight
4) Protect the underdog
5) Love without fear

Under each heading the white space called out to him to take concrete steps. After writing the first draft of his Personalized Action Plan, he pledged to himself that he would never reveal this silly list to Leah. Instead he would show her through a slow, steady march of progress that he could indeed change and that he still cared deeply for her.

When he noticed Chopper was stirring, he stashed the embarrassing little book away in the seat pocket and started looking over his presentation. He still wanted to be left alone with his thoughts and his laptop and insulated from Chopper's oratory. Luckily his friendly adversary looked too groggy for conversation himself.

Finally, the plane started its descent. Stephen resolved to complete the action points from chapter one and at least make it through a few more sections during his trip. But for now this inner-life stuff could wait until after a good sleep at the hotel. His presentation wasn't until the afternoon of the next day so he would have plenty of time.

As Stephen clacked down the staircase to the tarmac, a swirl of heat engulfed his body and a rush of hot wind kicked up from the airplane into his face. He was glad to be wearing an undershirt in this intense tropical sun and wondered why the plane didn't hook up to the jet way he noticed protruding emptily from the terminal.

Following the other passengers into the airport building, a sign informed him in awkward English that he would have to get a "visa on demand" before proceeding to immigration. He lined up at the appropriate booth and paid the Indonesian government $25 for the visa—permission to stay in their country 30 days. Next, a long line to immigration processing awaited him. When it was finally his turn at the brown booth, he unzipped his tri-fold document pouch and handed his passport, driver's license, boarding pass, and the receipt for his visa to the officer. He wasn't sure what the immigration officer really needed and the top of the man's head offered no clue. The officer pushed the unnecessary documents aside, flipped through Stephen's passport and found plenty of blank pages in the back to aim the stamp on. Ch-Clunk. The officer looked up at Stephen for the first time and said politely, "Welcome to Indonesia."

Stephen thanked the man, took his documents back and stuffed everything into his little pouch. He hadn't really wanted the modified fanny pack, thinking he could keep everything in his pockets. But Leah had bought it for him for his first international trip and now he was sort of glad to have it.

Next, the baggage area. The oblong carousel was surrounded by aggressive men in green and orange shirts hustling to carry bags and get tips from the tipping passengers.

"Hello mister," several of them called to him. "You need help with bag?"

Sure, why not. Stephen motioned toward a man with a laminated nametag proclaiming him Suparto. He walked with Stephen to the carousel, fully surrounded by a horde of people shoving ahead to get their bags.

"Where you going, mister?" Suparto asked. He was wearing a green uniform with the word Porlap written across his back and a wide smile across his face.

"Staying at a hotel here in Surabaya." Stephen pronounced the name of the city as best he could.

"Oh, Surabaya. Yes, Surabaya." Suparto responded, probably not knowing what to say next with his few words of English. Plus they were already in Surabaya so there wasn't much more to say. Suparto waited for the bags, pointing to each bag as it went by and asking silently with his eyes if that was Stephen's. He found the Indonesian porter charming, especially the way he enthusiastically picked up Stephen's one large black suitcase.

Suparto led the way through the second security check and

outside to the portico of the airport, where the temperature was once again unbelievably sweltering. Masses of brown-skinned people—sitting, smoking, talking, lining up at outside counters, calling out to each other, talking on their cell phones— overwhelmed his senses. He was glad he had one friend, Suparto, to guide him through the chaos. Stephen let Suparto lead and clear the way with the trolley. He could have carried the bag himself, but it was nice to have a friendly escort to lead him through the churning masses to where Stephen assumed the taxis would be waiting.

His relationship with Suparto was about as deep as his relationship with most people, he thought. Functional. *All my relationships are functional. Okay, okay, Stevey boy, get a hold of yourself. Just get to your hotel, finish going over your presentation, go to the office tomorrow and wow 'em, and then go back to your hotel room tomorrow night. Shake out of this funk for now and then you can open up this can again tomorrow.*

But he couldn't shake it. His life was so utterly functional. *I don't have any real friends. I don't do anything outside the norm. No excess. No risk. No adventure. Nothing spontaneous, living life like a pre-programmed robot.* Even the heat and the smoke of cigarettes and the loud noises of people chattering couldn't drown out his growing despondency. He re-affirmed he would at least do Action Item One while in Indonesia: do something spontaneous. What might that look like here in a tropical metropolis? Maybe he would go find a volcano after all and peer inside. He had enough time here to take at least one excursion. Maybe he would lose himself in a slum for one day and see how poor people really lived. Maybe he would arrange for a guided hike through the jungle.

Glancing through the crowd held back by a metal gate, he saw many men holding signs for their intended passengers. Taxi drivers were also hitting him up with offers to take him to wherever he wanted: Mt. Bromo? Malang? He shooed them away and Suparto kept leading him toward what he hoped would be an official taxi stand.

Man, it's hot here. Negotiating for a ride in broken English didn't sound fun, plus would probably get him ripped off. He envied the business people who strolled off the plane and walked right to waiting drivers.

As he was surveying the scene, with Suparto looking to him for direction, someone bumped him hard from behind. It was so jolting that it knocked Stephen to the ground and made him drop his carry-on bag and travel pouch, spilling the contents on the ground. When he turned around he saw a blur of a duffel bag and winced as he thought the person who collided into him was now going to fall right on top of him. Yet there was no impact. He heard Chopper's burly voice before he saw him. "Sorry, mate." Stephen looked up into his embarrassed and grinning face. "Didn't see you."

Chopper squatted down to help Stephen gather all the papers and tickets and documents that spilled out of his pouch. Then he stood up and stretched out his hand to help Stephen up.

"It's okay, Chopper. I know it was just an accident." Was this obnoxious jerk still trying to intimidate him? Stephen wasn't sure if Chopper did it on purpose, but he didn't have any evidence to make an issue of it. Did Chopper really not see him? *Do people really not see me?*

"So this is where we part ways, Mr. Stephen seatmate. I hope you have a great time doing your presentation or training or whatever."

"And I hope you find a great volcano," Stephen said tersely as he was brushing himself off and still feeling flustered.

Chopper stood there, looking uncharacteristically like he didn't know what to say next. "Have a good one," he finally said with a nod.

"You too," said Stephen. He watched gratefully as Chopper walked out of his life and into a line of waiting taxis.

Story of my life. People just don't see me, and the ones who do intimidate me. That's what the world would say about me when I'm gone: Sorry, I didn't see you. You were never even here. You took up space and breathed air and paid your taxes. Next. Whoa, okay, knock it off. Get to your hotel and shower off the grime of this city and you'll feel better.

But then, he didn't want to feel better. He wanted to keep feeling angry—it almost felt good, like an adrenaline high. As Suparto kept leading him on through the throng, Stephen felt a rush of rage inside. He hated that arrogant Chopper, but even more he hated his own pale persona. This was unlike him, but he wanted to do something quite unlike him. That's it, he thought, he was going to do Action Item One right now, whatever the consequences, and not wait until later. He looked around again at the milling crowd and the taxi drivers all looking for customers. He would do something unrehearsed right here, right now. That push from Chopper had come to shove, and he was going to shove his way into something spontaneous.

A scene from a commercial popped into his head where a guy pretends to be someone else to get picked up in a nice limo. That's it. He could at least do that. He felt that he might regret this, but for once he wasn't going to submit to his fears. Maybe one day this would be a funny story, but he refused to analyze himself and continued to march forward toward adventurous spontaneity. This was his orange exclamation point of no return. Right here. Right now.

He tapped on Suparto's back and led him back toward the drivers waiting for their riders. This time Suparto followed him, and seemed embarrassed that he led him this far away from his destination. *"Maaf mister,"* he said a few times. *"Maaf ya?"*

Yeah, yeah, follow me, Suparto. Stephen walked back toward the men holding the placards with names of passengers. One driver nicely dressed with a traditional Indonesian silk shirt was holding a sign with the name "Mr. Carlton Easley" printed boldly on it. Stephen nodded to the driver and said to him confidently, "Hello. I'm Carlton Easley."

CHAPTER TWO

Mustafal was standing cross-armed next to his parked motorcycle in the bike section of the Surabaya International Airport parking lot, his dark brown eyes peering behind black shades as Carlton Easley approached the luxury sedan that was sent for him from the company.

Mustafal was tall for an Indonesian and normally he would stand out in a crowd like this. Trying to appear relaxed, he purposely slouched while he watched his prey. He had imagined this moment for weeks, but when he actually saw the man he was about to abduct, a queasy feeling overtook his stomach and he suddenly felt like throwing up. Mustafal willed it back down, concentrating his hatred on his target and his objective. He could not let his two partners notice any second thoughts in the body language of their resolute leader. That was him—resolute—and this was his time. He needed them to follow through unwaveringly.

I hate this man.

He watched with disdain as the driver, submitting to the white man like a good little Indonesian servant, took Carlton's suitcase out of his hand and placed it in the trunk. Carlton put on his sunglasses and once even glanced Mustafal's way. *I hate this man. I hate this man.* He kept repeating it over and over in his mind, summoning the courage to take the first step of this risky journey. He actually felt a little sorry for the soon-to-be traumatized driver, who was now closing the door for his white master and smiling at him through the car window like an imbecile. This driver, like so many Indonesians, didn't have the courage to stand up to their exploiters. No wonder Indonesia was ruled by the *Londoh*, the Dutchman, for hundreds of years.

But Mustafal would not be the subservient yes-man of the *Londoh* any longer. He would rise up and strike a decisive blow against the forces of neo-liberal imperialism that were keeping his beloved developing country mired in third-worldness.

Mustafal strolled across the street toward his target. As he approached the car, still parked parallel along the sidewalk of the airport, he looked back and spotted his two partners. They were watching him closely from behind a shade tree and he wondered if they were having the same doubts about crossing the line of no return. Pretending to bend down and tie his shoelaces, Mustafal pulled a large nail out of his sock, then drove it in to the back tire as hard as he could with his thumb. Pressing the nail in hurt more than he had imagined, but it would surely leave a puncture big enough to eventually cause a flat tire. He backed away nonchalantly and could tell that no one noticed anything suspicious. With all the bustling activity at the international terminal, a man tying his shoes behind a car elicited no notice, not even from the driver and passenger of the vehicle about to drive off. His partners cranked their motorcycles to a start and left the parking lot. Strolling back to his motorcycle, Mustafal straddled it and waited for the car to drive off with the doomed tire. He would follow it until the car came to a lonely stretch of road where the kidnapping would occur out of public sight. A rush of adrenaline coursed through his body now that they were finally executing their well-rehearsed plans.

≈≈◘≈≈

Carlton Easley was feeling foul. The company driver was supposed to meet him at the international terminal. He had waited ten minutes already at this sweltering Surabaya airport and now his expensive suit was melting onto his heavy-set body. How hard could the explicit arrangements be to follow? After getting through immigration, grabbing his luggage and clearing customs, he would locate the company driver who would be waiting and holding up a sign with big letters welcoming CARLTON EASLEY. Yet the driver was a no show, and the only number he had on him was for the factory in Pandaan. And if he did get through, would they speak English? He was a stranger among strangers and his one link of communication, the driver, was missing in action. Now he wished he hadn't brushed aside his secretary's advice to activate an international plan for his cell phone before he left.

No choice but to try to contact someone at the factory. He walked briskly through the outside plaza of the airport, looking for some sort of public phone booth. Carlton attracted a lot of notice, not just because he was a foreigner, but also because he was walking so fast. These people were going in slow motion and he was not on their time. He was on his time. And his time was his money. And his money was being wasted at this backwater airport.

Taxi drivers were the only ones brave enough to approach the charging bull. They simply inquired, "Taxi, sir?" and he waved them off. After looking for five more minutes, he finally relented and slowed down to ask one of them for help.

A mustached man wearing plain clothes approached. "I driver. You go where? I take you there. Cheaper than taxi." The freelance driver made a motion with his arms as if gripping a steering wheel, turning it back and forth.

Carlton made a phone sign with his thumb and little finger and placed it to his ear. "Where can I find a phone?"

The man dropped his air steering wheel sign and made a phone sign in return. "*Telpon?*" he asked.

"Yes, *telpon*," Carlton said trying to hold down his disdain for playing charades. "Where *telpon?*"

The miming driver motioned for Carlton to follow him and led him to a little side office with a sign that announced *Wartel*. Carlton figured this was the public phone place, and although it wasn't air conditioned, he was at least thankful that a small fan appeared to be blowing inside the steaming booth. After fumbling through a couple of incorrect attempts, he finally got through and felt proud of himself for making contact.

"*Firdaus Rokok. Boleh saya bantu?*"

"Hello. This is Carlton Easley. Do you speak English?"

A long pause was followed by chattering commotion, which Carlton thought was probably the receptionist trying to find the lone English speaker.

After a few moments a weak voice answered, "Hello, may I be of assistance?"

"I certainly hope so. This is Carlton Easley at the Surabaya airport. Where is the driver who is supposed to pick me up? I've been here now for twenty minutes and the driver never came."

"I'm sorry sir. My English little little. May you please repeat slowly?"

Fuming that he had wasted all his verbal energy on second language ears, he had no other choice but to slow it down. He tried harder to sound more pleasant through a slightly clenched smile that could almost be heard through his voice.

"I am Carlton Easley. I am at the Surabaya Airport. There is no driver here."

"Yes, Mr. Easley. We are awaiting your coming. The driver will pick..."

"No. No," he interrupted. "The driver not here. Driver no come."

"Excuse me sir. The driver pick up you."

"No," he said louder. "Driver not at airport. Do you understand?"

"Yes, please hold," said the still polite voice. What choice did he have? He looked around through the plastic of the phone booth and already disliked this country. It was hot. He deemed the people incompetent. He knew liberal bleeding hearts accused him and his company of miring poor helpless third world people in nicotine addiction all the way to their graves, but they would probably die anyway from the pollution if the cigarettes didn't get them first.

The factory had fallen behind, there were major issues with quality control, and it was his job to whip it up into shape. Carlton was the right man for the job. His nickname around headquarters was "Hardly" as in the weak pun, "hardly easy." Most people behind his back just called him hardnosed. His nose actually was rather intimidating, large and dominant. It served him well to intimidate people almost as much as his bulging eyes. His physical presence was important, he felt, in a job that required hard-charging business insights and muted morals. After all, if he did his job right, his company would reap record profits even if it did send people to hospitals and graveyards. Now that smoking was going out of fashion in the

U.S., it was up to him and his colleagues to beef up the profit margin overseas. Asia was a booming market. Cigarette companies like his brought in huge sums of cash to make basketball courts for cash-strapped colleges, build walk-over bridges over impossible-to-cross roads, and promote their brands by having mini-skirt clad girls give away free cigarettes at rock concerts and malls. *Firdaus Rokok* was proudly displayed on billboards of every project and on banners at every event. He assumed most people here appreciated the extra help with their infrastructure. As far as the so-called dangerous side effects (his uncle smoked a pack a day until he was 93 he liked to say), people were going to smoke no matter what anyone did. If it weren't his cigarettes, they would die from someone else's. His conscience had dulled over time, and he doubted it would ever make a comeback. He never smoked himself and couldn't stand the smell when others did. Let others have their choices.

Today he just wanted to take the hour drive to Pandaan, check into the company guest suite or a nearby hotel, and relax his jet lag off in the afternoon before a scheduled welcome dinner in the evening. Maybe he could enjoy the company of an attractive young lady, which he had heard could be arranged by the managers. Tomorrow he would start throwing his weight around with the so-called leaders at the factory. Now his hours of relaxation were slipping away outside this infernal airport. He was tired from jet lag and felt like taking his frustration out on someone—he just didn't know how or on whom yet.

Finally, a new voice broke through. The English was better.

"Mr. Easley, this is Mr. Bambang, the senior manager. I understand the driver did not pick you up."

"Yes, yes, thank you, Mr. Bambang. Can you send another driver?"

"I'm sorry, we cannot find the driver because he is not answering hand phone. We are sorry for the delay but it will take too long I think to send another driver. Perhaps it better for you to take taxi."

"And just tell me how can I tell him where to go if I can't speak Indonesian?"

"Yes, I understand. Please is there a driver there that I can speak to and give directions?"

"Yes, okay. Let me go get a driver. Now you hold please."

He popped open the flimsy plywood door and exited the telephone booth store, feeling even fouler for having to engineer his own rescue. He spotted the same plain clothes driver who had pointed out the *wartel* to him. The man was sitting on a bench, smoking a cigarette and scanning the crowd for his next customer. Carlton tapped him on his shoulder. The driver looked up, flicked his cigarette out and stood up. Carlton made a motion for the man to follow him. The driver didn't seem to understand so Carlton tugged on his elbow sleeve and pulled it toward him as a sign to follow him. The driver seemed slightly miffed at being yanked on like that but followed Carlton anyway.

After a brief exchange over the phone, the driver walked out from the booth and said simply, "Five hundred thousand *rupiah*."

"Okay, whatever," said Carlton, nodding his head up and down in a yes. Whatever that meant or however much that was, the factory would surely pay it after they arrived. Carlton wasn't about to barter and bicker with this guy.

The driver looked pleased at the agreement and bent down to pick up Carlton's carry-on.

"No, I'll take this one. You carry that one," Carlton ordered, pointing to his larger suitcase.

Carlton paid for his phone call with the only currency he had, U.S. dollars, and the woman wearing a head covering behind the counter reluctantly accepted his five-dollar bill after examining it carefully.

The driver's face winced as he picked up and lugged the heavy suitcase to his dented-up car. Carlton didn't like using non-official transportation, but he was too impatient to waste time with another fruitless plan. He got in the back seat, carrying his leather briefcase with him. Off they went.

The air conditioning in the small car wasn't working very well, and now he wished he had chosen to sit in the front seat. He quickly removed his dark blue blazer and unfastened the top two buttons of his dress shirt. Still not enough air circulation. He thought about rolling down the window, but was afraid of the beggar people being able to get at him through a rolled-down car window. Plus there was the pollution. He decided just to suffer through.

What could have possibly held up his original driver? What could have been more important than picking up a visiting VIP from the U.S.? His only welcome in Indonesia so far was this sorry waft of air from a half-broken AC.

The driver tried to get the tense relationship on better terms. He tried out a few questions he had memorized in English, but Carlton fielded them off one by one with clipped answers. "Yes, once before...I am from Houston, Texas...Yes, I like Indonesia just fine...I have two children, both grown." The taxi driver must have surmised from the short answers that his passenger wanted to be left alone, or he had no more English ammo. He stopped trying and the two sat in silence on the road to Pandaan, with Carlton buried in his notes.

After about a half hour through the densely packed streets, Carlton felt a desire for contact again with his official hosts. "Could I borrow your cell phone for a moment?"

The driver turned around. "Hand phone?"

"Yes, hand phone, uno momento."

Carlton wasn't conscious of the fact that he had just spoken Spanish to an Indonesian, but it seemed to do the trick nonetheless. The driver extended his small cell phone to Carlton, and after a few minutes of fiddling with it, he got it to work. It rang at the factory too many times for his liking, and finally a voice answered. Before the voice could give the standard greeting, Carlton interrupted, "Yes. Yes. This is Carlton Easley. I am on the way to the factory. I want to speak with Mr. Bambang right now."

"*Halo ya? Sebentar,*" came a timid reply.

Another voice, a man's voice. "Hello, this Firdaus Cigarettes. How may I be of assistance?"

Didn't we just do this? "This is Carlton Easley. I am on my way to the factory. I must speak to Mr. Bambang right now." How much cultural nicety would he have to endure? Maybe the first person he would fire would be this second-rate translator who apparently sat a few feet away from the operator in case a foreigner called.

"Yes, Mr. Easley. I get Mr. Bambang right now."

He thought about biting out a, "No you're not. You're still talking to me," but he was afraid his snide comment would have to go through another round of translation. Instead he said nothing and waited, rummaging through his notes. Now his forehead had gone beyond sticky to soaking and he was desperate to ask the taxi driver for a higher notch of air con. He couldn't take it anymore and had to at least try. He pulled the driver's cell phone away from his face, pointed to the AC unit and said to the driver, "Air conditioning. More air conditioning."

The man turned his head and looked back at Carlton, but with a questioning look that showed he didn't understand the directive. The driver's focus on Carlton and not on the insane traffic made him fear for his life. "Never mind," he said and stuck the cell phone back to his face and kept waiting. The driver kept looking through the rearview mirror for some sort of facial clue as to what his passenger wanted, but Carlton gave none.

Finally, a voice broke through. "Mr. Easley, this Mr. Bambang again. We are awaiting your coming. We so sorry the driver not come. This very unusual because Mr. Gunadi very dependable. I'm sure he has good reason. Maybe he got accident."

"Well whatever he got, he didn't get me."

Bambang paused to understand and then continued, "We are sorry for the inconvenience caused, sir. I hope you find your ride to the factory now more comfortable."

At least someone empathized. He felt confident that he would be able to avoid staying at the lower-end company suite, get checked into a nicer hotel, cool off, take a shower, be treated to a welcome dinner, and finally collapse in bed. Maybe this wouldn't be so bad after all. The jet lag was already making him grumpy, but he could be forgiving. Heads were still going to roll, but tonight he would just recover from this day's unpleasant unfolding. There would be plenty of time for hard-hearted business tomorrow after he relaxed the tension away.

"I don't want any meetings today with the managers, and I would rather not stay at the company suite. Can you just check me into a nearby hotel?"

"Yes sir. We can do that."

"Great, and maybe just a dinner tonight but no official meetings."

"Yes, that was our plan."

"Okay, great." Carlton started to feel better about his plight. "Thanks."

≈≈□≈≈

Om Donri lay on his foam mattress bed, awash in the morning light, listening to the sounds of walk-by sellers peddling their breakfast concoctions and fresh ingredients for those who didn't want to go to the market themselves. These sellers typically won the race against the morning sun. It was only five AM and already the bright sun in East Java had beaten him awake by 15 minutes.

He missed Ibu Yuli in the mornings. For most of his adult life she had brought him a cup of strong black coffee to get his non-morning self started, and she always softened those harsh mornings with a soft kiss on the forehead. Now for the last eight years he woke by himself, showered, shaved, read his Bible over breakfast, went through his daily prayer routine, and by 6 AM he was ready to start his day. It used to be that they started their day together. He was grateful to always have the Lord, but it wasn't the same having his fried rice with a silent conversation partner. Didn't God tell Adam it wasn't good for man to be alone? It definitely wasn't good for Om Donri.

After breakfast he pulled his simple chair back from his small wooden desk, stacked ten papers deep with theological essays from his students. He sighed as he looked at how many he would be grading today. Not that he didn't enjoy reading the Biblical insights of his students into the book of First Peter, but he had read those same insights for over 20 years at the Baptist seminary where he worked as a professor in Surabaya. The seminary had been started by Baptist missionaries in the 1950's and was well respected among the minority of Bible-believing Christians in Indonesia. It was a small school, never more than 150 students. Called a seminary, it was more of a Bible college where high school students got a bachelor's degree in the Bible, enough to launch them into a pastoral role at small Baptist churches that grew here and there like tiny white mushrooms on the landscape of green Muslim Indonesia.

After a couple of hours of reading and grading, he walked over to the cupboard and fished around for a snack, finally settling on spicy peanuts. Refilling his favorite mug with extra sweet Java coffee and stretching his arms, he noticed his hands shaking more. He told himself again that the warranty on his elderly body was running out. Normally Ibu Yuli would have at least smiled at that tired little joke. But she wasn't here and there was no one to care. Back to work.

His once broad shoulders were starting to droop from old age, but his wrinkled yet kind face still had some spark of life in it. His eyes were black and his height was short like most Indonesians, but his frame was slightly more portly than average and his formerly thick black hair was thinning and grey.

Donri liked to tell new acquaintances that he was older than Indonesia. He always laughed hard when he said it whether they did or not. As an elderly man in his 70's, he could still remember some Dutch words from the days when the Netherlands ruled the archipelago. He was old enough to be called *Om*, the Dutch word for uncle.

Donri was a great storyteller and often held young pastors spellbound with his exciting tales of political upheavals and violent uprisings through the years. He had spent a stint in the jungles of Kalimantan—then called Borneo—and had a large treasure trunk of tales from his ministry adventures there. These stories had grown over the years, all for the glory of God, of course. The students loved all his "back in the day" tales and affectionately called him the Indonesian equivalent for "old school." He flung babyish nicknames back at them in witty retaliation. He was a better talker than he was a listener, and people gave him special allowances when he was a little too talkative or even crusty sometimes. He was now a little hard of hearing too, and sometimes rebuked his students for mumbling when it was only he who couldn't hear them.

Now he was in his last year at his beloved seminary. He wanted to stay on longer, but it had been made known to him in a very Indonesian roundabout way that his time there was at a close. He was being gently pushed out into the pastures of retirement. Some of the staff and students couldn't imagine the school without this familiar sight on campus, almost always wearing a traditional Indonesian silk-imitation batik shirt. They respected him, they loved him, and they put up with his quirks. His methods and ideas were outdated, but it gave everyone on the campus a benchmark against which to measure new philosophies of ministry. Some of the progressive thinkers might not be sad to see him go, for the sake of forward progress on new ministry fronts, but all would feel his absence. Everyone did at least respect the iconic figure on campus.

Now as he faced retirement, his greatest fear was that he would still be respected but completely irrelevant. No more would eager minds test his intellect, which he felt desperately needed sharpening against the dulling of old age. As an extrovert he craved company and always tried to surround himself with young ministers, some of whom wanted some mentoring from this ministry legend. He felt honored as an elder in Asia, and he enjoyed his respected role as statesman in the familiar educational environment. The future felt unclear. With Ibu Yuli gone the house felt so empty. No one greeted him at the end of his day nor grinned to hear his latest story of a ministry mishap. His three grown kids lived in other cities with their own lives and his quickly growing grandkids.

He knew he had to throw himself into something which would put him in contact with other people for most of his waking hours. There would always be preaching on the weekends for out-of-town pastors, but he yearned for more contact with the larger community. Maybe he would volunteer to be a neighborhood civic leader and people would be forced to drop in for a visit, if only just to get his signature to be able to overcome their latest bureaucratic hassle. Maybe he would spend more time doing free English clubs for kids in the poor kampung neighborhoods. He liked doing that, as he saw English as one of the keys that would open the door for young people to escape from poverty. His English was quite good, if he did say so himself, learned from interacting with Western missionaries who founded, supported and taught short courses at the school from time to time.

He had been teaching a weekly English club at an outlying village as a ramp-up to retirement. Tomorrow he would even take his small informal class on an all-day field trip, taking advantage of a school holiday. That experience would be energizing for him, he was sure. Maybe he could start doing more English clubs in other villages, too?

Donri would get a small pension from the Baptist denomination in Indonesia, enough to live on, so he would now have more time to spend doing things outside a ministry context. He knew he loved having young people around him. There was a double motivation of raising up the next generation for the challenges of globalization and having a fresh audience in front of him that would laugh at his jokes. He had been telling people that as he got older he was less interested in changing the world and more interested in changing the people who would change the world.

Donri checked the time by the clock on the wall, decorated on both sides with artful Indonesian shadow puppets, *wayang kulit*. He felt his role, like those heroic epic Indonesian legends, was drawing to a close, but he desired above all to finish well in his last ministry season in life. He started putting papers away, even though he really didn't have to yet, and got ready to depart his lonely house and start his day.

CHAPTER THREE

The driver reached out and gave Stephen a weak handshake. "*Gunadi,*" the man said as he retracted his hand and placed it back over his heart. Stephen mimicked the action clumsily. He wasn't sure if "*Gunadi*" meant "nice to meet you" or if it was the man's name. The driver then led him to a dark blue deluxe model Mercedes Benz parked alongside the curb. Whoever Carlton Easley was, he certainly had means. While the driver and the porter chatted together, Stephen remembered that he had communicated to his porter that his destination was Surabaya. Was that this car's destination, too, or was Carlton planning to go out of town?

He tried to slow his racing heart with measured breathing. Carlton Easley would make his way to his own car soon and Stephen would be exposed as an imposter immediately. He would be unable to explain his incomprehensible behavior, and could get into real trouble in the vulnerability of this foreign land.

No matter. He was going to do something spontaneous, Action Item Number One, and he was going to get it over with quickly. Stephen resolved he would at least ride along to the intended destination of this car, probably a five-star hotel or a business conference, before disappearing without a trace into the sprawling city.

The driver click opened the trunk with the beep of a key chain and placed Stephen's bag inside. Then Gunadi/Nice-To-Meet-You stuffed a tip into Suparto's hand which made Stephen suddenly remember he didn't have any Indonesian currency on him. It must have been a good tip. Suparto nodded a wide smile to both men and he bounced off cheerily in search of his next customer.

Gunadi started to open the door for his esteemed passenger and Stephen asked him, "Money changer?" It was obvious that Gunadi didn't catch the English as the meek man just smiled bashfully, opened the door for his guest and waited for him to get in. Stephen thought he could always get to an ATM later to pull out some *rupiah* after he played out his charade. He glanced across the parking lot at some taxis and hesitated, knowing this was his very last exit from predictability. He flipped on his sunglasses and sat down uneasily in the backseat, the leather interior seats creaking and squeaking to welcome him. Looking back at Gunadi through the slightly tinted window and at the people streaming by, he steeled himself. *Here goes.*

Gunadi started up the car and Stephen continued to scan the crowd for anyone who might be a Carlton Easley. Most of the people milling about were Asians, but there were a few Westerners sprinkled in, none of whom seemed to be looking for a missing driver.

Stephen wasn't enjoying spontaneity so far. He buckled his seatbelt and willed the car to take off immediately. Gunadi fiddled with the air conditioning controls. Although Stephen was nearly hyperventilating, he at least would have some comfort from the sweltering heat.

The car made its way through packed rows of the crowded airport parking lot. Stephen resolved again to hide inside the façade as long as he could take it. With the way he felt now, however, that wouldn't be long—certainly not all the way to Carlton Easley's intended destination. Maybe he could just jump out quickly at a long traffic light. But how would he get his luggage out of the trunk? He cursed himself for doing something so stupid, and felt the simmering panic attack wanting to fully uncork itself. He was trapped in the charade, strapped in the back seat and lurching toward some destination which would surely expose him as an imposter. They slowed at the exit gate and Gunadi paid the parking fee, then reached for an envelope on the dashboard and handed it back to Stephen without a word.

Stephen pulled out a letter which was printed on thick cotton stationery with the words *Firdaus Rokok* embossed in gold lettering across the top. It read:

Dear Mr. Easley,
Welcome to Indonesia. I entrust your journey comfortable. Because of preparations at factory today, I am send driver Mr. Gunadi to pick up you and I not accompany you. He take you to the company suite, and I meet you there tonight before the meeting. The meeting start at 7:00 PM and the managers looking forward to meet you, and so do I too. I will pick up you at 6:45 PM at company suite. Or hotel if you prefer. The driver take you there now to the place you want to go.
Best Regards,
Mr. Bambang

Stephen glanced at his watch: 10:30 AM Indonesia time. At least that bought him a few more hours of time before he had to bail. Or would it? When the real Mr. Easley arrived at the airport and didn't find his escort, how long would it take before he made the calls to *Firdaus Rokok*, whatever company that was? Maybe an hour? Did Gunadi have a cell phone that would instantly call his bluff? Would identity theft mean prison in Indonesia?

It's okay. You are escaping from your prison of predictability. Relax and ride this out a little.

The car blurred along the crowded streets with Gunadi's eyes aimed dead ahead in a tunnel vision style of driving. Motorcycles zipped by both sides and weaved through traffic within inches of the other vehicles. Stephen was mesmerized by all the crowds. Bicycle pedi-cabs carrying passengers holding bags from the market with skinny drivers trying to navigate around potholes. Children coming out of schoolyards wearing uniforms and holding plastic bags of juice with little straws poking out. Roadside food stalls crowding the shoulders of the busy roads with people eating while seated on top of plastic stools. Thousands of people everywhere, on major roads and tiny alleyways, talking, squatting, smoking, laughing, being. It was a dizzying eyeful for someone used to the orderly and well-manicured lawns of American suburbs.

The mind-boggling scenery was a brief diversion, but he was forced back to his frightening reality. What was his next move going to be? After about 15 minutes of riding along, he thought of an exit strategy and would improvise the best he could. He had to end this now—there was no other choice. It was unthinkable to show up at any meeting or company suite. Seeing a taxi parked next to a roadside food stall, he asked if he could stop.

"Can we stop here for one moment, Mr. Gunadi?" he asked. The question came out slow and loud in an instinctive attempt to be understood better. "I want to drink something."

The driver shot him a quizzical look as if he didn't understand. Stephen started pointing to the food stall they were about to pass and cut to the chase. "Stop. Stop."

The driver understood that and slowly applied the brakes. He looked over at Stephen again and unlocked the door from his side. "Mister stop?"

"Yes, mister stop. I want here to drink. I thirsty." He pointed to his throat and lifted an imaginary glass to his lips.

"*Silahkan, Pak,*" the driver offered. "*O ya silahkan.*"

Gunadi pulled the car into the tight parking area, more meant for motorcycles than cars, and Stephen bolted out of the backseat. He wanted to get out on his own before his driver could make a show of opening the door for him. The tropical heat slammed him as he stood up to survey the scene.

He walked unsurely to the rickety food stand and three men sitting on green plastic stools looked up from their coffee, snacks and newspapers. They were all smoking and watching him curiously. The small elderly lady who apparently ran the establishment also eyed him carefully.

He then remembered that he had no Indonesian *rupiah* on him. Maybe he could borrow some from nice Mr. Gunadi and pay him back when they got back in the car. Then again he didn't plan to get back in the car, ever. He would order first, and then ask Gunadi to open the car and the trunk so he could get his wallet. The next surprise move would be to grab all his stuff out and then make a break for a taxi he saw parked there. One of the men sitting on the stools was wearing a blue uniform with the same name as the taxi, and that man was going to be his savior.

From inside the food stand Stephen saw the elderly lady's wrinkled eyes squinting at him in the sun. She was wearing some type of traditional Indonesian dress, a large colorful cloth wrapped around her as a long skirt. "*Hello Mister. Boleh saya bantu?*" He got the first part and the second part must mean "May I help you," or "Are you lost, sir?"

He tried out a response of, "Yes. Coffee? Do you have coffee?"

With a quick affirmative nod, she scurried two steps backwards and started preparing the brew. The three men smiled, put down their newspapers and pointed to the last empty plastic stool.

He lifted his forefinger to make the sign for what he hoped meant "wait a moment" and motioned for Gunadi to follow him back to the car. Gunadi dutifully followed and saw that his guest wanted the car door opened. He pressed the remote button and the doors unlocked with a beep. Stephen rummaged through his carry-on bag still in the backseat for the wallet in his travel pouch, but in his panicked state couldn't remember which of the dozen compartments he zipped it into.

He cut a glance toward the coffee stand and saw that everyone was still staring at him. He also noticed the taxi driver was getting up from his stool and walking back toward his own vehicle.

Think, think. He had to do something quick. *Grab your stuff and go.* But didn't he at least have to go back and pay for his coffee first? Maybe not—he didn't drink any. Was that okay? The improvised plan was to grab the carry-on out of the back seat, the suitcase out of the trunk and run to the taxi. Leave the driver, leave the three men, leave the coffee, leave the unpaid tab, leave everything and get back to your reality. It was a lame plan, admittedly, but at least he would be in control once again. His meeting in Surabaya wasn't until tomorrow. He could take a shower to wash away all this stupidity and rest up at the hotel, maybe toss that self-help book into the trash and watch a movie. Tomorrow morning he would be fresh for his training and this episode would just be a bizarre asterisk in an otherwise uniform life.

Everyone was still looking at him, not coldly but curiously. The proprietor was setting the coffee on the slouching counter while the two remaining customers seemed more interested in him than in their newspaper articles. He assumed he was the first Westerner to ever patronize their favorite hangout. Gunadi was still standing at attention next to him, probably bewildered as to how to help his unpredictable guest.

Now was the moment. He had his carry-on hoisted over one shoulder and was going for the trunk to pull out his suitcase too. The taxi driver was now in his car and starting up the engine. *Go go go.* Gunadi looked confused, his head slightly hunched down on his shoulders. Stephen was already causing a commotion of curiosity by lifting his suitcase out of the trunk. *Just run for it while everyone already thinks you're weird anyway.*

Stephen stood there frozen in indecision under a hot tropical sun. *Just run.* His legs wouldn't budge—it would be too strange. Everyone was staring at him and what would poor Gunadi do if his guest just escaped and vanished from him, just like that? That wouldn't be right, but wasn't it equally wrong to go on impersonating Carlton Easley?

The taxi driver said his goodbyes to his fellow drivers through his rolled-down window and his car backed up out of the dusty car space and waited to merge into the mad traffic.

"You need suitcase, Mr. Easley?" Gunadi asked with a confused expression.

Too much indecision. Just do something, anything. Stephen surveyed his setting, first glancing at the food stall customers all in their same staring state. He then tried to make out what was on the other side of the roaring road full of insane traffic. It looked like just more food stalls on that side as well. A thought streaked through his mind to throw his heavy suitcase at Gunadi, knocking him off balance, and then make a mad dash across the road with his carry-on like a crazed Frogger and hope to find another taxi on the other side. That is, if he made it across alive.

That just wasn't Stephen. He put that thought out and looked into Gunadi's kind and worried eyes.

"Just looking for my wallet. I can't seem to find it."

Stephen could tell Gunadi was replaying the sentence through his mind, trying to translate it. Stephen simplified it down to, "No money," patting his empty back pocket. "Look for money to buy coffee."

Gunadi laughed his relief then reached for the suitcase to help heave it back into the trunk.

"No problem, mister," Gunadi offered. Apparently the coffee was on him.

Stephen sighed and heard the rippling of gravel in the parking area as the taxi was trying to make its way into the traffic. His getaway was getting away.

≈≈□≈≈

Agung was motoring and bumping along the busy roadway between Surabaya and Sidoarjo when he saw, of all people, a Western man at Ibu Karni's *warung*. He had just finished teaching his morning English class, and he was out doing an errand for his elementary school. He was considering stopping somewhere anyway for a mid-morning rice meal and he just couldn't pass up this chance to practice his English. Even though he was a part-time English teacher and should be fluent, he often felt ashamed at how bad his English actually was, especially his spoken English. Most of the Indonesian students in his afternoon classes at the elementary school couldn't tell, of course, but a *bule* would immediately know. Would this foreigner be aghast that he was an English teacher when he stumbled through a simple sentence? Agung decided that he wouldn't volunteer the truth about his job. Later in the afternoon, he would tell his students that he used his English that very day to speak with a foreigner, and hopefully that would motivate them to have more passion in their normally passive learning. He was surprised at how nervous he felt, but summoned his courage and parked his motorcycle under the shade of a tree along the busy road and close to the *warung*.

The customers looked up and instantly recognized Agung's friendly face and wide smile. His hair was black and his eyes dark brown like most Indonesians, but his skin was coffee and cream colored, light enough to be poked fun of by his close friends. They teased him that he was really Chinese and not Javanese, who were considered the authentic, indigenous inhabitants of the island. Agung's eyes were bright and inquisitive and his walk was energetic but not confident. Agung was a decent man from a decent family. He was enough of a dutiful Indonesian citizen and Muslim to keep a good name intact, but not too radical in any area of his life to make anyone nervous. Like a hundred million other struggling-against-poverty Javanese people who lived on the island, he was more or less content with his life. The Javanese cultural value of resigning to fate kept him on the straight and narrow, but his personality was mixed with a dab of curiosity that made him unique. When his school chums were crowding and clamoring around worn-out comic books, he was reading great tales of Indonesian heroes and historic legends. Growing up, he had read many Indonesian books in the small and stuffy library in Sidoarjo, and as his English got better he started going through the handful of English books that collected dust on the library shelves. He had spoken briefly with a foreigner in a mall once, a Mr. Brighton from Miami, Florida, and this was another chance he wasn't going to pass up.

As he approached, the English words of a possible conversation started to jumble together, but the start-up line came to him automatically: "Hello Mister! How are you today, sir?"

≈≈◻≈≈

"Uh, fine," said Stephen, his concentration suddenly broken. He was focused on all the other people fixated on him, and what they would do if he suddenly bolted, and he wasn't expecting a jolt of English from an Indonesian out of the blue.

"Hello, sir," said Agung again. "I would like introduce myself. My name is Mr. Agung."

Stephen wasn't quite sure what to do, but he surely couldn't be rude. Placing his carry-on down on the ground, he turned away from the car and stretched out his hand for a handshake. "Hello Mr. Agung, my name is Stephen...I mean you can call me Carlton Easley. Nice to meet you."

"It nice to meet you, too, Mr. Stephen Carlton Easley."

"You can just call me Carl for short."

"You can call me Agung. For short too."

The two just stood there smiling at each other, while the other gawkers looked on. A couple of stragglers moseyed over from an unknown location and inched closer to the conversation. Agung seemed to be the only one around who could make intelligible contact with the alien.

Stephen was doing his best to be polite, but the majority of his mental capacity was being taken up with figuring out his exit strategy. He quickly glanced over and saw the taxi driver had indeed taken off. Plan A was gone in a cloud of dust behind the taxi.

Agung broke through his thought process again. "Where do you come from, Mr. Carl?"

"Oh, uh, I'm from California. And where are you from, Agung?" He realized before it even left his mouth it was a very dumb question.

"Oh, I am from here, sir. I am Indonesian person. I born in Blitar but live in Sidoarjo."

Stephen couldn't think of anything better to say than, "Oh, really?"

By now two more people had come up, now forming a semicircle around the diplomatic ambassadors. "You ever go to Sidoarjo, Mr. Carl?"

"No, this is my first time in Indonesia." He felt himself starting to relax a little bit. This Agung guy was so friendly, with an eager childlike face and a toothy smile Stephen found disarming.

Just then Gunadi, the driver, said something in Indonesian. Stephen was about to be dragged away back into the false identity of Carlton Easley. No way was he getting back into that car. Stephen had a translator friend and could stall for time through this polite conversation until he came up with Plan B. The polite banter of what Stephen thought so far of Indonesia continued, and an idea began to bubble up in his mind.

He interrupted Agung, "Excuse me, could you translate something for me? I am so embarrassed but I haven't exchanged my money for *rupiah* and I need to pay for this coffee I ordered. My driver has offered, but I feel embarrassed. Could you ask this lady if she would take U.S. cash?"

"Oh no, Mr. Carl. I pay for it. You no need to worry."

"Oh, I couldn't do that to you, Mr. Agung."

He seemed eager to help this foreigner. "It is my pleasure sir." He pulled a few wrinkly bills out of his pocket and walked it over to the elderly lady, who kept her eyes suspiciously on Stephen as she took the money from Agung. Stephen looked over at Gunadi who seem confused that suddenly the new guy was picking up the bill.

"In Indonesia you can call me *Pak* Agung. This is how we say mister, Mr. Carl."

"Oh, thank you, Pak Agung." The banter continued and even in the presence of the easy-going Indonesian man, Stephen couldn't shake the fear of impending repercussions. What kind of trouble would he get into over this? Agung kept trying his best to impress the international guest, and Stephen was amused at his attempts at cross-continental connection. Agung asked him at one point, "I ever meet a man in Surabaya mall. Mr. John Brighton from Miami, Florida. Do you know him?"

The preposterous question almost flushed out laughter on Stephen's face but he held it in. "No, I haven't met him yet." The comic relief was at least good for his nerves.

Agung seemed to be trying to think of something else that would be of interest to his new friend. "Sidoarjo famous city in Indonesia for shrimp. Also for leather bags."

A couple more people shuffled up in their flip-flops and were listening. No one was as bold as Agung to step forward as a translator.

"The city known as city of shrimp because many shrimp crackers made there what we call *krupuk*. Like a fried shrimp cracker. And there is a street where you can find nice leather goods."

"Oh, really," said Stephen again politely, but more absently. His mind was still searching for an exit strategy and not for shrimp and leather.

"Would you like to see it with me? I can take you there."

I can take you there. Stephen's mind snapped to full attention. *You can take me away from this place on a motorcycle. Away from all these onlookers, away from this driver, away from this stolen identify.* Stephen suddenly had an overwhelming desire to eat fried shrimp crackers and buy leather goods.

"Yes, I would love to see it, Pak Agung." He looked over his shoulder at Gunadi, who was still watching him attentively. "Just let me tell my driver first. Maybe we can go together to your city and afterwards I'll take a taxi from your city to my meeting later."

"Oh yes, yes." He seemed genuinely pleased at becoming Stephen's personal tour guide.

Man, nobody in Sacramento would be this nice to a visitor from Indonesia.

Agung pulled his key ring out of his jeans pocket and twirled it on his finger. "I can take you on my motorcycle and back to your meeting. Up to you, mister. Sidoarjo not very far from here. Maybe we go to my house first and take a rest?"

"That would be fine." He didn't really care where they went or rested or ate or shopped as long as it was far away from the impersonation of Carlton Easley.

Stephen turned his attention back to poor Gunadi. The driver looked like he was trying to get a read on his guest, someone for whom he must feel very responsible. There were a few crevices of worry on the man's brown face.

The driver nodded to Stephen, and then turned to Agung as the official translator.

"I am so sorry," Stephen began. "Mister...I'm sorry, I forgot your name."

"My name Mr. Agung."

"No, I'm sorry, I forgot *his* name."

Agung smiled sheepishly and got the driver's name. "His name is Pak Gunadi."

"Oh yes, Mr. Gunadi." said Stephen. That elicited a smile from the driver, either because he was amused Stephen had already forgotten his name or his pronunciation was way off. No matter, this was the plan and he wasn't deviating. He was going to latch on to Agung for dear life. "My friend Agung here is going to take me to the meeting on his motorcycle. I would like to experience some Indonesian culture before I go to the meeting this evening."

The startling sentence was translated and it started a flurry of conversation between Agung and Gunadi. The driver obviously didn't approve and he walked out of earshot to make a call on his cell phone, which either wasn't getting good reception or else had a dead battery. Good thing he wasn't able to check in with headquarters, Stephen thought, as Carlton may have called in by now and exposed his ruse.

Stephen realized that he still had to deal with his suitcase. How would he possibly haul his large bag on a motorcycle? Maybe he could get away on the motorcycle and let the driver take his suitcase to the factory. He would never again see his suitcase, of course, but at least he would have his computer laptop bag with him on the motorcycle. A suitcase showing up at the factory and the owner never coming for it would excite a lot of interest, but probably no long term harm. There was a name tag on it but could that really be traced back to him on this overcrowded island? He could buy new clothes before the meeting tomorrow. He also considered coming clean and explaining everything, but could that even be translated intelligibly?

Gunadi walked back, and by this time there were about nine curious people standing around listening, all very interested in the volley of conversation. Some seemed to be offering their opinions. Stephen wasn't sure how Gunadi was going to handle this surprise move but he would keep charging ahead and away from the tentacles of this false identity.

"Mr. Agung, please tell my driver not to worry. He can take my suitcase back to the factory. You and I will visit Sidoarjo on your motorcycle, and if you don't mind you can take me to the factory in Pandaan tonight. I've never been on a motorcycle and it sounds like fun. Plus I really would like to experience some local culture."

Agung delivered the message, and the driver's face strained out a nod, registering his protest to the plan. Apparently he didn't have the power to veto his guest's strange request. The two of them negotiated more and Agung turned back to Stephen.

"He says it better if we all go in the car. He said he can take us to Sidoarjo for a little while but then we need to go to factory. No more than one hour. He afraid his boss be angry to him if you come too late."

Stephen's mind flashed to scenes of him sitting in his gray cubicle, slaving over his desktop, beat down lifeless by the tasks in his in-box. He wouldn't mind a little routinized boredom right now. So far to him it was winning hands down against spontaneity. At least this would be an interesting story at his funeral one day, so his eulogy wouldn't be a total snoozer.

Stephen hoped the quickly baked plan would work, but couldn't push out of his mind the worst-case scenario. He would soon be discovered as a Carlton Easley imposter and escorted directly to the police. What was he going to do, show his self-help book and little to-do list to the police and explain, probably with Agung as a translator, that he was pretending to be Mr. Easley to escape some existential angst and take more risks in his life? And then there was Bill's funeral and an adventure guide named Chopper he'd met on an airplane that pushed him over the edge. This Mr. Carlton Easley person was important and was wanted at some important factory. Important people don't wave off identity theft as an amusing little pre-midlife crisis episode. How could he possibly get out of this? He felt suffocated by all the very polite Javanese people around him.

In his mind Plan B was slowly becoming Plan C. Maybe he should just go to the shrimp city in the Benz and make his break there. He would at least be heading away from the direction of the factory.

"Okay, fine then. Off to Sidoarjo."

"I'm sorry, Mr. Stephen?"

"Let's go visit Sidoarjo together."

"Okay, I entrust my motorcycle to Ibu Karni first."

"Okay, that's fine. I'll wait for you in the car."

Gunadi opened the car door for Stephen, who felt a heavy dread of strapping back into the same mistake. He just couldn't think of any alternatives short of the truth.

CHAPTER FOUR

Carlton could see from the backseat that some sort of delay was slowing the traffic ahead. A long line of cars was being waved to the side of the road by two police officers standing under a shade tree.

He glanced down at his watch, which he had yet to set to Indonesia time. *Perfect, another delay.* He had precious little time to relax tonight and now it was being eaten up by a traffic jam in the middle of a highway. The pair of policemen came into his view. One of them was blowing a whistle, motioning every motorcycle and car to pull over while the other one looked like he was requesting ID's. Both of them were taking their sweet time.

What's wrong with this country? Carlton fumed to himself that with all the terrorist crazies running around, the police were spending their time checking for expired driver's licenses and vehicle registrations.

From the back seat he looked up at his driver, who seemed nervous, evidenced by the way he tightly gripped the steering wheel with and drummed his fingers on the stick shift. If this guy didn't have all his papers together, it wasn't Carlton's fault. Maybe it was against the law to take passengers if you weren't a real taxi or something. If his driver got nabbed, Carlton would just get out and find a real taxi on the busy road and let the police deal with the unregistered freelancer. Since they had already passed hundreds of taxis on the way to the factory, he assumed it would be very easy to flag down an empty one.

The car crawled ahead toward its turn for inspection, and the document checking police officer peered down through his large 1970's sunglasses. His stoic faced featured a dark down-turned moustache and he was dressed in a thick khaki-colored uniform, beige pants and high black boots. Carlton wondered how the police force could stand the tropical heat in long sleeves and pants all day.

The driver rolled down the window and waited for the directive from the officer. Carlton sat still in the back, trying not to be noticed, head down in his notes. He assumed that Indonesian police were corrupt and would find any reason to take a bribe. Even as he tried to appear uninterested, he felt an urge for a fight rising within him. *Just let 'em try to get a bribe out of me.*

The taxi driver opened his glove box and began rummaging through a stack of cluttered papers. While he searched, the policeman turned his attention toward the back seat and stared at Carlton.

"Excuse me, where are you from?"

"Oh, hello." Carlton looked up from his papers. "I am from America."

The officer was half smiling, but Carlton couldn't see the man's eyes from behind his sunglasses. It was hard to read if the facial expression was smug or just curious.

"America. Yes, America. Why you here?"

"What business is that of yours? Aren't you checking for driver's licenses or something like that?"

"Excuse me. My English not good," the officer said as his expression tightened into a definite frown. "May you please say again?"

Carlton caught himself, realizing that a tangle with this officer would only delay him more. He tried a word jumble game. "I'm sorry. My business that you want to know is that I work for the Firdaus Cigarette Company. Do you know that factory? Do you need to see my passport?"

Confusing the policeman with a barrage of English seemed to work. The officer's face un-tensed and he took off his sunglasses. Carlton pulled his driver's license out of his wallet and his passport out of his briefcase to make it seem that he was being asked for his identity cards as well. He leaned forward and handed his license and passport to the officer from the back seat, who took them and walked away from the car.

He seemed to forget all about the taxi driver's documents, which must have been a good thing, Carlton thought, because the driver was still rummaging through a tangle of debris in his glove box.

The policeman began speaking with his fellow officer, who was checking other people's documents next to his parked motorcycle. What was this about? The two of them looked at his Texas driver's license and talked for a bit, and the first officer slowly sauntered back to the taxi. As he did, the driver turned to Carlton and said, "I think he want money."

"He wants money? What did I do?"

"He want money," the driver quickly repeated. "He will find reason. Maybe 50,000 *rupiah* enough."

No wonder international businesses stayed away from Indonesia, Carlton thought. You couldn't even get down a public street without being hassled for a bribe. On another day, Carlton would have played along. Maybe it was just the jet lag or the frustration of roasting in this rattling car, but Carlton no longer felt able to hold back his combative personality. These Indonesians had pushed him around enough already today and he could feel his muscles tense and his face tightening. His temper clamored to be set free.

The police officer slowly bent down and handed Carlton back his driver's license and passport through the window. No expression and no reason given. Then he looked at the driver, who suddenly got flustered again and started searching for something official in the crevices and compartments of his car.

This is ridiculous. Let's just cut to the chase here.

He wasn't going to wait like a helpless victim until the police finished their little fishing expedition. Poking his head slightly out of the window, Carlton squinted into the sun and fired off his challenge. "You want money? Here, here is money." He opened his wallet, remembered he didn't yet have any Indonesian *rupiah*, and pulled out a U.S. ten dollar bill.

As Carlton waved the money out of the window, the police officer stepped back and scowled at it like he had just been offered a dirty tissue. Maybe it was the wrong move, but Carlton really didn't fear the man's response. He said to himself that the factory surely had higher-ups who would whittle this little police peon down to size.

The police officer didn't take the money but did an about face from the car and conferred with his partner. Now both of them ignored the other cars which roared to life back into the traffic. They both came marching back to Carlton's car. The driver stopped looking for his hidden paperwork and nervously eyed the approaching officers, trying to look as meek as possible.

The same policeman knocked hard on the car door with his knuckle even though the back window was still rolled down. He demanded to see Carlton's ID again while his partner looked on, arms folded across his chest and feet firmly planted in the dusty gravel.

Carlton wasn't sure what this was about but carefully placed his ten dollar bill back in his wallet and pulled back out his driver's license and passport and handed them out the window.

The officer clenched his hand around the passport and driver's license and stuffed them in his back pocket. He walked off in a huff back to his motorcycle, and his partner stayed behind, staring down Carlton. The first officer straddled his motorcycle, cranked the engine starter with his big black boot and spun off.

What? Carlton watched in stunned silence as the other policeman marched back to his own his motorcycle, straddled it and took off in the same direction.

Did these policemen really just steal his most important proof of identification—his passport and his driver's license? Where did they go? Were they coming back?

Carlton tapped the driver on the back shoulder for some explanation. "Where did he go?"

"Maybe he go, what you say, to court. To judge. If you no pay money now, you pay more later."

"But I didn't do anything, and I already offered him money!"

"You do it wrong way," the driver explained, not concealing his amusement at his passenger's predicament. He pulled out a cigarette and lit it as if for dramatic effect. Carlton hated his smirky attitude. "You no polite," the driver added.

A sweaty and exasperated Carlton felt like hitting someone. Cars were whizzing past happily with no more delays.

"But you told me he was going to ask for money."

"Maybe sir," he said as he took another a drag from his cigarette. "But not like that way. That not good way above ground."

"Maybe? Maybe?" Carlton could see a *Firdaus* cigarette box on the dashboard. He cursed the driver under his breath and hoped the man would die a slow painful death from his products. Instead of firing off a retort, Carlton would see to it that the man was shortchanged back at the factory.

"*Hati-hati* Mister," said the driver, looking flustered.

"You just *hati-hati* us to the factory."

Even in his anger, Carlton realized that rebuking the freelance taxi driver anymore for misleading him would not help them get to Pandaan any faster. He willed himself to contain his rage and started flipping through his notes again, as his mind boiled with thoughts of revenge. He tried in vain to remember some of the principles and precepts he memorized in his court-ordered anger management seminars.

The driver pulled back into traffic back onto the roughly paved road. Carlton asked with forced nicety, "So what do we do now?"

The driver said, "We go to factory if mister want, or to police station. I think better we go to factory and they send someone to police."

Okay, whatever. He was already in the country so he didn't need his passport until his departure date, and he wasn't going to be driving so he didn't really need his license for now. His only comfort was savoring the thought of that little petty police officer getting chewed down to size by his superior once the factory manager got to the station and everyone realized what an important person they had rankled. He wished he could be there for the berating of both officers. He was sure the police were on the payroll from the biggest factory in town, and they would both regret tangling with Carlton Easley.

"We go to factory," agreed Carlton, already unconsciously using simple grammar to make his English more understandable.

"Yes sir," answered the driver as he took another puff. He flicked the ashes out of the window and accelerated.

At last they came upon a smoothly-paved toll road leading out of the crowded and roughly paved streets of Surabaya. They were finally making time. Yes, he hadn't been picked up by his appointed driver in a nice car, and yes, he was sitting in the back seat of a beat-up car with a sub-functional AC, and yes, he had no ID on him. But all that would soon be sorted out and forgotten with an evening's relaxation.

After a few more minutes, the traffic slowed to a crawl again. What good is a toll road if it isn't any faster than the free ones?

He asked the driver what was going on, but the driver shrugged and said he didn't know. Every now and then the driver would eye his passenger through the rearview mirror, which bothered Carlton. *Keep your eyes on the road and stop looking at me.*

"Can you get us there faster? Is there another way?"

The driver didn't seem to totally comprehend, so Carlton repeated again slowly, tapping his watch a few times in sign language.

The driver saw the mime action through his rear view mirror and understood. "No other way. But I can drive on side of road and maybe get there faster. But can be dangerous and can get ticket from police."

"Tell you what, I will pay for whatever ticket you get and I will double your normal pay if you can get me there by five PM. I need to be in Pandaan by this evening."

"*Satu juta.* One million rupiah," the man turned and asked, with raised arching eyebrows, more of a question than a statement.

"A million? I said double the pay."

"One *juta*?"

"Double the pay, whatever that is."

"Yes sir," said the driver happily and obediently, pulling over into the left shoulder of the toll road and stepping on the gas. The man wasn't using a meter, but Carlton was sure that double the pay wasn't worth half this ride. The greedy little weasel had already gotten some free entertainment at

Carlton's expense and was now probably going to score a month's salary off him.

Carlton reached to get some more notes from his briefcase, but he wasn't sure if he would be able to read them as they drove rapidly over a narrow shoulder. He glanced out the window, wondering how the driver was going to maneuver when they got to a bridge and there was no more shoulder. They were whizzing by the cars stuck in traffic and he still couldn't see the cause of the delay ahead. He figured they would soon see it, and then nudge their way back into traffic and possibly save an hour.

Carlton tried harder to subdue his nervousness and concentrate on his notes. After a couple minutes he looked up just in time to see a sight that sucked out the wind from his lungs in a desperate gasp. The speeding car collided into a young man walking from between the deadlocked traffic onto the shoulder of the road. He held out his arm as if trying to stop the oncoming car while the other hand was holding a cardboard box full of some unknown items. From a blur, the boy's terrified face came into crisp focus through the windshield after his body was nailed with the left front of the car. The body jerked and spun around and flew about ten feet sideways, turning and tumbling over into the tall grass. Carlton's mind was imprinted with the image of the young man's terrified face as the car struck him. The cardboard box shot straight upwards and landed on the top of the braking car, plastic water bottles bouncing off the hood. The boy's leg was grotesquely twisted backwards, and it looked like part of his bone was sticking out through a patch of blood. It all happened in a millisecond, as the driver was screaming and screeching his brakes. Carlton could see and hear from his window the bloodied boy wailing in pain.

He jumped out of the car and dashed to the young man who was crying loudly. Carlton was relieved that he was at least making sounds. It appeared that the car had badly damaged his leg, but there were no major head injuries. He yelled at the driver who also got out of the car. "We need to get this boy to a hospital," he screamed. Other cars were now pulling over.

The driver only looked at him with huge, frightened eyes and then looked around to survey the scene. Suddenly the man lunged into a full run toward a grove of trees a few yards away. Carlton screamed after him, "No. Use my phone." But he kept running deeper and faster into the trees and overgrowth.

The boy's body remained face down and one of his legs was twisted in an impossible position. His flip-flops were still back at the point of impact. People spilled out of the first two cars that pulled over and now there was a small group of shocked people looking in horror at the young man, who was no longer crying and no longer moving. Was he dead or did he just pass out?

Carlton didn't know what to do and apparently the other onlookers didn't either. They just cupped their hands over their mouths and pointed.

"Someone call a doctor!" Carlton yelled in English, hoping that someone could understand that word.

After about two minutes that felt like twenty, with Carlton squatting next to the kid, some people started running through a large gap in a wall that separated the village from the edge of the large road. Carlton felt hope that the boy was from this neighborhood and these people would know where to take him and what to do.

A few farmer-looking men from the village ran through the tall brushy grass to the boy, who had still not awoken. The silence and non-movement were scarier than the loud groans. He was just lying in a crumple, and Carlton could see his face slightly bruised and bloodied from the impact of hitting the ground at such high velocity. The bottled waters that he must have been selling in the clogged traffic were strewn about in every direction. One of them, he could see, was smeared with blood, probably the one the boy was clutching when the car plowed into him.

As one man started to pick up the boy in a cradle position and another man helped, Carlton yelled out in protest, "Don't move him. Wait for the paramedics. You could hurt him worse." They glanced at him for a second, retorted something loudly, and lifted and carried the boy off into the same break in the cement wall they had come out of. The boy's legs were badly crumpled up and Carlton feared moving him in such a haphazard fashion could possibly paralyze the poor young man for life.

About half the men carried the limp boy back through the gap in the wall and half stayed behind, all staring down Carlton. A feeling of dread surrounded him. He now realized that the driver had run off, not to look for help, but probably to save his own life. He also realized how this looked, as if he had been driving that car. The other cars which earlier had slowed down to see what had happened were all now gone, taking all eye witnesses with them.

He started hard-charging against the unspoken accusations. "I did not do this. This is not my fault. My driver hit that boy, not me. Does anyone here speak English?"

"You stay here mister," one of the older men said loudly. "Police will come."

"I did not do this. Do you understand me?" As he said this he brushed his dirty slacks off, and then stood back upright, as straight and tall as possible, trying to show them he was the one in charge. "I did not do this." The Indonesians standing around looked more curious than menacing. They edged a little closer around him, a few still staring coldly at him. All of them were wearing flip-flops, most were smoking and some were carrying sickles, presumably for harvesting. The sharpness of their tools made Carlton feel uneasy.

He wanted to walk back to the car which had slid off the road diagonally into the tall dry grass. He started in that direction, but the farmer folk started murmuring something and moved closer to him, making a half-circle which blocked him off from the car. They must have thought he was trying to get away too.

Carlton looked into the face of the older man who had spoken English to him and asked again, "Can you translate my English for these people?"

"Little little," the man said with no emotion. "You stay here and police come." He snorted and spit into the grass.

Carlton just stood there in this intense heat, not knowing what to do next. He looked into the faces of these simple Indonesians standing guard, dark eyes peeking out of light brown faces and skinny bodies inside tattered clothes. In a second's flash he imagined himself back at his large apartment in Houston, sitting in his recliner with the AC on full blast, watching a movie on his large flat screen TV with his golden retriever at his feet, far away from the trash-laden shoulder of a so-called toll road, surrounded by a bunch of angry-looking Asians who thought he had nailed their neighbor. True, he did feel regret that the young man's lower body could be paralyzed. It could even be argued that Carlton's impatience bore some of the blame. Yet as the minutes ticked by and the heat bore down, he convinced himself that this was 100 percent the fault of the driver. Carlton asked the man to get to the factory quickly, not tear down the road at a rip-roaring speed. He was positive the kid would be fine, just a little shaken up, but fine. Young people are resilient. Maybe Carlton—or for sure the company—could even be counted on to help out with the hospital bills.

As the minutes kept crawling and the day grew hotter, any remorse or compassion Carlton had felt melted in the equatorial sun. Finally, he looked at the older English-speaking man and said, "I will not go anywhere. I just want to get back to my car to get out of the heat. Is that okay? I will wait for the police. I wait for police in car."

From over the man's shoulder he could see a woman running through the same large crack in the wall that the crowd went through earlier with the injured boy. She delivered some sort of news to the onlookers, and Carlton couldn't tell if it was good or bad. The report rippled through the interested crowd, more information was exchanged, and the collective eyes stared at him more intensely.

Maybe the boy was badly injured. Even so, he told himself emphatically that he was not to blame. *I just told the driver to hurry it up a bit. It was his decision to drive at a demon speed on the shoulder of the road, not mine.* "I did not do this, okay?" he said again out loud, knowing his English probably wouldn't be understood. "This is not my fault." It just felt right saying it so he kept saying it every few minutes in the face of the cold stares under the hot sun.

CHAPTER FIVE

Still no word from Stephen yet—no phone call, email, voicemail, nothing. Probably there was some logical reason, but Leah's mind told her that Indonesia was just too fascinating and home life with her was just too forgettable.

She had been busy all morning getting the kids' complicated schedule written down for her best friend Fiona. Telling the kids that Mommy was going to surprise Daddy in Indonesia was pretty cool news. They looked forward with unreserved glee to staying in the less structured home of Fiona. Lots of playtime was promised with Fiona's kids, who were around their ages.

Good ole fun Fiona, always ready to splash some color into Leah's routinized life. Leah replayed the conversation in her mind at the coffee shop when a surprise trip to Indonesia was strongly urged by her free-wheeling, free-spirited friend. You can always pay credit card debt off later, Fiona had said—your marriage is more important. The sweetener of the deal was that Fiona would take care of the kids and even the pets. "Just fly off to Indonesia and wow him!" she had demanded.

During their coffee shop conversation, Leah had painted the true, bleak picture of her relationship with Stephen. Fiona had sensed for a while that her best friend's marriage was dying, but didn't know how dead it actually was. As Leah shared, there were no tears or even much emotion, just a matter-of-fact death pronouncement.

Fiona countered vehemently. She kept telling Leah that the marriage vows and those two wonderful kids were worth one more shot. Leah couldn't really argue with that. If she did go to Indonesia, she could at least forever say to one and all that she had honestly tried to save her marriage before tearing it asunder.

She called Fiona three times to make sure she really could handle two extra kids with all their homework demands and extracurricular schedules. Fiona assured her every time that she was capable and on the last call said, "Just get to Indonesia, Leah. I'll take care of the home front. Get your man back on some tropical island."

Leah looked online to find out about the climate in Indonesia, and just as she suspected, it was hot. There was nothing online about whether she could get away with wearing shorts in a conservative Muslim environment. She decided to go half and half with cool summer clothes and outfits that would be more appropriate in a traditional culture. How they would get to Bali after she found him in Java, she still wasn't sure. That could be figured out later with the help of a travel guide book she would look for on the way.

She called Stephen's office to find his travel info from one of the secretaries there. The lady gave it to her without asking questions, and for that she was relieved. She really wanted to fly below the radar, and if Stephen's boss found out she was going, it might make the trip look less than professional. Stephen took this trip dutifully but grudgingly, and she didn't want to take any credit away from him for being a team player. By the time she arrived, it would be his last day of the trainings and then the two of them could maybe get a few days in Bali together. Would she just coldcock him in his hotel room with her sudden presence, tickets to paradise in hand? By this point could they even patch things together? Would Stephen really "go there" and admit that their marriage was lifeless and empty? Maybe if they got to Bali there would be no other distractions of his job responsibilities or the kids' needs or some household project or anything else to make avoiding the topic so easy.

She seriously doubted that Stephen would come out of hiding. In her mind this was the official point of no return. She would go to Indonesia, surprise him and make herself beautiful and vulnerable one more time. If he kept his distance, even one emotional iota, she would wall back up, pack it all in, and set her course for separation. All her friends and family would know she went half way around the world to try to save their marriage and Stephen didn't even meet her halfway. There would be some embarrassment, even shame, but she would be vindicated and released.

Honestly, the bigger part of her didn't want it to work. Building the protective barriers around her heart had taken years. To come from behind those barricades of low expectations would be vulnerable and painful. The divorce would be life-shattering but eventually they could all clean up the pieces. The kids would come live with her but she would always make sure they lived nearby Stephen so he could still be a part of their lives. She was mature enough to do this amicably. Maybe eventually she could find someone new and Stephen could too.

As she packed her suitcase, she pulled some of her cutest outfits out of the closet. *What am I doing?* There was still a faint flicker of hope in her heart. Maybe he would see her and be wowed, just maybe. A romantic image of their upcoming encounter in Indonesia played in her mind. There he is coming out of his training and making his way to the hotel, the five star Hyatt in Surabaya. There she is in the lobby, sipping on her tropical welcome drink and wearing her loveliest dress. The discovery. His eyes catch hers and turn away, but just for a split second, before they lock back on her and light up with joyful excitement. He runs to her. "Sweetheart, oh my goodness. I can't believe it's you! What an awesome surprise!" He embraces her tightly like in a heartwarming romantic movie.

In the more likely scene, one she could imagine more easily after all the years of their pretending, she walks up to him in the lobby wearing a simple but pretty outfit. He notices her and is more bewildered with shock than delighted with surprise. There is even a hint of disgust in his face and tone. "Leah...what are you doing here?" He asks a lot of questions with a furrowed brow wrinkled on his face. No hugs. Only questions of cost that would imply she had lost her mind. "I'm glad to see you, honey, but can we really afford this? Why didn't you call me first so we could talk about it together?" She would feel ashamed and stupid. And then she would fly straight back to America and officially and forever leave him. *That's what's going to happen.*

Those thoughts made her pick out several colder, more boring outfits. When she was finished packing, her various clothes choices were as varied as her moods toward Stephen. She did pack a modest one-piece swimsuit. At least she would try for a decent tan in Bali if all else failed.

She zipped up the suitcase and looked over at his clutter still in the corner of their room. So frustrating. *How many times have I asked him to organize all his stuff and he persistently ignores me?* She told herself his allotment of inconsiderate actions toward her was up, but he would get one last chance to see her, one last chance to pursue her. That was being more than fair.

She called Fiona one final time to go over some more details and get some more assurance that the plan wasn't totally insane. Fiona replied that it was indeed insane but still the right move. Leah was so grateful for a friend that she could be real with and that was willing to serve her in such an amazing way. Fiona always listened, even though she had plenty of dysfunction to deal with on her own home front. Leah wanted that kind of connection with Stephen, to be best friends with her husband. Shouldn't her marriage be the safest place on the planet for her?

She was able to get a flight late that Tuesday night from Sacramento that landed in Los Angeles with enough time to connect to a midnight Cathay Pacific flight to Hong Kong. Only a few hours layover in Hong Kong before the four hour flight to Surabaya. All in all over 24 hours of travel time, and the tickets were outrageously expensive on short notice, but she told herself again the trip was an absolute must. She still had a few hours to go before she left her driveway on this risky journey, plus another couple of hours at the LAX airport— barely enough time to pull everything together, and still plenty of time to change her mind. She was grateful that she had a positive connection that day with the kids even amid the packing chaos. They thought it was funny that Mommy was going to surprise Daddy and that she was leaving that very day. They were so precious, so young and full of unreserved hope. To them life was one exciting adventure after another, interrupted here and there by school assignments. She was older and knew better. Life was disappointing and you kept busy to keep the loneliness away. But this daring heroine still had one adventure left in her.

During the long travel time she would have plenty of time to think and plan, maybe even relax and catch a movie in flight. Maybe this wouldn't be so bad after all. Maybe she could totally unwind. Maybe she could get a good tan. Maybe she could salvage their marriage. Maybe this was the most foolish thing she had ever done in her life.

She dropped the kids off with Fiona Tuesday evening after dinner at their favorite pizza joint, sighing deeply in the dark of the driveway before pulling away to the airport. She would park the car in a long-term parking lot near the airport—forget the cost. She was going for broke, literally, as this trip might just break their rainy day savings account and put them way deeper into debt. They were already broke long ago in the most important accounts. Fiona told her that leaving Stephen would simply open up a new set of problems. Leah replied that if this didn't work she probably would welcome those new problems. This was the final straw as she simply couldn't live with the straw man any longer.

He better be knocked off his feet to see me in Indonesia. His face better light up. He better see what a good thing he has in me.

≈≈◻≈≈

Agung felt like a VIP riding along in an expensive car. Normally he rode his trusted motorcycle, or when a friend or relative was borrowing that, he got around on the bare-boned public mini-vans that snaked across the city. Those were always hot and crammed with at least ten people. If his friends could see him now, riding in style, sitting on leather interior seats with lots of leg room, and the AC on full blast, would they ever be impressed! He was a little nervous that he might get sick, *masuk angin,* with all that wind entering his body and without enough protection against it, but he willed himself to relish the experience anyway. It was probably too rude to ask them to turn it down.

Soon his friends would see him as he entered Sidoarjo. Agung would make sure that his guest Mr. Carl would stop in at his friend's leather store and maybe at a simple restaurant where he knew the owner. Perhaps they would run into one of his fellow elementary school teachers. Mr. Carl would be invited to come to the school and greet the other teachers, and the students would be excited to meet a foreigner visiting their campus. He imagined introducing Mr. Carl to the whole school assembly, with all the students sitting there wide-eyed, many of them outright giggling. The brightest students would read a speech or a poem to the honored guest in the auditorium. But there wasn't enough time to arrange all this today. Perhaps he could ask Mr. Carl to come tomorrow for a special meeting, which could all be arranged later with the other faculty members.

He wasn't brave enough to ask him yet, though. He knew that Mr. Carl had to be in Pandaan that evening for his meeting, so he thought it best to show him the road of leather goods quickly, and then escort him to the meeting. When he dropped him off, he would ask his new friend if he could invite him the next day to a special school assembly. He felt sure by then Mr. Carl would oblige, feeling the appropriate burden to reciprocate the favor of all this free touring.

≈≈◻≈≈

The four girls from fourth grade—Geni, Riza, Eni and Santi—were walking home from their morning elementary school, enjoying the leisurely stroll, joking and talking with friends and buying a few small snacks and juices from roadside vendors along the way.

Waiting to cross a busy street at a crosswalk, they watched the familiar sight of younger kids begging for coins from cars while the light was still red. Most of these young beggars had already changed from their school uniforms but they still recognized some of them from their school. The four girls looked down on this, because they felt like their classmates were doing it for extra spending cash, maybe for candy for themselves or cigarettes for their older siblings. It wasn't really for essential income for their families.

Their bored eyes watched one of the little beggar girls as she shook a stick-cymbal noisemaker at a tinted window in hopes for a coin. The window rolled down and to their surprise there was their teacher, Mr. Agung, opening up the window and dropping a coin in the empty plastic water cup of the little girl. They called out his name but he didn't hear them. They were shocked that he was not only riding in an expensive car, but a *bule* was sitting next to him, a handsome white man that Agung was chatting with. The window rolled back up, and Pak Agung and his foreign friend didn't notice their eyes full of wonder.

Now they were in a real hurry to get home. It would be fun to spread this news to their family and friends. They knew the information would stir a question in their community: "What was Agung doing riding in a car with a *bule*?" They all knew and respected Mr. Agung—he was a good teacher and had a good reputation in their community. What was the *wong cilik*— little person—doing riding with a rich *bule* in a big fancy car? Was there something mysterious and hidden about nice Pak Agung they didn't know? They felt privileged that they were the ones bringing this tasty morsel of gossip home.

CHAPTER SIX

Stephen nibbled his fingernails while riding in the back seat with Agung toward Sidoarjo. He was trying to concentrate on his exit strategy from Shrimp Town, but the driver had significantly increased the volume of the deep bass Indian pop music that was already ample enough. Over the noise, Agung was assaulting him with questions about life in America which also didn't help him think his way out of his pressing predicament.

At least they weren't heading toward the factory, but Stephen knew this quick tour to Sidoarjo would only buy him a little more time. The roads were a little less crowded and he noticed more trees than people for the first time. The peaceful scenery might help him think more clearly. Maybe he could escape out of the back door of a leather shop and find a taxi on his own. He had seen a few even on the less crowded streets. The downside of the taxi escape plan was that he would mystify Mr. Nice Guy Agung and would never see his suitcase again, though he had already resigned himself to that consequence.

As his new chattering friend continued the barrage of questions and the deep drum sounds kept rattling his chest, his scheming felt more and more futile. This wasn't going to work. He was not going to be able to escape from these two nice men unnoticed. A resolve started to grow within him to come clean.

He would admit his lunatic mistake, apologize profusely and then promise himself he would never do anything this stupid or spontaneous again. Chaz Wilton be cursed. It was time for honesty, or something at least close to that. He removed his fingernails from his mouth, ignored the last question and took two deep breaths. "Agung, could you translate something else for me to the driver?"

The line of questioning abruptly stopped.

"Yes, I be happy to."

"Please tell Mr. Gunadi I appreciate him driving me and I need to tell him something important." *I have got to just get through this.*

Agung translated the little tidbit and waited for the meat of the message.

"Uh," Stephen started. "Please tell Mr. Gunadi that there is some mistake. But I am not Carlton Easley."

"I'm sorry sir, I don't understand," responded Agung, more confused than shocked. "You not Carlton Easley?"

"No, I'm so sorry for the confusion," he said, hoping maybe he could get out of this by playing extraordinarily dumb. He had thinly escaped a lot of emotional quagmires with Leah before by pretending not to understand what she really had meant beforehand. He was at least practiced in this art of feigned ignorance so maybe he could do this after all. Agung hadn't yet translated the sentence to Gunadi because he still didn't understand it.

"My name is not Carlton Easley. My name is Stephen Cranston. I came to the wrong driver at the airport." At best they would chalk this up to an epic mistranslation.

"I'm sorry, Mr. Stephen. I don't understand because my English still only so-so. I thought you say you name Mr. Stephen Carlton Easley or Carl. Could you repeat more slowly? I confused until dizzy. Please say again because I don't understand."

"No, no. I am not Carlton Easley," he insisted loudly over the music. "My name is Stephen Cranston. There has been some mistake. I am so sorry. I just realized the driver has picked up the wrong person. I have never met Carlton Easley and don't know who he is. The driver has the wrong person." Blaming the driver was shameful but the desperate situation called for a drastic tactic. Though admittedly lame, it was the best excuse he could think of while under stress and the dominance of high-powered Indian pop.

Just then a wobble rippled through the car's underside followed by a thump-thump noise. Gunadi slowly pulled the car over to the shoulder of the road and all three men shifted their attention out the window.

"I'm so sorry, Mr. Stephen. It seem we have bad tire."

That much was obvious, but Stephen didn't really feel that inconvenienced by the flat, because he wasn't really trying to get anywhere except back to his hotel in Surabaya. Maybe this was as good a place as any to get out, make his confession clear and clean to Agung, have it translated to the driver, and then high tail it to his hotel. He would of course pay them something for their lost time and then flag down a taxi and get back to Surabaya on his own to prepare for his training seminar. At least this way he would have his suitcase with him. There was no way he was going to get out of this one unscathed and without embarrassment. If those were the only consequences of spontaneity, he could live with them.

Gunadi started the process of changing the tire. A couple riding on a motorcycle together, the man wearing a long white robe and the lady wearing a white head covering, pulled over to help him. These Indonesians were so friendly and helpful, and it made Stephen feel like more of a jerk deceiving them. But he stayed on course with his confession once Agung turned his attention away from the tire repair.

Stephen tried again. "You must understand, Mr. Agung. I am not the man you think I am."

Just then the Muslim man who had stopped to help abruptly opened the car door on Stephen's side. The suddenness of his car door being jerked open almost made Stephen fall out onto the road as he was leaning against it. Over his white robe the intruder was wearing a green velvety sash across his chest, with the letters IDF embroidered across it, sort of beauty-contestant style. The man was yelling something through a white scarf that covered his lower face. Stephen's mind raced for an explanation and for a second thought maybe the man was angry because he and Agung weren't helping change the tire too. Suddenly, the man shoved Stephen over as he barged into the car and slammed the car door behind him.

"*Allahu Akbar! Allahu Akbar!*" the man yelled with an ear-splitting scream. Before Stephen could fully process what was happening, the woman wearing a white head veil jumped into the driver seat and yelled out at the same time, *"Allahu Akbar!"* They both screamed it out again in unison.

Was this a robbery? A carjacking? The yelling man jabbed him with something sharp wrapped inside a folded white cloth. As the lady driver started the engine and turned off the music, the horrible truth started to invade Stephen's mind. He was not being kicked out. He was purposely trapped inside this car by two angry extremists.

Oh my God, I am being kidnapped by terrorists.

The female driver turned her veiled head toward the back seat and said something to the other captor. Stephen caught an expression of intense fear in her eyes. As she discussed something furiously with her partner, Stephen looked out the window and saw another robed man behind Gunadi, sticking something into his back that was also wrapped in cloth. Poor Gunadi was being forced at knifepoint to finish changing the tire by the third accomplice.

Stephen could almost hear his heart racing and he was sure he had never felt so scared. Agung finally said something with pleas and passion to the woman driver and the angry looking man on Stephen's left side. They blasted him back with something in Indonesian and he looked like he wanted to protest more but couldn't summon the courage. He only nodded his head up and down while looking down at the floorboards to signify he understood.

"What is happening, Agung? Who are these people?" Stephen finally asked, surprised to hear the spastic shaking in his own voice.

Agung's voice too was quivering. "They say this is kidnapping and do as they say or they will cut us with their swords. They make the driver fix the tire or they will cut him too."

The two kidnappers didn't seem to want Agung to talk to Stephen. They yelled at him again and he just nodded his head up and down submissively.

The one on Stephen's side looked into his eyes and barked, "You do exactly as we say, Mr. Carlton."

This was no random carjacking but a planned kidnapping. *They think I'm Carlton. They have to know they've got the wrong guy...I don't want to be tortured.*

The trunk opened and Stephen heard the tire-changing tools being tossed in the back. He felt his heart drop even deeper. What would they do now with Gunadi? This was a lonely stretch of road and not many people were passing. Would they kill him now and throw his corpse in the woods nearby? *Oh God don't let that happen.* Though not really religious, Stephen could think of nothing else to do except pray under his breath.

The angry man on Stephen's left side started talking harshly with Agung again. Stephen couldn't pick up any meaning, but he heard the word "Carlton" a few times in the intense exchange.

Agung, face now sweaty even in the AC-cooled car, turned to Stephen and said in a slow, low voice, "Mr. Stephen. They say this is kidnapping and they know that you is enemy of Islam. I told them no that is not true. You are Mr. Carlton Stephen Easley and nice man. They ask why are you going the opposite direction of Pandaan where you factory is. I tell them why and they say I am a liar. They will use their own translator with you because they think I am telling lies. They say I am an enemy of Islam too." Agung had tears in his eyes. "I say I am good man and not bad Muslim."

"No, no. Tell them I am not Carlton Easley. Tell them my name is Stephen Cranton. Remember what I was just telling you..."

"But if I lie they be angry to me, Mr. Carl. Please don't say lies. I think translator knows English."

Stephen considered jumping out of the car but Agung would have to go first and he didn't' know how to communicate that to him under the tense situation. Plus they might chase them down and use their weapons. He quickly reached for his wallet to pull out his ID. The angry kidnapper jabbed the sword or knife or whatever it was in his side harder. He felt his empty back pocket, remembered his wallet was still zipped away in a travel pouch hiding inside his carry-on, and lifted his empty hand to show that he wasn't reaching for anything to fight back with.

The third kidnapper opened the car door on Agung's side and jumped in. His frame was a little shorter than the first man, and he carried himself less aggressively. He was also wearing a robe with the IDF sash across his chest and his sweating face was half covered with a white scarf. With four grown men cramped in the back row, Stephen wasn't sure why the third terrorist didn't sit in the empty shotgun seat in the front, but maybe this was on purpose to make him and Agung feel even more trapped. If that were the case, it was working very well. He and Agung were now blocked on both sides.

"*Assalamalaikum,*" the one on Agung's side yelled menacingly as he slammed the door shut.

"*Walaikumsalam,*" Agung answered back.

"What are they saying, Agung?"

"Mr. Stephen, please no more questions or quick movements. I'm not sure why but I think they be angry to us." His voice was still trembling.

Stephen had remembered reading once that in a hostage situation the best thing to do was stay calm. Kidnappers are so hyped-up on adrenaline that they often do stupid things at the beginning without thinking. Better for the victim to go limp and be polite and let the initial emotional explosion of the capture pass. He would let them call the shots and know that they had the upper hand so they wouldn't need to use a heavy one to smash out any resistance. No more sudden movements from him.

Stephen could see out of the window, past the kidnappers' two parked motorcycles, a fat palm tree with several ropes tied around it. He couldn't see Gunadi, but he suspected that his ill-fated driver was bound on the other side of that tree. How long would it take for someone to find him in that cluster of trees next to a rice paddy? Could he scream out and be heard by a passing motorcycle? Or did they gag his mouth? At least they didn't kill the poor guy. The roads were busy enough but the rice fields looked empty. Hopefully a farmer would come by soon. Stephen felt guilty again for getting this nice man into his trouble, or rather Carlton Easley's trouble.

Stephen tried to look carefully into his male captors' faces to memorize them as the woman pulled the car from the shoulder of the road and into traffic. He could see them clearly from the nose up. They were probably in their twenties, the leader with a harsh face and the other with a more innocent and darker complexion. The brown eyes of the driver lady were peering through the veil, and he could tell from her voice and smooth hands on the steering wheel that she was also young.

"You are American infidel Satan," the angry one on his right yelled at Stephen. "You have humbled us and now we feel your pain. Now you will feel our pain, Mr. Easley."

The mashed-up quote would have been funny under other circumstances, like if he were watching it on TV. But this was real and he was honestly terrified, with this angry, robed man jabbing something sharp in his side. He just answered, "Yes sir."

"You will beg us for forgiveness for your country."

He didn't know how to respond to this. He just repeated again, "Yes sir."

"You will beg forgiveness for exploit the Muslim."

"Yes sir."

The fierce-looking man shouted with rotten, stale breath. Because they were all cramped together, Stephen felt the sharp weapon jabbing into his side even from under the bundle of cloth that the man was using to conceal it. Longer than a butcher knife, it must be some kind of machete or small sword.

He glanced at the man on Agung's right. His eyes were darting about under his prayer hat and he genuinely looked scared. Agung was quietly crying next to him.

Stephen marveled to himself that his kidnappers did not have him hooded and that he could see exactly where they were going. After about an hour, the sniffling stopped from Agung and the roads started to incline and wind through hilly and dense tropical scenery. Although it might be hard later to describe to authorities where he was been taken, as everything was so unfamiliar to him, he could at least memorize the names of signs or unusual landmarks they passed. It was a little hard from a cramped back seat trying to look through the windows without appearing too observant. But he did capture a few names of villages and stores in his mind, plus he tried to remember natural landmarks like caves and what appeared to be a teak tree forest they passed.

The mean captor's body was still tense and Stephen didn't want to agitate him, especially with that mystery weapon still pointed into his side. The other two captors seemed more nervous than angry. All of them rode together in tense silence, which seemed even more vacuous in comparison with the previous Indian pop music and hysterical Arabic shouting.

After another hour or so through endless curves, they finally made it to the summit of the tropical hill country. The car pulled over to a tight shoulder on the highest bend that looked like a picture spot for the spectacular vista. Were they planning on throwing Stephen-turned-Carlton into the steep ravine below? It would be a long time before anyone found his remains amid that dense forest jungle.

The three captors talked quickly and the mean one suddenly jumped and walked over to survey the edge of the ravine. Stephen's heart rate quickened. Were they going to grab him by the scruff of his neck and toss him into the valley below right here? Didn't they want to try for a ransom first...or was this ideologically-driven hatred toward the West, evil and simple, with no money needing to change hands?

Stephen took the chance of breaking the silence in the absence of their leader.

"May I know why you are mad at my country?" he asked in the direction of the unsure one on Agung's side. He tried to phrase the question as submissively as possible.

The garbed man either didn't understand the question or wasn't sure if he should answer it and looked for direction from the front seat. The lady driver adjusted the rearview mirror to get a look at Stephen's face. As she did, Stephen saw the leader marching back to the car, zipping up his fly. He must have just relieved himself on a palm tree and not been planning to end Stephen's life after all. Come to think of it, Stephen had to go, too, but he wasn't about to ask.

She looked like she wanted to answer Stephen's question but seemed nervous with her leader getting back into the car. This time he got back into the front seat instead, which pleased Stephen. No more sharp jab in the side. The two front-seat terrorists talked briefly and the leader then turned to Stephen, looking perturbed.

"You may not ask us anything," he barked, showing he was the top dog here. "You are our prisoner and you do as we say. We not answer you question. We tell you answer."

"Yes sir," said Stephen softly and looked down between his knees at the floor. He mulled over the remark which also would have been funny had he not been so terrified.

On they drove in silence for over an hour down the back side of the mountainous area, curving around the hills with some caves etched into the cliffs they zoomed past. Finally, the two-lane road started to flatten. Stephen surmised from the look of the expansive blue sky ahead that they were nearing the ocean. A seagull in flight confirmed his suspicion. It had been nearly four hours since the abduction, and since Surabaya was on the north side of the island, they had to be approaching the south coast. A stray memory entered his mind from the last time that his family had a day at the beach together. The pleasant thought made him feel deeply sad, fearing he may never see them again. He willed himself to keep these thoughts at bay, trying to stay in strategy mode, being watchful and keeping the clues in his mind that would lead toward his rescue.

After another half hour, the car pulled off a main street and onto a dusty gravel road which led them by small simple houses. A group of kids playing soccer in the middle of the road made way for the car. They looked at the fancy car with curious wide eyes and giggled to each other. As the car thumped over the two rocks in the road they were using for makeshift soccer goal posts, Stephen wondered if he should pound on the window and call out to these kids, at least attract some attention to this kidnapping, or perhaps jump out of the car now that it had slowed. He then thought better of it, as they wouldn't know exactly what he was communicating and the sudden move could bring down swift punishment. Not only that, he didn't want to bring negative consequences on Agung, and the terrorists would most likely catch him before he could escape. Passive mode was the safest bet.

The road got even more narrow and snaked through a field of tall brown stalks which he thought must be sugarcane. The car then pulled into the mouth of a gated driveway that led to a small dingy grey house. He kept noting to himself details of the surroundings as the girl got out of the car to unlock the gate. Before unlocking it she looked up and down the lonely street, presumably making sure they could do this clandestinely. That would have been impossible to do if there were anyone else around—pull a white guy out of a Mercedes-Benz in the middle of a sugarcane patch. Stephen never felt so fearful and isolated and alone, so far away from anyone he cared about. He brushed the thoughts of dread away again.

After the girl unlocked the gate the mean one yelled out something and then got out to swing the gate open. Stephen took in the tall and foreboding fence, with shards of broken glass cemented at the top. Corners of the fence were rolled with barbed wire where there were openings. Most of the other houses that he passed had low-lying fences that could easily be jumped. They had picked the one house in the village that most resembled a minimum-security prison. The quieter man held open the door for Agung and Stephen. He also asked politely enough for their cell phones. Agung handed his over and Stephen did too, even though it didn't have an international plan so he couldn't have made a call home anyway.

How long will it be before I can call my family? Are they going to hurt me? Will I get out of this alive?

CHAPTER SEVEN

Carlton wiped his forehead with the long sleeve of his damp dress shirt. He knew Indonesia would be hot, but not unbearably roasting hot. The noonday tropical sun beat down upon him as he stood waiting on the shoulder of the toll road with no shade in sight. He looked into the faces of the simple men and a few women that formed a semi-circle of growing spectators around him. Most were wearing long-sleeved shirts or light jackets; some even wore thick winter coats. One guy had a ski cap on. He asked himself a few times why in the world would anyone wear winter clothes in the humid tropics? Carlton's own blazer was left back in the car and he thought he probably wouldn't be putting it on again, unless he was sheltered inside an air-conditioned meeting.

But the heat was the least of his inconveniences now. Usually Carlton was a take-charge guy and took the lead even if he wasn't totally sure where he was going. One of his bedrock values, he often reminded younger associates, was that a wrong decision was decidedly better than indecision. Yet this far out of his cultural element, he felt dislocated from his managerial principles, adrift in a leadership vertigo.

A lean man in dull, tattered clothes pointed at him and said something that sounded almost cheery. Carlton shook his head to indicate he didn't understand. The man rubbed his thumb and two fingers together in a sign of someone twisting paper together, perhaps money. Then putting an imaginary cigarette to his crusty lips, he puffed with exaggeration.

How do they know who I am? So it had come to this again. "You want money," Carlton told the man. Then he rephrased it in question form, "Do you want money?"

The man didn't answer but smiled and puffed more on his air cigarette and then twisted the imaginary money together again. *"Uang rokok,"* the man responded with the same wide grin.

At least this made sense to Carlton as to why they were not allowing him to leave the scene or even rest back at the car. They probably figured out who he was by now, a wealthy supervisor from America here to inspect their local cigarette factory, the economic engine of the entire county. Surely they knew he had nothing to do with the hit-and-run by now, even though he kept reminding them from time to time in English. This was simple, and he could guess pretty accurately what *uang rokok* meant. He was here for no other reason than extortion. *Well at least they are speaking my language.*

He wasn't about to start handing out money randomly to scraggly strangers, but he had already decided to pick up the boy's hospital bills. *I'll do that and then some and then I'll be out of this unbearable place forever.*

"Where is the family? I pay the family for hospital bills."

No one answered.

He reached for his back pocket and pulled out his wallet to make them understand he wanted to help the victim. The police had already taken his ID but he still had some U.S. cash. And money always talked, even in a foreign language.

"Where is family?" he repeated, holding the wallet up.

The crowd stared wide-eyed at the uplifted offering. He immediately realized his mistake, thinking this was like waving a bloody carcass to a flock of hungry vultures. The wallet was stuffed back into his back pocket before outstretched hands could clamor for it. Instead he would focus his efforts on finding the official family spokesperson.

"Family?" he asked them all loudly.

The imaginary cigarette puffing man pointed to him and smiled brightly.

"You family?" Carlton snorted. "Yeah I bet you are. I can see you are wracked with sorrow over your loved one's injury." The man, obviously not grasping the biting remark, just kept smiling as if he had just been complimented. *"Uang rokok,"* he only repeated.

70

A long-faced man with his hands in his jacket pockets stepped forward and said something that sounded like *"kakak."*

"Kakak," Carlton repeated loudly, "Family? You *kakak?"*

A junior-high aged girl wearing a white school uniform approached and stood next to the somber man, looking up at Carlton with guileless brown eyes. "Yes, yes sir, we family," she said. "He is older brother and I am cousin."

Carlton studied the solemn man, still suspicious that he might be a charlatan. What if they were all total strangers to the injured boy and were trying to play the rich foreigner? The man kept frowning and looking indignant and then started saying something in a low tone to the young girl and the other onlookers.

Carlton would play along. After confirming if this man was the older brother, he would give the family a wad of cash. He realized that giving the family representative money in the midst of this semi-hostile crowd would be not only tacky but could provoke a strong reaction. It would be prudent to do this on the sly later.

In the end it always comes down to the green stuff, which had gotten him out of many jams before. A congressional subcommittee decided to look the other way when some prominent members got large re-election donations via select Super PAC's. A vengeful ex-wife with her potentially damaging revelations finally went away when she got enough money out of him. A sexual-harassment charge vanished with one large check. He knew how to act humbly for the cameras, but behind the scenes he knew what people really wanted. How many family members of cancer victims found it in their hearts to forgive cigarette companies after they received a large payoff, thanks to an out-of-control tort system?

As he liked to tell people, even the Bible says that money is the answer to everything. King Solomon or somebody like that said it. Money, plain and simple. Just give them enough money and they'll go away and stop bothering you. Sure it was bad that this man probably now has a handicapped little brother, but their family was about to see more money than they would ever see in their meager-incomed lives. One day they would consider this a big blessing of fate from Allah or whatever they believed in. Carlton would act apologetic and then slip a huge load of cash into someone's hand under the table. He just wasn't sure where the table was in this culture.

Without explanation, the alleged older brother started walking back to the cement wall with the cousin translator. Two more joined them and one of them put his arm around the man. The small group disappeared together into the large crack in the wall. Carlton wasn't sure what was going on or what would happen next. When would the police get here so he could file a report and get back to his life? There were still enough people on guard patrol to keep him from making a break for it.

Passing cars slowed down to get a peek at the wreck. By now it would be hard for them to figure out what had happened, with the injured boy gone. Seeing a car stopped sideways by the road with a white foreigner standing in front of it surrounded by a group of Indonesians was an interesting enough sight, though. He could see people looking out their windows and trying to solve the mystery, talking to their fellow passengers about what might have happened.

The day was getting even hotter and Carlton slapped at a large bug that landed on his sweaty neck. The brown faces continued to stare, curious to see what would happen next too. *Don't these people have anything better to do?* Once he smiled the best disarming smile he could muster, but it was only returned with emotionless stares. Waiting and staring and sweating. The sun must hang high in the sky a long time along the equator, he guessed, because it just kept beating and beating upon him.

This is ridiculous. He finally decided it was time to do something, even if that meant making a mistake. There were other things to attend to, and he wasn't going to stand around here all day, no matter what these people thought of him or what they tried to do. *I'll make my move and just let them try to stop me.* Eventually they would get their money and he could get back on track with the day's goals, mainly his much-deserved relaxation. He surmised the jet lag must be making him grumpy.

"I need to borrow a cell phone," he said, right into the face of the person who looked to him the least poor. "Cell phone," he said louder.

"Hand phone?" said the young man who was wearing a black leather jacket, but didn't appear to be sweating. His English response emboldened Carlton to take charge of the situation.

"That's right. I need to borrow your hand phone to make a call. I have to call the factory where I am supposed to be going." The man slowly pulled a cell phone out of his inside coat pocket as everyone watched. "And please tell these people in Indonesian that I had nothing to do with this accident. I was only a passenger, not the driver. The driver ran off somewhere."

The young man whispered to another presumable English speaker to get a consensus on what the foreigner just said.

The more direct he got, the more people seemed to back up. He liked that—playing offense and letting them play defense. "Please, tell them now. I don't want them to misunderstand." He thought twice and simplified his statement to, "I want them to understand I did not do this."

The young man, with the help of another auxiliary English speaker, translated to the crowd. As they weighed in with their opinions, Carlton searched for the number of the factory in his pants pocket. Thank God he still had it, he thought, a line of rescue from his false identity as accident suspect to the real identity of important boss. He wished he had thought of this sooner, borrowing a cell phone right after the incident and calling the factor immediately. Maybe he just couldn't think straight in the heat.

The small cell phone was hard to figure out and he tried to remember the lucky combination of initial digits he had used before on the driver's phone. When it wasn't working, he interrupted the young man, who was either in the middle of translating or fielding questions. "Please, can you help me dial this number? I must speak to factory and I can't figure out. I don't know how to use your phone. Your cell phone. Your hand phone." He shoved the device back into the young man's hand.

"Yes, yes," the young man said politely as his friend nodded in agreement. Carlton felt from his soft answer that the man believed him. It was good to have these two interpreters on his side, as that might come in handy later. Carlton gave the phone back to the man with the scribbled number and the young man quickly dialed it in and returned the phone to Carlton.

While the phone rang Carlton refocused his attention elsewhere, away from the staring spectators and toward small houses in the distance that lined a large rice field. To his great relief the phone was answered after a few rings.

"*Halo, selamat sore,*" came the answer.

"Yes, Hello. This is Mr. Carlton Easley. Is this Mr. Bambang?"

"*Sebentar,*" came the timid reply. "*Sebentar mister, ya?*"

He wiped his sweaty face again with his sleeves while he waited, wishing he would have remembered to bring a handkerchief to the tropics.

After a few minutes came a greeting. "Hello? Oh yes, this Mr. Bambang. I sorry they answer phone in Indonesia language. They thought you Indonesia person."

The over-effusive apologies for everything were really grating on Carlton's nerves. He held a sarcastic response back and said, "Yes, Mr. Bambang. I am having some more trouble."

"Oh. I sorry to hear that sir."

Great, more apologies. "Yes, I did find the other driver but I do not know where he is now. He hit some kid selling water bottles on the side of the toll road and now there are a bunch of people here thinking that I was involved. The boy may be injured but it was not my fault. You need to get down here right away and sort this out."

"I'm sorry, sir, Mr. Carlton. I not understand. You say driver hit boy?"

"Yes, that's right. And now he is in the jungle or the forest or whatever you call it here."

Bambang took a second to process this, then asked, "Where you at, now, Mr. Carlton? You in jungle too?"

"I don't know where I am," he said sharply. "I am not in the jungle. I am on the side of the road, the toll road." The terse sentences rocketed out of him like the rat-a-tat of a machine gun. He didn't mean to blurt out his anger, knowing that bursts of verbiage from a loud American wouldn't help matters now. The humility card would need to be played until he figured all this out. "I'm sorry. I'm not sure. I am on some sort of toll road."

"Okay, Mr. Carlton is on toll road. Where is driver now? Driver with you or in jungle?"

Didn't we go over this already? He would have to take charge again after all. "Look, Mr. Bambang, I am going to tell you the mile marker, the uh, kilometer marker where I am on this toll road. You will come here and pick me up and talk to the police when they get here."

Carlton felt proud of himself for thinking of a good strategy like this in the midst of all these bumbling people. He also felt a whole lot better that he could be located by someone on his side. He looked down the road and saw a small green sign. Luckily there was some GPS coordinate on his life—a kilometer marker. He couldn't make out the number but pointed it out to the few people still watching him. "What number does that say? What kilometer is this?" he asked toward the two English speakers still gawking at him curiously.

"Kilometer two six," one of the men said without looking. He must have lived here his whole life.

"Kilometer two six," Carlton repeated into the phone as clearly as he could.

"Okay, Mr. Carlton. We send someone right away to six. You please stay there."

"Don't worry," said Carlton sarcastically. "I won't go anywhere." Then before Bambang hung up he quickly added, "But you come too. I need you here." He hated sounding so helpless and needy but that's what he was in this God-forsaken moment.

He hoped it wouldn't take too much longer for them to get there and get him out of this nightmare. The money-grubbing police were probably also on their way to investigate the accident, he assumed, and he wanted the people squarely on his side on the scene first. The factory he was sure had a "special relationship" with the police and he would be able to get out of this quickly and salvage his day.

As he looked around the trashy side of the busy road, he saw that more people had come from the same break in the wall to gawk at the foreigner and the scene of the crime. He hated being stared at, especially by people who were whispering and probably casting blame on him. He stared back at them. *I've got nothing to be ashamed of. I am as innocent of this as you are.* Determined not to look down and convey any sense of guilt, he held his head up and looked right back into their brown little darting eyes. Strangely, he derived some measure of pleasure staring them down long enough to make them look away.

"Go ahead, stare," he mumbled. "I'll stare right back."

After a few more minutes of staring and sweating, a new clump of people emerged from the large break in the wall. Someone was leading the way, a tense-faced man wearing a felt black hat and marching straight toward Carlton. When he saw Carlton, he flicked out his cigarette and picked up his pace.

Carlton braced for impact. Who were these people? Was this an Indonesian lynch mob? They certainly looked angry enough to do something rash. Perhaps it was the family of the boy. His heart, which had already been subjected to one stressful procedure, pumped fast to keep his brain oxygenated.

The semi-circle became a full circle around him. The leader stepped to his face and started saying something excitedly, which of course Carlton couldn't understand. He looked around for one of his former translators, but he didn't see their faces in the small crowd.

He looked back into the man's quivering face, which was either pleading with him or scolding him. Carlton thought it had to be the boy's father. The crowd nodded their heads and murmured approvals at the man's ranting.

True, he was sorry for what happened to this man's son, but he was not going to be bullied. As the jabbering went on and the crowd echoed their affirmations, he lifted back his head and shouted with all the strength he could muster, "I did not do this!" The people took a collective step back.

He then looked directly into the probable father's eyes and yelled, still at full volume, "I did not do this. Do you understand that?"

The crowd was stunned silent, as was their leader. The man thought for a second, then reached out and tugged on Carlton's sleeve as if he wanted Carlton to follow him. Carlton noticed for the first time the man had tears in his eyes.

"He want you to come to his house and see his boy and what happened to him," someone in the crowd called out.

Carlton looked down and saw that it was the young teen translator again.

"No," Carlton shouted back, not to the translator but to the father, thinking the man would at least understand that universal word. "We wait here," he said while stomping the dry ground and pointing to it. Carlton congratulated himself for quick thinking in the midst of a stressful situation. This was his zone, and he had always prided himself on rising under pressure that would make other men wilt. The course of action, short of police intervention, would be to wait for Bambang to arrive. He was not about to get dragged by these crazy people into their hysterical household.

Others beside the leader began pleading with him, motioning toward the crack in the wall. *No way am I going with you lunatics.* He planted his feet firmly on the ground and folded his arms across his chest to say a very loud "No" with his body language.

"Police," he said loudly. "Police."

As if on cue, a police car came into sight in the distance down the toll road. Carlton saw it first and pointed at it for benefit of the crowd. They parted slightly and half looked behind them at the approaching squad car. Carlton groaned audibly, as he was hoping Bambang would get here before the police. Now it would get complicated and he would be forced to become an official witness to this whole sorry mess and do his reporting through a bad concoction of English and Indonesian. This mob would say God knows what to the officer. None of them had been there to see what really had happened.

The police car was slowing on the shoulder of the road, and Carlton at least preferred the law to a lawless mob. He decided he would approach the officer first and stay on the offensive before these simple townsfolk gave their version of events.

As he started up the small grassy embankment to get to the officer, he had to shield his eyes from the blinding sun with one hand. With his other hand he waved to get the attention of the officer who was now stepping out of the police car.

Carlton quickly recognized the officer's face and let out a long sigh. It was the same officer who had taken his passport and driver's license earlier. The officer bent back into the car to grab something off the seat, and Carlton turned and headed back into the crowd. He slunk in the middle trying to hide himself, which was not easy to do with his large frame and skin color.

He decided that, after all, he *did* want to visit that poor unfortunate boy right now. As in right this very instant. He already knew firsthand these Indonesian police were conniving opportunists and would somehow pin this on him, especially that one miffed cop. If he would be extorted to pay, at least the money would go straight to the family and not into the pockets of these shameless officers, little boys in great big uniforms.

He half-jogged to the crack in the wall, and the villagers at first did a double take—looking toward the officer who was still engrossed with something inside his car and then toward this bizarre white man now charging into their neighborhood. The group consensus was to follow Carlton, and they had to hurry to catch up to the *bule* who had no idea where he was going.

Carlton walked quickly down the dusty, busted-up road, looking to the left and right at all the people gawking at him from the shade of little roadside shack-looking cafes. *What do these people do all day? Shouldn't they be at work or in the field or something?* He immediately judged them as lazy, wasting their time sipping coffee, chatting with friends and smoking cigarettes. He could see from the packs on the counter that at least they were smoking his cigarettes. *I would die of boredom in this village if the smokes didn't get me first.*

He stopped suddenly, and a couple of villagers in step behind him almost knocked in to him. He spun around and asked, loudly, "Where boy? Where sick boy?"

"*Di sana,*" one of them said, pointing in the direction of an unpainted plywood-walled house at the intersection of two narrow roads.

"Let's go," he said confidently. People on both sides of the road stopped frozen in fascination. The only people moving were the half dozen people who had become his unofficial entourage. "Let's go and get this over with," he whispered to nobody in particular and directed his steps to the tiny house. Chickens scattered at his approach and a little boy peeped wide-eyed through the open window.

As Carlton got to the front stoop, he heard a lot of commotion coming from the inside. On the side of the porch were discarded water bottles and garbage scattered across a piece of scorched earth where they must burn trash.

He took a deep breath, steeling himself for the inevitable hysteria of relatives whipped up into a frenzy.

As he stepped in the dark of the front room, he immediately saw the injured boy surrounded by his friends and relatives. They gasped and made some other indistinguishable noises upon his entrance. Carlton replied with a forced smile the best he could. A coffee table was pushed aside and the boy was laid on a small beat-up wicker sofa. A washcloth was draped across his forehead, and his head was lifted to see the foreigner.

An old man wearing a plaid wrap cloth around his waist and a black oval-shaped hat on his head struggled up from his squatted position next to the boy. His eyes blazed indignantly as he pointed a bony finger at Carlton. Through a spittle-filled mouth with most of the teeth missing, he started spewing at Carlton with some sort of rebuke.

Must be grandpa, Carlton thought. "Take it easy, old guy. I'm here to help."

Still blank stares and no one said a word—just the sound of grandpa's angry lecture rifling through the hot and humid air. Carlton looked down respectfully until the old guy could get it off his chest. The bare concrete floor absorbed his attention during the animated speech as he thought through his next move.

When the tirade was over, he looked up and tried consciously to change his dispassionate smirk into a compassioned look of concern. He repeated, more slowly, "I'm here to help." *Where is that little girl translator?*

He pulled out his wallet and the sudden movement seemed to startle the group, like he was about to pull a gun on them. *Let's just cut to the chase.* He could see the boy had pulled through and just needed to get to a hospital and the bone would be reset and all would be just fine. He held his wallet up toward the mob of relatives and asked with a lift in his voice, "Help? I give money and you take boy to the hospital. Want go to hospital?"

A woman with a tear-streaked face stood up and walked in front of Carlton. *Must be dear old mom.* She said something that sounded gut-wrenching and pointed back to her son. Others came around her to hold her up.

"Yes, yes, I help." He bobbed his wallet up and down in front of her face for her to get the point. "Hospital. Take son to hospital. Take son to doctor. I pay."

She wiped the leftover tears from under her eyes with a clutched kerchief and the harsh expression softened on her lined face. *"Terima kasih mister, ya"* she said with a sniffle as she reached out and took the wallet out of his hand. "Thank you mister."

CHAPTER EIGHT

As they escorted him into the house, Stephen studied the tiny front yard and stole glances down the street for any markings he might need later. He tried hard to memorize everything, marveling again that he wasn't hooded. These people may be daring extremists but they were terrible kidnappers.

The leader pulled Stephen's suitcase and carry-on out of the car and dropped them on the cement front porch. He stayed outside like a sentinel, maybe to stand guard or to go on some other terrorist errand.

When the four of them got into the dimly lit front room, the female pulled off her head covering, revealing a surprisingly friendly, lovely face. She motioned them to sit in the rattan furniture, and announced "I will get us some refreshing." Her hair was straight and dark black and she flipped it off her neck for air circulation as she tossed the head covering on a chair.

The kind statement perplexed Stephen. He was bracing for anger and beating and torture. During the long car ride, he had imagined a black banner in Arabic hung on the wall with a handy-cam mounted on a tripod to videotape his execution. Yet he was being treated like an honored guest by a gentle Asian beauty. She pointed for her partner and Agung to be seated in the small couches at the front entrance of the house. Stephen and Agung sat there dazed, not knowing what to say or how to behave. A couple of minutes later she came back into the room with a tray of lemonade drinks and a tin of cookies. "Please," she said, "take some refreshing."

They took away my freedom but at least they are offering refreshments.

The timid terrorist took off his white prayer hat and sat on a chair next to the sofa where Stephen and Agung were still sitting stiffly. The kidnappers both looked at their captors as if they were expecting polite conversation now. "Please," she offered again, "have some refreshing." Without the Muslim headgear, his tormentors just looked like a nice couple of people who wanted nothing more than to have the neighbors over for a cup of tea.

Agung leaned close to Stephen and whispered softly, "It's not polite in Indonesia to drink right away when the host offers. Wait for them to ask again."

Stephen thought it bizarre going through cultural niceties while being kidnapped, but he went along. He waited for them to offer again before he would take a drink. It did look good in this humid and airless room, and he could feel his undershirt starting to soak through to his cotton button-down.

He looked around the room, stuffed full with odd knick-knacks on all the shelves and sagging furniture. It reminded him a little of his grandmother's old house with the same homey yet musty smell. *No more thoughts of relatives and home. Stay in the game here.*

The mean one suddenly exploded into the room carrying Stephen's luggage, startling everyone. He closed the door and looked out the window to see if anyone was watching. When he was satisfied all was clear, he turned his attention to his hostages and a look of disgust engulfed his face.

He shot an angry look at the two other captors, both of whom had already discarded their face coverings. Then he yelled sarcastically through his face covering to Stephen and Agung, "Are you comfort? Do you need something else to make more comfort?"

Stephen wanted to quip "How about my freedom?" but no way would he let that one fly. He stayed in his I-don't-want-any-trouble mode by quietly studying the floor.

"Here you want drink?" the mean one practically shouted. He placed his foot on the glass coffee table and with the front tip of his shoe flicked over the drinks and the tin of cookies to the floor. "You no guest here," he yelled. "You my hostage!"

He then darted down the hall and could be heard rummaging around in the back rooms.

The strange foursome—the two kidnappers, Stephen and Agung just sat in the little guest receiving room in an awkward, polite silence, while the lemonade dripped onto the floor and over the scattered cookies.

The mean one quickly burst back into the room and for some reason was holding up his embroidered sash. "We the IDF," he screamed as everyone stared at him in bewildered silence. He looked over the room and then yelled something in Indonesian to his partners. Whatever he said they didn't like, and the girl protested back to him. He ignored her.

"You not guests here," he snarled at Stephen and Agung, switching back to English. "You my hostage. You do as I say and not act like guests."

Stephen wasn't exactly sure how to follow that command, and he just nodded his head up and down slowly. *Whatever you say. You're the boss.* The leader had sense enough not to reveal his face as easily as his kinder and more dimwitted partners had done. He was obviously the brains of this terrorist outfit.

He barked something to his partners and they got up slowly and submitted to his order. The woman solemnly and submissively began cleaning the mess. The quiet one escorted Agung down the hall to the first room and the leader walked Stephen to his room at the end of the hall. Without warning the angry man suddenly shoved Stephen into the wall, knocking a framed picture from the wall, its glass shattering around their feet. Before Stephen could straighten himself up and recover, the leader wrapped his chest sash around Stephen's neck and began tightening it. He growled, "We the IDF. You do as we say." The choke hold was released gruffly and Stephen gasped for air.

Before Stephen could answer or even think about defending himself, the leader threw him into his room and he tumbled down hard to the floor. The door lock clicked.

Stephen lay motionless for a minute, his body feeling the pain of hitting the hard floor even more than being shoved against the wall. The sensation of being choked stayed with him and he tried to breathe deeply to regain his emotional composure. He finally opened his eyes and crawled to a thin foam mattress on the floor.

Now Stephen was all alone with his thoughts, for the first time in several hours. He sighed and looked up at the ceiling patched with mold spots. *Am I going to be attacked again? Is something worse to come?*

The thought was disconcerting and he surveyed the room to get his mind away from imagining torture. It didn't take long to inventory the sparse room. One woven mat on top of the white tile floor. One foam mattress with no sheet cover. A long, cylindrical pillow on top. A rectangle window covered with bars that was too high to look out of. One fluorescent light bulb emitting a dim light with a low hum. That will get annoying fast, he thought. Besides that, there was nothing else. No TV, table, bed, bathroom, AC, fan or any other furnishings.

How stupid. Impersonating a total stranger who was destined to be kidnapped in Indonesia. He thought of who this mystery man might be and what he did to get people so angry at him. Maybe besides being expected at a factory in Pandaan, Carlton Easley was covering up some alter identity and had been exposed, like a CIA operative under the guise of a businessman? Or maybe there was some connection with organized crime? Stephen also regretted that his new friend Agung wasn't contained in the same room. More than just wanting friendly company, he wanted to apologize again in person to the kind man for getting him into this terrible predicament.

He thought of Leah. She would just start wondering why he hadn't called yet. He remembered that he had forgotten to call her while traveling, even though he promised he would, no matter what time it was in California. It had now been a few hours since he landed and she would probably be looking at his itinerary and checking her emails. If she were worried enough and figured out a way to reach the company in Surabaya, they would say he was a no-show, which would of course worry her more. He got up to pace around and once more checked the door. It was definitely locked.

But if Leah did know what was really happening, she would be *really* worried. Maybe frustration over lack of communication was better than the trauma of her husband getting kidnapped.

The word stabbed his soul. *Kidnapped.*

The screen of his mind re-flashed the images of foreigners in poor quality web videos about to be beheaded. *Executed.* He thought of his children growing up without a father and began to tear up.

A couple of hours later he heard faint footsteps coming toward his room. He braced himself and hoped it wasn't the leader ready to yell at him some more and maybe take the first slice with that sharp dagger. Instead, the door opened slowly and the female poked her head through. "*Maaf, Pak, saya mengganggu.*"

She realized quickly from his puzzled expression that he didn't understand a word of what she said. She smiled to herself at the thought of speaking to her guest in her native language and repeated, "I'm sorry I bother you, sir, Mr. Carlton."

"No, no," he said. Stephen felt relieved that a friendly captor was paying him a visit after much solitude, yet he remained slightly suspicious that this was some sort of good cop/bad cop mind game.

"I bring you snack. Maybe you tired from your journey. "Our leader..." she stumbled over the words, "...not really angry. He just want to show you he the boss."

"Oh, I believe he's the boss," Stephen said as she placed the drink and snack on the floor. "Can you tell me your name?"

"No cannot."

She just stood there, way too gentle and bashful to ever be convincing as a terrorist.

"Why I am being kidnapped, Miss...Miss whoever you are."

"My name Mbak Dina," she volunteered, apparently not realizing she had just broken her own rule.

She looked back at the door, still slightly opened, as if to see if anyone were close by, listening. He saw a struggle in her face and after a long pause she said, "You have snack first. Later we talk why you here. But you not be here long if you cooperate." With that she smiled and nodded, walking gracefully backwards out of the room.

Minutes crawled by, but he wasn't sure exactly how many, as they had taken his watch during the car ride. Claustrophobia and a desperate need for human contact began to suffocate him. He wondered where Agung was and hoped he was still in the house. That was selfish, he knew, as the man should be home with his own family, but Stephen wanted at least one person one hundred percent on his side. He wasn't sure what to think of this sweet captor lady who may be part of a mind game strategy. Maybe she was trying to soften him by using a sweet and innocent Bambi routine. But why?

His thoughts echoed in his head under the dull hum of the fluorescent bulb overhead. Here he was in solitary confinement, a punishment he heard that prisoners feared above all others. They would rather be kicked and beaten in the prison yard by their fellow inmates than locked up all by themselves for time without end. It was the worst torture ever devised by man. Would this solitude drive him mad? Would he have hours of solitary confinement or days or weeks or even months? God, not years. Plenty of time to be with his thoughts, which had seemed to turn on him lately. Plenty of time to go down his Personalized Action Plan—what a joke.

The first hours were already unbearable. His skin was sticky and he wanted a bath. He couldn't bear this for more than a day. Would they let him take a bath? Would they even let him go to the bathroom? He really needed to go for the last few hours but he dared not ask permission yet.

Another hour, maybe two passed. He slurped every sip of his drink and nibbled every crumb of his crunchy cheese snack. Outside he heard the faint chants of the call to prayer from a distant mosque loud speaker and once heard some villagers walking by. He thought he could scream out to them, but if he did, would the main guy get angry and do something rash and painful again? It was getting darker outside. He sat on his mat with his back against the wall, wondering what would happen next. Was Agung still next door? What ever happened to the real Carlton Easley and why was he being kidnapped? More questions that couldn't be answered.

But mostly he thought of Leah, Randall and Tristan and missed them. He longed to be able to see their faces. What were they doing right now? He wanted so badly to play with them again, hold his wife. Did they know how much he loved them? He vowed to be a different man if he ever got back home.

~~☐~~

On the first short leg of her trip from Sacramento to Los Angeles, Leah was wedged into a middle seat, but on the long flight from LAX to Hong Kong she got an entire middle row to herself. She could spread out her purse and reading materials all next to her and still have plenty of room to try to get in a semi-comfortable position. It was dark and most of the other passengers were sleeping. She felt antsy and walked up and down the tight aisles to get some circulation in her legs. The flight already felt long through an unending night, and she still had several hours to go before landing in Hong Kong. She cleaned out scrap paper from her purse and organized her wallet. She watched a couple of shows on the in-flight entertainment system and listened to some music on her iPod. She flipped through her *Woman's Day* magazine a few times, rummaging through articles on pre-holiday weight loss, new fashion fads, recipes and beauty tips.

But she refused to read the one article on rekindling your marriage. *It should be Stephen reading this article, not me. I shouldn't even be flying out here.* It felt dignified for her to have the self-control to not read the article, like she was salvaging some piece of self-respect.

Yet, after a long stretch of boredom, she finally relented and read the article, which made her feel more mad than hopeful. She read the article quickly and could have probably written it herself, it was so clichéd. *In fairytale land you can rekindle your marriage. But our flame has been a dead pile of ashes for a long time.* The article was infuriating. How come men's magazines don't have articles about how to rekindle your marriage? Why do women seem to always carry the burden of strengthening a weak relationship? It wasn't fair.

She stashed the magazine in the seat pocket and flipped through the in-flight entertainment options again. She finally settled on a romantic comedy. The handsome man in the movie realized what a good thing he had in his girlfriend and pursued her in dramatic fashion at the end. Leah's insides already felt queasy with all the meat-heavy meals on board, and the happy ending didn't help. *Why can't Stephen be more like that? Why am I even doing this?*

She took an Ambien pill that Fiona had given her, knowing that probably wasn't a good idea with only four hours left of flight time. She just had to try to get some rest. Yet even under its influence, her racing mind was active enough to fight off medicated slumber. Finally, in the last two hours before arriving in the sparkling city of Hong Kong, Leah drifted off and dreamed fitfully of the upcoming reunion with her missing-in-action husband.

CHAPTER NINE

The *Firdaus Rokok* factory of Pandaan, East Java, stayed on standby for several hours during the mysterious no-show of their visiting VIP guest Mr. Carton Easley. Bambang, the head factory manager, rode with the company's second driver to kilometer marker six on the toll road right after Mr. Carlton's call. They found no wreckage there or hints of a hit and run, just some local goat herders cutting tall grass for their flocks. He asked them if they had seen a *bule* or a driver run off into the woods, and they shrugged their shoulders. Looking up and down the road he saw nothing unusual either. After another hour of searching along the toll road he gave up and ordered the driver to take him back to the factory.

Unfortunately Bambang didn't have the phone number that Mr. Carlton had called from, because his guest had called the factory phone which had no caller ID feature. If he would have called Bambang's cell phone, the number would have been captured and could be redialed. Pity. The original driver, now missing for several hours, was not answering the company cell phone, but Bambang kept trying it anyway.

It was now late afternoon, and Bambang calculated it should have taken them at the most an hour to get out of the airport, another hour through the main road and the toll road, and then just a 20 minute jaunt from there to the factory. Whatever delay had befallen his American guest had added a few hours to his already long journey.

Bambang considered going to the police department as Mr. Carlton had said something about a car accident. But he wasn't quite ready, emotionally or financially, to get the police involved yet. Perhaps Mr. Carlton would show up at the factory eventually on his own. All would be explained soon.

Now back at the factory, Bambang knew he had to start making decisions. People were looking to him for orders and he could feel them whispering about him behind his back. Technically, Mr. Carlton was coming only as a consultant, but his opinions would carry weight and would determine the career paths of many when he reported back to the mother company in America. Bambang was *capek*—physically exhausted—from preparing the grand welcome for the VIP, and now the guest of honor was missing. He felt uneasy at the possibility of botching this somehow. And if Mr. Carlton showed up in a surlier mood than he was already reputed to have, heads would surely roll. Output had been falling behind and profits were sagging. Would he become the fall guy for the company's recent financial predicament, losing his own job over this? He had worked so hard to get to this place in life—it didn't seem fair for his career path to be dependent on one man's opinion, especially one who didn't understand anything about Indonesian culture and context.

In his office, Bambang fielded some questions from the assistant managers. Should he let them go home now, or wait it out with him? Would their jobs be in jeopardy too?

He walked with them to the factory floor break room where everyone was congregating since news of the missing consultant/supervisor had broken. Now was the time for action. As much as he didn't want to, he had to start making some decisions, some of which he feared could get him into trouble later. Bambang himself realized that he was a prisoner to the Indonesian cultural tendency of *takut salah*, fear of making a mistake. It often slowed down his actions and he had to fight against it again and again to get to the top. Most Indonesian people could afford inaction but he couldn't if he wanted to keep rising. He steeled his mind for decision-making mode.

His first decision was that they would wait before officially alerting the police. When it was time to play that card, he would do so carefully. He had plenty of contacts in the Pandaan police department and knew which ones were good and decent men and which ones were in the force for the money. The first step would be to ask his neighbor, who was a police officer, in a very casual way how his day went. If there were an extraordinary traffic jam or a hit-and-run, that would come up naturally in the conversation without raising suspicions.

The next decision to tackle was what to do with the extra staff assembled for the welcoming of Mr. Carlton. His guest had already communicated he would rather stay at a nearby hotel than in the company suite. But would he still want to meet with the senior leadership team during dinner? He probably would be so tired from the long journey and the extra delay that he wouldn't want a welcoming reception, no matter how small. Bambang made an announcement that they could all go home and welcome Mr. Carlton the next day. They seemed relieved to be able to leave, but he could hear some of them talking to each other in excited whispers as they left the break room in pairs. Maybe the *bule* wouldn't come after all and they could all just relax and get back to status quo work habits.

As the meeting ended he realized he needed to play this down. There was a perfectly reasonable explanation for his driver and his international "liaison" as they called him—but really a supervisor—to be missing for this long. Maybe there was some sort of car trouble on the toll road after the first call, and by unfortunate coincidence the driver's cell phone battery was dead. That was his working theory, but he didn't really believe it himself. He walked down the long hall from the factory floor to his simple office, fretting and hoping Mr. Carlton would be forgiving that he was unable to be found.

≈≈□≈≈

The grist for the rumor mill in Agung's packed *kampung* neighborhood kept conversations whispering through the alleyway-sized streets late into the night. What was the respected teacher doing with a foreigner in a nice car? Was he in trouble? Or maybe a new job? Why hadn't he come home after teaching his morning classes? Agung wasn't answering his cell phone. This odd behavior contrasted sharply with his dependable and predictable personality.

Two proposed theories ran through the tight-knit community, where close bridges of relationship carried heavy gossip traffic. One was that something terrible had happened to Agung, and the other was that he was doing something terrible, like drug dealing. Why else would he be riding around with a rich foreigner? That theory was a lot juicier than maybe he got into a simple motorcycle accident.

But for his family, his disappearance wasn't newsy chit-chat. They worried that he had gotten into an accident and maybe at that very moment he was sprawled out on some road, unconscious and unable to reach them. They were literally worried sick—his mother had vomited twice already.

All of their frantic text messages to his cell phone stayed unanswered. They knew his character deeply and were sure that he wasn't mixed up in something bad, contrary to the buzz in the *kampung*. He was probably trying to help a foreigner, maybe as a translator. Agung was diligent in school and they felt confident he was the best English speaker in Sidoarjo.

What should they do next? It had now been almost 11 hours since anyone had heard from him. The general consensus around the tiny kitchen table was to stay at home and wait for him to return. If he didn't show up tomorrow they would split up and go in search for him, checking his usual hangouts. There were enough people in the house to split up into three search teams. They only had two motorcycles but could borrow one from a neighbor and go off in three separate directions. The stark light of a low watt light bulb hung over their discussion, giving the meeting the feel of a war planning session. Agung's father nervously puffed out clouds of cigarette smoke. The unspoken rule was that the younger children didn't speak in serious family conferences like this, and they stood somberly around the table, some of their friends behind them in the outer ring by the doorway.

Normally when they all felt nervous someone would say something light or humorous to break the tension, trying to regain a sense of emotional balance. But they were feeling too heavy even for that. Most were quiet. Some started offering silent prayers to Allah for Agung's safe return home. All agreed they would do the second round of evening prayers together at the mosque down their street.

≈≈◻≈≈

Mustafal cleared his throat while his two partners looked on with wide-eyed awe. Standing in the small kitchen near the only phone in the small house, he readied himself to make the first call to the factory. He wanted to use a landline instead of his cell phone to make sure the call was clear and terrifying. It was already past the afternoon shift but Mustafal was sure Pak Bambang was still there, worrying frantically about his American puppet master. His two partners watched with horror and fascination from the kitchen table. Mustafal was afraid Pak Bambang would recognize his voice, so he practiced it a few times a few octaves deeper. To further cover his identity, he also put a handkerchief over the mouthpiece. His fiancée Dina said that wouldn't help at all, but he waved her away. He was going to do this his way—confidently. He had no practice in real kidnappings of course, but he had seen plenty of movies where someone was nabbed and eventually ransomed.

If Bambang demanded to hear Mr. Carlton's voice, his cousin Karniawan, nicknamed Happy, would go and fetch him. Then Dina would meet him in the hallway and sweet talk him to be nice and obedient on the phone and not give away anything, followed by Mustafal who would threaten him with his life before he ever got on the phone. That was the contingency plan. Mustafal hoped Bambang would be so relieved to hear that the missing supervisor had been located, he would trust the kidnappers and wouldn't demand any proof of life. He imagined the factory to be in disarray by now. The higher-ups would surely be open to hearing the kidnappers' demands and want to get this over with quickly. It wasn't like they were demanding a helicopter or a million dollars U.S.— they just wanted fair working conditions and a livable salary. The factory would at least be shamed into doing that much, and Carlton Easley would surely sign his name to it. He seemed like a pushover so far. The American undoubtedly wouldn't want to draw attention to the conditions of his sweat shop of a factory and how the workers were so fed up that they actually planned a kidnapping to get some leverage in their desperate plight. Like all shady companies, they would go to great lengths to creep away from the public spotlight.

Cupping one hand over the mouthpiece before he dialed, Mustafal made the shush sign with his other hand. It was unnecessary—they were already speechless. He carefully pressed the numbers and the call was cheerily answered with, "*Firdaus Rokok.*"

Going down a few octaves forced him to clear his throat before he had the vocal wherewithal to speak. This was the second point of no return. They could still dump Carlton Easley off in the front of the factory and speed off and no one would probably ever know. But now, putting his voice on this phone, he was putting his life on the line, too. He would be traceable. What if the receptionist immediately recognized his voice? How many people didn't show up for work today? Would they be able to put two and two together quickly?

"We are the Islam Defenders Front, and we are holding your supervisor, Carlton Easley, as hostage," he growled in *Bahasa Indonesia* with the most menacing voice he could muster.

A silence on the other end, and he could hear scurrying in the background. After a few minutes he could hear Pak Bambang's meek voice break through. "Hello, who is this?"

"This is Islam Defenders Front," he barked again, taking the handkerchief off the phone quickly and wiping the sweat from his brow. Mustafal's heart was racing but he tried to play it fearlessly, especially with his two cohorts watching so closely. If they thought he was at all nervous, they would be petrified.

"Yes," came the timid reply. "What do you want?"

"Pak Bambang, we know you are looking for Carlton Easley and we know where he is."

"How do you know my name? I didn't tell it to you."

He shook off the question and stayed on the offensive. "I am speaking to the manager of the factory, am I not?"

"Yes, you are. This is Pak Bambang. Where is Carlton Easley?"

"We will ask the questions here, Pak Bambang, and we will give the answers. We will contact you soon. Just be ready to meet our demands and Mr. Easley will be delivered back to the factory safely. If not, be ready to receive his mutilated corpse at the front door of your factory."

Mustafal clamped the phone down on the cradle and wiped his forehead again with the sopping handkerchief. Happy's eyes were wide in shock and Dina shook her head with a disapproving look. He already knew they wouldn't approve of the death threat at the end, but these corporate types had to know that they meant business. Before either partner could protest, he jumped up to sit on the kitchen counter, gaining the physical high ground. Then he lectured them again on the need to play this as real Muslim terrorists so that no one would be suspicious. Radicalized people, he told them, care more for the end goal than the right or wrong of the means to get there. Dina argued that they should make all tactical strategy decisions as a group, and that the plan was never to issue a death threat right away. Happy fiddled nervously with his hands and looked like he wanted to be somewhere else. Mustafal was always the most eloquent when backed up into a corner, and he persuaded them through a litany of lawyerly points to see things his way. Dina stubbornly stuck to her guns that from here on out they would make major decisions together and Mustafal conceded the point for now. He knew that he could say that now and do what he wanted later, as long as it was followed up with a sincere apology.

"I wonder what's going on over there now," Mustafal asked them to distract them and lighten up the tense mood. "I'm sure they are glad to know he is alive but scared to death of our demands."

"You didn't need to threaten to kill him," Happy said quickly, surprising his older cousin. Mustafal was flustered that his right-hand man was second guessing his confident leadership, but before he could argue with him, Happy grabbed a lemonade from off the counter and walked into the living room. Mustafal jumped down from the counter and started after him, but Dina put her hand on his shoulder. "Don't," she said pleadingly. "You've done enough today."

"You will thank me one day for this," he shot at her in an impolite lower-level dialect of Javanese. "Right now courageous leadership is required and that is what I am providing. Plus you agreed to this, remember?"

Before she could fire back a rebuttal, he stomped out the kitchen door that led to the small courtyard in the back. Lighting up a cigarette, he began angrily pacing back and forth in the weedy grass. He could see from the corner of his eye that Dina was still watching him through the kitchen window and was probably whittling some choice words into weapons. He kicked a rotten mango out of his way to show he was upset and not to be messed with.

CHAPTER TEN

Carlton reached into the gaggle of relatives to try to retrieve his wallet, but the family members had already surrounded the boy's mom and were excitedly chattering to each other. He scanned hands and bodies but couldn't see his billfold in the commotion. One lanky man bolted out the door. *Does he have my wallet?*

Frustrated, Carlton tried to follow the man with his eyes but the rest of the family started tugging on him. It looked like he was being recruited to lift the boy off the wicker sofa. Everyone grabbed a limb, an extra guy under the broken one, and Carlton assumed he was supposed to carry the head. They heaved and hoed in Indonesian, moving the boy out the front door and forcing Carlton to walk backwards.

"You take him to hospital, and I will pay," he said through labored breath. "I just need my wallet back."

The relative holding the boy's good leg said something indistinguishable through a mouth still puffing on a cigarette out the side. The injured boy rolled his head back to look upside down directly into Carlton's eyes as they were crossing the door's threshold. It was the first time Carlton really looked into the kid's eyes, and the gaze of passive sadness gave him the willies.

Now where? The man who had exited earlier was now backing a rusty pickup truck toward the crowd. Other bystanders peeled to both sides of the narrow road and motioned with their hands for the driver to back up. "Stop," one said loudly. Dust kicked up into Carlton's mouth and made him cough right into the boy's face.

"Sorry," he offered. The boy just rolled his head back and looked up at Carlton with the same sad and somber face.

The living stretcher made more commotion and someone unfolded a few canvas rice bags and placed them carefully over the layer of dirt in the bed of the truck. Then the boy was lifted, shifted and placed up on top. Carlton did his part deftly, then spun away and took a few steps from the crowd. They were either excited or agitated—Carlton couldn't tell. The animated mom turned to him to say something while pointing to the front seat of the truck. Apparently he was being invited to ride shotgun.

No thanks. No way am I going with you crazies. He thought about his wallet which still held a wad of U.S. cash. There was probably enough in there to pay for the boy's hospital bills if they took foreign currency, and maybe even enough left over to pay for the whole family to stay in a nice hotel in the big city for a week. His credit cards were in there, too, but he assumed they wouldn't be able to figure out how to use them. Plus there were a few other random items, like health insurance and loyalty cards, all easily replaced. The crooked cop still had his driver's license and passport, the two most important forms of identification. Those he would get back for sure once the police realized whom they had messed with. He started to think he could get by on this foreign soil without his wallet. One call to the factory to be located and picked up, and he would be treated like Carton Easley again. Later he could replace his credit cards and he was sure the factory would loan him some personal money in the meantime.

"Bathroom?" he asked the mom who was already in the center seat, pressed against the gearshift and waiting for Carlton to get in. Her sweaty face moved its attention off her son in the back of the truck and turned to Carlton to understand what he was saying. The engine of the pick-up fired to a start and they were ready to whisk the boy to the hospital.

"Bathroom? Restroom?"

"Toilet?" a non-riding spectator asked in clarification. Carlton saw it was the same junior-high girl who had translated earlier.

"Yes, toilet." *Do I really have to be that specific?*

The mother clicked some sort of huffing noise and a general consensus of disapproval rippled through the ranks as the request was translated by the girl. *"Di belakang,"* the mother said while pointing toward the front door of the house.

The little girl translated that to "behind back."

Now was his chance. He strode quickly through the front door to the back of the house, which didn't take long, and pressed open a back door. Spotting an alleyway that led away from the house, he scurried to it and walked at a fast clip to get away from all the madness. His pace was hurried but not frantic. The neighborhood watch association would probably get curious seeing a white man enter their barrio, and he didn't want to make them any more suspicious by running at full speed. A couple of kids poked their heads out of open windows and jabbered at him.

Carlton kept walking, kept sweating, kept making turns. After a few minutes he slowed his pace. He wondered how long they would wait with the truck in idle until they figured out he was a no show. Hopefully not too long. He only would have gotten in the way. Let them do things their way.

He stepped carefully on the uneven sidewalk which was made of large cement blocks that also served as a ditch covering. Every third or fourth block was missing and he had to be careful and really watch his step. Finally, he opted to walk on the side of the road, freeing his attention to scan the neighborhood for some sort of business where he could use a phone. So far the industry in this place looked like roadside food stalls, greasy motorcycle repair shops and the occasional store selling building supplies. A few pedi-cab rickshaw drivers, half-napping on the benches meant for their passengers, looked up at him curiously. Some inside the food stalls watched him with a wait-and-see attitude from their coffee and newspapers.

He committed to himself to not waste time with these gawking bystanders. Instead he would take charge again, searching for a person with enough means to both speak English and own a cell phone.

Finally, he spotted a security post perched on the corner of two sleepy streets. A thin man wearing a white security uniform stepped out onto the street and looked over at Carlton, who cut to the chase and asked for a phone. The guard didn't understand and went back inside the booth to turn down his TV volume. He appeared again and for some reason had a clipboard in his hand.

"Police? Are you a police?"

"Police?" the man repeated the question with the same inflection, squinting in the sun.

Good enough, Carlton thought. "Yes, take me to the police. I need to use a phone to call my factory."

"Yes, yes," said the guard, not sounding convincing that he actually understood most of what Carlton had said. He motioned toward a wooden bench in front of his security post, and Carlton, not knowing what else to do, plopped down on it. At least it was under some tree shade. The guard nodded his head up and down a couple of times and then disappeared back into his post. Carlton hoped he was going inside to call the police station, and he assumed he would have to wait outside. *I've gotta be the most exciting thing that has happened to this guy all year.*

He ran his fingers in the deep grainy crevices of the wooden bench, which wobbled on one side. It had never been finished or painted. Carlton muttered to himself that they had just nailed together some old chunks of wood they found somewhere, and didn't bother to measure or cut it properly, or even apply finishing. *That's the way they do things around here.*

He hoped that he would hear the security guard talking on a phone but no such voice came out of the little booth. Craning his neck around and pressing his face against the dusty window, Carlton tried to find out what the man was doing in there. He only saw the white-uniformed back of the man hunched over something.

Carlton turned back to the action on the lonely road, willing to give this guy only five more minutes. Even under the shade, he continued to sweat on the rickety bench. He bent down and rolled up his suit slacks to get a little more air circulation to the bottom of his thick and sticky legs.

A gaggle of school children walked down the street, looking up from their moving huddle of conversation to the sweating foreigner in their midst. Their young innocent faces did not hide their fascination at seeing him sitting there, and a couple of them looked like they were working up their courage to speak to him in English. He didn't feel like talking. *Just go on about your business and stop looking at me like I'm some kind of zoo animal.*

"Hello mister," a cheery little boy said. His friends congratulated his bravery with laughter. Carlton could tell that if he responded they would stop and surround him and poke him with more questions. His best move was to just nod and parcel out a tight smile and maybe they would leave him alone and move along, nothing to see here.

Carlton focused his full attention down on the weeds growing out of a crack in the black and white striped curb at his feet. The kids would eventually get over their curiosity and go on their way. He could hear them murmuring to each other when the guard came out of his post. The man barked several words with lots of long "O" vowel sounds to them, which Carlton hoped was the Indonesian equivalent of shoo. Carlton looked up to see the guard holding a brown plastic tray with two steaming coffee glass mugs. The clipboard was gone and now the man was serving refreshments. He placed one down beside Carlton precariously on the bench. The kids were still standing bunched in a clump, staring at him.

Carlton wanted a phone or the police, not a group of giggling pre-adolescent spectators and especially not coffee on a hot day. More wasted time felt infuriating to Carlton, but on second thought it had been a long time since he had anything to parch his thirst, and he had better drink something while he had the chance. He purposefully didn't make eye contact with the little fascinated bystanders as he lifted the cup to his lips and murmured thanks to the guard. All eyes were on him as his pursed lips endured the first steaming sip.

"Hot, mister," one of the kids helpfully pointed out. "Hot. *Hati-hati.*"

"I can tell it's *hati-hati,*" he said tersely, still without granting them the respect of eye contact. The glass mug was placed firmly back down on the bench to announce that the show was over. Carlton turned to the guard now watching him with an expression somewhere between amused curiosity and caution. "Please take me to the police right now," he said clearly and slowly. Carlton noticed a large patch on the man's white uniform shirt that announced SATPAM. "Do you understand what I am telling you, satpam?"

The guard looked to the kids, either for a translation or for moral support. Or maybe they were enjoying some inside joke, judging from their spurts of laughter. A couple of the youngsters said something to the guard, but it didn't matter to Carlton what they were discussing. He decided he was going to escape from his zoo cage and find the police station on his own.

As he started to walk away, he lost his step off the curb and the back of his leg hit the bench. The wobble caused the coffee mug to dump over, emptying the rest of its steaming contents onto the ground. The glass shattered on the curb and some of the kids started their giggling again.

The guard squatted down to attend to the broken glass and Carlton stooped down to join him, not quite as adept as the guard in balancing in the squat position, but he managed. He picked up a few of the larger pieces and threw them into the open ditch sewer as the guard was doing, and somehow this was even more hilarious entertainment for the children. *Shouldn't they be in school right now?*

Carlton mumbled a soft "sorry" and the guard answered *"tidak apa apa,"* in a politely forced sort of way. His attention stayed on the glass as did Carlton's, and the kids continued to giggle on.

In that moment, Carlton Easley again juxtaposed his comfortable life back in Houston, where he was a very respected man, with the humiliation he had stooped to now, a disoriented and sweating white man sorting through the grass for broken shards of glass on a sweltering hot day next to an open sewer, without a host in this third-world country, without his wallet or ID, and now without his dignity. *If my enemies could see me now.*

He suddenly stopped what he was doing, stood back up again, and made a decision. He would be in control again. He would stop cleaning up for anybody and he would stop being pushed around. He would regain the high ground and some modicum of dignity and very likely swear off Indonesia forever.

He stood erect, straightened out his damp dress shirt and tucked it back neatly inside his pants. If he still had his blazer with him he would have put that on too as a power move. He ran his hands through both sides of his head to straighten out his matted-down hair and patted down the swoop of his receding bangs. His audience watched with fascination.

The guard stood back up, apparently satisfied with the cleanup effort, and Carlton looked dead into his eyes with a look of menacing authority.

"Phone now," he demanded.

The guard and the kids looked on, none of them seeming to dare a response.

"Do any of you understand English?" he said flatly. "Take me to a phone now." All the humiliation of this wretched day made him forget any pretense of politeness.

The guard turned toward the group of kids and conferred with them. After some murmuring and looking back to the demanding foreigner in their midst, the guard turned. "Please, you follow," he said flatly.

Finally, we are getting somewhere. Carlton smiled and unfurled his hand out as if to indicate, *Please, you first.* The guard didn't return the smile but stepped into his post, and came back out quickly, fastening his baton to his belt. He started walking down the street without looking back to see if Carlton was following.

What's his problem? Carlton dutifully followed, but kept a professional distance. The gaggle of kids followed along too. *Does anyone in this town have anything better to do than watch me?*

The security guard clipped quickly down the busted-up streets and past small rickety houses, cutting turns and entering alleys here and there. Not many people were out in the heat of the day except Carlton, his guide and the trail of chattering kids. The guard was always a good few paces ahead and Carlton became winded in the pursuit. The kids didn't seem to mind the brisk walk by the way they were cheerfully yakking and poking each other. Carlton wished again he had brought a handkerchief to wipe away his sweat, which had already won the battle for his dress shirt.

Finally, they came to a little shed-like store, unfinished poles holding up a sagging tin roof. Carlton peeked in and saw it was some sort of building supply shop, mostly offering painting supplies and dusty bags of cement. The guard turned to Carlton at the front and mimicked the exact same gesture Carlton had used for *after you.* He had a sarcastic look on his face that Carlton didn't like, but he wouldn't show that he was upset by it. He took the high road again and smiled back innocently as if to show appreciation.

A serious and stern old man whom Carlton guessed was the owner looked up from the newspaper he was studying at his disorganized desk. He eyed Carlton cautiously and a stocky younger man, presumably the owner's son, appeared from behind a row of shelves. The younger man was wearing flip flops, long denim shorts and a white T-shirt two sizes too small with the words "I Be Friend In Your Ever World" boldly printed on the front. They both stared at Carlton who now realized he was totally on his own, as the guard and the kids were still standing outside. *Fine, I can handle this myself.*

"Excuse me," Carlton said politely enough. "May I use your telephone?" He straightened out his hair again as best he could to look more professional.

Nothing moved except a cloud of cigarette smoke that was wafting its way to the ceiling in the light of an antique lamp on the desk. Both men just stared at him blankly, as if an extraterrestrial were speaking to them in alien gibberish. Carlton cut to the point again. "Telephone. I need to use your telephone, may I?" He flashed them a telephone sign with his pinkie and thumb. *When is this day ever going to end?*

The father-son duo finally broke from their statue-like trance and looked at each other, the old man still seated and the son standing at attention. Carlton was feeling impatient and noticed a pack of *Firdaus Rokok* cigarettes on the cluttered desk. So this was his customer base, his constituency, his people.

He reached for the cigarettes to make some sort of contact with them, to show them a connection with himself and the mighty cigarette company. Maybe they could even break from their busy schedule and bring him straight to the factory and he could cut out the phone call all together. Those cigarettes might be his only clue of communication with these simple village folk, he thought.

The old man jerked back and gasped out a yelp when Carlton made his sudden move. The noise threw off Carlton's concentration in his lunge for the cigarettes and he accidentally knocked over a glass lamp from the desk, sending it crashing onto the cement floor in thousands of shards. The son cried out something and the guard came running in from outside.

More broken glass. This is all I need. The old man put one hand over his heart and his mouth drooped open in incredulous amazement. The son and the guard started talking things over furiously. Carlton regained his composure and checked his hands for cuts. A couple of the kids poked their heads inside and snickered.

He wasn't sure if he should try to clean up the mess but he wouldn't know how to ask if they had a broom and dustpan. By the looks of the unkempt place they didn't—dust covered every item on the shelves and coated the floor. The three men kept gibbering to each other and the old man got to his feet.

"Sorry about that, I can pay for that. I just need to use your phone, please. Or could you take me to the factory of this cigarette company?" He reached again for the pack of cigarettes and as he did the security guard grasped him from behind by his shoulders and seemed to be steering him to the chair vacated by the old man.

"Get your hands off me," Carlton yelled while trying to spin around in the slick shards of glass. He intended to face-off squarely with this meddling security guard, but the man squeezed more tightly onto his shoulders and Carlton couldn't quite wiggle free. He was much smaller than Carlton but felt much stronger. Carlton was forced to sit down in the chair and the guard and chunky son flanked him from behind on each side, pressing his shoulders down so he couldn't stand back up.

The old man finally started speaking, looking very agitated and flapping his wrinkly jaws at Carlton like he was lecturing a child. Carlton breathed deeply and knew he needed to cool down before he did something rash. He felt like tearing down the place with his bare hands and then lighting it on fire with a *Firdaus Rokok* cigarette, but first he had to regain the emotional composure of the man in control. His position of prominence would eventually be restored. For now the six-figure salaried executive would have to endure the long-winded rebuke of a simple Indonesian shopkeeper.

The firm hands stayed on his shoulder and kept pressing down. He took another deep breath to remain calm and not fling them off. He watched as the old man walked to a corner where a telephone was mounted.

So that's where it is.

"You must pay for lamp" a voice said from overhead.

The sentences out of the younger shopkeeper's mouth startled Carlton. He tilted his head upwards and around to see the man's face, who was looking down on him sternly. "Why didn't you tell me you could speak English?" Carlton demanded.

"You just wait here. We make sure you pay. My father call police to make sure you pay and security guard say you have very bad temper so we make sure."

"What?" Carlton snorted. "This is all about money? I assure you I will pay for your very cheap lamp." He reached back instinctively for his absent wallet and both men pressed him back into the chair more firmly.

He had just about had it with these people. "I was just going to get my credit card and pay for this and be on my way."

"We not take credit card here, mister. Just cash."

"Well I don't have any cash. I just have a credit card," he shot back angrily.

Then he remembered he didn't have either. His wallet was on its way to a hospital in a pick-up truck full of hysterical village people.

"Please you wait for police."

He pressed up into the hands still pressing him down. "I am not going to wait here to pay five bucks for a broken lamp." The chair creaked nosily under the jostling and strain of the quickly-won tussle that ensued.

The old man finished the phone call and ambled back over to the action.

Carlton took a third deep breath and closed his eyes. He hated these people—this petty little guard and this old man and his power-tripping son, all of whom seemed to delight in lording over a foreigner. He hated this airless, closed-in, claustrophobic, dusty paint store. Most of all he hated this country and wished he had never come here.

106

For now there was no other choice but to submit under the mini-dictatorship of his captors. *Just calm down and bide your time. You are Carlton Easley. You are a VIP, a Very Important Person.*

He forced himself to relax his body and they loosened their grip when it was clear he was going to submit to their demand to wait for the cops. What would the police be able to do? He didn't have any money on him. Maybe he could give them his expensive watch, worth several hundred dollars more than the lamp. Hopefully the police would be able to put him in touch with the factory quickly and get him to his VIP footing.

The minutes ticked by and his three personal guards said nothing. The old man went back for his smokes and Carlton grinned to himself. He would have the last laugh after all, maybe in a few years. The two other men finally stopped hovering over him and made themselves comfortable, the son sitting on a stack of cement bags and the guard squatting down beside him. Carlton wondered how he could squat on his hams in that position for so long.

He looked around the little store, the tiny aisles crammed with building supplies. It appeared the place had never been painted, which he thought ironic for a paint supply store. He glanced outside. The children had lost interest and had finally moved on. It was just him and these three men and time. Carlton stewed in his thoughts.

Finally, the tense boredom was broken when someone entered the shop. All four men looked up to see a tall policeman enter the premises. The three Indonesian men jumped to their feet to greet him and quickly formed a huddle, looking back to Carlton as they conferred together. He sighed to himself loud enough so they could hear him.

Give me a break. I'm a hardened criminal. I broke a lamp.

After a few more minutes the policeman, also wearing the same type 1970's sunglasses his other nemesis officer was wearing, strode up to Carlton with the chubby shopkeeper's son by his side. He barked something in Indonesian and motioned for Carlton to stand up. Carlton stayed put and looked up into the man's face with indifferent defiance.

The officer said something again and the young man delivered the translated verdict: "You under arrest for hit the boy with car."

≈≈▢≈≈

Johanna Grazen's car door was opened by her part-time Indonesian driver and she slipped into her U.S. government-issued black vehicle. It was the end of another mundane day at the U.S. Consulate compound in Surabaya. She was in the back seat, still feeling it was too uppity for an independent lady like herself to have her own driver, and glanced around the property. She always felt like saying "On James' to the driver but she knew he wouldn't get it, even if she had tried to explain the Western humor to him.

The consulate was an unassuming building encased with tall fences and barbed wire. Plexiglas was recently added to cover the fence and shield the facility from the frequent volleys of tomatoes launched by angry young mobs on Friday afternoons. Many rotten missiles had sailed through the narrow fence slats and had started to stain the paint on the face of the building.

The security staff pushed the heavy gate open and waved her through. She waved back and her driver navigated their way into the maddening traffic of Surabaya.

Johanna was in her early 40's but most people guessed her in her early 30's. Maybe not getting married helps you look younger, friends joked with her at times. Sometimes Indonesians would ask her point blank why she wasn't married. Over time she accepted that they were just being curious and friendly, and she would give them the pat answer that she just loved to travel too much to settle down. They marveled at this statement, and she could never tell if it was because they pitied or envied her.

Her serene face looked absently out the window at hordes of motorcycles while her driver concentrated on the road. The motorcycle drivers, sometimes with two or three other passengers riding with them, were trying to inch forward and flow through the traffic on both sides of her car. Even with all the chaos of traffic and relentless pollution, the place was beginning to feel familiar and almost home-like. Tonight she would celebrate her one-year anniversary of moving to Indonesia with some friends from work by going out to her favorite restaurant, a little Italian gem in walking distance from the consulate. *One year already. Amazing.*

It took a few months for the initial malaise from disappointment of moving to Indonesia to subside. Overall she liked her job at the U.S. consulate, enjoying the role of liaison between the state department and U.S. citizens living in East Java. The administrative paperwork part of the job she could live without. Before she got dispatched here she was hoping for an appointment in the Latin American world as she was fluent in Spanish. Yet she got placed as far away from her last assignment in Venezuela as possible, something that she suspected would happen. In the wisdom of the U.S. State Department, employees were moved around and out of their comfortable surroundings, for fear that they will "go native" in their host countries and eventually turn against the foreign policies of the U.S. government. Though she was friendly with the Venezuelans, and even got into a serious relationship there, she never felt tempted to adopt all their political sentiments.

When she learned she would be moving to the ends of the earth, she was hoping for a post at the U.S. embassy in the metropolitan capital of Jakarta and not at its lesser known stepsister, Surabaya. The vast polluted metropolis would have never been her first, second or third choice. The sprawling capital of East Java felt to her like one big overwhelming traffic jam. But when she moved a year ago to her new location, Johanna resolved to get as familiar as possible with the new surroundings. She knew if she looked hard enough she could find some hidden cultural treasures in the concrete jungle, and one day she would look back on this time with fondness. At least most of the people she met so far were extremely friendly.

She was also a little disappointed at the slow pace of her career track. The job relocation felt like a lateral move when she desired a vertical upgrade. Like most of the other State Department officials she knew, she was good at biding her time as she slowly climbed the bureaucratic ladder. One day she would be rewarded for her patience and hopefully break through the glass ceiling to arrive at full ambassadorship.

She was at least enjoying Java more than she had expected. Spending her weekends exploring mountain villages, volcanoes and beaches while a live-in maid took care of all the chores on the home front made her friends in the U.S. jealous. As a single lady fully capable of tidying up her own home, she felt a little funny about having a "helper" at first but got used to it and loved the fresh-from-the-market cooking every day. The friendship with her maid was also helping her advance in language fluency and, best of all, it made the house feel not so lonely. Employing her own driver was strange at first too, but she got over it quickly because the traffic was so insane and she was afraid she would kill somebody in it, most likely somebody on a motorcycle.

Johanna continued to stare out the window at the quickly darkening and congested city, past bright humongous malls which overshadowed tiny dingy houses. Hordes of people could be seen down every alleyway in this city of three million people. The whole island, roughly the same size as her home state of Tennessee, was cram packed with 120 million people. She often told friends back in the U.S. to imagine everyone west of the Mississippi River suddenly moving to Tennessee and that's Java. They were able to cram so many people onto this small island because they were all stuffed into millions of these tiny dwellings. She had visited Indonesian people in their cramped *kampung* neighborhoods and always came home to her large abode with a full-time helper and part-time driver and felt a slight twinge of guilt for having it so good.

A chirp of her cell phone interrupted her thoughts and let her know it was a text message from the office. She didn't even feel like reading it after a long day, a tedious one of mainly administrative busywork. Johanna paused for a few more seconds in her thoughts, and then glanced down to read the text message from her secretary, Ibu Dewi. It simply stated that an American businessman was being held by the police in Pandaan. *Pandaan? What in the world would a businessman be doing in that little bump in the rice paddy?*

Instead of texting back a response, Johanna called Dewi back to confirm and get more details. There wasn't much more than what was indicated in the message, and the police were not releasing any details. Johanna directed Dewi to reschedule all her appointments for tomorrow, which she had already pre-emptively done, because she would need to be in Pandaan the next morning. Their policy was to meet with any American detained within 24 hours and to notify the family immediately. U.S. citizens getting arrested in Indonesia didn't happen that often and this was her first one. There were only about 200 American families in all of East Java, and almost all of them were law-abiding folks aware of Indonesian expectations.

"Tomorrow we go to Pandaan," Johanna told her driver in *Bahasa Indonesia*. "I have a meeting there." Her driver looked at her through the rearview mirror with slightly raised eyebrows at the odd and out-of-the-way destination.

"*Ya Bu.*"

Johanna felt grateful for the chance to be plucked out of a Thursday full of mundane administrative tasks and dropped into something much more exciting, like meeting with an American outlaw.

PART II

THURSDAY

CHAPTER ELEVEN

An early morning call to prayer, blaring through distant yet still potent mosque speakers, awakened Stephen back into the same bad dream. His jet lag, adrenaline and repeated dreams of getting choked all added up to a fitful few hours of sleep. The thin foam mattress was a weak cushion against the hard tile floor. He tried as best he could to sleep with the long cylindrical pillow, but his awkwardly stretched neck longed for a more rectangular pillow. It did at least offer him the only decoration in the room, a flower design on the faded pillowcase.

His body ached, his breath reeked and his mind struggled to orient himself to his new reality in the morning light. Lifting himself from the floor to stretch, he was surprised to see a plastic cup of water and some sort of breakfast package by the door. It must have been brought there during his one good deep sleep cycle, probably by that kind girl Dina. The other two didn't seem to care if he ate or drank anything.

Stephen had difficulty puncturing the cellophane lid of the plastic cup with the tiny straw provided but finally got it through. It was good that the straw was so narrow as he needed to partake slowly and make the water last. Who knew when he would get another drink? He unwrapped the green banana leaf around the breakfast package to find a fried egg on top of fried rice. His stomach felt too queasy for a greasy fried breakfast but he ate anyway as he thought he would need his strength for the day. Although the meal was slightly spicy, he held back from downing all of his limited water at once and sipped with self-control.

An hour went by as he stared at nothing in particular and his bladder begged him to use the bathroom. He wasn't sure how long he could hold it, but he definitely didn't want to go in his own room. There was no way he could urinate out of the small rectangle window on the wall—it was too high up.

He finally found the courage to knock on the door. Maybe Dina or the other gentler one would come and let him go relieve himself. He began tapping on the locked door and calling out, "Excuse me. Excuse me."

Quick footsteps clipped down the hall and the mean one swung open the door. "What you want?" he demanded with indignation.

"I would like to go the bathroom," Stephen replied softly.

He hesitated for a second, as if he were considering denying the request. Then he grudgingly said, "Okay, you follow."

Stephen followed down the short hall and could see down the corridor Dina and the other one in the living area watching TV. It sounded like music videos. He figured they would be memorizing the Holy Koran or something this early in the morning, but they looked like a few teenage friends hanging out and watching MTV on a lazy summer day. Only one other room could be seen off the hallway and he assumed that Agung was still locked inside it. He looked at the small window over the door but there was no light coming through. Maybe his friend was still sleeping or maybe he was gone. He thought about calling out something to his unfortunate tour guide, but decided against it when he looked back at the tall body of the mean one walking in front of him. The cracked picture frame now hung back upon the wall reminded him how quickly his captor's anger could erupt.

The head terrorist opened the door for his hostage and Stephen looked into a small room with water on the floor. He saw no toilet but a square tank containing water in the corner and a small circular drain in the corner. He hadn't been oriented yet to bathroom procedures in Indonesia but this smelled like the right place. He wasn't going to ask the mean one about how to use this thing so he decided he would figure it out on his own. He closed the door behind him, hating the feel of water under his socked feet in a bathroom. The small water tank in the corner was full of what looked to be clean water so he couldn't pee in there. His only other choice was the drain, so he went for it. When he finished, he sunk his hands into the clean water tank and wiggled them around inside the cool water to clean them off. That felt good so he splashed his face with more water and started to run his wet hands through his matted hair to cool off. The mean one must have heard because he barked through the door, "No bath. Pee pees only."

"Just a moment," Stephen shot back. He took the scooper which was set on the ledge of the water tank and filled it and poured it out over the drain to flush. Not bad for a first try, he thought.

Stephen came out of the bathroom shaking wet hands and from his vantage point in the hall he could see all three of them eyeing him carefully.

"Excuse me, sir," he said to the leader while still feeling pressed by his intimidating presence in the small hallway. *Stay on the offensive.* "May I ask some questions about why I am here?"

Even if they got mad, anything was better than the stone silent boredom of his uncomfortable and bare room.

The others said something to the boss in Indonesian before he had a chance to respond to Stephen's request. They started arguing and he couldn't tell who was winning. It became obvious when the mean one turned back to him and said flatly, "No."

Stephen was escorted back to his room and had another hour or so with his thoughts and himself. He mainly wondered and worried about his family. He figured if there were a ransom request it would have been directed to Carlton Easley's family and not his own, or probably to the factory. So far no one in the world knew he was impersonating this mystery man. Stephen's own company may have chalked this up to a missed flight, but by now surely Leah would have expected a call.

The footsteps of someone coming down the hall and turning the lock of his room jolted him out of the thoughts of home. Jumping up from the foam mattress, he was relieved to see Dina opening the door. "You may come and ask question for five minutes." She pointed to the front room without making eye contact with him. Gone was any friendliness in her voice or manner.

"Thank you, Dina" he said, suddenly feeling unsure. Earlier he longed to be out of his stuffy cage and desperately wanted to ask some of the questions that nagged his mind like the mosquitoes in his room the previous night. But now he wondered if the sudden approval to his request was a mind game, or maybe he was about to be assaulted again and that's why she was keeping a cold distance from the captive.

"Please not say my name," she whispered, glancing down the hall.

He followed her gaze down the hall and saw the mean one with his arms folded, already looking perturbed. His two partners must have won the argument, but they probably got a lecture about not revealing their identities.

As they entered the living room the other male turned down the volume of the wood-paneled television set and the mean one kept staring at him sternly while positioning himself in front of the TV. The volume was down, and Stephen could see through the leader's legs that they were in fact watching music videos. After taking his stance he refolded his arms across his chest.

"I want no trouble," said Stephen, looking back into the mean one's face to placate him even though he seemed not to need any assurance from Stephen. "How can I help you with your goals? I just want to go home back to my wife and family."

He had spoken in English quickly and he could tell that they were still trying to decipher what he was saying as best they could. He said it again, more slowly and simply to the point. "I want to go home to my family. What do I have to do?"

Stephen assumed he would hear ransom demands now but the three of them seemed unsure of what to say next, looking at each other in silence. Dina finally said something to the others, either translating what he said or offering her opinion. He knew he would be shooed to his tiny room again so he decided it couldn't hurt to ask more questions and let them tell him when to go back. Since there was no response he went to his second most pressing question.

"Is my friend Mr. Agung still here?"

"Pak Agung here," the quieter male said. It was only the second time Stephen had heard him speak.

"May I speak with him?"

"No," the angry one said. "We let you know how you do our goals and we let you know about Pak Agung."

Two strikes but he wasn't out yet.

"May I know where I am, then?"

"You are in on the south coast of East Java," said Dina, who shot her leader a superior look and smug smile.

The man blasted her back with an angry barrage of Indonesian. While she argued back the softer one shifted his legs back and forth and looked down to the floor. Stephen saw an opportunity to exploit the tension between the three of them. The meaner the boss was to their captive, perhaps, the more the sidekicks would be on Stephen's side.

"Do not worry, sir," said Stephen, looking pleadingly toward the leader. "Even if I knew this city's name I still don't know where I am. I have never been to Indonesia before. I have never even looked at a map of Java." He thought that sounded genuine, even if he was lying a little bit. He did glance through a *Lonely Planet* guide to Indonesia at the L.A. airport bookstore right before he bought that ridiculous self-help book.

The leader said something tersely in Indonesian and the girl translated it reluctantly. "He says go back to room and you be called if we need you." Stephen finally struck out, but he felt there was more tension now between the three. His budding strategy made Stephen feel a tiny bit more powerful. Backing away obediently, he made his way down the hall to his room. As he passed Agung's door he wondered about his new friend's condition but decided against calling out to him. He had pushed far enough today.

Stephen opened the door of his own tiny room and immediately felt hot and claustrophobic upon entering. Taking a seat back on his mattress, he looked up and realized he had forgotten to close the door. *I'm not closing it.* He would let them do that if they wanted it closed. He would let them do most of the work in this kidnapping thing. It was clear the whole abduction was in confusion and he wasn't going to help them one bit. He could hear the television volume turned up again, unsuccessfully trying to cover up their heated conversation. It sounded like Dina was pitted against the leader. No one came down the hall to close his door so at least he had some form of distraction.

The argument died down, the television droned on, and Stephen was alone with his thoughts again, staring into the emptiness of time. It felt ironic how much he wanted to be left alone at his own home, desiring above all to relax after a long day at work. And now he had all the isolation he wanted and yet he craved human contact and conversation.

He yearned for his family while his thoughts continued to drift back to his previous life evaluation. What if he never saw his kids and wife again, the people that he loved the most? And how could he be so distant with them? Maybe there was more to just wanting to relax that made him shut down at home. It was much easier for him to throw himself into work where he knew the rules and how to succeed than to come home where emotional vulnerability was required. His marriage was dying, he knew that. It had no real soul. Leah complained the most about him being "emotionally distant," but he had an artful way of avoiding conflict and putting just enough gas in the marriage machine to keep it running but never any real tune up's. As long as they weren't fighting they were doing okay, Stephen told himself. But he knew Leah had given up fighting long ago. He had entrenched and barricaded himself too cleverly to ever be found vulnerable and out in the open. She had no choice but to try to pursue him, which was futile, or to hurl herself into her kids' lives which was not only socially acceptable but gave her lots of admiration from other mothers. She could never really reach him or pin anything specific on him. That's where they had drawn the truce line long ago. Do your thing and I'll do mine and let's not fight too much because that's unpleasant for our home and bad for the children. His kids would also say that he was always there for them, but still too young to realize that being just physically present wasn't what was required emotionally.

All the thoughts ganged up on him and he craved some relief, or at least something lighter to pass the time. But he had nothing. Four bare walls, a foam mattress, a long pillow and a floor mat. Just him and time. If only he had a book to read—he would even succumb to finish reading *Fear Not and Live Hot!* He started thinking about the chapter exercises in that book that had gotten him into all this trouble in the first place. *Now's a good a time as any for some soul searching, I guess.*

Maybe the material would be helpful, but it was tucked inside his carry-on that had been confiscated by the terrorists. He wouldn't mind some handrails through this path of self-exploration, even from the self-help book that had gotten him into this quagmire. Anything better than this dreadful boredom and self-loathing.

He stood up to pace, wanting to stretch his achy legs and focus his thoughts. If he ever did get out of this place he would work down his Personalized Action Plan, focusing on the last to-do of loving without fear. He just wanted to hold Leah again and tell her he was so sorry for being so distant with her. Looking into her eyes, he would have a heart-to-heart conversation with her. He would scoop up his kids in his arms and tell them over and over how much he loved them. There would be a real heart connection with his family. He would unglue his face from his laptop and gadgets and look Randall and Tristan in their surprised eyes and actually play with them.

The door remained mostly open, and he sat next to it for greater air circulation. As time crawled by he reviewed how he had gotten into this situation and schemed how he could possibly get out. Only 48 hours ago he had said goodbye to his wife and children, then rode on a grueling trans-Pacific flight, met an obnoxious man who pushed him over the edge to do something stupid and spontaneous, and as a result was kidnapped under a false identity and had no way to prove who he really was.

But maybe there was. *Of course, my wallet.* He would show them his ID—the real Mr. Stephen Cranton without a trace of Mr. Carlton Easley. Why didn't he think of that before? He remembered it was still zipped inside his travel pouch inside his carry-on in the front room.

A foot appeared in the crack of the door, and fear obliterated his hopeful musings. The mean one barged into the room. "Mr. Easley, it time to tell you our demands," he said evenly and without anger. "Please follow me."

Stephen quickly followed him down the hall and was overjoyed to see Agung now sitting on the couch, seemingly unharmed. Stephen was motioned to sit next to Agung who smiled and squeezed his hand. Across the coffee table three empty chairs were aimed at them. The three captors filled them in one by one. Apparently, they were trying to make this look official, but it looked to Stephen like they were contestants on a game show.

He whispered to Agung, "Hello, how are you friend? I am so sorry I got you involved in this."

"It's okay, Mr. Carl. It not your fault." Even as a hostage the man was irrepressibly polite. The misnomer reminded Stephen again who he wasn't. He would blurt out the news as soon as he was given the chance to speak, backing it up with the proof of his tucked away identity cards.

The leader kept his gaze on Stephen who kept looking away to seem meeker. This guy could have won the intimidation contest even against a guy like Chopper. This angry terrorist could suddenly inflict a painful blow, if nothing else to show his half-hearted partners that he was still the boss.

The leader took a drag of his cigarette and got right to it: "You government keep the Muslim down and we want the Muslim up. You hurt the Muslim and now you must help the Muslim."

A silence hung in the air along with the smoky puffs of the man's cigarette.

"Okay, I understand," Stephen lied. Then he tried his turn at leading the conversation. "And I need to tell you something."

The leader started to react, and Stephen assumed it was more of I-am-the-boss-here and I-will-ask-the-questions. He dropped the humility and meekness and forged ahead before he was stopped again.

"I am not Carlton Easley. My name is Stephen Cranton. I am not who you think I am."

The three captors all looked at each other silently and Dina finally whispered the translation. Their faces showed they still didn't understand what he said and he kept going while they were off-balance.

"If you will look in my carry-on bag, you can find my wallet and you will see my ID, my identity cards. I was telling this to Mr. Agung here right before I was kidnapped. I was picked up at the airport by the wrong driver. This is a mistake. I am not Carlton Easley. I have never even met him. My name is

Stephen Cranton from Sacramento, California. I repeat, I am not Carlton Easley."

The leader's face dropped, either unhappy with this disclosure or with Stephen taking charge of the conversation. He snorted out a laugh to show Stephen's claim was ridiculous and nodded toward his partners with a large roll of his eyes.

"You lie," he shot back to Stephen. "You are Carlton Easley. We waiting you much time."

Stephen had to play his hand carefully, honoring this angry man while at the same time nudging him toward the truth. "You can look at my bag and see."

The man huffed and walked to the carry-on, still propped against the wall next to the front door. He unzipped the pouches and rifled through the contents. Finally, he retrieved the travel pouch and threw it across the room to Stephen, apparently for effect.

Stephen reflexively caught the pouch in mid-air. He unvelcroed and unzipped the pouch but didn't see the wallet or his passport. He searched it thoroughly but they were gone. Clearly this was a mind game and anger burned inside him.

"May I please have my documents? You already have put them somewhere else and you already know that I am Stephen Cranton and not Carlton Easley."

The leader spun around, kicked the carry-on over, and pointed back at Stephen. "You lie again. You are American liar. We know how you love come here and get rich and make us poor ones."

Stephen looked into the man's cold eyes. This personification of evil had taken his documents and was hiding the plain fact from his own partners. He knew he had snatched the wrong person and didn't want anyone to know his mistake. Stephen felt like lunging across the room and tackling him. Why not? He didn't see any knives or swords or whatever they were using earlier anywhere around. Maybe his partners would turn against their boss, too, if he just suddenly leapt across the room and attacked.

A doorbell chime from the front gate startled everyone, and they looked at the door as if they had all been suddenly frozen by an ice spell. The leader shot a glance at everyone and pressed his finger over his mouth for the quiet sign. Everyone but Stephen froze, who was boiling with enough frustration to try something rash.

"Let me call my family or I will scream and the person at the gate will hear me."

The same buzz chime again.

The statement must have emboldened Agung, because he cleared his throat and translated the sentence so there would be no mistake of the demand. Dina jumped up, grabbed Stephen by the hand and said "Yes, yes," as she tried to walk him down the hall.

He planted his feet into the floor and said, "I want a yes from him," pointing to the leader.

"Yes, yes, go back to room and you telephone," the leader quickly responded, not having enough time to brow beat his hostage back into submission.

Stephen felt like he had pushed enough so he obeyed. Once down the hallway he felt like screaming out anyway, but he still didn't know what violence these people were capable of. He would needle them little by little. So far they were sloppy in the way they were imprisoning him, compared with abductions in movies he had watched. Maybe he could just bolt out of the door and no one would stop him, before they had time to scramble for their weapons.

Whoever came to the gate had left quickly and probably didn't suspect a thing, walking away when there was no answer. Stephen had lived up to his side of the bargain by not screaming and they had better live up to theirs.

He sat down again in his lonely room, back against the wall under the one window. Quick footsteps clomped down the hall and this time they remembered to close and lock the door. Only an hour would be given before he started demanding to call Leah. He didn't want to wake her with such terrifying news—what time was it in Sacramento? He didn't even know what time it was there. If he did get through, he would first assure her that he was all right and unharmed. Break it to her slowly that he had been kidnapped, wait for her to react, and then answer her most pressing questions. A measured and calm disclosure would hopefully elicit compassion from her more than anger over why he did such a stupidly spontaneous thing. His emotions ranged from greatly longing to hear her voice again to dreading her terrified reaction.

The reserve of his energy was spent honing his mental strategy game. These were obviously not professional kidnappers. No one with any experience in this realm would so quickly show their faces to their hostage or let him see the route to this safe house. It seemed to him by now that they weren't going to torture him. They had him—or Carlton Easley—here for some reason and it would be revealed soon enough. It had something to do with "helping the Muslim." But it was also about money, as they said something about them becoming poor because of him.

He thought of poor Agung again and felt sorry for the kind man who just got mixed up with the wrong guy at the wrong time. At least they hadn't hurt him yet.

Still no offer for the promised phone call. More time passed without any human contact. His last conversation had been chaotic, but at least it was something. Now he was all alone again. A musty smell in the room, mingled with the smell of trash fires from outside, made it difficult to breathe.

Time and thoughts. Time was one thing in his former life that he never felt like he had enough of. His whole life felt like a to-do list that had to be checked through. No art, no heart, no passion filled his soul. He just made it to the end of every day with as many boxes as needed to be checked before enjoying a bit of entertainment in the evening, sleeping poorly and then going through a revised checklist the next day.

When did my heart die? Was I ever alive?

The self-exploration was just too gloomy, so he switched back over to his mental and exit strategies. Surveying the steel bars that were fastened with screws over the rectangle window again, he surmised he would need a long screwdriver, or at least a tool like a kitchen knife to unfasten the screws and remove the bars. But if he could lift himself to the height of the window and remove the bars somehow, he still wasn't even sure if he could get his head and shoulders through the small opening. Or the idea was still appealing to make a full run for it out the front door in the middle of a conversation. Maybe the door would be unlocked tonight. But could he navigate himself back to the civilization of Surabaya through hours of sugar cane fields, hilly roads, rice paddies and slum neighborhoods?

Why did the leader swipe his wallet? Why not just admit they got the wrong guy? How could that possibly help their cause in the long run? What would his company do now that he was late for his presentation? Would someone phone Leah? How long would it take for a missing Westerner to attract attention?

The kidnappers told him that they wouldn't hurt him, but wouldn't all kidnappers say the same thing to keep their hostages docile and submissive? Maybe they were just toying with him with the bumbling terrorist routine and eventually were going to dump his body into a ditch along these dusty streets. Maybe Dina was a plant that was there to give him a sense of false hope that he could turn her.

Plenty of time to chew on these questions. Plenty of time. Strategy and soul searching filled his mind until there was a knock on the door. It slowly opened and Agung poked his head in.

"Agung! Please come in, I'm so glad to see you." Stephen stood.

"I glad to see you, too, Mr. Carl," he said politely and with a kind smile. "They say I can visit you for ten minutes and check on you."

"Please come and have a seat. And remember my name isn't Carl. How are you my friend?"

Agung weakly bent down and sat on the floor, and Stephen followed.

"I'm fine. But I so embarrassed this has happened to you, sir."

"And I'm so sorry this has happened to you. I'm sorry that I got you mixed up in this"

"Mixed up?"

"I mean involved."

"Oh yes, I see."

Stephen was ecstatic to talk to a friendly ally, and yet felt the pressure of ten minutes passing quickly. He wanted to get straight to the point but knew he needed to show a little compassion to the kindly man first.

"How are you holding up?"

"I'm sorry, what you mean holding up?"

Stephen made a mental note to stop using so many American idioms. "I mean how are you doing in this situation?"

"I fine, sir. But I feel embarrassed that these people take you hostage. But they ask me to tell you something important and that's why they let me see you."

Stephen gave Agung his undivided focus, causing Agung to divert his eye contact and look down to the floor. Whatever this news was, it wasn't good. But if it was bad news, he was at least glad that Agung was the messenger and he had a few precious moments together with him.

"Go ahead and tell me." He braced his stomach.

"They say sorry but you not allowed to call your family yet. They have to do something first but no family call yet. No call to wife."

The news caused his already knotted up stomach to clench up even more. He felt flush and closed his eyes. Hatred for his captors reignited in his soul, especially for the leader. A scene of Stephen strangling the leader in his sleep played in his mind. Maybe he would get his chance—they did leave the door unlocked once. He hated that his wife would be worried, not hearing anything from him for over two days now. He should have at least called her en route but of course that was like good ole inconsiderate Stephen to drop that ball. She was already concerned about him going to a country that she feared was a breeding ground for terrorists. Her worst fears were being realized and he couldn't comfort her.

Probably seven more minutes with Agung. He pushed the hatred aside to get back to a pressing point.

"Agung, remember when we were in the car before we were kidnapped? I told you I am not Carlton Easley but my name is Stephen Cranton. Do you remember that? That's what I was trying to tell our kidnappers."

Agung finally looked up from staring at the floor. "Yes, I remember that but I still confused."

"It is confusing. I pretended to be Mr. Carlton Easley but I am not really him. That's what I was trying to tell the three of them. I was supposed to be in Surabaya yesterday evening leading a training for my International Courier Services company. They are probably wondering what happened to me."

Agung looked at Stephen as if he either didn't understand or didn't believe him.

"You say you not Carlton Easley? But why you pretend to be Carlton Easley?"

Stephen knew that the complex truth would be hard to put into simple English—after living under the constraints of fear and predictability his whole life, he decided for one insane moment to impersonate someone else, someone that was destined to be kidnapped a few moments later. A more understandable reason was required, at least one he could squeeze into the remaining minutes.

"I made a mistake at the airport and was picked up by the wrong driver. His car was supposed to be for someone named Carlton Easley and I got in the wrong car."

Agung looked confused. "Was driver holding a sign that said 'Carlton Easley'?"

This hole would be more difficult to dig out of than he originally thought. "No, he wasn't. He was just standing there and he said that name, but I only heard the word 'easily.' I said, 'Surabaya?' and I thought he said, 'easily,' like 'yes, I can easily get you there.' So I went with him, not knowing that he was waiting for someone named Mr. Easley. I never looked at the sign. Later I found out that I was in the wrong car."

Stephen felt proud of himself for coming up with that one so quickly. And Agung seemed to buy it, or at least get disoriented in the rapid-fire narrative and accept it because he would not be able to untangle a complicated knot like that. He nodded his head up and down in cautious understanding.

"Oh, I see," he said after a long pause. "That is, what you call it…unfortunate. So you thought you get in car that will get you to your destination in Surabaya, but driver was picking up someone named Mr. Easley."

"Yes, Carlton Easley. It was a terrible mistake."

"Yes," Agung shook his head up and down again. "Yes, terrible mistake." The two men traded looks of understanding and sympathy in the silence.

Agung spoke again. "So now what we do?"

"I have no idea, Agung. I have been thinking about that but I'm not sure what these guys want. Can you overhear what they are saying?"

"Sometimes. They argue a lot. I don't think they agree with each other and the one named Mustafal is leader of the group. Dina is his girlfriend and the other one named Happy, the cousin of Mustafal."

"Happy? I am being held hostage by someone named Happy?"

"Yes, his name Happy," he answered matter-of-factly, not seeing the humor in it.

Stephen wasn't sure how many seconds were left with Agung so he needed to use this time to get the most important information.

"Can you tell why they are holding us?"

"They say they Muslim terrorists."

"But what do they want from us?" Stephen asked.

"I don't know. They not say yet. They only say you cannot call your wife. But if they are terrorists, they not very good Muslims. Because they never *sholat*. I still *sholat* even here, but we have been with them two days and not once they *sholat*."

The two of them could both hear someone walking down the hall briskly.

"Agung, quickly, what is *sholat*?"

The door creaked opened. Agung looked at Stephen before he looked at the person opening the door. It was their newly named leader Mustafal and their time was up. Agung said to Stephen quickly and quietly, "Pray."

Stephen wasn't sure if *sholat* meant to pray or Agung was telling him to pray. He automatically started to pray silently, which he had done more in the last two days than he had in the last twenty years.

Mustafal stepped inside the doorway and said something in a low, growling voice to Agung, who nodded and followed him obediently out of the room.

CHAPTER TWELVE

Om Donri descended from the van, taking a little longer than a younger man would have, and told the driver he would be back in less than an hour. Today's driver was a kind-hearted friend from his church, willing to take the kids on today's outing if Donri covered the gas. Normally Donri made the hour drive from Surabaya to Pandaan on his trusty and well-maintained motorcycle but today was a special day that needed extra seating.

Donri waved him farewell and looked back to see the man light up a cigarette, probably thankful that no church folk would be around who might frown on that sort of thing. The van inched ahead to find a better parking spot along the busy road in Pandaan, and Donri entered the alleyway which was not wide enough for a car.

The journey from the main road through the *kampung's* narrow sliver of streets to the English center normally took him a couple of minutes on his motorcycle but would take him about ten minutes to walk. Along the way the old man greeted everyone he saw with a nod and the *monggo* Javanese greeting, which was usually reciprocated with a double *monggo* in return. It was actually kind of nice to be on foot, and to hear some people go beyond the expected cultural greeting and call him by name. With those he would stop and chat and inquire of their children. He had become a weekly visitor to this *kampung,* and he was pleased when he heard a few English greetings from the younger ones with their proud parents standing nearby. Om Donri believed that English was a key to these little ones' success, unlocking the world of technology and business for them in a brave new world. His lectures on the challenges of globalization surprised people expecting to hear a rant about how Indonesians are leaving the ancient traditions. At 72, he was pushing them into the future.

For the most part he looked forward to leading his little English club, and the role gave him an almost celebrity status in this sleepy little neighborhood of Pandaan. Today he would be even more of a hero, taking a van full of kids on a field trip four hours away to the southern coastal town of Sendang Biru. Most of these kids had never been more than one hour away from their homes and had never even seen a beach even though they lived on an island. Just like faith, he often said, poverty was a lack of options.

There would be a buzz in the *kampung*, he was sure, as the kids were getting ready for their exotic trip. They were already excited to have a school holiday today but now they actually had someplace brand new to explore. After the long drive, the plan was to park the van at a hidden little beach near Sendang Biru, picnic and explore a cave there. Donri could hardly wait to see the amazed looks in the young kids' faces after they got out of the van and beheld the South Java Sea for the very first time. After playing for a while at that beach, they would go by van to the main beach and take a boat across a small strait to the nearby island of Sempu. This tiny island was a nature refuge, and after giving a governmental guardian a small tip for permission to enter, they could all hike across it to a pure white sandy lagoon that offered a breathtaking view of giant waves crashing against black coral cliffs. Their world would expand today in an unforgettable way and that vista would be the climax of today's adventure.

On through the narrow *kampung* roads he walked, simple houses on both sides, with plenty of people to greet. It was taking twice the time he had estimated because of all the stopping and chatting. More kids than usual were out playing because of the school holiday. The cramped passageway suddenly opened into a rice field which gave him a view of Mount Arjuno. He looked up at the majestic, ash-covered mountain and thought he would soon be like the old volcano, no longer active. But while his feet still carried him where he wanted to go, he would serve the Lord and the poor. Not only that, his mind was way too active for him to stay at home doing nothing all day during retirement.

On the other side of the rice field and down two more crowded streets sat the small tutoring center used for his free English class. The club started with a dozen diligent students and swelled quickly when word got out that the old teacher was funny and full of good stories. Donri had to limit the number to 25 because they just couldn't cram another little body into the borrowed classroom. Sadly, he had to impose another limit for today's field trip because of limited seating in the van. Only those students with perfect attendance over the last six months would be able to go, which worked out to ten lucky adventurers.

There were already two kids standing out front of the rental house-turned-tutoring center and Donri unlocked the door for them. The three of them moved the few single-seat desks to the back room and spread out woven mats in the main room to make space for everyone.

While they waited, Donri erased the white board and grimaced when he saw scribbles of poor grammar on the whiteboard leftover from the owners of the place. They were selling bad English and people were buying it. He offered these poor *kampung* kids, unable to pay for a private course, better English for free. But he was at least grateful that the owners let him use the place without cost. They were willing to do that, he assumed, in hopes of drumming up more business from his few students who came from families with modest means.

Donri looked with satisfaction at the new colorful posters on the walls describing simple English objects like fruits and household items. He had suggested to the owners that they put up some educational decorations and he was pleased to see they did. He had always thought Indonesian classrooms were dreadfully bare and boring, and the teachers usually didn't do much to spice up their lessons with creativity. Donri felt that education wasn't something for people just to endure but should be something that sparked the imagination and intellect into action. That mindset should even be reflected in how a classroom looked. He told the owners this principle and they seemed to have heeded his advice. Donri was freer in sharing his opinions than the typical Javanese person and he was especially delighted when people actually took them to heart.

Some more students soon trickled in, some with their parents who chatted with Donri about the day's plan, and they all waited excitedly for the departure time. This was going to be a day to remember.

≈≈◻≈≈

Johanna Grazen was driven through moderate traffic on Thursday morning to the main police station in Pandaan. After conferring with the police captain and the arresting officer, she walked to the small holding cell of Carlton Easley and got a first look at him through the rust flaked bars.

She was expecting to see a young hitchhiking hippie but was surprised to see a semi-professionally dressed and heavy-set man sitting on a cot and staring at the floor with his elbows resting on his knees. The large man looked up at her and mumbled a hello with the intonation of a question.

"Hello, Mr. Easley. My name is Johanna Grazen and I am the citizen liaison from the U.S. Consulate in Surabaya. We received a call that an American was being held here. It's our policy to meet with any American citizen that has been arrested within twenty-four hours."

Carlton struggled to lift himself out of the low-lying cot and reached his hands through the bars for a firm handshake. "You've got to get me out of here," he urged while pulling Johanna toward him. "I don't know if these cops are looking to extort money or if they're just crazy. I am here in jail for knocking over a lamp on accident. They have violated my rights of due process and wouldn't even let me make a phone call. I've been in this holding cell since yesterday and I will not stand for this. We will bring the full force of the United States government down on these third world thugs."

The barrage of information and inflated threats made Johanna take a slight step back, more to get her personal space back than to process the information. But the intense man was still able to grip on to her hand through the bars.

"Uh," Johanna stuttered after wrenching her hand free. "Let's, uh, start from the beginning here." Carlton's bulging eyeballs popped out with a wide-eyed crazed look which Johanna found disconcerting. She forced herself to forge through as a professional. "The police told me nothing about a lamp but that you are being held for a hit-and-run incident."

"What?" he yelled, "I have told them a thousand times that I had nothing to do with that!" A fury of emotion uncorked from his large body. The crazed man stomped around in a circle, balled his fists up and shook them, yelled out curses upon Indonesia and pressed his chubby face between the bars, threatening the policemen at the station like a professional wrestler out for blood or fame.

This guy is completely nuts. Johanna turned her attention to the policemen in the station who were all startled by the tirade. Their quiet conversations and newspaper reading suddenly stopped as they watched the cell with a hunter's motionless stare. She knew she had to calm her new client down before they all came over with batons and the whole situation got out of hand.

"*Maaf, ya? Maaf,*" Johanna called out loudly toward the tense policemen. She pressed her palms together and lifted them in an apologetic, prayer-like gesture. "*Saya cuma mau berbicara dengan orang ini sebentar dan saya minta maaf atas ketindakanyna yang kurang sopan.*" They still were observing Carlton intently but at least they weren't marching over to the cell which made Johanna feel relieved.

She turned back to Carlton, now sitting back down on the cot, still fuming. "Mr. Easley, you have got to calm down here. That kind of an outburst is not going to help you any."

"What did you tell them?" Carlton asked without looking up.

"I said I needed to talk to you for a minute and I apologized for your behavior."

Carlton shot up from his cot and squared himself in front of Johanna, grabbing the bars. "You apologized for me? Don't you do that again," he said in a low, gravelly voice. "They should be apologizing to me, not the other way around."

Johanna didn't know how to respond and she felt the best tactic now was to change the subject to less explosive matters.

She nodded her feigned agreement and pulled out a notebook and clicked her pen open. The interview started off with general questions about who Carlton was and where he was from, why he had come to Indonesia, and then gingerly on toward the events that led up to his arrest.

Carlton spoke quickly and Johanna kept up as best she could on her notepad. It only took a few minutes of questioning for her to be convinced that Carlton's story was probably true. It also didn't take her long to judge that the man wasn't crazy but just a hot head who probably brought much of this on himself. Carlton didn't show one sign of decorum or respect for the culture or people around him. Johanna was put off by the condescending tone of the sweating man and the way he kept looking over her shoulder when she talked instead of making eye contact. It was as if he were waiting for someone more important than her to come walking into the police station. Johanna was there to help him, and yet he seemed almost bothered by the interview. She could understand that this businessman wanted to get back to his own life again, but why did he have to treat his one ally in this mess like an inferior? The guy was an "Ugly American" even to his fellow Americans. It made Johanna want to work slower for spite but she resisted the temptation and pressed ahead again professionally.

Johanna started into her next question but Carlton cut her off. "Miss Grazen, is there any way you can call the factory so that they can explain everything? I have been here for over 12 hours now. The name of the manager on duty is Mr. Bambang. He can assure the police that I was being driven here by a driver and was not operating that vehicle. Why is it so hard to get a phone call to that factory?"

"Okay, I think we're finished here anyway. I can try to make a call now."

"I'm pretty sure I know why," said Carlton, ignoring Johanna's statement and answering his own question. "This is about money."

Johanna ignored the comment and walked to the nearest window to make the call. It would look like she wanted to make the call in a place with good reception but the truth was she didn't want the overpowering man bossing her around from inside his cell. She was well out of earshot but she could see that Carlton was straining to hear.

Johanna flipped her cell phone open and got the number from information, then punched the number in. After the official *Firdaus Rokok* greeting she asked, *"Boleh saya berbicara dengan Pak Bambang?"* with what she thought was flawless enunciation.

"Oh, yes, wait just moment," came the answer in English. She could never pass for an Indonesian on the phone, no matter how hard she tried to mask her American accent. They always answered back in English if they had the proficiency.

A few seconds ticked by as Carlton looked like he wanted to reach through his cell bars and grab the phone away from her if he could. He was drumming his fingers on the bars and the only other sound was the rustle of some newspapers being read by the police officers. The show was over and they were pretty much ignoring him again. Good thing.

"Hello, this is Mr. Bambang. May I help you?"

"Yes, hello Mr. Bambang. I understand that you are waiting for a Mr. Carlton Easley."

"Have they found him?" Bambang asked excitedly.

"Yes, I am with him now."

"Thank God. We been so worried. Where are you now?"

"I am at the police station in Pandaan. He says he is a visiting supervisor for your factory, is that correct?"

"Yes that is correct. May I know who this is?"

"Oh, yes. I'm sorry. This is Johanna Grazen from the U.S. Consulate in Surabaya."

"Oh, thank God you found him. We so worried when the kidnappers called. How did he get rescued?"

"Kidnappers?" Johanna said with confusion and she looked back over at Carlton.

"Yes, the kidnappers called and said they will call later with their demands."

Johanna kept looking at her client, who had sat back down and was brooding on his cot. Carlton looked up and caught Johanna's confused gaze from across the room.

"I am with Mr. Easley right now, Mr. Bambang. We are at the Pandaan police station."

"Thank God he has been found," Bambang rejoiced again. Johanna could hear him announcing the good news in Indonesian to the people in the background.

Johanna was trying to find some trail of logic, and couldn't even think of her next question. "We are at the police station and he is being questioned here for his role in hitting a boy on the side of the toll road. But there was nothing about a kidnapping."

"I'm sorry, what you say?"

"I think you may have been crank called."

"What?"

"Prank called."

"Excuse me?"

"Why don't you come to the police station and we can sort this out. I said we haven't heard anything about a kidnapping. We'll wait for you here. Mr. Easley is here and not going anywhere."

"Okay, we come right away. We did not call the police yet but I am glad they found him. Did you say there was a car accident? We not find Mr. Easley on the toll road where he say he was."

"Just come down to the station and let's sort it all out."

Carlton's perturbed face indicated he wanted an immediate explanation. Johanna decided to give him just a portion of the conversation. She felt a little ruffled from his gruff manner and wasn't in the mood for an attack of his sharp questions.

She walked over and said simply, "Mr. Bambang is on the way now."

"'Bout time," Carlton snorted.

Johanna didn't answer that but walked over to an empty desk, picked up a copy of the day's *Jawa Pos* newspaper and scanned the pictures and the headlines. One of the police officers smiled at her, but she looked down at the newspaper and smiled at it instead. She knew better by now than to act too friendly toward certain Indonesian men who seemed too friendly.

She couldn't concentrate on making sense of all the newspaper articles in Indonesian because her mind was consumed with trying to figure out how this caged man could have gotten into so much trouble in such a short time. Hit and run? Kidnapped? This was going to be an interesting day. She sent a text message to Ibu Dewi saying she probably wouldn't be coming to the office today after all. So far this mystery was definitely more intriguing than processing visas and passports.

≈≈□≈≈

Agung's family once again called all the friends, relatives and workmates they could think of on the second day of his disappearance, but still no one had heard anything. The entire family, especially his mother, was nearly frantic. His dad tried to calm her down with a lot of reassurances but he was worried too. She sensed that he was just trying to put on a brave face which made her spiral into even deeper despair. The dapper and well-respected man got ready for work, drank his coffee, smoked his cigarettes and read his newspaper as usual, but he couldn't push the fear for his son out of his mind. At first they thought it was some sort of miscommunication but after all this time they started to fear one of the theories of *kampung* gossip was true; not that Agung was doing something terrible but that something terrible had happened to him. It was just too out-of-character for Agung to disappear and not tell anyone where he was going. Something bad had happened.

They talked through his steps on the day of the disappearance. Agung had taken his niece to her pre-school in the morning on his motorcycle, then taught at his elementary school and went off campus later to do an errand for the principal. He may have stopped at a *warung* for a mid-morning rice meal, but they had checked all of his favorite spots and none of the owners remembered seeing him that day. He simply never came back to the school—vanished just like that.

Their only lead was that four elementary school girls said that they had seen their teacher yesterday riding with a *bule* in a nice car, smiling and chatting away. Were these little girls lying to get some attention? Did they see it wrongly or rightly? Why would he be riding with someone they didn't know and not even tell them?

To the clusters of relationships in the *kampung* this was all just interesting gossip but to the family it was a cloud of fear that grew darker and darker with time over their small household.

Should they call the police? They didn't want to have to pay to get adequate police help, but it had been almost 24 hours since anyone had seen him. His cell phone wasn't picking up either, although his mother kept calling it, almost obsessively. He was such a nice boy, not one to get into trouble, she said repeatedly.

They went to the mosque during noon prayers and asked the *imam* for special prayers for Agung. Normally not ones to do the *sholat* prayer at the mosque, the whole family showed up wearing their white prayer garb and ready to petition Allah for Agung's safe return home.

CHAPTER THIRTEEN

Stephen felt unbearably hot in his stuffy room, but there was no other choice but to bear it. Looking up through his small window at the bright sunlight, he surmised it was mid-day on the equator.

Before the trip he had looked forward to doing some sightseeing while in East Java, especially catching what he read was a spectacular sunrise over the active volcano of Mt. Bromo. There would be no such excursions on this trip. Now his only scenery was the inside of a bare 10 by 8 foot room. He had measured it several times with his size 12 feet, and had counted the tiles at least a couple of times to cross check his calculation.

His thoughts wound through the subjects of his longed-for family, lifeless marriage, his aging parents and lack of connection with them as well, his own stupidity for getting into that car and then finally back around to an escape strategy.

The latch of the door unlocked and interrupted his thoughts. He looked up to see Dina entering his room with what looked like lunch. She placed a triangular shaped package on the floor along with a napkin and two plastic cups of water. She looked back at him, smiled kindly and started to back out of the room while nodding her head up and down. Stephen smiled back, with pleading eyes, beckoning her to stay just a bit longer.

"Please, eat with me," he said with his clearest enunciation.

She responded with something he couldn't understand and left quickly, closing the door behind her. He wanted her in the room for some more information but mainly for human contact amid the boredom.

Stephen sat with his legs crossed and focused on the pyramid of mystery food wrapped inside another tightly folded banana leaf. Inside the package was a fist-size ball of rice with chicken and vegetable-like ingredients he didn't recognize on top. A small plastic baggie of some sort of sauce plopped to the floor between his legs. Tucked inside the food there was a mini spoon. Immediately he tested the utensil's usefulness as an instrument of escape, bending it back and forth to see if it could be used perhaps as a screwdriver. No go.

His thirst was greater than his hunger and he was grateful for two cups of water this time. With the small straw he punctured the cellophane lid in one quick strike, like a nurse inserting a needle into a patient's vein. Getting the straw in with one try made him feel proud, as it had taken him three attempts at breakfast. Next he started in on the food, which he decided to eat slowly to savor every bite. Stephen carefully opened the little plastic baggie of sauce and dripped it over the rice and bits of chicken and vegetables. It was spicy stuff but overall the meal was good and a nice distraction, at least something to do besides brood and strategize.

He sipped slowly and ate on through the burning sensation, then noticed something shiny at the bottom of the rice. He dug at it with the spoon, and was shocked to see a small silver key covered with the saucy rice.

His mind exploded with wonder. A key? Was this the key to his freedom? Dina must have put it there. Why didn't she just hand it to him? What door or lock did it open? He searched the wrappings for any more clues but there weren't any. Stephen felt a surge of hope that there was someone on his side in all this. Or was it still some sort of mind game? He turned his body away from the door so a sudden intruder wouldn't be able to see his precious treasure, and placed the key in his mouth to wash off the rice and sauce. Then with the napkin he wiped off the sticky key and folded it into his sock.

This secret tool set off in him a cascade of ideas—how, when and where to use it. It was a small key, ill-fitted for a regular door. Maybe it was for a window or a padlock to unlock something he would need later. Would she reveal the rest of the escape plan or was it up to him to improvise? It was pretty risky for her to sneak it to him so he couldn't assume there would be more aid coming.

He finished off the remains of the small-portioned lunch and started on the second water glass to wash away more of the spices still agitating his mouth. He stood up to stretch and placed the wrappings of the meal in the corner. More pacing. More strategizing.

Armed with the new ammo and after a few more minutes of thinking through his limited options, he finally decided it was time to make a move. He didn't want to wait to see if Dina's missing key would be noticed and they would come searching for it on him. If she tried to offer any more insider help, she could endanger her own life or even his. That real possibility, plus the humdrum boredom, was making item number two on his Personalized Action Plan—to take a risk—a lot more appealing.

He knocked confidently on the door and called out, "Excuse me, excuse me."

He was glad to see Happy's child-like face as the door opened. "Hello Happy. I need to go to bathroom. Restroom."

"Toilet?" Happy asked, not seeming surprised that Stephen knew his nickname.

"Yes, toilet."

Happy opened the door and led him down the hall to the bathroom.

Stephen closed his eyes briefly and told himself he had to do this now, and would allow himself to feel the fear later. It was time to take a risk, just like getting into Carlton's car. Even more than fearing not or living hot, this was about fighting for his family.

Before Happy could react, he shoved past him and ran at a full sprint toward the front door. Through his peripheral vision he could see Dina lounging on the couch and watching music videos, but there was no sign of Mustafal. He jiggled the door lever and found it unlocked, pushed the door violently open and tore toward the gate. There was no time to grab his shoes off the porch so he ran out with his slippery black dress socks clinging to his fast moving feet.

He cleared the short, empty driveway in a few strides. The Mercedes Benz was no longer there. Had Mustafal left in it? No time to wonder.

The front gate was padlocked. He checked and it was indeed locked. The key! He reached down, yanked it out of his sock and jammed it into the padlock. It fit perfectly. He glanced behind him and saw Dina and Happy appearing in the doorway, yelling something at him. The lock popped open easily, he flicked the gate latch and then slid open the gate quickly.

With a surge of energy he slid the gate back closed, and the thought came to him that he needed to lock the gate behind him. Maybe they didn't have an extra key and this would buy him more time. He closed the gate latch and poked the padlock through the hole as Happy ran toward him, screaming loudly. Stephen barely had the time to clamp the padlock closed into the gate latch. As Stephen's hand was withdrawing through the gate's bars, Happy got there and reached through the bars, grabbing Stephen's arm. Dina was still on the front porch, watching with shocked but likely feigned amazement.

Stephen flung his arm free from Happy's grasp and started running. He knew his captors would not be able to scale the gated fence quickly with all the glass shards and barbed wire he saw at the top, but he still glided off as fast as a spooked deer. Dina, he guessed, was not in a hurry to get him, but her partners would surely come charging down the road after him any second.

He bolted down to the first turn-off from the road. At the lonely juncture he looked back and could see Dina and Happy, still trapped in the front yard and yelling through the gate. He turned and ran down a side dirt road and kicked up a trail of dust in his wake, arms pumping through the hot, humid air. A row of houses was ahead and he ran right by them, not daring to stop so near his captors. He came to a sugar cane field and found a trail which led to a poorly paved, pot-holed road. He took it in the direction that led to more houses, and he felt a little safer being a good five-minute run from the hostage house.

People on their front stoops called out things at him as he shot past their small houses but he dared not stop yet. He would ask someone for a phone but wanted to be a little farther away from anyone who might be on Mustafal's side. Kids ducked around corners to peer at the strange white man running at full gallop without shoes through their sleepy neighborhood. Some laughed. A commotion trailed him as chickens scattered and people kept calling after the running foreigner. He wasn't sure if it was greetings or questions but he kept running as fast as his socked-feet could take him. His body was on fire, chest pounding and lungs breathing in the air of freedom as deeply as they could.

After one more sugarcane field trail he came to a nicer paved road that ran along a beach. Apparently his first impression had been correct and Dina hadn't lied to him—this was a seaside community. Stephen felt confident his captors had lost his trail and he slowed his pace down to a brisk walk. He looked through a break in the dense grove of palm trees at the tropical beach. The majestic sound of the waves crashing onto the beach filled him with the exhilarating joy of freedom. He had escaped. No more threats and no more choking. He was not going to get captured again by crazed terrorists and he was going to be reunited with his family. He imagined Leah's relieved face and the pride that Randall and Tristan would have in knowing their dad took a gigantic risk to get back to them. *Thank you, Chaz Wilton.*

As he walked along the shoulder of the road, villagers carrying loads of sticks and baskets of tall grass passed him. All of them smiled and some would look him over, notice his shoeless feet and call out, *"Mau ke mana?"*

He didn't know what it meant but kept smiling back. He tried once to parrot it back to an older farmer and the man responded by chuckling heartily. Stephen politely laughed back but kept up his pace, feeling elated to be free and fearful of being nabbed again.

The walk continued along the beach road and he hoped it would lead to a more populated area. The houses he had passed earlier were so poor and simple he doubted if any of them had telephones. Plus he wanted to find someone that spoke English to help him through the phone calling process and he figured a translator would be more easily found in a town than a village.

He knew he looked ridiculous, a sweaty foreigner power-walking down a shady road without any shoes on, but he dared not stop yet. He tried to look as confident as possible, as if he were meeting a friend in the middle of this Indonesian village. Maybe a racquetball appointment? Knowing how out of place he looked, he tried to ignore the wide-eyed stares of the villagers. His heart was beating at a more normal rate now but his mind kept on racing.

Ten, twenty more minutes of walking and he came to a more lonely stretch of road, without a soul in sight. Ever so often a car would pass and Stephen would duck into the overgrowth of the side of the road, making sure it wasn't a Mercedes-Benz trolling with the search party inside.

As he continued to walk, his socked feet hurt more and more from walking on the rough surface. He wanted to catch his breath for a moment and think about his next steps from a safe spot. Ducking into some dense overgrowth, he fought through it until he came to a large palm tree grove that opened up into a better view of the beach.

He came to a grouping of large rocks under a canopy of coconut trees and climbed on top. The cool breeze under the shade felt refreshing and the view of the pounding waves was spectacular. Impossible rock formations jutted out of the water and the horizon stretched on to forever. Stephen felt so grateful to be alive and he caught himself offering a prayer of thanks to a long-ignored God.

He took his socks off to pick the debris and pebbles out of them while his weary body enjoyed resting on the smooth boulder. He had the whole beach to himself and for the first time since the kidnapping, he felt safe. He could stay in this spot as long as he wanted and if anyone did try to approach, he could see them coming from far away.

He slipped on his picked-over socks and surveyed his situation. His clothes were intact but sweaty. No wallet or shoes and no carry-on or suitcase. His only choice ahead would be to rely completely on the generosity of others to use a phone and get him back to Surabaya. Grateful to be free, he wanted the same for his unfortunate friend Agung.

He scooted back down the rocks and decided to walk along the beach instead of the main road so he wouldn't have to be concerned with a Mustafal sighting. Plus it would be easier on his feet. As he strolled along he tossed a few rocks into the pounding surf and wondered at the beauty of this tropical beach. If the world knew this place was here, this little patch of paradise would be overrun with expansive and expensive beach resorts. A very skinny fisherman was the only human he saw and he tried out a *"Mau ke mana"* greeting but the old man looked back at him puzzled and turned his attention back to his bamboo fishing pole. Stephen didn't bother asking the man for a cell phone.

He walked on for another half hour or so to what he hoped was civilization. He remembered that Java was the world's most densely populated island but it sure didn't feel like it now. Palm trees and ocean stretched out for miles and miles.

The beach and the road wound closer together and he could see some farmers walking along the shoulder of the road but they were too far away to see or notice him. He debated whether to stay safe at the ocean's edge or take his chance on the busier road where an English speaker with a phone might be riding by.

He finally decided that he would have to make a move before the afternoon got any closer to dusk, so he made his way back to the nearby road. As he climbed up to the shoulder he heard a car coming down the road and ducked behind a couple of palm trees to make sure it wasn't Mustafal.

A blue Mercedes Benz ambled down the lonely road. *It is him.* Through the trees and as low as he could crouch, Stephen saw the car moving slowly toward his direction, with Mustafal's searching face looking out through the rolled down window.

Oh my God. The feeling of peace and beauty Stephen had slowly let himself enjoy vanished into an instantaneous flash of fear. He stayed low and dared not move as the car crept past. Mustafal must not have seen him but Stephen stayed as still as a statue for several minutes after the car was long gone.

Now what? The madman was still on the hunt. What would Mustafal do to him if he found him? So far Stephen had not seen any gun. If Mustafal came after him with another knife or sword, Stephen could surely outrun him.

He straightened up and jogged quickly back along the beach. Now he really needed a phone and he would ask the next person for help, fisherman or not. He kept looking back at the road for a Mercedes sighting. If he saw it, he would dive into the surf since there was nothing to hide behind on the sand. Hopefully Mustafal would miss him again.

On he trotted, feeling an emotional whiplash from swinging from serenity back to terror again so quickly. Up ahead he saw a group of kids sitting on a large blanket next to the ocean, laughing and singing along with an elderly man who was nicely dressed in a traditional Indonesian shirt, untucked and silky.

Civilization! People! Time to bust up the picnic.

Stephen ran at a full gait toward the group, recognizing the lyrics of the song they were singing together as he ran. "If you're happy and you know it, clap your hands..." *English!* These people knew English.

The kids looked up startled as the raving foreigner charged them. The older Indonesian man jumped to his feet and positioned his body between himself and the children.

Seeing the startled children, Stephen realized he must look to them like a demented Western hitchhiker. He tried to catch his breath before he explained his predicament to the older man, who kept a kindly but authoritative gaze on Stephen.

"I'm so sorry," Stephen stammered. "I'm sorry to interrupt you, but do you speak English?"

"Yes," said the old man, whom Stephen guessed was in his 70's. "What is the matter?"

"I, uh, I am being chased and just escaped...." Without warning and surprising himself the most, Stephen burst into tears. The kids circled around him with wide-eyed wonder. The old man put his hand on Stephen's shoulder, which didn't help his composure any but instead made the sobs come out even stronger and louder.

The old man kept his arm around Stephen's shoulder until he was finished. "Tell us what happened," he said calmly. His pronunciation was pretty good and Stephen felt great relief that the man seemed to be an excellent English speaker.

"I'm so sorry. I've been through something very traumatic and I didn't mean to cry like that."

"It's okay," said the man with a calm, comforting voice, "It's okay."

"Yeah, is okay mister," said one of the kids, looking up at Stephen with an angelic expression of compassion. She had two long braids and big brown eyes, and the sight of her sweet little face made Stephen feel a tad bit safer. Maybe that good cry helped.

"My name is Stephen Cranton and I am from the United States. After arriving at the airport in Surabaya yesterday I was kidnapped by three people and taken to a village not far from here. They kidnapped me and one other Indonesian man and I just escaped. The other is still there."

The old man looked like he was catching every word. One of the girls started tugging on the old man furiously and asking him questions and the man bent down to have a talk with her. Stephen wondered what could be so important in the middle of his narrative, and he used the pause to look back to the road from their beach spot in case Mustafal was coming.

The old man straightened back up. "Was the name of the man with you Agung?"

Stephen felt startled at the mention of Agung's name. Were these seemingly innocent looking people on the kidnappers' side somehow? Or maybe there was a nationwide manhunt for Stephen and Agung?

"Yes, it was Agung. How did you know that?"

"Here, please sit down," said the old man, motioning to the two thatch mats they were using for their picnic.

Stephen obliged, thinking these sweet kids were not likely with the kidnappers. "Thanks." The kids formed a circle around both men, with big eyes and bodies leaning in to hear the conversation.

"My name is Donri," the old man began, "and the kids here call me Om Donri. I teach an English club in their neighborhood. Today we came to this beach for a field trip and my students say that one of their neighbors, Pak Agung, has been missing. They said they saw him riding in a car with a foreigner yesterday. This one here says it was you." Donri pointed to the girl who was tugging on him earlier, and she nodded her head up and down excitedly.

"Uh, yes, that was me yesterday." Something about the little girl's beaming face reminded him of Tristan. The thought of his family made Stephen feel like crying again but he tightened his eye muscles to stop the dam from cracking open. "Agung was helping me as a translator when we were abducted, when we were kidnapped, about eleven o'clock yesterday."

"And you say Agung is still there and you escaped?"

"Yes, Agung is still there." Stephen felt sorry again for his kindly tour guide.

"And these people who kidnapped you, they are still looking for you?"

"Yes," Stephen said, feeling another jolt of fear.

"We need to call the police."

"Yes, for sure." Stephen felt relieved that someone was definitely on his side, someone with an air of authority. Donri said something to the kids and they all jumped up, started folding the mats and gathering up their picnic supplies. The tallest boy in the group grabbed the guitar and the smallest girl in the group held Stephen's hand. He wasn't sure why, but it suddenly made him feel very protective. He had been acting like a victim for the last 24 hours...but now he felt emboldened. Maybe it was just safety in numbers, but whatever it was he wasn't going to let anything happen to these kids and he would fight to get back to his own.

"Come on, I left my hand phone back in our car," said Donri. "It's not a far walk from here and hopefully the reception is good."

Donri started marching off in the same direction as Stephen had been traveling, with the road on their right side and beach on their left, toward enormous rock formations ahead. Stephen felt relief that they were getting farther and farther away from the hostage house.

"No shoes?" Donri asked when he noticed Stephen's feet clad in only socks.

"I left them back at the hostage house when I escaped."

Donri nodded a compassionate smile. "Do you think you could help the police find that hostage house?"

"I've done a lot of running and walking since I escaped but I think so."

"And do you think Agung is still there now?"

"I can't imagine him being anywhere else. It wasn't that long ago since I escaped and I'm sure they have tightened up security since then."

Donri was marching at a surprisingly good clip with the kids trailing behind him. Like Donri, none of the kids looked like they were dressed for a day at the beach. All were in long pants and many were wearing long-sleeved shirts too. One of them was even wearing a jacket. Stephen filled Donri in with details of his capture and captivity. The kind-faced man nodded along and asked more questions about Agung and the location of the house.

When they got closer to the towering rocks Donri said, "Our car is just up ahead in a parking area beyond those rocks and our driver is waiting inside the car. You can use my phone and the driver can take us to the nearest police station, although I'm afraid I'm not sure where that is."

"Can't you just call 911?"

"Sorry, what's that?"

"It's uh, never mind," Stephen said, looking at the road again for the Mercedes. "I really appreciate your help."

"No worries, as my Australian friends say."

"Well, I wouldn't even know how to contact the police in this village, or much less anything else. I feel quite helpless."

The kids started singing more English songs as they walked, apparently not sensing they could be in danger.

"Well, I wouldn't say you are helpless."

"I sure feel that way."

"I was just thinking," Donri said, looking out over the ocean before he looked into Stephen's face as they walked together. "This is such an amazing coincidence. Here we are together on an island of over one hundred million people and after you escaped you found us, a small group of people at a picnic. One of them knows the person you were captured with. Of all the people on this island, we are probably the best to help, how you say, connect the dots."

"That is lucky."

"Blessed, I would say."

"Okay, blessed." Stephen didn't dare debate a man who was bringing him back to civilization.

"I think God is also on the side of your friend Agung. Little Siti here says that his whole family is very worried and many people in her neighborhood were looking for him last night. They have been praying a lot. God cares about them too. About all of us."

Stephen wasn't in the mood for a sermon but the old man was in the driver's seat. He just politely nodded along until they could get back to the car and to the phone. He was thinking more about his worried wife than a concerned God at the moment.

"Just up ahead." Donri pointed down the beach and Stephen could just start to see the beach's parking area, with a glimmer of sunshine bouncing off a car windshield.

Now that safety and communication were just a five minute walk away, Stephen's emotional state swung from fear back to elation. What could Mustafal do now? He even allowed himself to feel some pride for taking a risk, taking care of Action Item Number Two. He had boldly escaped from crazed terrorists and would be reunited with his family soon. They would be proud too when they heard the tale of his uninhibited bravery, a great story for his new and improved funeral eulogy one day.

"Why are you smiling, may I ask?" Donri inquired.

Stephen didn't want to expose his hubris so he thought for a moment and came up with another good-sounding reason for smiling. "I was just remembering when I was brought here by Mustafal and his partners. They didn't cover my head with a hood so I was able to see the mountains and the beautiful scenery but I couldn't enjoy it because I was too scared. This is the first time I have ever been able to enjoy those mountains," he said, motioning to the range in the distance. "Quite beautiful."

"Ah, yes. I've always loved the hills and mountains here. So beautiful and they give a great view of the ocean. It always reminds me of how little I am and how big God is."

Stephen sensed that Donri wanted to steer the conversation back toward spiritual matters. He tried to think of something to interject but he was too late.

"Some people believe in themselves. But I am too old and have too many experiences of letting myself down frequently. If I believed in myself, I would be very disappointed by now."

Stephen wasn't sure what that had to do with mountains but he wasn't going to stand in front of a speeding sermon. Donri nodded toward the majestic mountains and said. "'I lift my eyes to the mountain,' the psalmist said, 'and where does my help come from?' It doesn't come from there, my friend." He looked back dead aim at Stephen to emphasize his point. "It comes from the Lord, the maker of heaven and earth."

Stephen didn't know exactly how to respond to the stare down of some ancient truth, or if he were even being asked to respond. He just nodded back to Donri and smiled as if he agreed. Their walk continued.

Just get me back to your car and phone, old man.

CHAPTER FOURTEEN

Dina inhaled a deep breath while leaning against the kitchen counter, arms folded and foot tapping rapidly. She was replaying in her mind the fight with Mustafal when he returned with some groceries and discovered that their prized possession Carlton Easley had escaped. He rebuked both his partners harshly for allowing something as simple and important as the spare gate key to go unguarded. She didn't really have a good answer for him, at least not a truthful one. During the tirade she tried to deflect his ire, saying that one of them must have left it out in the wide open where Carlton could have easily picked it up when he spoke with them in the living room. That made him even madder and he shot back that it was definitely not him, as he would never have done something so stupid. Satisfied his partners had been sufficiently scolded, he warned them to guard Agung tightly. Then without any more explanation as to where he was going or what he was doing, he tore out of the house. She followed him out to the front porch and saw him grab a small black duffel bag from the side of the house which she hadn't seen before. No answer was given when she asked what it was. He then reversed the Mercedes out into the road, pulled the gate closed and locked them all in with his own key, and finally grunted loudly for dramatic effect before taking off in solo search for Carlton Easley. Dina was fuming in the wake of his childish fit. *How could I ever have fallen in love with such an inconsiderate man?*

Back in the kitchen, she thought of more clever put-downs she should have fired back during their heated exchange. Though she would never admit of course that she herself had given Carlton the key, she still could have returned more verbal fire. Especially after he called her the worst thing one could be called in Indonesian, *kurang ajar*, literally "less than taught," an insult that condemned someone as an uneducated imbecile. But she just stood there and took it along with Happy who kept his gaze on the floor during the angry lecture. Stupid she could handle. *Kurang ajar* she would not tolerate from anybody.

She would not take this anymore. No more orders from someone who called her such things. She would overcome her once tender feelings for a strong-willed Mustafal and show some strong will herself. She would call off their wedding—no way could she spend the rest of her life with a husband who treated her this way.

Dina felt a surge of adrenaline in making the decision. It felt good, so final, so empowering. Her foot stopped tapping and she pushed herself off the kitchen cabinet, standing tall.

A second decision quickly followed. She strode confidently down the hall to Agung's room. After unlocking and opening the door she announced, "You are free to go." Agung looked shocked to hear his emancipation, and stood up slowly and unsurely. Happy followed her into the room, looking even more shocked than Agung. They were both staring at the powerful goddess with reverent awe.

She was in charge now, not Mustafal, and it felt great. "I'm so sorry, Pak Agung," she offered in Indonesian. "My fiancé Mustafal, my, uh, ex-fiancé Mustafal, had a crazy idea and I am so sorry we got you mixed up in this."

"So…you are letting me go?"

"Yes, I'm afraid we are not very good terrorists."

Agung processed that for a moment then gingerly asked, "May I have my phone back and let my family know that I am okay?"

"Sure," she replied, pointing down the hall toward the living room with her thumb. Agung quickly found his cell phone inside his bag which they had stashed in the corner of the room. He said he would send them a quick text message to let them know he was okay and would call them later. He looked too intrigued with what was happening in real time right in front of him and probably wanted to know more before answering his family's frantic questions.

Happy continued to gape at Dina with the same shocked expression. She read it not as a protest but more of fear as to what the consequences would be at her sudden coup. He was especially intimidated by his hard-charging cousin and she put her hand on his shoulder to soothe him. "Don't worry, Happy, it's going to be okay. I just can't do this anymore. You and I should have never done this. We should have stood up to Mustafal earlier."

She then turned down the TV and sat down opposite of Agung on the thin-cushioned wicker couch. He must have switched his phone on mute as she could hear it continually vibrating in his hand. His poor worried family. Happy was the last one to sit down on a chair in the corner, and he did that slowly, while keeping his eye on Agung. He looked uneasy fraternizing with their former prisoner.

The stares bounced from face to face, the three of them trying to get an emotional read on each other. Agung spoke his thoughts first. "Where is Carlton...Mr. Carl?"

"He escaped."

"I heard all the screaming when he ran for it, but may I ask where he is now?"

It was clear to her that Happy wasn't going to contribute to this mutinous conversation so she continued. "We don't know. Mustafal left to search for him." She looked into Agung's kind and concerned face. What the unfortunate man didn't know yet is that they were all prisoners of Mustafal now. There were only two keys to the front gate lock—Carlton had one and Mustafal had the other. The high fence around the property was too high to climb over and its barbed wire and shards of cemented glass would severely punish anyone who tried. The three of them would simply be stuck together until Mustafal came back. When that did finally happen, she almost looked forward to seeing Mustafal's angry and distorted face when he saw the three of them chatting together like old friends.

"How long will he be gone?" Agung asked.

"We don't know that either."

Agung seemed more confused than perturbed by her unhelpful answers. Happy was still tight-lipped and watching the proceedings with caution.

"Then what we are doing here?"

"We need to figure out a plan. Mustafal has the key to the gate and the fence is near impossible to get over. Mr. Carlton has at least a half-hour head start on Mustafal and I'm sure we will be called if he is found."

"So Mustafal doesn't want help from you to find Mr. Carlton?"

"No, he warned us to stay back and guard you."

Agung half smiled that the three of them suddenly had the secret, upper hand. Dina smiled back. The new found power felt so liberating. She was the one calling the shots while Happy stayed in neutral and Agung tried to follow along. She decided to hold back the part about her stashing the key in Carlton's lunch—no need introducing new evidence that could be turned against her when Mustafal returned and tried to wrestle back the reins of leadership.

"If Mustafal catches Mr. Carlton and comes back," she thought out loud, "we need to all pretend like everything is normal and you are still our prisoner."

"Shouldn't we at least try to get over the fence and try to find Mr. Carlton first, before Mustafal does?"

She considered the suggestion and admired Agung's courage to not only think of his own safety but also want to help rescue his friend. The three of them walked outside and examined the imposing fence and gate for weak spots. The entire perimeter was covered with enough barbed wire, cemented shards of glass and sharp spikes to keep the most diligent of burglars outside and them inside. Dina never realized her uncle was so paranoid, to have such a perimeter of security around a house in the middle of a lazy, friendly village. There were no ladders either, or trees leaning against the fence that could be scaled. Happy rummaged around the house and yard for things like bamboo poles that could be cobbled together to build a makeshift ladder, but found nothing of use.

Agung examined the thick padlock of the front gate. He gave it a few whacks with large rocks and metal objects he found around the yard but it didn't crack. The only thing that would cut it open was a strong hack saw, he announced, but they could find no such tools there either.

The three of them sat down on the stoop of the front porch together, sweaty, tired and dejected from all their efforts to escape. Dina said she would go inside to make them something to drink while Agung finally conceded to call his worried mother.

~~□~~

Agung's family exploded with excitement when they suddenly received a text message from their missing loved one. Several shouts of *Alhamdulillah* were lifted toward heaven. His shorthand sentence announced that he was all right and would explain everything to them a little while later. They tried to call back but he didn't pick up. Their furious avalanche of questions in thumbed shorthand also went unanswered. That was a bit worrisome and cast a mysterious shadow over the celebration. The cell phone was passed around and family members read the message from the tiny screen themselves for hidden clues. A wave of great relief was met by an undertow of profound puzzlement.

Finally, about a half hour later he called them, asking forgiveness for not being able to call back immediately and assuring them that he was safe and well. Right now he needed their help to find an American businessman named Carlton Easley or he might go by the name Stephen Cranton. The *bule* was somewhere near Sendang Biru and in danger. Don't involve the police yet. Why not, they demanded. Agung responded that all would be explained later, but for now he needed to be picked up at a house in a village near Sendang Biru. Just get on the road and he would text the exact address to them later.

Before they could even respond with more follow-up questions, he begged their patience once again. Just get on the road, details to follow. This was so bizarre—why in the world was Agung linked up with this *bule* and in danger way down on the south coast of Java? But they sprang into action as there was no other choice but to help.

Agung's mother had a nephew who lived near the south coast and who always felt close to Agung. He was called first, given the news and urged to start driving to Sendang Biru as fast as possible. The estimated coordinates would be called in later. The rest of them made an impromptu plan to load up double and triple on borrowed motorcycles, one team on an immediate four-hour journey toward Sendang Biru to pick up Agung, one in the same direction to ask around for the mysterious *bule*, and one in a pedi-cab *becak* to comb the streets of Pandaan to drum up more volunteers for the search in case those teams needed backup. The intriguing and exciting mystery would soon be solved, but more importantly for them, their beloved Agung was alive and safe. Or at least they hoped he was safe.

Only Agung's mother stayed back at the kitchen headquarters to monitor developments and to be there in case someone called the home phone. As neighbors entered the kitchen, she would share the news with them, which was greeted with praises to Allah that Agung had been found, followed by promises of more prayers for his safe return. From the tiny house into the well-worn streets flowed a stream of exciting gossip about Agung's whereabouts, his mysterious Western companion and the possible danger they were in together.

The *becak* posse rounded up over a dozen more search-and-rescue volunteers for the Sendang Biru mission. They all gathered at Agung's house as more gossip zigzagged down the narrow streets. The only new development Agung's mother had to report was that Agung had just texted in a request for a ladder. That message was forwarded to the cousin who was closer and already on the way, then discussed and dissected among them as to why a ladder would be needed. Agung's mother honestly had more onlookers, question askers and volunteers than she knew what to do with, but she wanted to hear back from the advance teams before she sent them out or mapped out any further strategy.

No one could remember anything this exciting happening in their *kampung* in a long time.

Dina walked onto the front porch carrying a tray of lemonade and Agung looked up at her and smiled his gratefulness. "Some of my friends and relatives are on the way to help with the search," he announced in Javanese.

"Great," she said, setting the glasses down. It felt good to have more people on her newly switched side, but there was still plenty to worry about. "They aren't calling the police, are they?"

"No, I told them not to. They are just on the way to help get us out of here and to help us find Mr. Carlton."

"Okay, good." She sat down on the porch and took a sip. The sun was roasting. "Why don't we go back inside and wait?"

"Great idea." He picked up his glass and nodded his thanks again. He was so kind, considerate and complimentary—much more than Mustafal. His Javanese was definitely smoother than Mustafal's, much more polite. Not only that, he was kind of cute too. Maybe anyone would fare better than her harsh fiancé in comparison at the moment, though.

They stepped inside and settled on the sofa. Dina adjusted her seat cushions and granted the men cultural permission to drink. Agung took a deep breath and drank slowly, leaning back and looking semi-relaxed. He also looked like he was still trying to comprehend his new identity as prisoner but no longer hostage. Happy remained upright on the thin sofa and still looked conflicted between his own two identities.

They sipped in silence until Agung finally asked, "May I ask a question?"

"Sure, go ahead," said Dina while taking a deep sip.

"Who are you people?"

The question made her laugh and cough up some of her lemonade. It also broke some of the tension from Happy's face. "Well I guess we have some time here while we wait," she said, wiping her face. "Got time for a story?"

Agung toasted her with his lemonade glass, indicating that he did.

"We are factory workers at *Firdaus Rokok*," she started and then paused for effect, as if she were about to tell a long

Indonesian legend. Agung settled back as best he could into the wicker sofa. It looked like his curiosity at knowing the identities and motives of his inconsistent kidnappers was about to be sated.

Dina began with her friendship with Mustafal as fellow cigarette factory workers, their journey toward courtship, and his obsession with the disparity between the workers on the floor and the managers that watched from above in their air-conditioned office perches. She said at first his fire for a cause was attractive because so many other guys she knew were so culturally passive and this was a man who acted like he would change the world. She painted her story from a palette of Indonesian and Javanese, choosing the word from each local language that was the most substantive at communicating her thoughts.

She moved on to Mustafal's hatred for visiting Western supervisors, and she could tell from Agung's facial expression that he was fascinated with her story. It felt nice to have his attentive focus, and Happy seemed to be relaxing more and getting more into the story. The story was indeed an interesting one, as her own role in it was so out of character for her, and she felt certain one day she would be re-telling it to her friends. She could imagine Happy doing the same in his good natured way, that is, if they didn't land in prison.

With plenty of time, a true captive audience, and a nice-looking, kind-hearted guy giving her his full attention, Dina slowed the tale down to color in more details.

"Mustafal hated these wealthy Westerners who came on supervising visits. They came in nice cars, stayed in the air-conditioned hotel suites near the factory, and sidled up to some of our female co-workers who hoped to become the mistresses of these rich men. Mustafal especially hated this. The supervisors did their 'supervising' in as little time as possible and then it was off to the nearby golf resort or a date with a willing factory worker who fancied herself up for the evening.

"When they were at the factory, these *bules* and the local managers who sold their souls to them would walk to the overlook plank and peer down on the thousands of us workers below rolling cigarettes and stuffing them into *Firdaus Rokok* cigarette cartons. They never once came below to talk to us, not one word of thanks. We sweated it out all day making cigarettes which Mustafal said made these foreign devils rich and our countrymen addicted and sick.

"Mustafal worked at the factory for nine years, starting as a roller like everyone else and then after two years as a stuffer of 12 cigarettes to a box. He hoped one day to go up to the next level of quality control. That work was better than rolling thousands of cigarettes every day, but the pay wasn't much better and it was still in the same sweaty factory. The managers were so stingy that they only turned on the fans during the hottest part of the day, and even then we could barely feel a waft of a breeze. Of course, Mustafal said, the air conditioners were always on full blast in their upstairs offices."

Agung was still drawn into the story, but from time to time would look toward the front door. Dina wondered if he was scared that Mustafal would bust in at any minute and ruin their little chat session. She also wondered if Mustafal was becoming less of a monster in Agung's mind, now that he was beginning to understand his motives.

"He had once tried to get a better job but soon found that impossible. He was ambitious enough to be pretty good in English, but when he applied to hotels and banks, they could tell he was from a slum *kampung,* and that he probably had no experience relating to wealthy people and foreigners. He went to many interviews in an old suit he borrowed from one of his relatives, and they could tell with one look that he didn't belong in their organizations. I tried to tell him the suit was outdated but he said it was fine. He would go into an interview and he always knew from their condescending looks when he walked in the room that he had no chance. The rich would always get richer and the poor would always get poorer in Indonesia. That's the way it would always be in Indonesia, he said. We thought he was peculiar for being so bothered about this issue and we tried to persuade him to resign himself to Allah's fate for his life, but he felt like there was potential in him that would never be realized because the system was rigged against him from birth. He wasn't much of a believer in fate but it did seem that the cards were stacked against him. He does believe in Allah, though, and prayed every day that he would be given a fair chance."

"Did he ever make a turn to radical Islam?" Agung asked. Happy was now leaning back on the couch pillows, fully absorbed in the story, too. As if suddenly summoned, the wailing of the call to prayer cranked up and could be heard garbling out of the closest mosque speakers.

"No, not even close. He got more agitated and started thinking of organizing to get power in this life and ignoring the afterlife. He bided his time, talked here and there about organizing to get more pay, but most of us preferred to keep our heads down. We knew that the managers could fire any one of us and there would be plenty of others who were willing to take our place, grateful for the low pay. He knew he was stuck, and he tried to make the best of it, and he usually did, concentrating on...well, me, and our possible future together."

She tried to hide any facial expression as she said this and could tell that Agung was trying to read her.

"Then one day he snapped," she said, pausing to take another sip. "One of our co-workers had been fired for falling behind the quota, the magic number of 4,000 a day, but this was because he was ill and afraid to stay home and miss out on the meager pay. There are no paid sick days at the factory and if you were gone more than four days they simply found someone else. Mustafal was frustrated by how casually they fired our friend, just showing him the door without a thank you for the hard work he had given them for years. Plenty more rollers where he came from, and if he couldn't meet the quota two days in a row, they'd throw one more person on the pile of unemployed workers. Who cares about his family and what other means of income he could find in Pandaan? The managers were just heartless. They only thought about quotas and money and nothing else. The magic numbers of 5,000 people each rolling 4,000 cigarettes a day in 12 hour shifts were the only numbers they cared about."

Happy looked like he was doing the math in his head, counting silently while looking at the ceiling.

"This is when Mustafal really started talking more about organizing. At break time he would casually drop a rumor of people organizing or striking in the near future. If the potential convert's gaze averted his, he left him alone. Mustafal would tell me later the coward didn't have what it takes to make a change. If there was a flash of fire in the man eyes, he would invite them into further conversations. His first recruit, maybe because they are close cousins or maybe because he was the most easily swayed, was our friend here, Happy."

Happy looked up and smiled proudly.

"Why do people call you Happy?" Agung asked.

"My real name is Karniawan but my friends started calling me Happy when we learned the English word in elementary school."

"Well, because his smile is so wide and he is so happy, as you can see." Dina patted him on the knee.

Happy smiled wider still. He looked proud to be an important part of the story.

Dina continued. "Then he recruited me. I, like him, didn't have the money to get into college after graduating even with good grades in high school. I had the national test scores necessary to get into state-run university, but my family couldn't afford to lose a wage earner to higher learning. I accepted my fate, spent a lot of time watching Western movies and TV shows, dreaming about a better life, and did my shifts in the factory. Celebrity gossip became my hobby as well as trying to read English novels."

"I hoped Mustafal would propose soon to show everyone he really was serious about his commitment and my reputation." She looked down at the ground, hesitating. Should she bare her heart to this man? She looked up from the floor into his kind face. He looked so absorbed in every one of her words, and the undistracted gaze flattered her.

"I secretly thought that I would start to think about moving on if he didn't show his commitment soon. I liked the spark in his eyes when he talked of serious matters, even when I didn't agree with his views. I liked that he had some drive in him, and didn't quietly acquiesce to his life circumstances as our culture and theology dictates. If nothing else he was a lot more interesting than the other simple guys I had dated."

"Talk show," Happy said with a huge grin, referring to a popular new entertainment phenomenon in Indonesia where people openly shared their intimate emotions on television with the guidance of a psychologically experienced host.

"Oh, does this feel like one of those talk shows?" she asked, smiling brightly and looking slightly embarrassed.

Without waiting for an answer she continued. "I was also frustrated at conditions and exploitation at the factory and it opened my mind to consider Mustafal's proposition. I was nervous at first, but he assured me the risks would be minimal and that we would not go to jail if we got caught. We spent long hours walking the small streets of my *kampung* and went on errands together while he talked me into the brilliance of his plan. I liked his passion, and figured it was worth the risk. I just hoped we wouldn't be publicly shamed if we did get caught."

"I can certainly understand that," Agung interjected.

"I preferred the relaxing times with him when it was just the two of us together talking about life rather than his obsessive scheming with the kidnapping plot. But I knew I had to take them both together—I could never separate revolutionary Mustafal from my boyfriend Mustafal."

She surprised herself with all the honesty. She had a lot of strong and contradictory feelings for this man who often infuriated her. It felt good sorting out her complex emotions in story form, like she was reading a story about someone else, far away and from the high altitude of common sense.

"Talk show," Happy called out again. It didn't have the same humorous effect as the first time, but Dina and Agung smiled politely at him. He laughed at himself unabashedly.

"Mustafal knew organizing and even striking could only get to a certain point, another impasse, and he wanted to launch a new stage that would bring quicker, more dramatic results. He called a gathering with Happy and me to go over the plans. He only trusted us as his inner circle, although others at the factory were sympathetic to his leanings."

Dina reached into the back pocket of her jeans and pulled out a folded sheet of paper, their top secret plans for the kidnapping. She unfolded it and handed it to Agung, who reached over the coffee table and took it out of her hands. She let their touch linger for an extra second as he took the note from her hands. She got a deeper glimpse into the eyes of her captive and liked the way he boyishly looked away.

He started reading it to himself without being asked, his mouth murmuring silently. Happy's attention turned back to the television still playing music videos on mute. After a few moments of scanning the document Agung looked up and read one portion out loud: "Mustafal and Happy will tie the hostage's hands with duct tape while yelling at him in Arabic." He looked up to Dina and smiled. "I was wondering why the Islam Defenders Front were screaming Arabic greetings of peace to us in the car. I guess you guys don't really know Arabic that well."

Happy snapped away from the videos. "We didn't know that another Indonesian would be there—you. We thought it would just be him so it would be okay to yell at him in any kind of Arabic to scare him. Mustafal made us practice it over and over until it would, as he said, 'strike fear in the hearts of the infidels,' but I never thought it would. And we really don't even believe in infidels."

"Yes, I did find the Arabic peace yelling rather strange," smiled Agung.

Dina giggled loudly.

"I think it worked to scare you and Mr. Carlton," added Happy.

"Yes, nicely," Agung said while not looking up and still reading on.

"And Mustafal said that I must be called Abdullah and not Happy. Happy doesn't sound scary enough."

"That's true," Agung tried to say without laughing. His obvious restraint made Dina giggle even more.

He continued reading the plan out loud: "Phase five. Drive Mr. Easley to the safe house, secure him, and then start the ransom negotiations at the factory."

"Mustafal said it would probably take less than a week, and that they would pay quickly, so as not to be embarrassed by the lapse in security. Happy and I didn't agree, but as usual, Mustafal won the argument."

Agung nodded and continued. "When the factory finally agrees, Mustafal will meet in person with Mr. Bambang to collect the ransom. He will be wearing a full face covering and bring the contract, already signed by Mr. Easley."

Dina explained, "This contract would state that *Firdaus Rokok* submits to the demands of the IDF, which had to do more with workers' rights than propagating a purer form of Islam. I told Mustafal that that would seem very suspicious, but he said that everyone would want to get it over with so quick they wouldn't be thinking very critically. He assured us he would throw in a few religious demands in the contract to cover our tracks."

"And another thing," said Happy, voice slightly rising, "He kept saying over and over that the cigarette company would come to our terms quickly just to avoid the embarrassment of their foreign guest being kidnapped."

Dina and Agung both tried to find the additional point in the simple reiteration of what was just said. Dina could see Agung replaying the sentence through his head, too. She looked over at Happy, now getting reabsorbed into the music videos. She felt sorry for him getting dragged into this, only because his simple personality was no match for his older cousin's forceful intellect. She hoped that Happy wouldn't serve jail time only because he was so easily swayed. She should have swayed him away from getting into this poorly planned kidnapping plot and she hadn't.

Agung kept reading until he came to his next question. "Does your uncle know that we are here, that his house is being used as a hostage house?"

"No, he is away in Jakarta on business and I sometimes house-sit for him while he's away. I feel so bad for this and hope he never finds out. It was he who taught me how to drive."

Agung nodded and kept reading, "Phase Six: Burn the costumes, show up for work the next day, and be as shocked as everyone else that all this happened. Enjoy new pay raises along with everyone else and never brag a word of this to anyone.

"This was solemnly promised over the graves of various dead relatives," said Dina. "And then we would all live happily ever after," she said while rolling her eyes.

"He was pretty sure that it would go as scheduled, but he told us to be ready for any contingencies in case something unexpected happened," she added. "If that happened, we could abandon the plan and just blend into the masses of people on the roads that day and no one would ever suspect a thing. That's at least what he said. He is usually right."

Dina felt her soul purged with the full confession, and wondered if Happy felt the same. Her partner's face hinted at an internal struggle. Maybe he was still torn between who would have his allegiance. She knew that even if her mild friend did side with Mustafal later, he would not be able to stop her now. She kept charging ahead.

Dina turned and looked apologetically into Agung's eyes. "Please forgive us. I didn't really want to do this from the beginning and I shouldn't have gone along with Mustafal. I never knew that another person would be kidnapped too. Your family must have been so worried when you disappeared."

"I'm still single," he quickly added. He was grinning now and looked like he had already forgiven her.

Happy shifted in his spot and stared down at the white tiles. Looking up, his unsure expression revealed his uncertainty about her sudden leadership. She decided that instead of pleading with him, she would give him a definitive order to follow so his mind wouldn't be consumed with the issue of allegiance.

"Happy, we need to clean the house of any evidence that we were here. Pack up everything and bring it all to the front room. My uncle can't know we were here. If Mustafal texts you, let me know and we will just text him back and make him think everything is the same and we are still here."

Agung stood to stretch and get his new emotional bearings. He fished his phone out of his pocket and attended to more unanswered text messages.

She smiled at him both sweetly and apologetically. "Would you mind helping us with that?"

Agung smiled back. "No, I don't mind at all."

"Good, let's clean up everything first and then try one more time to get over the fence. We need to do everything we can to find Mr. Carlton. Hopefully we can get to him before Mustafal does."

Agung corrected her. "I think his name really is Stephen." His statement was met by a confused look by Dina. Happy was already down the hall and beginning to clean up and clear out all evidence.

CHAPTER FIFTEEN

Carlton was pacing in his cinder-block cell when a short Indonesian man entered the police station and timidly scanned the room. Any new person coming or going was a welcome distraction since Carlton had already memorized the small, cluttered station and every face in it. He wondered right away if the unassertive visitor was Bambang. The man was nicely dressed and his wide eyes peered from behind his glasses like a nervous little bird.

Carlton stood up and hoped the movement of his large body would get the attention of the man, who was still waiting to get the attention of an officer. Johanna Grazen still sat with her back to Carlton, reading the same Indonesian newspaper, and didn't notice his movement or the new visitor entering the station. *This has gotta be Bambang.* Carlton had never seen the man, but his fidgeting made it seem like he had something to fear. And he did. He had done a terrible job of hosting an international visitor, one who had the roundabout authority to fire him. This so-called leader's lack of leadership caused Carlton to be stranded at the airport, surrounded by money-hungry villagers on the side of a blazing hot highway, detained inside a building supply store with a crazed old man, and now locked up in this dinky cell by petty officers bent on humiliating an American. Carlton set his sights on Bambang, narrowing his eyebrows and scoping him like a sniper getting ready for a hit. *You are going to pay.*

Bambang still didn't see him, but Johanna Grazen finally noticed the visitor and stood up to greet him near the entrance. The two shook hands and chatted like they were old friends. Bambang nodded up and down, his short little body dwarfed by

Johanna's average height. She was smiling and even patted Bambang on the shoulder once during the friendly banter. Did these two already know each other? What in the world could be so amusing—some inside joke? Carlton clenched his jaw and gripped the bars until his knuckles became almost white.

His two official advocates still didn't see him, but his movement and the gripping of the bars did get the attention of one of the officers nearby. The policeman waddled over with his thumb tucked in his belt and started saying something to Carlton, who ignored him and kept looking at the two people who could rescue him from his nightmare. The officer said something else, which sounded like a threat, then retreated back to his desk to read his newspaper.

Johanna and Bambang were now in a more serious discussion, and at one point Johanna pointed out Carlton's cell, like a guide in an aquarium pointing out the killer whale exhibit. Bambang smiled with embarrassment and timidly waved to Carlton, who just stared him down, not feeling or looking grateful. *Get over here and get me out of here now, you moron.*

Bambang didn't come. He kept chattering to Johanna and to another officer who joined the conversation. Every now and then one of the threesome would look over at Carlton, and when they did he would frown more solemnly and grip more tightly. They were talking about *him*—how dare they shut him out like this?

Carlton finally cleared his throat, and called out loud enough to be heard across the station, "I need to be a part of this conversation."

The conferring stopped and all three of them turned to Carlton. Johanna looked politely perturbed. The officer soured and looked like he was ready for some police brutality while Bambang fiddled with his eyeglasses. His two allies looked to the officer for direction and their three-way conversation kept going, totally shutting out Carlton again.

Infuriating. *Get over here right now.* Carlton had suffered intolerably, and now at the hour of his freedom, his rescuers were stalling. Settling back on his cot, he breathed deeply to concentrate and get the upper hand over his anger. He had already exploded once and that definitely did not help his case or cause. He remembered one anger management method was to try to think of something else, like the proverbial happy place, but he soon became distracted and couldn't help fantasizing about anything except retaliation against all three of them, especially the police officer. How would they feel stuffed in this monkey cage? Would there be some way to pursue a case of wrongful imprisonment in the Indonesian courts? *Nah, the whole system is probably rigged.*

After a few more moments Johanna casually walked over, looking over a piece of paper that looked like an official report of some kind.

"You want the good news or bad news first?" Johanna asked in an attempted friendly voice.

Carlton was not in the mood for a jest. "Just give me the news please," he said flatly.

"We have cleared up the fact with the police that you were not driving the car. Pak Bambang was able to confirm that he ordered you to be driven from the airport, and that the car that struck the boy was being driven by someone else."

"You guys are some amazing detectives," he said, voice dripping with sarcasm. He really didn't mean to let that barb fly but it was too late to retrieve it now. Over Johanna's shoulder he could see the officer approaching.

She stepped out of his way and the officer unlocked the cell, opening the heavy door for Carlton. The thought of escaping the musty smell and breathing fresher air was invigorating. Yet he exited the cell slowly, on purpose, to show them all that they hadn't got the better of him.

"Okay, now that we have cleared this up, what is the other news?"

"Two more things. First, you need to pay for the lamp you broke at the building supplies store."

Unbelievable. "Fine. What else?"

"One last thing before they release you and hand back your driver's license and passport," Johanna started slowly. "They are requiring you to go to the scene of the crime at the toll road and tell them what happened so they can file a police report."

"*Requiring* me?" he half shouted. And then he repeated it, slightly more controlled. "*Requiring* me?"

Carlton marched straight over to Bambang and now all the officers in the station were looking at him with bemused interest. "Come on, Mr. Bambang. You will take me to the factory now. I have had enough of this nonsense."

Johanna stayed put in the background and Bambang looked unsure how to respond. At first he stretched out his hand for an introductory handshake with Carlton, whose balled fists stayed planted on his hips. Bambang awkwardly retrieved the unrequited hand and pushed his glasses back up his nose. Looking around the room at the other people there, he said gently to his guest, "Yes sir, Mr. Carlton. We just need to go to the place on the road where the boy was hit and then I will take you to your hotel. I take you there after we go with police. The police captain will take us himself."

Carlton leaned forward slightly, crossed his arms and looked directly into Bambang's twittering face. He could feel his own eyes sockets twitching with subdued anger, the effect of which made Bambang look even more terrified. "I am not going anywhere with these police," he gritted out in a low growl. "I have already spent the night in this stink hole and wasted many hours just so they could play games with me. We are going to my hotel now and you will drive me. They will be lucky if I don't get the courts involved with this harassment." He hoped his directness with Bambang would make the police feel intimidated in the periphery.

"Yes, yes, I see. We just go to make the report first."

Carlton unfolded his arms, shifted, and cleared his throat. "Please come with me, Mr. Bambang," he said as he took a step toward the door. He turned back to Bambang as he was walking out. "It seems you don't understand yet. We are leaving right now and we are not making any stops." Righteous anger over the abuse of injustice gave him a new surge of energy.

As Carlton started walking away, the officers perked up and looked at each other like two football referees not sure what call to make. The police captain took a step closer and said something in Indonesian to Bambang.

Carlton was in the doorway now. Bambang called after him, "Mr. Carlton, the police say we can ride in their car. We go now with the police captain."

"The police can say anything they want to," he shot back without looking, walking briskly in the direction of the two non-police cars in the parking lot. "We are leaving. Let's go. I am going to take a shower and get some rest and that's that."

Carlton wasn't sure which of the cars in the small parking lot was Bambang's, and he looked back at him for an indication. The police captain was nearing Carlton, getting his keys out of his pocket. Bambang was about ten steps behind Carlton, frozen in the entrance of the police station. Two officers were standing behind Bambang, mesmerized by the unfolding conflict, and Johanna was somewhere out of sight behind the logjam.

The captain opened the passenger door of his black and white squad car for Carlton. Bambang was looking back and forth at both men, unsure which one of them should have his allegiance.

The captain called out something in Indonesian, and Carlton didn't know if it was directed to him, his fellow officers, or to Bambang. He ignored it and made his demand louder and more bluntly, "We are leaving now, Mr. Bambang, and I suggest that you come get in your car and drive me to my hotel if you want to still have a job."

Carlton could read in his manager's flushed face that he clearly understood the threat. He himself was semi-enjoying the showdown and wanted to teach the timid man a lesson in unyielding leadership. Keep charging forward and people would move aside eventually—always happened. Bambang stepped forward, freeing the two officers behind him from the doorway. Johanna Grazen walked into the parking lot. The captain said something else to Bambang, who looked like he was going to throw up as he walked over to Carlton.

"Just a moment, Mr. Carlton. We go with these men first. They say we must, and then we can take you to your hotel," he pleaded gingerly. "It just take a moment."

"I'm sorry, Bambang. I don't have any more moments. We are going to my hotel now. You can bring my ID cards back to me there." Carlton opened the door for himself on the driver side, quickly realized his mistake, and stomped over to the other side of the car to the passenger side. He could hear one of the officers snickering.

"I really think you should go with these men first, Mr. Easley," Johanna called out, offering her opinion about the standoff for the first time. "It's only going to make matters worse."

Carlton ignored that advice too. He unrolled the window and shouted "Let's go," to Bambang, who was frozen in his tracks again, same nauseous look on his face. Both policemen made their way to his side of the car and one of them tapped on the window while the police captain looked on with his arms folded.

It was a beautiful and bright blue day, a cheerful backdrop to a tense standoff.

Carlton looked up at the enemies that surrounded him and caught a glimpse of Bambang behind them. The apprehensive manager leaned over, placed one hand on the car and with a violent, retching sound, threw up on the grass. Johanna rushed from the doorway and pulled out a small pack of tissues from her purse. She gave it to Bambang, who was still leaning over, and patted him on the back. Carlton looked down at the floorboards and let out another sigh of curse words, sounding like air coming out of a punctured tire. He slowly rocked back and forth in the passenger seat and pressed his feet firmly into the floor board of the car to keep himself from exploding with rage again. *Somebody please get me out of this unending nightmare.*

The captain came over and conferred first with Johanna and then with Bambang, who was wiping his mouth with Johanna's tissues and trying to compose himself. Carlton had finally gained emotional mastery over a potential, full-blown temper tantrum. He sat stoically in the car, staring straight ahead.

After a few minutes Bambang slid nervously into the driver's seat. He placed the key in the ignition and said softly, "Police captain send his men to give us police escort. We only must stop at the kilometer where child was hit."

"He wasn't a child," Carlton said while still scowling and staring straight ahead. "He was almost full grown." The car started up and idled. "And speaking of kilometers, why didn't you come get me at kilometer twenty-six?"

Bambang turned into Carlton's gaze, his wide eyes made wider through the slight magnification of the glasses. It reminded Carlton of a frog.

"Oh, so sorry sir. I thought you say go to kilometer six."

"To six?" he growled. "I said two six. Twenty six." *Totally unbelievable.*

Before further disciplinary action could be taken, Johanna came around to Carlton's side and leaned down to say something through the crack in the slightly rolled-down window. "I don't think I can help you anymore, Mr. Easley. I will be going back to the consulate now and I think I can fill out the report by myself."

Johanna waited an awkward moment for a response but didn't get one from Carlton, who was too overcome with anger toward Bambang to speak or make eye contact.

The sirens on the two police cars fired up. One pulled in front of Bambang's car and one pulled in behind. Bambang eased the car out of the parking lot, being careful not to look his distinguished guest in the face. Carlton brooded and presented his best poker face to show that none of this bothered him, but inside he was seething. *What did I ever do to deserve this?*

≈□≈

After the longest flight of her life, a grueling fifteen-hour haul, Leah surprisingly didn't feel that sleepy when the plane finally touched down in Hong Kong. The Ambien only afforded her around two hours of sleep hours toward the end of the flight, so she credited her energy to the thrill of embarking on an adventure. Either that or maybe jet lag hadn't caught up with her yet from her hasty exit out of Sacramento.

She strolled down the jet way into the shiny and sleek Hong Kong airport and scanned the corridor for an internet kiosk. She already had a hotel room near the airport that she had booked on-line, a place for a quick nap and shower, but for now she just wanted news from home, something from Fiona about how the kids were doing. There'd better be an email from

Stephen in her inbox, offering a heartfelt apology and explanation for his information blackout.

Finally, a computer opened up at the stand-up kiosk and she logged on to her web-based email. She scrolled down through the usual spam promises of cheap prescriptions and tips on stocks that were about to take off. Her eyes finally settled on an email sent from Chuck, Stephen's boss, and she clicked it open.

Leah,

Have you heard from Stephen? I got word from the office in Surabaya that he never showed up for the training. He hasn't tried to contact us yet. Have you heard anything from him—travel problems or something?

Please email me back to let me know you got this.

Chuck

Leah felt the moisture leave her mouth. She re-read the email to make sure she got it right and her mind churned for logical explanations. *Maybe there was plane trouble and he is grounded somewhere...here in Hong Kong even? Maybe he had car trouble in Indonesia and didn't make it to his meeting, or maybe he just got sick on the airplane or something?* None of that made sense—she knew that. It had already been over 30 hours since he landed in Indonesia. If he were sick or stranded, he would have definitely contacted someone by now, especially his only contact in Indonesia. Something went wrong.

She couldn't help but think of worst-case scenarios and checked the CNN website while cringing to see if there were any plane crashes. None were reported in the news. She couldn't think of what else to search for and typed his name into a search engine. Nothing appeared but genealogy sites and some musical artist with the same name. She steeled herself with a resolve not to panic.

She shot off a quick reply to Chuck but downplayed her fear. She hadn't heard anything but she was sure there was a good explanation. The fact that she was on her way to Indonesia to find him and do shock treatment on their ailing and failing marriage was not mentioned.

Checking flight schedules on-line, she discovered that the next flight out of Hong Kong to Surabaya was the one she was already on. She couldn't get there any faster. Next she sent an email to Fiona. She was worried—no one had heard from Stephen. Don't tell the kids. No need to worry them. Just give them her love. Please let her know if she heard anything. She would keep checking her emails while in Hong Kong and again once she arrived in Surabaya, Friday morning Indonesia time.

With no more information to find or share, she pulled herself and her carry-on to the shuttle pick up point. The ride was free but it was a half hour to the hotel. At least the airline let her check her heavy suitcase all the way to Surabaya so she wouldn't have to deal with it until then. Besides that there was not much more to be thankful for. Leah was all alone in an unfamiliar mega city, with plenty of time to wonder and worry.

≈≈▯≈≈

Carlton hunkered down in the front seat of Bambang's car and refused to get out when they got to the scene of the crime. *You can lead this old horse to water, but you ain't getting him to drink.* Bambang, looking like he was going to throw up again, didn't argue and got out of the car. He directly stepped over to the two police cars, now pulled over but with their sirens on mute.

Carlton turned his focus to the police lights ricocheting their blue imprints off the same cracked wall where his ordeal started yesterday afternoon. The memory of the accident and its aftermath pained him. He wasn't going to get out of this car, no matter what they did to him, short of brute force. He would go limp like some hippy activist protester, and he smiled to himself at the thought of these scrawny policemen trying to haul his 260-plus pound body.

He quickly wiped the smirk off his face and tried to pretend he wasn't interested. Crouching down further into the seat and slightly sideways, he could see, through the reflection of the side view mirror, Bambang speaking with the officers.

He would not show them he was paying attention to their games.

One of the officers was speaking into his walkie-talkie, probably asking for backup for this dangerous mission. *Give me a break.* They had violated his rights of due process over and over and he wasn't going to help them with one iota of cooperation. Zero. Why did they need him to testify to something that was totally obvious? That young man was hit by a freelance driver—all they had to do was trace the registration from the car they must have already towed away. Surely they could do even that in this backwater town.

Carlton was going to get to the factory a day late and tired from a horrific ordeal. He knew it could seem unfair to unleash his pent-up fury on somebody, but his patience was wearing thin. He watched Bambang kowtowing to the officers and probably offering some sort of apology for his guest's belligerence. Obviously this Bambang was a weak invertebrate of a man, Carlton concluded, and could not be trusted with the reins of leadership. Yes, change would come to *Firdaus Rokok.*

One officer broke from the conference and sauntered his way to the passenger side window where Carlton had barricaded himself. The officer was barking into his little radio the whole time and Carlton steeled his back and stared straight ahead, still giving no indication of attention or concern.

The officer lightly knocked on the window with one knuckle but Carlton didn't move or respond. A second, louder tap also did not get a budge out of Carlton, who was secretly enjoying the showdown. A couple of seconds went by and the officer suddenly jerked the door open, causing Carlton to almost fall out of the car and to the ground. He caught himself with his elbow on the center armrest and straightened up again, squinting in the distance and pretending the surprise move didn't ruffle him.

The door was now ajar, and the officer blasted him with an angry barrage of Indonesian. The other officer came over, looking incredulous too, with Bambang timidly following. Carlton stared straight ahead and didn't flinch.

The officers turned their anger on Bambang, who sounded like he was apologizing profusely. Carlton felt satisfied and could only hope that this measly manager was learning a real life lesson in the school of hard knocks. Show weakness and others will dominate you. Carlton was careful to show merely a stonewall face and suppressed all urges to smile smugly. The rant went on and finally Bambang squatted down in front of the car door that was still cracked open.

"Mr. Carlton, these man have something to say to you and very angry and feel disrespect that you not answer them. They say they get call from hospital, from accountant at hospital, and some group of village people try to use credit card with your name. They say you give permission."

"What?" Carlton shouted, shoving the door all the way open. The sudden outburst sent Bambang off his heels and tumbling down the embankment of the road. The two officers rushed over. One helped Bambang to his feet and the other pointed his baton stick in Carlton's face.

"Get out car," the officer yelled, his baton trembling. "Get out car."

Carlton knew it was time to obey. He pushed himself out of the low-lying seat slowly with his hands up over his head. "Now take it easy. I didn't do anything. Mr. Bambang fell over. I did not push him."

The officer was still trembling with anger and pointing his baton in Carlton's face. The other officer holding up Bambang was climbing back up the embankment. "Just get me to the factory and we can work all this out there," Carlton offered in a conciliatory tone, concentrating hard to not clinch his jaw as he said it. His hands stayed over his head in the don't-shoot-me posture.

A few villagers poked their way through the same crack in the wall and were now cautiously approaching the scene. Bambang was saying something in a pleading voice to the officer still inside Carlton's personal space. He looked pathetic with grass and roadway gravel plastered to his body. The policeman seemed to ease his anger and trembling as Bambang went on and on. Carlton surveyed the situation and whispered in his attempt at a soothing voice, "That's it. Listen to Mr. Bambang. He knows what he's talking about."

Carlton's added commentary seemed to re-infuriate the officer and he now looked angrier than he did at the beginning.

He stepped closer to Carlton, planted his feet on the asphalt shoulder for a better footing and lifted his face into Carlton's until the two men's noses almost touched. He snarled something in Indonesian and Carlton could smell his strong, stale breath. Carlton looked dead into the man's eyes and consciously showed no fear. *I may appease you momentarily but you will never intimidate me.*

The standoff lasted a few seconds, neither man moving. Bambang seemed at a loss to know what to do, as did the other officer. Cars whizzed by and their tailwinds tussled the hair of both men, but still neither moved.

A larger group of gawking villagers were now on the scene, surrounding the two men. It looked like a fight was about to break out. "Mr. Carlton Easley," one of them yelled out, in what almost sounded like a cheer.

Expensive clothes ruined, a day and a half wasted, hungry, thirsty, tired, threatened, persecuted, smelling bad and whiffing in the bad breath of an Indonesian officer right in his face, it took every fiber of Carlton's being to not lay into the officer with two fists of his fury. The only tactic from his anger management course he could remember on the spot was to always count to ten before you reacted in a stressful situation.

By the time he got to eight, the officer suddenly eased back from the standoff and smiled. He whispered something to Bambang who was right behind his shoulder, staring into the showdown with wide yet tired eyes.

Bambang reluctantly translated the message and Carlton braced for impact. Was he going to be handcuffed and brought back to jail, this time for resisting arrest?

"Police say to stay in car. We all go to hospital together to make sure you do pay bill of boy hit by car."

Carlton blinked, fumed and counted off his last two digits silently in his head. *They have won the battle but I will win the war.*

CHAPTER SIXTEEN

The beachcombers stayed on their trek toward their van with the children in a large wiggling clump, laughing, veering off course and throwing seashells and pebbles at each other. Donri trudged on, not saying much anymore, maybe because he was winded. Stephen kept his attention through the trees and toward the road, watching for any glimpse of Mustafal in a Mercedes Benz.

Up ahead and to the right, a large hilly rock formation with trees and trails connected to the beach and towered over all other scenery. To the left Stephen caught sight of a van parked facing the beach and he assumed it was Donri's.

The kids ran ahead to explore the trails of the tall rocky hill, apparently having lost any fear that there was a kidnapper on the loose. Donri looked up and smiled and pointed at the beautiful formation which must offer a spectacular vista of the entire beach. *"Gua Cina,"* he said to Stephen, then quickly realizing he needed to translate. "China Cave."

"Oh, there is a cave up there?" asked Stephen, trying to appear interested, but more concerned with getting into the safety of a van and away from the beach.

"Yes, popular tourist object," said Donri. "Most well-known tourist object in this area. Many people come on the weekends and explore this cave and enjoy this beautiful beach. Today not so crowded. Just us."

Stephen looked back toward the van and now that they were closer could see a man reading a newspaper and smoking a cigarette in the driver's seat. Must be Donri's driver, Stephen thought. He felt relieved to have even a larger number of people with him, and that he would soon have a cell phone in his hand.

"Would you like to see it?"

"What's that?"

"*Gua Cina*—the China Cave."

"Oh, uh, thanks Om Donri. But I'd really like to call my wife before I do anything else."

"Oh yes, yes." Donri seemed embarrassed that he was offering sightseeing to a man who had more pressing concerns. "The kids play at cave while we make phone call."

The two men crested the hill toward a flat sandy grove dotted with shade trees that served as the beach's parking lot, and Stephen noticed a motorcycle coming down the pot-holed lane from the main road toward them. It occurred to him for the first time since his escape that Mustafal might not be the only one coming for him. Was Happy on a search mission too? That partner in crime seemed too docile to be able to capture anyone, but were there any other people in cahoots with the mastermind? He felt sure Dina wasn't seriously on the hunt as she had helped him escape.

The man on the motorcycle passed them, parked next to the van and took off his helmet. He nodded and smiled widely at them, un-straddled his motorcycle and looked like he wanted to come over and make introductions. Stephen wasn't in the mood for any more interruptions, and he whispered to Donri on the side, "I really need to call my wife and get back to Surabaya."

The old man seemed either confused by the statement or maybe he didn't quite hear it because of its low volume. Either way it was too late…the friendly villager had approached with a big smile on his face and was asking Donri questions in Indonesian.

Great. Stephen backed away from the conversation and got the attention of Donri's driver, who had been absorbed in the newspaper and hadn't noticed all the commotion yet. The man startled, threw his newspaper down, flicked his cigarette out the window and hopped out of the van. He ran around to the other side of the vehicle and was already nodding his head up and down yes before Stephen had said or asked anything.

These people are just way too friendly.

"I'm with him," said Stephen to the nodding driver, motioning over to Donri who was suddenly engaged in a lively conversation with the motorcycle man. They were probably discussing the kidnapping, thought Stephen, which was a good thing as the man was a local and could probably help them report all this to the police more quickly.

The driver got consumed in the conversation too, and his smile evaporated into a deep concern. Stephen felt emboldened by having three adult advocates now on his side and no longer being the lone escapee running from his captor. He was also thinking of Agung, yet his most pressing concern was getting a call out to the outside world.

He waited a minute more and then inquired toward the huddle, "Could I use a phone now?"

"Sure, sure."

More Indonesian chattering. The driver was dispatched to retrieve something from the van and he came trotting back with two cell phones in his hand. Donri punched some numbers into one of them while the driver in vain tried to turn the other one on. Stephen figured the driver's phone battery must be dead and when Donri grimaced at a message on his screen he knew that wasn't good news either.

"Um, Mr. Stephen, I'm so sorry but I'm afraid I am almost out of *pulsa*. I'm not sure if I can make a local call and for sure cannot make an international call."

Whatever *pulsa* was, there wasn't enough of it. So much for being blessed, and he for sure wasn't anywhere near lucky.

More chattering. The motorcycle man stayed engaged in the long conversation and listened intently. At one point he started fishing in his jacket pockets for something. Stephen hoped he was about to pull out his own cell phone, but when he kept patting his pants pockets and looking inside his wallet he assumed the man was trying to find a scrap piece of paper to take notes on. It looked like none of them could come up with a writing utensil. One of the English club boys wandered up to the parking area from the cave and asked what was going on. Stephen felt more and more impatient as the strategizing session continued, but he knew he had to wait until they made a plan. Once he got back to civilization he would be his own man and in control once again.

Finally, the young boy scampered off toward his friends and Donri broke out of the huddle. "Mr. Stephen, we sorry to keep you waiting. We are trying to make a plan. This man here named Pak Kadir has a friend who is a policeman in Sendang Biru. That city is about 20 minutes away so we want to call to report to police more quickly. We want to contact the police but unfortunately my phone it almost out of *pulsa* as I already said, and our driver Pak Yohanes has a phone which has dead battery. We will have to drive there to police station and you can try to call your family from there. We are also concerned with the kids here. Did you say that the people who kidnapped you have a weapon? Do you think they are still looking for you? Do they have guns?"

The sobering thought jolted Stephen that these precious kids could be in danger with Mustafal still on the prowl.

"He used some sort of sword or knife with me, but it was wrapped up and I didn't see any gun."

"That's a relief. Let's go get the kids and then go to the police station together and from there you can call your family."

It sounded like a reasonable plan to Stephen, to get out of there as fast as possible and to the safety of a police station. The four men made their way quickly to the large rock formation and spotted the kids climbing up and down the trail that led to the mouth of the cave. The little guys were having a grand time, looking out over the ocean's horizon, throwing rocks into the water, collecting seashells and poking in and out of the cave. Donri called to them loudly and they reluctantly started climbing back down.

"This is the first time they ever go to the beach," Donri said as they waited. "They were very excited."

It was indeed unfortunate that their once-in-a-lifetime beach picnic was being cut short, but he didn't feel like he needed to offer an apology as he was sure Donri was as concerned with the kids' safety as he was.

The kids were nearly all gathered up and Stephen turned back toward the beach's makeshift parking area. On the dusty road that led from the main road to the beach, he noticed a car in the distance slowly rumbling down the road with a cloud of dust being kicked up behind it. He squinted to get a better look and his heart dropped. It was a dark-blue Mercedes Benz being driven by Mustafal.

Stephen yelled to Donri and ordered everyone back up the trail to hide in the cave. They didn't really understand what he was saying and looked to Donri for the translation. Stephen grabbed Donri's elbow and pulled him in the direction up the trail. "It's Mustafal, the man who kidnapped me," Stephen said frantically. "We must hide right now."

Donri got it and yelled it out in Indonesian to the kids. Some of them screamed and all ran frightened back toward the mouth of the cave. The driver and the motorcycle man brought up the rear.

Stephen continued to help Donri up the steep trail and looked back to see Mustafal's car almost at the parking area. He was sure that from their vantage point, tucked behind the trees of the trail, they could see him more easily than he would be able to spot them.

The Mercedes lumbered to the edge of the sandy parking area, right at the crest of the hill overlooking the ocean, and stopped. Stephen crouched down at the cave's entrance behind some large rocks and watched while everyone else besides Donri stayed back in the darkness of the cave. He could hear some kids behind him crying and the two men trying to calm them or at least quiet them down. Donri was squatting down next to him in the opening shadow of the cave while Stephen stayed flat on his belly and peered from between the two large rocks he was using as cover. It all happened so fast that it took a while for his emotions to catch up with his stone frozen body. The only sound was his heart pulsating against the gravel of the trail. He dared not move or speak.

Mustafal sat in the Mercedes for a long time before venturing out and looking around. He was smoking a cigarette and carrying a black duffel bag which he placed on the ground before he walked over to the crest of the hill and looked out over the ocean. Twice he peered in the direction of the cave but Stephen doubted that Donri and he could be spotted in their covered, darkened position. The two other guardians were still back in the cave's darkness, along with the kids who could no longer be heard crying.

Mustafal was obviously disappointed not to have re-captured his Western captive by now. Stephen could tell by his quick, jerky movements. He stomped over to the van and cupped his hands against the windows to peer in on both sides. He examined the parked motorcycle as if looking for clues about his escaped prize. He checked his phone for messages and sounded like he was cursing out loud when the wind brought his voice in their direction. Finally, he picked up the duffel bag, settled on the hood of his stolen car and placed it on his lap. He waited and watched the ocean.

Stephen assumed this was his new lookout point, and it was a fairly good one, offering his nemesis a wide swath of the beach on both sides of the rock formation. Maybe Mustafal was just waiting there until the driver of the motorcycle or the van returned so he could casually ask them if they had happened to see a Westerner. They had, of course, and were all huddled and hiding together.

The minutes ticked on and Stephen wondered what Mustafal's next move would be and what in the world was in that duffel bag that he was still clutching. Donri kept squatting beside him in the shadow of the cave, and Stephen marveled that the old guy could squat down that like for so long...these people must have some serious hamstrings. He was grateful that for now Donri was no longer talking or sermonizing and instead seemed to appreciate the seriousness of the situation. The old man remained as quiet as a church mouse.

Stephen could hear the kids shuffle from the back of the cave toward the opening but the loud crying had stopped. Even if one of them suddenly started wailing, Mustafal would probably not hear them with the distance and the whipping wind between them. As long as Mustafal stayed put, they would too. Hopefully it wouldn't be too long or that Mustafal would suddenly decide to go cave exploring, especially if there was a weapon inside that bag.

After about a half hour that felt more like three, Mustafal suddenly jumped down from the hood, stretched and started walking around again impatiently. He had the duffel bag with him and carried it to a patch of trees and overgrowth, dropped it there and then began to relieve himself with his back turned toward the beach.

Stephen made his move quickly, jumping up from his crouched position and darting into the cave. Donri without a word followed him and the two of them felt their way along the slick walls and ducked their heads because of the low overhang. Their eyes needed adjusting to the inky black darkness and they could hear the kids before they could see them. Donri pulled his *pulsa* depleted phone out of his pocket as a dim flashlight and it was enough to help them walk more confidently than their slow waddle.

The cave didn't go all that far back, but a large opening in the rear made an excellent hiding place for a large group. Stephen was also grateful that it was dry—no slimy things like bats, which he had dreaded when he had entered. The ground was compacted with dry, solid sand. When they came upon the group, some of the kids were still sniffling. Donri aimed his cellphone screen at one of the little girl's faces to get a better look and tried to comfort her by patting her shoulder. He started the conversation in a hushed whisper and it was clear he was still in charge.

The Indonesian flowed frantically and Stephen felt flustered and impatient that the obvious next step wasn't being taken, to call the police on Donri's phone. Finally, Donri turned to him and in the same hushed tone began, "Mr. Stephen. We think we have a plan."

Stephen cut him off. "That's great but I think the first thing we need to do is use your phone to call someone, don't you think?" The darkness shrouded Donri's face and Stephen couldn't tell if the suggestion registered. "Can we use your phone to at least call someone on the outside first, domestically, before Mustafal decides to go exploring in this cave?"

"Uh, yes, we can make a local call with my phone I think, but we still need to have a plan while we wait for someone to arrive."

"Okay, then let's make the phone call first and then talk about that plan. It doesn't look like my kidnapper is going anywhere."

Donri took it all in, thought for a moment, and turned back toward the cowering group. Some of the kids were still holding each other and lightly crying. Stephen could just start to make out their frightened faces now that his eyes were more used to the darkness. Donri spoke mostly to the men and it sounded like some sort of back-and-forth debate ensued. Yohanes the driver and the motorcycle man Kadir started talking too loudly for Stephen's comfort but he was encouraged when Donri finally started punching some numbers into his phone and waited for a response.

Stephen took the moment to crouch down and smile into the faces of the scared kids. "It's going to be okay," he said gently and slowly, hoping they could understand. "We're going to get you out of here." Some of them nodded their little heads up and down as a response and other expressions stayed frozen in fear. The dark cave was creepy enough already without there being a bad man brooding outside.

Donri kept punching different numbers in and waiting. "I'm calling the information number to find the police number in Sendang Biru," he finally offered. Stephen thought once again why they couldn't just call 911 but let it go. "This man Pak Kadir says Sendang Biru is about 20 minutes from here," Donri said with the phone to his ear, naming the motorcycle man again and probably forgetting he had already given that information to Stephen earlier.

Donri finally got directory assistance on the phone. Stephen heard him use the word "*polisi*" and felt relieved they were finally getting somewhere and that there was definitely a signal even from inside the cave. Donri punched that number in but apparently the police station in Sendang Biru wasn't answering. While he waited, Donri started another long conversation with Yohanes and Kadir and afterwards turned back to Stephen.

"Mr. Stephen, you and I will wait for the police to come to this cave. We need to get the kids out of here safely and home with Pak Yohanes. They are very scared hiding in here. If this Mustafal is waiting outside, he will not know who they are and hopefully not bother them so Pak Yohanes can take them home. Also Pak Kadir will go with them toward Sendang Biru to report to the police exactly where we are."

It sounded like a solid plan to Stephen. "That's a good idea to get these kids out of here now. Do the police know we're here?"

"Not yet. But I will keep trying to call them on this number and Pak Kadir will report everything to the police as soon as he accompanies Pak Yohanes and the kids to Sendang Biru. Don't worry, I promise I will keep trying to call."

The crowd crept back to the mouth of the cave with Stephen and Donri leading the way. Stephen crouched down to his previous hidden position behind his rocks. Mustafal was sitting on the hood of the Mercedes, still with the duffel bag cradled on his lap. It looked like he didn't notice their stealth movements, or if he did he didn't let on. Donri whispered some last minute instructions to the men and the kids. It sounded like his words were mainly to calm the frightened children, who were going to have to go past a bad man to get to their van and pretend like they were just having a carefree picnic day at the beach. The soothing tone of his voice didn't seem to be working—some of them started crying harder when they were nudged toward the light at the entrance of the cave. One of little boys even started wailing and Mustafal looked up right toward their direction.

Donri noticed him looking and crouched down in his former shadowy spot. He whisper-yelled a barrage of Indonesian to them, and the men quickly nodded their heads up and down to indicate they would follow whatever it was he was telling them. The kids didn't look like they were going to be able to do this and some were on the verge of hysteria, with the little boy still crying loudly.

Stephen watched the scene unfold as if it were in slow motion, and he was at a complete loss to know what role he should or could play now. He felt protective of the kids, yet helpless to know how to guide them toward safety out of this bizarre predicament. He could only peer from his low vantage point, both at the crying kids and their two-wide eyed escorts, and back to Mustafal, who stayed on alert like a lion ready to pounce on his prey.

Donri kept on whispering instructions as the two men guided the children and tried to soothe them and lead them down the rocky trail away from the cave. It was a steep descent. Stephen could hear both men trying to shush them in a comforting voice as they navigated their way down the rocks and back toward the trail at beach level. Mustafal was watching with rapt attention but he hadn't jumped up from his perch yet. He would have no way of knowing that his former hostage was somehow connected to this group, and Stephen prayed they could all slip by him without arousing any suspicion. Would he try to talk to them? What would they say if he did?

Why am I so scared? We've got the numbers on our side. He wished he had a rifle or something to aim at Mustafal's head until the kids got into that van and got on their way safely. But for now he was a sniper without a gun, powerless to do anything but scope out the dangerous situation.

The two men crossed the beach with the kids timidly trailing behind them, some of them looking up at Mustafal a little too often. They all climbed the sandy hill toward the parking area and Mustafal smiled at them and looked like he was trying to make small talk. The kids hurriedly scooted into the van and Mustafal kept trying to engage them in talk while Yohanes opened the driver's side door and climbed in. He answered back quickly before shutting the door and starting up the engine.

Kadir walked straight toward Mustafal and struck up a conversation with him as the van started pulling back out of the parking area. Nice diversionary tactic. Stephen could see the kids petrified faces looking at the bad man from their windows. He hoped Mustafal didn't notice their stares as Kadir was engaging him in conversation. Mustafal jumped down from the hood and struck out his hand for a handshake which Kadir reciprocated. Both men placed their hands back on their hearts to finish their cultural greeting and they talked in a cordial manner for a few minutes. Mustafal didn't seem suspicious or agitated at all as the two continued to chat. Stephen once again found himself praying, this time an offering of gratitude that the kids made it to the van safely, along with an urgent intercession that Kadir would be able to pull this off and get to the police station quickly.

The two observed men said their goodbyes and Kadir straddled his motorcycle and took off from the parking area, kicking up sand as he left. Mustafal settled back into his position on the hood, picked up the duffel bag and continued in his post as lone lookout.

"Donri," Stephen whispered. "Let's go back inside the cave."

"Okay." The two men slowly crept backwards into the cave while Mustafal was looking in the opposite direction down the beach.

They gingerly stepped toward the back of the cave while Donri lighted the way with the dim screen of his cell phone.

"Try not to use that thing too much because we may need to save the battery," Stephen said once they got back to their previous spot.

"Yes, no problem. Good idea. I will only use it when we have to."

"What happened?" Stephen asked. "What did you tell them to say?"

"I just tell them to say that one of my students received a call that his grandmother died and she was very upset and needed to go home right away."

"Great idea. That would explain to Mustafal why the kids looked so scared."

"Yes, well, I think I got the idea from God. I can't really think that fast."

"God gave you an idea to lie?" Stephen asked with a smile on his face, which he quickly realized couldn't be seen in the pitch black darkness.

"Yes, well, it is wrong to lie normally, but I think God gave me the idea because He is concerned for the children. It's like a story in the Bible when Rahab the prostitute lied about the spies she was hiding from the enemies of Israel..."

Stephen cut him off. "Yes, I see your point and I'm glad you got that idea, but let's try to call the police again."

"Oh yes, yes."

Donri fumbled with the phone some more and said he might be dialing the wrong number as the police station still wasn't answering. He tried to call directory assistance again. While he did that Stephen crept back to the mouth of the cave for another Mustafal scoping. Still sitting on the hood, still clutching on to his duffel bag but this time he was looking at his cell phone. *If only I had his phone number—I would love to call him right now and spook him, tell him the police are on the way and that he's going to go to prison for a very long time.*

193

Stephen crawled backwards into the cave, picked some more rocks and sharp twigs out of his socks, and felt along the wall toward Donri. He could barely make him out again, especially as the cell phone was put away.

"I'm sorry, Mr. Stephen. I tried to call directory assistance and I think I have the right number but still there is no answer at the station. I don't know why. I suggest we pray."

Stephen felt flustered that his simple goal had been blocked for so long, to get a call out to the outside world, and it came out in his voice more than he wanted do. "We can pray later. I need to call my wife now. Can you help me with that?"

A long pause as Stephen could only guess the expression on the helpful man's face.

"Yes, I understand you want to call your wife. Let me check to see if there is enough *pulsa* on this phone to make one international call."

"What is *pulsa* anyway? Is that minutes?" Again, the strain from Stephen's ordeal made the question come out sharper than he had anticipated, making it sound more like an accusation than a question.

Donri answered in measured tones as he punched some more numbers into the phone. "*Pulsa* is when you have enough credit on your phone to make a call."

"Okay, so like pre-paid minutes," Stephen answered more cheerily, hoping the upward lift of his intonation made him sound more appreciative.

"Yes, let me check," said Donri as he punched some more numbers into his phone and waited. "I'm so sorry, there is only 6,000 *rupiah* left."

A quick calculation made Stephen realize that was less than a dollar and would barely be enough to get a call out of this village, much less off this island and over the sea. The new-found appreciation turned back to frustration that made him feel like kicking the wall of the cave if he were still wearing his shoes.

"Maybe we can pray now?" Donri asked, also with a little more cheer in his own voice.

Stephen couldn't argue with that as he could think of no other options. The two of them settled on the packed sand of the cave floor and Stephen suddenly realized how exhausted and famished he was. The adrenaline of the last few hours had kept him going and it now felt like his body wanted to collapse into ten hours' worth of slumber. His eyes had adjusted to the darkness again and he could see some tiredness in the old man's face. This must be an ordeal for him as well, thought Stephen, although he seemed to be handling it more calmly.

"Thanks, Om Donri. You have been too kind to me. Sorry if I haven't sounded grateful. I do appreciate your help. We can pray now if you'd like to."

"Yes, I would like that. Would you?"

"Sure, no objections from me."

Donri placed his hand on Stephen's shoulder and led them in a long, lumbering prayer, mostly for God's wisdom in their ordeal. He took his time praying for each player involved—the English club kids, for Yohanes and Kadir, for Agung's rescue, for repentance in Mustafal's heart and finally for peace for Stephen's family, which Stephen genuinely appreciated.

CHAPTER SEVENTEEN

Agung's cousin reached through the gate's bars and clasped his little cousin's hands tightly. Beaming and looking like he wanted to cry, the hulking man kept saying how grateful he was that his beloved Agung was alive. He had been praying for a safe reunion since he got the news from Pandaan, and he noted that twice. Agung really appreciated all of that but even more the ladder that his two cousins had brought with them, a tricky balancing act on a motorcycle with two passengers. As they hoisted and passed the ladder over the gate, Agung promised he would pay them back for what they had paid for it on the way. They waved off his offer, saying it was more than enough payback that Agung was safe.

Even with the ladder now on their side of the gate, the tricky part for Agung, Dina and Happy would be clearing either the barbed wire and glass cemented to the top of the thick fence or the sharp spikes sticking out on top of the gate. Agung hadn't thought of this previously, but they really needed two ladders—one to get over the fence and one to get back down. As it was, whoever tried to climb over the fence would be stuck at the top in a tangle of wire and glass or sharp spikes. Various ideas were put forth about how to overcome this obstacle, with much gesturing and many assurances from his two cousins that everything would be okay.

"Can we talk for a second?" Dina asked Agung in Javanese.

"Sure," he responded, stepping away from Happy and his two cousins who were still strategizing the break-out plan. They walked together to the shade of the front porch.

"What is going to happen when we get on the other side of this fence?"

"What do you mean?"

"Do you think after we find Mr. Carlton...I mean Mr. Stephen...that you could not let anyone know that Happy and I had anything to do with this kidnapping?" She paused for a second and looked away, like she was trying to stop from crying. "I don't want to go to jail."

Agung suddenly felt strong and powerful protecting this vulnerable beauty. "I'll make sure nothing happens to you," he said with some uncharacteristic flair. "After we find Mr. Stephen, I will tell the police that you and Happy tried to help us escape the whole time and that you were just playing along. We can think of a story to tell them that keeps you out of trouble and then we will blame the whole thing on Mustafal."

Her worried expression morphed into one that revealed conflicting emotions. Agung realized he couldn't appear too eager for Mustafal to go to prison. Though she was surely mad at her ex-fiancé, Dina probably didn't want to see him go to jail quite yet. Come to think of it, she hadn't yet communicated with him that she wanted to break up and probably felt some anxiety over that too. But Agung felt no such qualms over Mustafal's fate and would be fine if he were locked up for a long time. Yet now it was time to backpedal slightly. "We can think later about how to keep everyone out of trouble. The important thing is that we find Mr. Stephen before Mustafal does."

Happy approached them holding out his cell phone. "It's a text from Mustafal," he announced with a tight expression of worry on his face. "He says for you to guard Agung and that I should meet him at China Cave to help him find Mr. Carlton. How should I answer him?"

Agung and Dina looked into each other's eyes, silently strategizing.

"Stall him," Dina finally said. "Ask him how he expects us to get out of here when he took the only key to the gate."

"Here, you type it the way you want it," Happy said, placing the phone into her hands and obviously feeling uneasy about answering back with sarcasm.

Agung and Dina conferred some more and concocted a makeshift plan. They would text back Mustafal as Happy and say that he would try to get over the fence as soon as possible and join him at China Cave.

That would take a long time, of course, and keep Mustafal waiting for Happy at China Cave for as long as possible. Hopefully, while Mustafal waited there, Mr. Stephen would be found by them, Agung's cousins or his other posse of relatives still on the search. Dina expressed her thankfulness that Mustafal was too stingy with his *pulsa* to ever call, which would give them time to decide how to reply to each of his text messages.

Agung promised Dina again that he wouldn't report any of this to the police and would try to shield her and Happy from any legal consequences. She brightly smiled her gratefulness and looked like she wanted to hug him. That would be a huge cultural impropriety, of course, so they just looked at each other with awkward and bashful appreciation.

Happy's cell phone, still in her hand, buzzed again with another text. Mustafal was demanding to know why it was taking so long to answer back, coloring his question with a few expletives. She had to tap into her Javanese inner peace to answer as Happy would and not nip back at him. In text short hand she typed that Happy would be there as soon as he could get over the fence because the key was now in his possession. Dina would stay back and guard Agung at her uncle's house as he had asked.

"Hurry," Mustafal answered back. "I don't like' waiting here out in the open with a stolen car."

Dina typed back Happy's response, "I'll be there as fast as I can." She repeated it out loud, rolling her eyes for effect and then smiling mischievously at Agung. He was completely taken by her beauty—her long shiny black hair, her pearly white teeth, her smooth soft skin, her deep brown eyes—all making his heart beat slightly faster. But what he liked the most about her was her spark, and he promised to himself to not let anything happen to her.

The three of them walked back to the fence together where Agung's cousins were still discussing ladder strategy on the other side. The younger cousin asked Dina why her uncle was surrounded by so much security out in the village. She didn't respond, either not knowing the reason or too consumed with the task at hand to explain her uncle's protectionist personality. She looked up at the sharp obstacles and then at

Agung, who suddenly felt a need to impress her with his bravery. He placed the ladder against the adjoining space between the gate and the fence and mounted up the ladder first while Happy held it secure at the bottom. The cousins were telling him to just jump over and they would catch him on the other side. Easy for them to say that as they weren't about to step on glass or over barbed wire. He placed the toe of his shoe between two large shards of glass, got his footing on a gap between the barbed wire, delicately held on to a spike of the gate for balance and suddenly jumped backwards over the barbed wire like a trained high jumper. He dismounted down from their arms with a proud grin on his face.

"There is no way I can do that," announced Dina. Happy heartily agreed.

Agung assured them that they could—they just had to trust that he and his cousins would catch them both.

"It's not being caught on the other side. It's getting over the fence like you did," protested Dina. "We're going to have to think of something else."

"We need to get out of here before Mustafal comes back," Agung answered back calmly. He knew that fact would register with her and make her be more willing to at least try.

As the discussion ensued another text message beeped in from Mustafal. Dina read it with an exasperated look on her face and passed the phone back to Happy. "Here, you answer. He keeps demanding that you get to China Cave quickly. Just tell him you are still trying and will get there when you can."

Happy punched in his version of her message into the phone and tucked it away in his pocket. Then with a determined squint in his eye, he took a deep breath, scaled the ladder and followed Agung's example to high jump backwards over the barbed wire. Agung and his cousins barely had time to position themselves but easily caught his light frame in their arms.

Dina was now by herself inside the compound. Happy, Agung and his cousins pleaded with her from the other side of the fence to coax her up the ladder. Just then another message from Mustafal came in. Happy read it aloud, another demand to know what the status was and why it was taking so long.

"Ask him what his problem is," Dina shot back. "Not only did he take the keys and lock us all in, he took our only form of transportation with him. How does he expect you to get all the way to China Cave, to run on foot?"

Happy looked unsure as to which part of her answer he should include in his reply.

Agung felt increasingly confident to play the role of leader, in front of his supporting cousins and especially in front of Dina who somehow looked both helpless and angry at the same time. He was going to have to improvise from their original plan and get Happy there more quickly, or else Mustafal might go off in search of Mr. Stephen by himself again. Decisive leadership was needed and he would have to pull himself out of his indecisive personality to take charge.

"Happy, tell him you have just gotten over the fence and will now try to borrow a neighbor's motorcycle. Also tell him to just wait there and you will try to be there as soon as you can." Then Agung put his hand on Happy's shoulder and looked him dead in the eye. "I forgive you for being part of kidnapping me and Mr. Stephen, but now I need you to be strong and make this right. We need to get Mr. Stephen safely back and you have to help us. If you do that, I will not report you and Dina's involvement in this kidnapping to the police. Do you understand?"

Happy nodded that he did.

"You will now borrow my cousin's motorcycle and go meet Mustafal at China Cave. Then you will pretend you are helping him look for Mr. Stephen. When he's not watching, text us and let us know what he's doing. The rest of us will try to find Mr. Stephen and get him back to Surabaya. Hopefully we can do all this without the police who will start asking all of us lots of questions. Oh yeah, and remember that Mustafal still thinks that Mr. Stephen's name is Mr. Carlton. Call him Mr. Carlton so Mustafal won't ask too many questions and realize that you are siding with Mr. Stephen. Can you do all that?"

Happy paused, putting all the sentences together and looking like he was trying to draw from some hidden reserve of inner strength before answering. "Yes," he finally responded confidently.

"Good, now go to Mustafal. We will get Dina out of here and text you on my phone. Don't text us with him around or he will start asking who you are communicating with. Remember to let us know where you are and what he is doing."

Happy was offered the motorcycle and keys by an obliging cousin and he cranked it up. "Be careful," Dina called out to him, "and keep your phone on mute so he won't hear us texting you."

He nodded, drove off and didn't look back. Agung turned his attention back to Dina as his relatives offered suggestions of how to get her over the gate.

"You can do this," he assured her.

"I can't," she countered.

The cousins offered more suggestions and Agung finally decided he would have to go back over the fence himself to help her scale it. He explained his intention to his relatives and they gripped the ladder between the bars and hoisted it upwards with Dina pushing it up from below through the bars.

Agung got to the top and it looked a lot tougher now to jump down with only one person to catch him, a thin person whom he surely didn't want to squash. He decided to secure himself at the top, holding on to one of the gate spikes as he lifted the ladder and placed it on Dina's side. Then he told her to climb it and he would help her over.

She looked up at him like he was crazy while he tried to coax her up with a pleading smile.

Up the rungs she went, into his arms, and with the helping hands of the cousins the ladder was lifted over to the other side. She grimaced at the top with all the barbed wire and glass around her while he held her. Aside from the safety concerns Agung was thoroughly enjoying himself as the hero. After the cousins gave the thumbs up that the ladder was securely positioned, Agung guided and encouraged her down one step at a time. Then he climbed down himself, and he and Dina were celebrated on the ground with applause. Dina gave all three men an appreciative smile.

"We need to find Mr. Stephen before Mustafal does," Agung said with a certain and steady voice, making it clear that he was still in charge of this operation.

"That's a great idea, Agung, but how do we go looking for him?" No trace of the appreciative smile was still visible. "We don't have any transportation."

Agung suddenly realized that their only transportation had indeed driven away with Happy and now they were all on foot. He felt flustered with everyone looking at him and expecting a wise answer. Decisive leadership wasn't easy.

He fumbled through his thoughts for a moment. Remembering what he had just told Happy to tell Mustafal, he exclaimed, "We will borrow one from a neighbor!"

Dina was incredulous. "I don't know any of these people! I've only visited my uncle here a few times and never once met any of his neighbors. They're not going to let strangers borrow their motorcycles."

"Let's see if there are any *ojek* motorcycle taxis around here."

"Are you crazy? Out here in the village?"

Agung was starting to feel frustrated with Dina for challenging every idea without offering any suggestions of her own, and especially in front of his family. She didn't look so pretty now with a scornful scowl on her face. Maybe it was just the stress.

"Well, I guess that means we will have to search on foot. Mr. Stephen ran off without any transportation, and so can we. We'll make two teams and go off in two different directions. Dina, you and I will stay together and head west down the beach and ask if anyone has seen a *bule*."

He turned to his two wide-eyed cousins. "You guys go east along the main road by the beach and also ask people if they have seen a *bule* walking past. We will let you know if Happy texts us." They nodded their excitement at the orders and embarked on their mission.

Dina's smile came back. "I'm sorry I was cranky with you, Agung. I think I'm just tired from going through this ordeal, and I'm kicking myself for ever agreeing with Mustafal in the first place. I really appreciate your help."

He found it easy to forgive her while she was looking up at him with those beautiful brown eyes.

"It's okay. It's been a long 24 hours. Let's go find Mr. Stephen."

He turned toward the road and without warning she placed her hand in his. A pleasant sensation fluttered through his body. He didn't know if it was a small thank you squeeze or something more but it sure felt great. He clasped back.

A beauty by his side and an adventure ahead. Agung thought that this was the best day so far of his rather uneventful life.

~~□~~

By the time the police-escorted caravan arrived at the hospital, Carlton was so angry he could not bring himself to even speak to Bambang, his only ally in this country. He stared straight ahead in the parking lot and tried to concentrate and drown out the white noise of Bambang's insistent pleas for patience and calm. He would do things as he saw fit and hoped this irrepressibly polite man would just stay out of his way.

The mustached policeman yanked open the door and motioned Carlton to follow. The gruff manner indicated this was a demand and not a request. Carlton tried to think how he would play this. He hated every living soul and every single thing about Indonesia, but he knew he had to keep all those feelings in check to be able to get through this as fast as possible to assume control again. He had decided in the passenger seat of Bambang's car that he was no longer a prisoner to the petty power plays of the police. Dragging his feet and being belligerent, which he had already tried and felt like doing again, would only energize them and imprison him once more inside their spiteful game. Instead he would take charge and throw them off their heels with a sudden burst of confident Western leadership.

He jumped out of the car with a big smile on his thick face, and the instantaneous awakening from his comatose state seemed to frighten Bambang while bewildering the police at the same time. They probably thought from his rapid pace that he was making a run for it, but he was actually making a bee line to where he thought the hospital's administrative office might be. He would pay the full bill, play nice, and give them absolutely no more reason to hold him. Then he would fire Bambang for his weak leadership and get out of the country as fast as he could, saying farewell to supervising or consulting or whatever exactly it was he was supposed to be doing at the factory. Once back in the U.S., he would dare the home office to reprimand him for not finishing his duties, countering with a demand for some sort of financial compensation for his ordeal. That was leadership. The best defense is a good offense. *Take charge and take note, Bambang.*

With the police and Bambang trailing him, Carlton got to the information desk in the hospital's main lobby. It was a sleepy place, with a large courtyard off to the side of the lobby. There were visitors lounging around on the benches and the grass, and many of them noticed the large foreigner charging into the premises. His sudden appearance certainly got the attention of the three petite ladies working the welcome counter. They looked at him, and then at each other, probably trying to silently decide amongst themselves who had the best English. Carton made it easy for them by speaking slowly and deliberately.

"Where is boy who hit by car yesterday? I pay his bill right now."

He reached for his back pocket and felt it empty, recalling again he was without his wallet. A quick spike of frustration was followed by the delightful remembrance that his wallet was inside this very hospital, somewhere hidden among those scheming relatives of the injured boy. He could get his wallet and life back in one fell swoop! Bambang and the police made it to the reception desk, and Carlton raised his voice to the welcome desk staff to show them who was in charge among the various visitors before them.

"I want to pay the bill of young man hit by car. Do you know where his room is? I want to check on him."

The administrative staff seemed taken with the sudden scene in front of them, as now three police officers and another Indonesian man suddenly appeared with the domineering foreigner.

Carlton went louder and slower. "I want to see boy hit by car."

The bravest receptionist of the three softly cleared her throat. "Excuse me sir, do you look for the boy hit by the car yesterday? He is in room 146, in class two section. To pay bill you must visit cashier office."

"Fine, to room 146 we go." Carlton looked for signs leading the way and didn't bother to explain what he was doing to his thunderstruck escorts.

It felt empowering to his weary soul to be in charge again, even if he didn't know exactly where he was going or what he would do when he got there. Carlton felt a real smile emerging from underneath his fake one.

CHAPTER EIGHTEEN

Less daylight was coming through the opening of the cave. Stephen and Donri had settled back in the far end of it so their conversation couldn't be heard by their malevolent watchman. Stephen felt grateful he wouldn't be spending the night in this uncomfortable place, assuming that Kadir had already made it to the police station with his urgent report and that police officers were now on the way.

"Do you think you could try to call the police station again?" Stephen asked Donri who still seemed strangely unmoved by the whole ordeal. "Is there enough *pulsa* to make that call?"

"Yes, there should be enough for another call. Let me try again." No answer.

"Are you sure you have the number to the police station correct? Could you call directory assistance again to make sure?"

"I did that once and I'm afraid another call to them will use up all our *pulsa*. Let's try again a little later. Hopefully Pak Kadir will get there soon and report everything. Whatever is happening, God knows we are here and He is on our side."

"I would feel better if I knew the police were on the way. Who knows if Mustafal might enter this cave with a weapon?"

"Yes, I can understand that concern. Let me try once again." Still no luck.

Either the entire police force of Sendang Biru had cleared their headquarters and were dashing toward the cave, sirens blazing, or they were on some sort of collective coffee break outside of their station. Stephen suspected that the more likely scenario was that Donri was punching in the wrong number, an understandable mistake for a well-meaning older man. Once again Stephen felt the cultural frustration of being powerless in a situation he did not fully understand. He decided to give it a few more minutes before he pushed Donri for more phone tries.

A long moment ticked by in the darkness as both men rested against the smooth cave walls. In the silence Stephen could hear Donri's measured breathing, like he was deep in thought or praying again silently. A breeze from the ocean wafted all the way to the back of the cave and the cool air felt refreshing on Stephen's weary body.

Finally, Donri spoke his thoughts. "Pak Kadir has probably reached the police station by now. It will take him a few minutes to report what has happened to the police and then at the most fifteen more minutes for them to get here because they will be traveling fast. So I assume we have no more than a half hour in this cave together before the police arrive."

Stephen was relieved the man was dealing in the concrete world of math and time calculations instead of the subjective realm of faith. "That sounds about right."

"It doesn't seem our friend Mustafal is going anywhere so I suggest we use the time to get to know each other better. Tell me more about where you are from and about your family."

Stephen felt it couldn't hurt having a chit chat and might make the wait time go by faster. He gave a brief description of his job, a little on Sacramento, his kids' ages and how long he and Leah had been married.

"Congratulations for fifteen years. My wife Yuli and I were married for forty-seven years before she passed away eight years ago."

"I'm sorry to hear that Om Donri."

"Yes, it's been hard living life without her. But you must go on. And God gives me strength. Are you a man of faith, Mr. Stephen?"

"I have my own beliefs." Stephen still didn't feel like delving into matters of his personal religious convictions, which were vague at best, so he tried to deflect the conversation back toward their current predicament. "What do you think will happen to Mustafal when the police get here? Do the police shoot first here and ask questions later? And what do you think Mustafal is doing out there anyway?"

"I guess what happens to this Mustafal is up to God and the police. The only people we are responsible for are ourselves. I wonder what God would have us do in this situation."

"I'm not sure what God would have us do in this situation," Stephen said with a forced smile that went unseen in the darkness, "but I know I am waiting right here until the police come. I'm not leaving with that crazy man out there who hates me. He choked me and threw me against the wall once. Who knows what he would do with a second chance and a real weapon in his hand."

"Fair enough. We wait."

Silence filled the dark space between them. After a few moments Stephen could again hear the rhythmic breathing of Donri and it sounded like this time he was napping. How could he sleep at a time like this? Either he possessed a deep well of calm based out of his deep religious convictions or he was just old, bone tired and needed a rest. Stephen decided to use the time to creep back to the mouth of the cave and sneak another peek at Mustafal.

He did so slowly, careful not to make a noise or movement that would arouse Mustafal's attention. At the entrance of the cave he belly crawled to his previous look-out post behind the two large rocks and peered through the trees. Mustafal was still sitting on the hood of his stolen car, this time with the duffel bag open on his lap. From the bag he pulled out a folded towel and carefully opened it up, looking over his shoulder to make sure no one was looking. It was some sort of black object, and when it was fully unfolded from the towel, Stephen immediately recognized it as a gun. Mustafal admired it and rubbed his hand against the black barrel while Stephen could feel his stomach turning knots.

Mustafal popped off a couple of pretend shots toward the trees around him, looking down the sight, finger carefully on the trigger, then ending with a fake kick back. If he weren't a terrorist he would look like a grown up kid playing with a toy gun. Stephen knew this man was truly capable of violence and he dared not move a muscle, having never felt so scared in his life. After a couple of minutes Mustafal wrapped the gun back inside the towel, placed it back in the bag and then pulled his phone out of his jacket pocket. He pressed some buttons on it, probably texting someone, and seemed frustrated and impatient. Stephen's best guess was that he was waiting for an accomplice like Happy to arrive at this well-known spot in the area. When he was reunited with his partner they would resume the search for their missing prize together.

Stephen hoped Donri wouldn't suddenly wake and decide to join him at their lookout point. He didn't want any more movement that could give their position away during the waiting game, especially now that a gun was in play.

Suddenly Mustafal looked down the dirt road, focusing on something that Stephen couldn't see from his vantage point. Quickly zipping up his duffel bag, Mustafal jumped down from the hood of the car and kept peering down the road. Whatever it was spooked him and he trotted off to the base of the trail that led toward the cave, still glancing back toward the road while carrying the duffel bag.

Stephen could see that it was a car, and then a set of lights on top revealed it as a police car. They arrived even faster than Donri had estimated.

Mustafal was about 30 feet away down the trail, still cutting glances back toward the police car. Stephen could make out the faces of the two officers now pulling their car into the parking area. It looked like they were talking to each other and not looking ahead.

Mustafal looked up toward the cave again and Stephen in horror realized what was about to happen. Clutching his duffel bag against his chest, Mustafal quickly climbed up the trail using his one free hand to grab on to rocks and tree roots to scramble up. In a split second Stephen rolled off to the side of the trail into some overgrowth but he would still be easily spotted in plain sight by anyone at a normal walking pace. He hoped Mustafal would zip right by in his mad dash to enter the cave, not noticing his recently freed captive.

Stephen pressed his body as hard as he could into the overgrowth and could hear Mustafal almost upon him now. From his peripheral vision he saw a shadow cross into the cave. He knew Mustafal had entered the cave but couldn't tell if he had been spotted or not, nor what Mustafal would do now. He surmised Mustafal would do what Stephen had done, watch the action from the shadowed security of the cave and plot his next move. If he did that, Stephen would surely be seen off to the side. Another scenario was that Mustafal would hide deep in the back of the cave and come upon a harmless old man napping.

It was decision time and Stephen knew he had to act. He could jump up and yell for the police and hope Mustafal wasn't watching, but that might get him shot in the back. Or he could stay put, wait and sneak his way down the trail while Mustafal was hiding. He could still be shot in the back if he did that. Stephen felt the beginnings of a panic attack start to choke out his breathing and he willed it away hard, turning his head slowly sideways toward the cave to see if Mustafal were there.

He was and his cold eyes stared into Stephen's, pointing his gun with one hand at Stephen's head and placing one finger over his lips in a shush gesture.

Stephen nodded his submission and stayed flat on the ground, barely believing what was happening to him. Mustafal turned his attention to the police car and crouched down. He motioned for Stephen to follow him into the cave. Stephen did so slowly, keeping his eye on the gun. This was his last chance to jump up and yell to the police before he entered Mustafal's dark dominion again. The gun pointed at his face made the decision simple and Stephen crawled toward the cave at the snail's pace but with the adrenaline of a runner. Every now and then he could hear Mustafal whisper some sort of angry curses at him but he kept his head down and his body inching forward to obey. It felt like he was climbing inside his own tomb, but he couldn't summon the courage to flee or flight back.

Once he got inside the darkness of the cave, he felt thoroughly ashamed of himself and looked up toward his conqueror. Mustafal snarled at him, peered once more at the police, and motioned for Stephen to follow him deeper into the cave, continuing to point the gun at Stephen's head and pressing his finger against his mouth for his captive to remain quiet.

They got about five steps in, into the blackness of the cave, and a sharp pain exploded on the side of Stephen's face. At first he thought he had been shot, but then he realized Mustafal had hit him with the butt of the gun flat against his cheek. He wobbled with pain and lost his step, knocking against the cave wall and collapsing to the ground.

"You be quiet," Mustafal warned. "If you call help I will shoot."

Stephen cradled his throbbing cheek and checked his face for blood. There was none, but he fully believed Mustafal's threat, remembering when he had been thrown against the wall back at the hostage house and choked. It was the same type of intimidating power move and it worked again to paralyze him with fear. He could barely breathe and knew there would be a large welt of a bruise on his face later.

Stephen suddenly remembered Donri back somewhere in the cave, and assumed the commotion aroused him from his rest. Mustafal seemed to prefer this vantage point, deep enough in the cave to stay hidden but still close enough to the opening to watch for the police. Stephen hoped Donri would stay put in the back part of the cave, not venturing out which might startle Mustafal and cause him to start shooting. Stephen kept his head down and tried to think of what to do next, but could think of no defensive strategy except to stay obedient and very still.

Mustafal glanced down at his docile hostage, tucked the gun into his armpit and pulled out his cell phone with the other hand. He was distracted with text messages and Stephen thought this would be a good time to strike, to catch him off balance, grab the gun and yell for the police. Yet the moment passed. Mustafal pulled the gun out and aimed it at Stephen while punching in a text message.

"I want no trouble," Stephen said, looking back down toward the ground.

"Shut up," Mustafal hissed.

Silence ensued and Mustafal fidgeted with his phone and sent out another message. Either Donri was staying put in the darkness to listen or still deep in a nap, an unlikely possibility with all the noise. Mustafal had to be worried about a stolen car sitting out in the open like that, Stephen guessed, although he didn't know yet that their position had already been reported. The police would enter this cave any moment, weapons drawn, and what would Mustafal do then? He was probably just thinking the police were here by coincidence and would soon mosey on, and he could get back to being in charge again and bring Stephen back to the hostage house. That was not going to happen. The police already knew there was a foreigner along with another Indonesian man in the cave. Mustafal was about to be brought down, but would he go down fighting in a blaze of gunfire?

≈≈□≈≈

Happy pulled the borrowed motorcycle to the shoulder of the road to read the text message when his phone vibrated. In short-hand Indonesian it read, "I found Mr. Carlton and we are in China Cave together. Get here immediately." He started to respond, but remembered that he needed to send a text first to Dina and Agung to let them know. He sent that message, and then started another one to Mustafal to let him know he was on the way. As he thumbed it out, his phone vibrated with another message from Mustafal: "Be careful. The police are here too. Hide in the woods nearby and wait for them to leave before you come to the cave."

This was getting complicated and he didn't know what to do. Now that the police were at the cave, should he continue on? There was a real possibility that he could go to jail for his role in the kidnapping if he were caught. Dina would know what to do. He sent her a text message to ask, and she responded that he should just go hide in the woods near China Cave as Mustafal asked. Watch, wait and report.

Okay, he could do that. He would find a hiding spot for the motorcycle in the woods and just hide nearby and watch.

≈≈□≈≈

The squawk of voices over walkie-talkies could be heard drifting into the cave and getting closer. The police were here and probably climbing up the trail. Stephen had only seen two officers in the squad car, but by now maybe they had backup.

"Hello, hello? Anyone in there?" a booming voice asked. "This is police."

The message was in English, which must have puzzled Mustafal and confirmed to Stephen that the police definitely knew he was in there. Mustafal was gripping his gun with both hands and aiming it toward the mouth of the cave, a wild expression of fear on his face.

"Yes, we are in here," shouted back Donri suddenly and very loudly. He must have heard the announcement, and came out of his hiding spot to answer. But did he know that Mustafal was in here with them? If he did, his shouting was either exceedingly brave or incredibly foolish.

Mustafal's move. He yelled something in Indonesian toward the officer and cocked the gun. He shouted out again, louder and with more intensity, while Stephen stayed as flat as he could on the ground, his hands over his still-sore head, awaiting the gunfire.

"We are in here. Don't shoot," Donri called out from the blackness behind them.

"Donri, stay back. He has a gun," Stephen yelled out. His outburst was answered with a hard kick to the back of his head from Mustafal. Stephen winced with pain but yelled out again, "Stay back, Donri."

Voices got louder and more animated from the walkie-talkies and Stephen imagined at least two officers crouched down at the mouth of the cave, maybe more, aiming their guns. Mustafal threatened them with an angry barrage of Indonesian. Donri seemed to have taken heed to Stephen's warning and hadn't come fully forward yet.

The officer yelled something and Mustafal answered back angrily with even more volume. Stephen's head throbbed with pain and he kept his body flat against the ground and braced for an eruption of gunfire any second amid the intensity. *This is happening. This is really happening. I could get shot. I could die right here.*

No response from the officers except the squawking radios and then Mustafal yelled out something again. Whatever he said caused them to back away and Stephen could hear the voices from the walkie-talkies trail off.

Mustafal then turned his attention to the back of the cave and called out something. A moment later Donri appeared and Mustafal greeted him with a swift kick to the groin, sending him down hard as he coughed and gasped with pain. He landed and rolled over right next to Stephen who whispered, "I'm so sorry Donri." The old man didn't answer but rocked back and forth in his agony. Stephen reached out to pat him on his shoulder and Mustafal started shouting something to both of them.

Donri slowly reached for his wallet out of his back pocket and handed it to Mustafal without looking. Mustafal snatched it, grabbed the bills out, stuffed them in his pocket and kept on yelling out toward the police officers. Stephen could see him in the dimming light take a few crouching steps toward the cave's opening, gun aimed. He flung the wallet through the mouth of the cave as hard as he could and Stephen could hear it land into the bushes. It must have been a proof of life for the police, Stephen thought, the best Mustafal could do without Stephen's own wallet. That one Mustafal had stashed elsewhere.

Another threatening burst of Indonesian erupted from Mustafal toward the police. He then backed up, turning his attention to his two hostages. He demanded something of Donri who seemed reluctant to answer and Mustafal bent down and roughly turned him over to search him. Donri went limp and Mustafal finally retrieved what he must have been searching for, Donri's cell phone, their only link with the outside world.

Mustafal scanned it for messages or other clues, and then asked something else from Donri, kicking him to emphasize his further demand.

Donri, still flat on his back, responded in a gentle manner with his palms up toward Mustafal and whatever he said seemed to placate him. Mustafal paced around in a tight circle, tucked the phone inside his jeans and pointed the gun back toward Stephen and demanded something, expecting Donri to translate. His attention then turned back to the entrance of the cave and he crouched at a bend in the wall that offered the best vantage point. He yelled out something to the police again and pointed his gun toward the entrance. Still no response from the officers.

"Come on, Mr. Stephen. He says we must go back to the very back of the cave." Donri started to help himself up but was having trouble and Stephen jumped to his aid. Donri thanked him and they made their way, feeling along the walls. With no light from a cellphone screen anymore there was only deep pitch blackness.

CHAPTER NINETEEN

Carlton cleared his throat and knocked loudly on the door of room number 146. There was no answer so he pushed the door open, revealing an old man wearing a gown and lying flat on a wrought iron bed. The man looked back at him with wide-eyed puzzlement. He was all by himself and there were no signs of the mob of relatives that had confiscated the missing wallet. Carlton assumed he didn't know English and didn't bother him with any questions. He stepped back into the hall to look at the number on the door, just to make sure he had it right. As he did Bambang and the two officers arrived.

"No, no, Mr. Carlton," said Bambang breathlessly. "This is 146 class three. The boy you hit is in 146 class two."

Carlton wanted to curse the hospital for its inane layout and confusing class system, but then Bambang's last comment registered. "I did not hit that boy, Mr. Bambang," he roared while turning to the police officers to make sure they understood. "You know that. The driver hit the boy."

"Oh yes, yes," replied Bambang softly. "The boy whom your driver hit is in room 146 class two."

"And it was supposed to be your driver in the first place, not my driver."

Bambang looked unsure as to how to apologize for that and just gave back his standard, "Yes, yes." Carlton didn't respond but looked back into the faces of the officers, trying to convey his fearlessness. "Okay, then, Mr. Carlton. Let's proceed to room 146 in the class two section."

Carlton marched next to Bambang in silence while the two police officers trailed behind. Every now and then he could hear them snicker to each other, evidently getting their kicks out of this absurd situation. Bambang led the way through the courtyard walkways toward the new section, which looked like a slight upgrade from the sparse class three.

"Normally a family in the village would have to go to the cheapest section, class three. But because you say you will pay the bill they upgrade to class two. Class two more expensive than class three. Still not nice like class one or class VIP but at least better care than class three."

"Yes, I get it."

Bambang didn't detect the sarcasm and kept going. "The hospital want to make sure that you will pay the rest of bill before they will let boy stay any more days in class two. That is kind of you to offer to pay boy's bill, Mr. Carlton."

Carlton started to say that he didn't offer but rather his wallet was commandeered in the mayhem, but he let it go at that. Besides, they were almost at the correct room and he would now get his wallet back, pay for whatever class of treatment these people wanted and get long gone.

Bambang opened the door first and a group of visitors lounging on straw mats in the grassy courtyard perked up. Carlton followed him in and the officers stayed outside.

A half-dozen people were crammed into the tiny room, which didn't look much better than class three except for some charts hanging on the wall. Bambang made introductions and they all immediately recognized the white visitor. The mother jumped up and started speaking with animation. He couldn't tell if it was anger or thankfulness so he took a step back, out of her breath range, and looked to Bambang for the translation.

"She says thank you for your coming. She says that boy must be in hospital for many days but doctors say he will get better. She also says hospital want to talk to you about paying bill."

"Yes, I understand," Carlton said with a smile that came out more as a smirk. Both policemen entered the room, one of them talking into his crackling radio. Carlton decided he would continue with his shrewd strategy of shock and awe. Curiosity got the better of the people that were loitering outside and they crowded around the open window when the police entered.

"There is one problem here, Mr. Bambang," he said loud enough for the whole room and the outside gallery to have his attention. "This boy deserves better treatment at this hospital. I would like to upgrade him to first class."

As Bambang translated Carlton tried to read the expressions of the police officers, looking for some shock or at least awe. One of them stared forward blankly as if unmoved by the announcement of Carlton's generosity and the other one stayed consumed in his radio communication.

A loud cheer went up in the room followed by a question from the mom. Bambang translated the inquiry. "She wants to know by first class do you mean section one or VIP section?"

"I mean VIP, the very best for this poor boy." He really meant just a one class upgrade but it felt good announcing the most audacious offer, especially in front of the officers. He would work out the reimbursement later, if not in Indonesia then back at home office.

A louder cheer went up.

The police seemed completely unmoved by the celebration, now in their own private little conversation, which disappointed Carlton. The whole point of this theatrical exercise was to show them how small they were and how big he was. Now it all felt pointless.

"Mr. Carlton," Bambang whispered. "Are you sure? VIP treatment very expensive here and boy could be here for many weeks."

"Yes, I'm sure," he answered back loudly. The mom knelt by her son's bedside, looking like she had tears in her eyes, and shared the happy tidings. The officers called Bambang over for a chat.

All other eyes were on Carlton, who was feeling awkward being the object of adulation in a roomful of adoring onlookers. The officers finally broke out of their huddle with Bambang and he stepped over to explain. "Mr. Carlton, more good news. They have found the company car, a Mercedes Benz that was supposed to pick you up at the airport."

"That's a relief," said Carlton, with sarcasm that once again Bambang didn't detect.

"Yes, it is. What's more, the driver has been found too, but a long way from the car which was found at a beach very far from here."

"Car jacked by joy riders, huh?"

"Excuse me sir?"

"The people who stole the car took it to the beach, I assume?"

"No, the driver says that you were in the car when the car was taken near Sidoarjo by terrorists."

"What?"

"The driver says that you were in the car when the car was taken near Sidoarjo by terrorists."

"I heard what you said but that doesn't make any sense. I have been in this God-forsaken city the whole time."

The two police officers broke in and shared more information with Bambang and had more questions. Carlton turned his attention back to the mother and tried out some simple English with pantomime to retrieve his wallet. She understood right away and pulled it out of her purse, unwrapping it from a scarf before handing it over to him delicately. He smiled his thanks and tried to find the cashier's office himself to pay whatever a pre-paid VIP monthly hospital package would cost. The police and Bambang were too consumed in their conversation to notice him leaving but the mother followed. She stepped ahead of his pace and led the way to the cashier's office, apparently sensing his intended destination, and kept smiling at him along the way to show her appreciation.

Sure, lady, I'm your sugar daddy.

They wound their way to the cashier's window, which Carlton would have never found on his own, and the mother got into a long conversation with the female accountant sitting behind the glass who eyed Carlton suspiciously. He looked around to bide the time, seeing nothing much of interest in the tiny hallway. After a few minutes Bambang rounded the corner by himself, looking out of breath.

Carlton actually welcomed the distraction. "Hello Bambang. Where are the police?" he asked cheerily enough.

"They will meet us back at the factory. The company driver, Pak Gunadi, is there now and giving a report as to how he was captured by the terrorists. They are waiting for the company car to be towed back to the factory. The police would like us to be there as they follow developments on the terrorists holding you hostage in the China Cave."

"Bambang," Carlton broke in. "I am not in a Chinese Cave. I am standing right in front of you!" His mood, which was starting to brighten when he thought the bill would soon be paid and he would soon be on his way back to a five-star luxury lifestyle to recover, darkened back into a cloud of anger. Now he would be again held hostage, not by terrorists but by the same spiteful and incompetent police force.

"Yes, Mr. Carlton, I know. The police know that too and they believe that you is you."

"Great detective work."

"But the whole thing doesn't make sense and they want us all back at the factory to, how you say, sort it out or get to the bottom of it?"

"However you say it, it's an incredible waste of my time. Either your driver is lying or this is some sort of set up."

"I'm sorry, Mr. Carlton?"

"I'm sorry, too. I'm sorry I ever came here. I have barely slept in the last two days and I badly need a change of clothes and a shower and shave."

The mother interrupted and presented Bambang with a print-out of the bill. Carlton could see his eyes get big as he looked at the figure at the bottom. The mother started explaining and pointing to the bill and pointing back to the cashier's desk.

Bambang gulped slightly and looked up into the stone face of his international visitor. "Mr. Carlton, the hospital estimates the boy will be here for two weeks. For VIP room you must pay up front and for estimated costs of doctor, medical treatment and medicine. You pay for the whole cost ahead of time. If it is less than that, they say they will refund that amount to your credit card. They only need your signature to make payment today. You okay with that?"

Carlton noticed that Bambang left the actual total amount out of his explanation, which he estimated would be astronomical. He was always good at sensing when someone was covering something up even when they answered with a barrage of words. He decided right there on the spot to play this differently. Time for another leadership lesson.

"Tell them I changed my mind. Tell them because of these outrageous charges I will pay for the lowest level only, for class three treatment and not a penny more."

≈□≈

Dina and Agung were both winded from their long walk and search. During their journey Agung had cracked a few jokes to try to break the tension of their somber mission to retrieve Mr. Carlton/Mr. Stephen. But all friendly banter had ended when a text message from Happy announced Mustafal had found Mr. Stephen and the two of them were at China Cave. A follow-up question from Happy let them know that the police were now involved.

By the time they received that news they were already about 15 minutes from the house in the opposite direction from that beach so it would take them over an hour to get there at a good clip.

How to play their next move was tricky for Agung. He felt obliged to help Mr. Stephen yet wanted to protect Dina from a fate of life behind bars. He also wanted to show that he wasn't scared of her ex-boyfriend—yet he actually was because he knew the unstable and angry guy was liable to do something desperate at this point.

Since his initial phone call to his mom, Agung had been sending text messages to his family instead of calling to conserve his *pulsa*. Yet this new development was too complicated to explain completely in thumbed shorthand. He would have to make a second phone call, especially now as the police were involved. Up ahead on the side of the road he could see a raised bamboo *pondok* hut used for resting villagers and small communal meetings. He suggested to Dina that they rest there for a minute while they plotted their next move and he made a phone call.

Dina agreed and he helped her climb on to the waist high platform, then excused himself so he could make that call. He wanted to do it out of earshot because he was going to call his mother and didn't want to sound like a momma's boy. She would surely get emotional and barrage him with a dozen more questions, which she did. He walked far enough away from the *pondok* to not be overheard yet not too far away to make it look like he had something to hide. From his peripheral vision he noticed Dina was straining to hear their conversation. *So embarrassing.*

As he was nearing the end of the talk with his frantic mother, he decided he would have the rest of the conversation in front of Dina to show that he was not a scared little boy but a man in charge again. He casually strolled back toward the *pondok*, giving his mother specific instructions to call off all search parties including his cousins and send them all back to Pandaan. It was too dangerous for them here. He would find his way home but there was something he needed to take care of first. He didn't tell her that it was actually someone. Against his mom's protest he said he needed to go now and that all would be explained later. Just call the others and tell them the search was off. More words of pleading and further questions poured forth but he hung up manly enough and looked into the face of Dina. She was leaning against one of the posts of the *pondok* and smiling down at him. A breeze from the rice field brushed her smooth black hair to the side, and she looked like a beautiful Javanese princess from some epic Hindu legend. But this was a real-time present story, and it was up to him to prove himself the hero.

He helped her down from the platform and then explained his quickly evolving strategy. They would walk together toward China Cave, keeping off the main road, and then hide somewhere out of sight from the police but with the cave in view. Maybe with the help of Happy's intel they could sneak up on Mustafal and rescue Mr. Stephen. They would not report to the police themselves for the obvious reason that if Mustafal were caught, he would surely confess all, and especially so when he found out that his fiancée had turned on him.

As they walked along they discussed more than once the idea of contacting Mustafal directly through his cell phone. Just tell him that the game was up and to come out of the cave with his hands up. Dina knew him best and she said he was too erratic for that type of logic. He would go down fighting, she assumed, hurting as many people as possible in a fit of rage.

"What if I just called him and told him I have a new boyfriend," she asked playfully. "Do you think that would flush him out of hiding?

Agung enjoyed the flirtation, but imagining Mustafal's jealous rage kept his mind out of the clouds. This was serious and potentially deadly. He also thought of poor Mr. Stephen, scared to death and likely having a very bad first impression of Indonesia.

~~□~~

Happy parked the borrowed motorcycle behind a clump of trees off a narrow side road that was mostly used for dumping trash. He found a trail that led toward China Cave and walked it slowly, continually looking behind him to make sure he wasn't being followed and scanning ahead for any signs of trouble. Mustafal texted him once and asked where he was. He sent back a message that he was getting close. Now he was supposed to keep stalling Mustafal, find a hiding spot close enough to the action but far enough away from the police presence to not be seen, watch out for Mr. Stephen while he scouted for Dina and Agung, and then text back all the latest developments. How was he supposed to do all that when he was feeling so much stress?

He noticed a patch of bushy overgrowth ahead that might make a good lookout post because it clumped around a stump of a hill that tilted toward the ocean. He enclosed himself inside the dense overgrowth, covering his upper body with leaves and branches for extra cover, and could see the stolen Mercedes Benz clearly with a police car parked next to it.

From his vantage point he could see the opening of China Cave faintly and the head of the trail that led up to it more clearly. He knew from the earlier text message that Mustafal and Mr. Stephen were in the cave together and the police were nearby, but there was still no sighting of them yet.

A car pulled down the road and Happy could make out that it was a second police car. His heart raced while his body froze. The car rolled up right behind the Benz and two officers hopped out, one looking inside the stolen car and the other scanning the area, like he was searching for something or someone in particular. Both of them had their hands on their holsters which terrified Happy—they had come here ready to apprehend someone. One of them looked directly in Happy's direction which frightened him but he still didn't let his body flinch and shake those branches.

Both of the officers crouched down behind their squad car and started talking into the radios that they had unclipped from their shoulders. They were calling for more backup! Soon the whole beach would be searched by the entire police force of Sendang Biru and he would be caught and arrested and spend the rest of his life in jail. He felt like crying but he didn't dare let his eye muscles release any tears. Sobbing would flutter the bushes and someone might see him.

His cell phone vibrated inside his pocket, probably another text from Mustafal, but he dared not reach for it. Now he felt grateful that Dina insisted he turn it on mute when he was leaving her uncle's house.

Not a lot of people looked up to him—he could tell that— nor did they appreciate his limited talents. But he was a good hider. Always was. He could do this. He could wait in this spot motionless for hours if he needed to and be a good scout.

The cell phone vibrated again. Maybe Dina but more likely Mustafal. *Nope, not going to touch it. You're on your own, cousin.*

CHAPTER TWENTY

Stephen and Donri gingerly found their way back to the farthest recesses of the cave, far out of earshot from Mustafal. The back of Stephen's head was still sore with pain from Mustafal's assault and his eyes tried in vain to get used to the cold black darkness. He could tell from Donri's labored breathing that the brave old man was still in pain too.

"Donri, are you okay?"

"Just a little hurt. I will be okay."

"I'm so, so sorry I got you into this."

"It's not your fault, Mr. Stephen. It's the fault of Mustafal."

"Yes, I guess it is. Let's rest our backs against the wall for a minute."

"Okay, you may need to help me down."

"Of course." Stephen felt for Donri's elbow and guided him downward to the ground.

"Can you tell me exactly what happened back there? Or do you need to rest some first?"

"Yes, I can tell you now." Donri let out a long exhale. "Mustafal threw my wallet out of the cave to prove to the police he had two hostages in here. They must already know about you. He told them that if they tried to enter he would kill us both with his gun."

"I believe him."

"I think he needs us to stay alive so he can have something to bargain with. To show he is serious he might kill one of us but not both." The analysis wasn't very comforting for Stephen. "Don't worry," Donri said with a hearty chuckle, apparently reading Stephen's mind. "If he executes someone, it will probably be the old Indonesian man and not the esteemed visitor."

Stephen couldn't bring himself to laugh at Donri's morbid joke as there might be some truth in it, but Donri laughed enough for the both of them anyway. Stephen was amazed the old guy still had a sense of humor after all that had happened. "What else did Mustafal say?"

"He saw the last numbers I dialed on my phone and demanded to know why I was calling directory assistance and who I called next."

"What did you say?"

"I lied and said I was trying to get the number of a friend who lived nearby that I planned to visit later today."

"Did he buy it?"

"What's that?"

"Did he believe what you said?"

"I think so. He seemed more worried about the police coming into the cave than questioning me anymore. He didn't even ask why I was in here in the first place."

"Well, I guess it worked," Stephen exclaimed with a wide smile that couldn't be seen in the darkness. "Another good lie."

"Yes, I'm getting pretty good at those today," Donri said and Stephen imagined a wide smile on his face. "But I give all the glory to God."

At that Stephen had to let out a laugh. Donri patted him on the shoulder and Stephen reciprocated. The light moment was a good tension breaker, but Stephen's mind quickly fixated on what just happened and what they should do next. "How did the police get here so fast do you think?"

"Either it was a coincidence they were patrolling the area but more likely Pak Kadir got to the police station more quickly than we had estimated. Maybe after he reported what happened, they alerted a police car that was already in this area to check it out."

"That seems reasonable. But why weren't the police answering their phone?"

"I'm not sure. Perhaps I was dialing the wrong number or they were already busy planning to get here and had no one to answer."

"Well, no matter now," Stephen said as he massaged the back of his aching head and felt the bruise on his cheek. "The important thing is that they are here now. I hope this can be over soon and that the police can find my friend Agung, who is probably still being held in the house I escaped from."

"Well, as I said before, I believe God is on our side even in this."

"And I'm grateful I have a man of faith on my side."

"Thank you," Donri said after a long pause. Stephen could hear him shifting in his place and probably turning his gaze to his listener, even in the darkness. "That brings us to my previous question, Mr. Stephen. I take it you are not a man of faith?"

Uh oh. Stephen had gotten the sermonizer started again. He had other more pressing concerns right now than his personal belief system, but this old sage and spiritual question asker kept circling around to this same topic. This felt different than when Stephen's private space and philosophy were challenged by Chopper on the airplane, because the interrogator was a stranger. Donri was becoming a friend, an ally in this fight. He felt a sense of indebtedness to the old man. Plus a spiritual conversation could be a good distraction from thinking of which one of them Mustafal might shoot to show the police he was serious. He decided not to deflect the question and was thinking of a true answer when Donri offered, "Unless of course that is too private a question."

"Well, honestly, in my country that might be too private of a question but I don't mind being honest with you."

"I don't mean be so forward, but as I said before I don't believe in coincidence, and maybe this is an important question even in the middle of our trouble. I always like to give my students deeper questions rather than trite answers."

"Okay, fair enough. I guess I think of myself as basically a good person."

"That's good to hear but still not what I asked. Are you a man of faith?"

"You mean religious?"

"No, someone can be religious and not be a man of faith. I have known plenty of those. I mean, when you are going through something difficult like this, do you feel you are on your own and everything depends on you and your strategies, or do you feel like there is someone stronger you can lean on?"

Stephen thought for a moment before answering. "I guess I kind of believe that God is always there for us. It's like they say, God helps those who help themselves. So it mostly depends on us, but He helps us along the way." He was sure Donri had heard that Bible verse before—or was it an American proverb?

"I see."

There was silence between them and Donri was either deep in thought for his next response or he didn't want to pry anymore. Stephen made it easier for him to volley back the theme if he wanted to. "How does that sound to you?"

"Hmm. Well honestly that sounds like, how do you Americans say, like a bunch of baloney?"

Stephen was charmed with the old man's candor. "Oh yeah?" he said back with a spark of jest in his tone. "How so?"

Another long pause. "Either God is with us or He isn't. If He is with us, then there is always someone stronger right next to us we can lean on. If so, we would always cry out to Him when we are in trouble. If He's not, then have faith in your own thinking and strategy and leave God out. But there is no really in-between ground. You either trust in Him or you don't."

Stephen thought about firing back with charges of false dichotomies, weak premises or any other ammunition he could remember from debate class in high school, but the guy was so genuine in his beliefs, so sincere. Taking Donri on, especially in their predicament, would be like taking issue with an exquisite museum exhibit.

Donri continued. "I say we cry out to God and watch him deliver us. I believe He is with us in this dark cave, not in an abstract way but in a real here and now way."

"Okay, I see your point. Why don't you do the praying for both of us? I think you have more practice than me."

"I'm sorry, Mr. Stephen," Donri said with some emphasis. "Not like that. God wants to get your attention, right here and right now, even before He rescues us. He already has my attention but He wants yours. He loves you and wants you to experience His love and power, even in this place. You yourself can call out to Him."

Stephen wasn't sure what to make of that or how to respond. He thought about it in the silent darkness which offered no other distraction. Calling out to God in prayer felt so personal, so intimate. He wasn't comfortable enough to do that himself, much less in front of a seasoned pro. Besides that, he didn't feel worthy, since he spent most of his life keeping God at a cordial distance. He didn't know how to convey all this to Donri and he was trying to formulate an honest yet understandable answer. Finally, Donri broke in again. "I'm sorry, my new friend," he said, more softly. "I sense that I have pushed too far. Old men do that sometimes without realizing it. Maybe we should just give God a chance and watch Him come through for us?"

Stephen was still feeling exposed and wanted to think of his next answer, an intelligible one devoid of clichés. But their conversation was interrupted by the scraping of footsteps coming their way. The screen of a cell phone could be seen approaching and then the outline of Mustafal's body, holding the phone in one hand and the gun in the other. Stephen grabbed for Donri's arm and pulled him into a tighter huddle. They both looked up while Mustafal bent down menacingly over them, the light from his cell phone casting his face in an eerie glow.

He demanded something of Donri with a growl, placed the phone face-up on the ground in the middle of their tight triangle, then pulled a folded knife out of his back pocket and pointed it toward Stephen. It was the kind of knife that had lots of tools folded in with it, more apt for a backpacker than a terrorist. He grunted toward Donri which must have been his indication for the old man to serve as translator again.

"He says that if he shoots us, the police will hear and might come inside the cave. But if he cuts us they will not know. He says he will cut us if we don't do what he says, and if we try to run from the cave, he will shoot us."

Mustafal squatted down and stared hard into Stephen's eyes to emphasize his threat. Stephen had no trouble believing him.

"The best thing for you is to let us go, son." Donri calmly said. Stephen was surprised that he was answering back in English, either for Stephen's benefit or because he was too mentally exhausted to keep on translating. "You know how this is going to end. The police are going to bring you to jail and if you harm us, you will never get out of that jail."

Mustafal apparently understood the counter-threat in English and answered back with fast-paced verbal jousting, spittle flying from his face.

Donri remained calm. "Besides, you can't hurt me. I'm already a dead man. And you will be too unless you surrender to the police." He then repeated the phrase in Indonesian, apparently to make sure Mustafal got the point. What in the world was he doing? Was he trying to dare Mustafal into a fight?

The effect of Donri's words electrified Mustafal into a rage, which he directed at Stephen instead of his debating opponent. Mustafal pressed the tip of the small knife into Stephen's chest and Stephen dared not move.

Well maybe this old guy doesn't have anyone or anything to live for, but I do. He had to fight for Leah and his children. "Yes, yes, we will do as you say, Mustafal. We will do as you say." Stephen held both hands up, sucked his chest in and away from the knife and lowered his head as a sign of submission.

Mustafal and Donri argued back and forth in Indonesian and Stephen scooted away from their heated exchange. Mustafal's distorted face spewed out his threats and Donri answered back with a calm tone and demeanor. The old guy was either out of mind or bold beyond belief. Why argue back with the madman? Why not just submit?

At one point in the argument, Mustafal pulled out his gun and shook it toward Stephen who was praying under his breath and promising himself he would be a different man if he ever survived this.

Finally, Mustafal tucked the gun into his pants pocket and gave Donri another tongue lashing in Indonesian, the loudest Stephen had heard yet. Apparently this was the last word in the argument as Donri didn't respond. Then Mustafal turned to Stephen. "You stay here or I cut you. You try escape and I shoot you. Tell grandfather to shut up."

Stephen nodded his head and looked toward the ground to show he would not argue further. Mustafal stomped back toward the front of the cave, taking their only light source with him, and the inky black darkness returned. Stephen formulated his questions while they waited in silence, feeling flustered with Donri's foolhardy response to Mustafal's own foolishness.

Before Stephen could question the strategy of bold truth telling, Donri was the first to ask his question. "Do you know why he kidnapped you? Is it for money or for a symbol maybe?"

Stephen put his questions on hold and pondered that. Honestly he wasn't sure. "He told us he was a Muslim terrorist and he hasn't asked for any money yet. My friend Agung probably knows more by now. He is still locked up with Mustafal's two other partners. He hasn't let us know his demands yet, but I think it is probably ideological more than financial." He wondered if his English vocabulary was going too high in his explanation.

"Yes, ideological is always stronger than financial," Donri answered slowly and thoughtfully. "This is a man who believes something very strongly, enough to take great risks."

"What were you arguing about with him?"

"I was just trying to reason with him, explain his options to him. The fact that he was arguing back shows that he was at least considering what I was saying. He didn't like what I had to say but I think he knows deep down it's the truth. The best course of action for him is to surrender and then hope for the best for himself. But that not might help him with his ideological goals, so he feels divided. Plus he is very scared. That's why he keeps yelling at us, to show us he is not."

Stephen considered the psychoanalysis and had to admire it. "Very insightful, Donri."

"Thanks. Though theology is my field, I like to think of myself as a student of psychology too."

"I can see that. What do you think he will do now?"

"I don't think he knows yet. Only God knows, and as you Americans like to say, your guess is as good as mine. What is your guess?"

"I guess we'll find out. I just want to get back to my family. I'm praying for a safe return to them and for Agung too."

"Glad to hear you are praying. Always a good option."

Stephen chuckled. "I think I've prayed more in the last 24 hours than I have in the last two decades."

"And I think God has noticed. We should also pray for Mustafal."

"Why's that?"

"Well, Jesus said to love your enemies. Not always easy, I can say from experience. Let's pray that he comes to his senses and doesn't do anything else so foolish. I have to admit, I kind of admire the guy."

Stephen was taken aback, but his expression of shock went unseen in the darkness. "Why in the world would you say that?"

"He is a man who believes something so deeply that he is willing to take great risks. Not like the rest of us. I don't agree with his methods, but I have to admire the strength of his convictions and his willingness to carry them out."

"Well, I think he is an evil man for the way he has treated us and I hope he gets what he deserves."

"Ah yes, justice, getting what one deserves."

He sensed that the theologian-philosopher-psychoanalyst wanted to take the conversation in a direction toward the merits of justice versus mercy, but Stephen was too tired, thirsty and physically weak to delve into another deep discourse. The more pressing need was to focus on their immediate predicament and prepare for Mustafal's next move.

"I assume it is dark by now out there, Donri. Will the police try to storm this cave later tonight, do you think? Do they have night goggles here?"

"I'm not sure what those are."

"Glasses that help you see in the dark."

Donri paused before answering. "I doubt the police have those here out in the village, but we have them."

"What do you mean?" Even as the question left his mouth, Stephen realized he had just walked into another sermon trap.

"The eyes of faith. Seeing into the dark and still moving ahead."

Man, this guy is good. Slightly annoying, but good.

In the space of the silence that followed, Stephen tried to think of a way to guide the conversation back to safer, shallower waters. "Two weeks ago I would have never imagined myself hiding in a cave, being kidnapped by a madman and discussing strategy with my new friend, an Indonesian seminary professor of all people." Stephen laughed and Donri reciprocated weakly.

"We never know where the road will take us, and that is one thing you can count on in this life, my friend," Donri finally answered, a bit too loud for Stephen's comfort level. Stephen definitely didn't want another Mustafal intrusion.

"So what do we do now?" Stephen asked in a whispered tone, trying to give Donri the hint to talk more quietly.

"Well, we've already asked God to help us, so I suggest we wait for Him to do what He does best." Donri was talking still at full volume.

"What's that?" Stephen intoned in an even lower voice, barely an audible whisper, emphasizing his pressing concern that they could still be overheard.

"What was that?" Donri responded, even more loudly. "I couldn't hear you."

Stephen leaned even closer toward Donri. He was starting to feel exasperated with the old man. But every time he sparred back, he felt affection for him, like a kindly old grandpa that people bestowed with forgivable allowances. "I was asking what it is that God does best," Stephen repeated, even more softly.

"Rescue people," Donri stated confidently.

PART III

FRIDAY

CHAPTER TWENTY-ONE

With no watch or light reference in the pitch blackness, Stephen could only guess the time. It felt like the middle of the night. Donri had settled back into sleep with his back against the cave's wall. Though exhausted, Stephen still couldn't sleep. He kept thinking about next steps and what would be the end of this showdown. Thankfully Mustafal hadn't paid them another nightly visit and he had to assume his captor was crouched low and aiming his gun at the mouth of the cave while watching for moving silhouettes against the night sky. Either that or he had snuck off somewhere into the darkness and slipped through the police's perimeter.

Stephen imagined that a large police force had gathered outside and were surrounding the cave, yet prudent enough to not suddenly storm in and cause Mustafal to start shooting blindly. They were probably plotting their next move, too.

Suddenly a crackle of noise split the silence, startling Stephen and waking up Donri. A garbled voice spoke through a loud megaphone. The police were finally making contact! Stephen hoped that Donri had pulled out of his deep slumber enough to make out what they were saying.

The amplified voice spoke again and Mustafal shouted something back angrily. So he hadn't exited the scene and was still in charge of this cave and Stephen's nightmare.

A few seconds ticked by and Mustafal started yelling again.

"What's he saying?" Stephen whispered.

Donri must have straightened himself up and was leaning in to hear because when he answered back his voice was just a few inches away. "The police told him that if he surrendered and came out nobody would get hurt. He answered he would kill both his hostages before he did that. He also demanded that they bring something to eat and drink."

More yelling by Mustafal.

"Not good," Donri answered before Stephen could ask. "He said he is going to show them what he is capable of if they don't believe his threats."

"What does that mean?"

"I'm not exactly sure but it doesn't sound good."

They could see the light from Mustafal's cell phone screen bouncing toward them and Stephen's body tensed up. Mustafal barked something and they both stood, Donri requiring a little help from Stephen.

Mustafal yelled out something in Indonesian and circled around behind Stephen, pressing the barrel of the gun into his back. Stephen's hands instinctively shot up and Mustafal slowly marched them both forward toward the mouth of the cave. Stephen was too afraid to ask for a translation with a gun in his back and kept his hands folded over his head. It was tough to walk forward still in his socks and in the darkness but he managed not to stumble which might cause the gun to release its payload into his back. When they got near the opening there was a faint light from the moon to brighten the path. Donri was walking parallel to Stephen and not answering back to Mustafal's hissing and threats.

They came to the cave's entrance, and Mustafal wedged his body in between the shoulders of his two captives. He waved his gun up in the air and shouted something loudly in Indonesian, stinging Stephen's eardrums. Was he going to kill one of them right now in front of the police to show them he did indeed mean business?

A bright light from the trees and bushes suddenly washed over the three of them, blinding Stephen temporarily. He wanted to cover his face with his hands but thought better of moving a muscle in this standoff and instead squinted his eyes tightly. Mustafal shouted something else to them, and then pointed the gun right at Donri's temple.

Oh God no.

There was no click or discharge, but plenty ranting in Indonesian by Mustafal.

The police answered back through their megaphone and Mustafal wrapped his free hand around Stephen's chest with his gun still pointed at Donri's head. He tugged on them from behind and Stephen understood his intention for the three of them to retreat back into the cave.

The amplified voice answered back again and Mustafal turned around and screamed out his response. Stephen ignored the pain in his ears and concentrated on not tripping over something. When they were far enough away from the entrance, Mustafal pushed them away from him and said in English, "Go to back."

Stephen obeyed and helped settle Donri back down to his previous spot. Again Donri didn't have to be asked before he gave the translation. "Mustafal told them he would kill one of us if they didn't do exactly as he said. He repeated his demand for some food and drink to be brought and left at the entrance of the cave. He also asked for a flashlight and a cell phone. Not sure why he wants an extra cell phone as he already has one. But I do know he wants to show them that he does have two hostages in here. That's why we were brought out. He said if they met his demands, nobody would get hurt."

"And what did the police say?"

"They said they will do what he says."

"That's a relief."

"Mustafal warned them that if they tried to do anything tricky or to deceive him, he would kill one of us to show that he is serious."

"I believe him."

"Me too."

"But don't worry, my friend. As I said before I think the old man will be the first to go."

Stephen imagined Donri smiling as he quipped that line. He was continually amazed at how the old guy had a sense of humor even in this high stress situation.

"Well, I guess that means we will get breakfast soon," Stephen said, wanting to change the subject to something not so morbid. "Or at least he will."

"Yes, someone will, hopefully us. It could be a long night."

"It already has been. But I'm really glad I have you here with me, Om Donri."

"And I'm glad to have a new friend too, Mr. Stephen."

≈≈▯≈≈

After the umpteenth time it vibrated, Happy finally decided to sneak a peek at his cell phone. He calculated it was about 3 AM, the darkest it could possibly get on this moonlit night. Most of the police were focusing their attention on China Cave, and only one officer stayed behind in the triangle of three police cars parked together. The other officers were hiding and taking their positions in the bushes nearer to the cave. The lone officer left behind was now standing at the front of the police car perimeter, peering into the darkness toward the stalled action. Happy made his move, slowly turning himself in the undergrowth, pulling out the phone and arching his body over the screen so no light could escape and give away his position. There were several messages from Dina and several more from Mustafal, both of them wanting to know where he was, what he was doing and what was happening. He didn't feel like responding because he felt so nervous. What if the officer closest to him suddenly looked over and saw a faint light in the bushes? If he were caught he could go to jail.

Suddenly he heard an amplified voice, and at first he thought it was coming from his own phone. Had he accidentally pressed the speakerphone button just as Mustafal called? But then he realized the voice was coming from a policeman calling out to the cave on his megaphone. A few minutes later Mustafal screamed out some sort of response, but Happy couldn't make out exactly what he had said. A police officer turned on his powerful flashlight from his staked-out position toward the entrance of the cave. There was Mr. Stephen and an older man standing together, with Mustafal right behind them, yelling out something and waving a gun. When he did get a gun? That was never in any of their planning—Happy would have remembered that.

The policeman answered back on the megaphone that they would do as he said, whatever that was. With all the police attention riveted on the cave's entrance, Happy bravely sent one message on his cell phone to Dina, to inform her that Mr. Stephen had been found, that he was at China Cave with Mustafal, and that the police were here also so don't come. Call off the other search parties too. He checked to make sure the phone was still on mute, then tucked it away back in his front pocket. He then had to decide if he would make a run for it in the darkness while their attention was on the cave, or if he should keep hiding in the bushes.

The phone kept vibrating back, undoubtedly from Dina, which made concentrating on the decision at hand harder. After weighing his options, and imagining more police possibly on the way, he felt that staying put would be the safest decision. He would no longer move at all, not even to answer his phone, and would become one with the scrub brush. He could wait this one out.

≈≈□≈≈

After their recent ordeal and chatting for about a half hour more, Donri fell back asleep again, resting against the same smooth contour of the cave wall. The old man had some serious inner peace to be able to drift back to sleep so soon after all the action. Stephen was badly in need of some sleep too, but his thoughts were hammering away inside his mind and keeping him wide awake. His hunger and thirst also fought away the slumber. Stephen wasn't sure if the police met Mustafal's demand for breakfast, but if they did, none of it seemed to be for the hostages.

If Mustafal's motivations were merely financial, he would cut his losses and get the best deal for himself. But there was no room for bargaining in the man's temperament and thinking. As Donri said, his reasons were stronger— ideological—and he was hell bent on carrying out his mission, whatever it was.

What is your mission? The question seemed to come from somewhere outside of himself, piercing him out of the cave's darkness. Instead of swatting it away, as he normally would, he embraced and pondered it. There were no other distractions or comforts in the darkness anyway.

What is my mission? To be brutally honest with himself he would have to admit that he was mission-less, living inside a very small story. He was trudging through his days, and usually half asleep at that, just punching in and getting by, hoping for a little entertainment at the end of each grinding day. He and Leah had very little emotional intimacy and he surely wasn't fighting for his kids' hearts either. *When did my heart die? Why can't I be more like Mustafal, believe in something so strongly that I am willing to die for it?*

He turned his head toward Donri even though he couldn't see him. *Or like Donri here. I don't agree with all his beliefs but he is so passionate about them, so full of life. He's living so full of purpose.*

Stephen again thought of Chaz Wilton and envied even him. *All of these men have something I don't, a fight to live for something bigger than themselves. God, what's wrong with me?*

As if on cue, subconsciously sensing that someone was two feet away pondering life's deeper questions, Donri started stirring. He yawned aloud, sounding like a squeaky hinge. Stephen couldn't see him in the darkness but it sounded like he was stretching too.

"Stephen, are you awake?"

"Yes. Good morning."

"Good morning to you."

"Well I hope it is anyway."

"Yes." Another yawn. "Me too. Were you able to sleep?"

"Not really. Too many things to think about, although I am so tired. It was just me and my thoughts for the last few hours."

"I'm sorry to hear that."

"Donri, can I ask you an honest question?"

"I love honest questions." The query undoubtedly energized the kindly theologian as Stephen could now hear a lift in his voice. "What's on your mind?"

"I was thinking about what you said earlier, about not believing in coincidences. Maybe someone is trying to get my attention."

"What do you mean someone?"

"Well, I'm not sure if I am really ready to say this, but maybe God."

Donri paused before answering. The moment felt so real and raw to Stephen that he hoped Donri wouldn't answer back sternly with something religious but rather respond gently to his honesty.

"I sure believe God speaks to us all the time. Why would that be hard to admit?"

"I don't know. I guess I can believe that there are greater reasons out there for things happening but I'm uncomfortable with the idea of a personal God."

Another pause and Stephen spoke again before Donri could answer. "Anyway this question came to me a few minutes ago, and I don't know the answer to it. This question formed in my mind: 'What is your mission?' I thought maybe, that voice was coming from somewhere outside of me."

"Like God maybe was speaking to you?"

So easy for him—the old preacher swam in this spiritual stuff every day. But this was hard for Stephen, to sort through his complex and contradictory thoughts and to be able to even formulate them aloud. But he really did want an exclamation point on his life when this ordeal was over, with or without Chaz Wilton's help, and he knew he had to honestly wrestle with these questions to get there.

"Okay, I can admit that. Maybe God was speaking to me. Maybe even a personal God. But why would he ask me a question and not give me the answer?"

Donri breathed out heavily through his nose and Stephen perceived it as more of a muffled chuckle than a sigh. "Do you know what God's very first question to mankind was, according to the Scriptures?"

"I'm afraid I was never a star pupil in Sunday School. Our family didn't go much and it's been a long time since I darkened the doorway of a church..." Stephen caught himself in the idiom. "Since I attended church."

"Yes, that's okay." The shift back into sermon gear came through in Donri's voice. "Now they say that when an omniscient God asks you a question, it's not because he is seeking information." He paused and let Stephen ponder before continuing. "The first thing that God asked man was, 'Where are you?'"

Another thoughtful pause which Stephen was grateful for. This was deep stuff.

"Adam was afraid and thought he could hide from God. And God asked that question out of heartbreak, not anger. He was grieved that the one He created was hiding from him. He wanted a close relationship with mankind. He still does. That's why He sent Jesus to us."

Stephen nodded, though it couldn't be seen, and settled on the word "close relationship." He had never thought about God much except as an ethereal presence in the sky somewhere, more of a philosophical something than a personal someone. Always there for you but never really there. *Kind of like me. I've created God in my own image.* The thought jarred him, again like it had come from somewhere or someone else, and it was pulling out the posts of the fence of logic that had insulated him from religious, other-worldly matters.

"I'm an old man and you are still young." Donri interjected. "Let the One who has been seeking you find you. You can come out of hiding because He cares for you."

Another long silence followed, with nothing else to do but ponder what the old preacher man had just said. Stephen knew that Donri's deep questions and pointed advice were coming out of a heart that wanted his best, so he at least had to give this sermon a fair shake. If God was going to this great length to get Stephen's attention, he could at least be genuinely attentive.

"You know," Stephen finally said while sifting sand through his fingers from the cave's floor. "In a lot of ways I have been hiding. You're right. Hiding right here feels very familiar to me. I hide from my wife. I hide from people getting too close to me. For a long time I've been hiding from anything real, from God, I guess you could say…"

"That's a good place to start, my friend. To let these questions God is asking you to *masuk*, I mean uh, penetrate you."

Stephen wasn't sure what to say to that and he kept sifting the sand.

Donri continued. "If you ever read the Bible you will see that Jesus often gave questions to people when they came to him with their questions. Sometimes he told stories in response. I don't believe God always gives us the easy answers, because He wants a relationship with us, like Jacob wrestling with God all night to get a blessing from him."

"I'm afraid I don't really know that story."

"Oh, there are so many good stories in there. You should read them sometime!"

"Yes, I should." Donri's enthusiasm for his holy book felt contagious.

"Now let's get back to your first question. What is your mission?"

The question felt so vulnerable, and Stephen suddenly felt a pull to hop back down a safer bunny trail of logic and reasoning. "You know, Donri, I am in a lot of stress right now and this could be some sort of a foxhole conversion."

"I'm not familiar with that term."

"It means...well, that doesn't really matter." He was going to do this—come out of hiding. Stephen forced himself back to the question at hand. "I don't know what my mission is. How can I?"

There. He said it. He didn't know his purpose in life and he once again hoped Donri wouldn't stuff a thick sermon down his throat. So far he felt safe to share, feeling comfortable in the back and forth exchange instead of a one-way monologue from a spiritual expert. Maybe it was the cave's darkness that was bringing out all this brute honesty.

"Thanks for your sincerity Stephen. I admire that you can wrestle with these questions, even here in this circumstance. I can't give you an easy answer to that. God asks me the same question, and it reminds me again of Jacob wrestling with the angel of God all night, which you can read about later. Jacob came away from that experience changed and received a new name as a result. He was a completely new man after that encounter with God."

"Wow," was all Stephen could think to respond.

"Yes, and maybe you are meant to be here to wrestle not just with these questions but with God himself."

"Whoa," Stephen replied, feeling a bit silly with his mono-syllabic answers. But Donri's insight stopped him cold and he couldn't think of a more intelligent rebuff on the spot. Was God really trying to engage with him, Stephen Cranton of Sacramento, California? Was that what this trip and kidnaping were all about? Stephen halfway doubted that, imagining that anyone going through a stressful situation like a kidnapping would also start suddenly pondering life's deeper questions.

"You and Mustafal are men of such passion," Stephen finally managed to say. "I do want to get there."

"Well, I don't know about Mustafal because I think he is misguided. But for me, passion isn't something you go out and get. It's not about how to find passion. It's about...."

Stephen sincerely wanted to hear Donri continue but they both heard Mustafal's voice coming toward them, his weak cell phone light leading the way. The altar call had ended and it was now back to reality.

CHAPTER TWENTY-TWO

Johanna Grazen slipped out of bed, quietly trying not to wake up her sleeping cat Nuzzles who was curled up on her favorite blanket in the corner of the room. If the chunky feline were summoned from slumber, the meowing alarm for food wouldn't turn off until Nuzzles received her morning food offering. Johanna didn't feel like dealing with all that in the middle of the night so she tiptoed downstairs to the living room. Once there she realized she left the novel she was reading on her nightstand, but she didn't want to risk reentering her room with Nuzzles still sleeping. Johanna wished she could sleep so soundly, but her mind was already racing after a bizarre day dealing with an obnoxious American and trying to sort through misinformation about a kidnapping.

She glanced over from the couch at the light glow of her desktop computer and considered powering it fully on. Checking emails probably wouldn't have the same soothing effect as the historical romance novel she was reading, but she thought she might as well try. Maybe she could do an internet search on "Carlton Easley" and find out more about her latest unappreciative client. While the machine booted up she brewed a cup of non-caffeinated herbal tea. Settling down at the desk, she scanned through her emails and her eyes settled on the email last sent to her office account. She read it twice and it got her mind fully cranking. The email was from a woman named Leah Cranton who said no one had heard from her husband for two days on a business trip to Indonesia. The worried wife had found Johanna's email on the consulate website, listing her as the official liaison of ex-pats living in East Java. Leah said that her husband had never shown up at the Surabaya branch office where he was supposed to conduct a training. She was on the way there now, apparently to look for him. His name was Stephen Cranton. Leah requested a quick response to her email, wanting to know what her next step should be and when someone would be considered a missing person in Indonesia.

The email seemed legit, and reading between the lines she imagined the woman was near frantic. Johanna fired back a quick reply, saying she would check into it first thing in the morning, and gave her personal cell phone number. She told Leah to call once she arrived at the airport in the morning, and that she could come straight to the consulate if she hadn't heard anything yet. Even though this step wasn't required protocol, she would want someone to go the extra mile for her in a crisis.

She googled both names, Stephen Cranton and Carlton Easley, but didn't find anything of relevance. There was nothing related on the *Firdaus Rokok* website either. After finishing off her tea, she decided that she better go back to bed as she would need her energy in the morning. Slipping back under the sheets, Nuzzles stirred and starting meowing for food as she had feared. "*Aduh*," she whispered, the Indonesian version of a sigh she had picked up from her co-workers.

Johanna flipped the sheets off and thought to herself that even without Nuzzle's insistence, she probably wouldn't have been able to get back to sleep anyway, not with Leah Cranton's email on her mind. Nuzzles seemed pleased that she was getting out of bed early and rubbed her plush fur against her legs.

She brewed a stronger concoction of caffeine and then scanned the morning *Jawa Pos* newspaper which had already hit her doorstep in the pre-dawn. She flipped through it for a while but it couldn't really hold her attention. Instead, she looked out the window into her small courtyard and replayed questions from the day before while sipping on her coffee.

The biggest question in her mind was if this were the beginning stage of a new surge of terrorist plots in Indonesia. In a recent security briefing she learned that the CIA had been picking up chatter about more Americans being targeted for terrorist attacks, but nothing about kidnappings. So far Indonesia had been spared that particular brand of terrorism from the Middle East. There had always been security threats, especially when anti-American sentiment got whipped into a frenzy by religious zealots, and the embassy in Jakarta was in the habit of sending out vague security warnings via email to American citizens living across the islands. Like most of her fellow citizens, Johanna had grown numb to those general warnings to avoid large crowds and vary daily routines. But what if large-scale terrorist attacks or widespread kidnappings were being planned and hatched from East Java and this was just the beginning? Shouldn't the outpost of the United States government in Indonesia do everything it could to take a preemptive strike against it?

These were the questions that captivated her mind as she stirred her strong coffee. She decided to make an easy breakfast, frying up a little bacon she had found, not always easy in Indonesia. It was going to be a long day, and after a short night's sleep, she was going to need both protein and extra caffeine to get through it.

≈≈◻≈≈

As the first light rays of dawn appeared on the horizon, Happy's phone vibrated in his pocket yet again. He had been ignoring them, at his count a total of twenty-five missed calls and unanswered text messages. The police were still absorbed in the long stand-off near the cave's entrance which was now several hours old. The one officer that was supposed to be guarding the rear perimeter had grown bored and started reading a newspaper, probably yesterday's, that he found in one of the squad cars. Happy was feeling bored too, sitting still and uncomfortable in the bushes through the pre-dawn hours. Maybe as long as his phone was on mute and he didn't make a sudden movement, he could chance a quick peek at it.

Most of the notifications were missed calls from Mustafal and a few from Dina. Then he read a long string of angry text messages from his older cousin. Where are you? What was taking so long? The police are here and I need your help. The last message was the longest, and probably took a long time for

Mustafal to type out on a simple cell phone. The police had surrounded the cave (which Happy already knew of course) and he was holding Stephen (whom Mustafal called Carlton of course) and an older man named Pak Donri inside. Mustafal wanted an immunity deal with the police and needed Happy to serve as the go-between, someone he could trust as a negotiator. If the police didn't want to negotiate he would kill one of the men inside the cave. After that they would surely want to. Happy needed to approach the police, say he received a message from his cousin, and volunteer as the head negotiator. Lastly, Happy shouldn't bring the phone with him when he talked with the police because there was too much incriminating evidence on it. Mustafal would give him a cell phone that he had demanded from the police, one clean of all their previous phone logs and text messages.

Happy regretted the decision to look at his phone because now he had an even heavier decision to make than whether to run or hide. Would he go along with this new demand?

As he was thinking it over, a new text message vibrated in, a warning from Mustafal that if he didn't get any help from little cousin he would surrender and tell the police about his involvement in the kidnapping too. Mustafal was always so persuasive with his arguments, and if those didn't work he often resorted to intimidation. The threat left Happy frozen with fear, feeling too cowardly to go along with the plan and too petrified of the consequences not to. He decided to text Dina back to let her know his position and predicament.

As he started to write out a long and complicated message to Dina, whom he imagined to be very anxious for any update by now, the police officer closest to him started stirring. The man tossed the newspaper he had been reading back into his squad car, stretched his arms up, and started walking toward Happy's direction. Had he seen the movement of Happy fiddling with his phone from his peripheral vision? He wasn't walking like he was tracking someone—it was more of the leisurely pace of someone just enjoying the beach scenery. Happy hunkered down as much as he could without twitching a muscle as the officer continued his saunter straight toward the clump of bushes. Then the officer planted both feet squarely in front of the hiding spot and started to reach for something.

Happy closed his eyes and waited for the Indonesian "Come out with your hands up" command. He braved one eye open, fearing to see a gun pointed at his face but saw the man was instead reaching for his zipper. The officer was about to relieve himself in the bushes, looking casually over the horizon toward the beach and not down into the dense greenery, his target area.

Happy had suffered much humiliation over his life, primarily because of his limited mental capacity. Growing up, other kids often teased him that he was *kurang pintar*, less than clever. Yet he still possessed a modicum of personal pride and, despite his modest intelligence, he always tried to conduct himself with a higher than average personal code of ethics, going along with a kidnapping plot notwithstanding. For Happy there were some lows that he was not willing to sink to, and getting urinated on by another man definitely was on that list.

"Stop," he yelled out frantically. "Someone is in here!"

The police officer jumped back in fright, nearly losing his balance but recovering quickly. Zipping back up, he commanded the bushman to identify himself and drew his weapon. Happy fought his way upwards out of the thicket with his hands up.

"What are you doing in there?" the police officer demanded in a harsh hue of Javanese.

"I'm sorry, sir, I got a text message from my cousin..." As soon as the words left his mouth Happy realized he was revealing too much truth.

The officer kept the gun pointed at Happy's chest and glared at him with a silent stare that meant keep going.

"I, uh, I came here because the police are here and my cousin said he needs my help. He is the one inside the cave."

"Keep your hands up and come with me." The officer motioned with his gun for Happy to walk in front of him back toward the police cars.

"I didn't do anything wrong," Happy protested, and then felt tears welling up and wanting to join in with his pleas of innocence. "My cousin called and said he needed my help. I can be your go-between with him because he trusts me. I can be the negotiator."

The officer was unmoved by the offer of assistance. "Keep your hands up," he repeated as they marched together toward base camp. The officer called for backup into his radio while he kept his gun trained on the suspect's back. Happy could see a couple of officers rise from their hiding spots near the cave and make their way down the incline of trails back toward the beach parking area. After so many hours of stakeout, they were probably excited about any new development worth examining. Happy couldn't control his emotions anymore and the tears found release. By the time he was led to the middle of the triangle of police cars, he was sobbing.

The apprehending officer patted Happy down, finding only his motorcycle keys and his cell phone. Two other officers kept their guns pointing at their sniffling detainee while the first officer handcuffed him and then immediately started reading through the text messages on his telltale phone.

"Who is Mustafal?" the first officer demanded. "How do you know him?"

"I didn't do anything," Happy protested, trying unsuccessfully to sound indignant as he sidestepped the question. "Why are you arresting me?"

The officer repeated the question and gave Happy a yank by the handcuffs as the other officers clipped their handguns back into their holsters. "Just answer the question," one of them snarled.

"He is my cousin. He asked me to come and help him. I can talk to him if you'd like. I didn't know he was in trouble."

The first officer kept scrolling down the text messages and more questions started popping out. Who was Dina? Why was she looking for Mustafal too? What had they done? Who is this man named Stephen? Or is it Carlton? Obviously they had found a goldmine of evidence on the phone.

"Can I speak with my lawyer?" Happy inquired politely. All three officers laughed. That was a good one.

"You need to answer our questions."

Happy didn't want to do that, as that would get him into even more trouble. He wanted to pretend that he was an innocent bystander, and that his cousin had called him to come and help and he didn't know anything about any kidnapping. That was going to be hard to do with all the overwhelming evidence of the string of text messages. If he were clever like Dina or a good liar like Mustafal he could talk his way out of this and explain it all away. But he couldn't. He was just Happy. He started crying again.

~~□~~

Agung and Dina's hiding spot, behind a tight clump of palm trees, was close enough to the action to see most of what was happening. They looked toward the tall rock cropping that held China Cave in its thick belly and debated their options, keeping their voices to a whisper. The cave's entrance was now easier to see in the soft morning light, but their decision of what to do next was no clearer.

When Happy was nabbed by the police, Agung favored still waiting it out and watching from afar. But when they saw Happy crying as the officer questioned him, Dina repeated her resolve that they had to come out of hiding and help him. She felt they owed him that, but Agung wasn't convinced.

"If we wait any longer, it will be too late. He needs our help now."

"But if we help him, you could get in trouble too."

"It's too late for that. I don't think any of us can avoid the consequences now." She looked past him through the trees into the huddle of police officers now surrounding Happy. Her eyes sparkled in determination that he knew could not be easily slowed down. "But I don't see any consequences for you, Agung. You haven't done anything wrong."

"Yes, but I want to do the right thing here. Just follow me and let me do the talking. I will tell them we were just walking by and wanted to see if there was anything we could do to help."

"Okay, whatever. Let's just go now." He was hoping for a little thanks for his newfound bravery to approach the police, but she was too concerned for her distressed partner to think of anything else.

He sidestepped backwards from the trees to the edge of the beach and then started walking on the sand, to make it look like they just happened to be strolling by. He held her hand as they climbed the embankment to the parking area and one of the officers saw them coming.

"Get back," he yelled at them. "There is a man with a gun in the cave."

They scuttled up the hill and ran behind the officers, crouching down low. Agung thought they were doing a pretty good job of looking like innocent bystanders. Happy wouldn't be able to see them from inside the huddle, but Agung could hear them questioning him and heard Dina's name mentioned once. Was Happy already spilling everything to them?

"Go back," the officer commanded. "Get back." He was pointing to the back perimeter of the crime scene. The two of them ran behind the triangle of police cars and crouched down again while the officer followed.

"What are you doing here?" he demanded.

"We were just walking by and saw all the police here. What's happening?"

In short statements the policeman informed them that there was a crazy man in the cave holding two hostages. They looked and acted shocked. "Stay here," he ordered, "and keep your head down."

Apparently no suspicion had been raised that the two of them might be involved in this in any way. The officer made his way back to his fellow policemen who were still asking their crying suspect a series of questions.

"Now what do we do?" Dina asked.

"This was your idea to come here," Agung whispered back, sounding angrier than he meant to.

"I know, but how do we help Happy?"

"Let's just keep our heads down, like the officer said. If Happy sees us he will call out to us. We can stay here for a while and try to hear what he is saying to them. That will give us some time to think about our next move."

She cast him a worried glance. "Okay, I just don't know what to do."

"We'll think of something," Agung assured her.

≈≈□≈≈

Happy kept crying under the insistent questioning from the police, all the while enduring the uncomfortable posture of having his arms handcuffed behind him. A volcano of truth started to rumble inside him, and he couldn't quite summon the will power to keep it stuffed back down. Finally, after more intense questioning, it erupted. Yes, he knew the gunman in the cave, named Mustafal, and he had indeed helped him kidnap the man with him now, an American named Stephen who was supposed to be Carlton Easley. He was so, so sorry that he ever went along. Please, please have mercy.

The effect of the sudden confession caused the officers to stop their interrogation and look to one another, as if to silently decide what to do with all this fresh intel. The honest words and tears continued to pour out of their suspect turned informant, and one of the officers patted Happy's shoulder with a comforting hand. Happy's crying eventually downgraded back to a sniffle and he wanted to wipe his nose with his sleeve but his arms were still pinned behind his back.

The officers conferred together out of Happy's earshot and one of them stepped back toward him. "There is one thing you can do to make this go easier on yourself. Help us get the hostages out of the cave. You know Mustafal and he might listen to you. Just do as we say now and later during the plea bargain we will let the judge know that you helped us in his capture and arrest."

"Yes, yes," Happy said, liking the sound of the words "plea bargain." But then the afterthought followed of facing down Mustafal's harsh interrogation inside the cave which could be just as effective as the police's outside. *Sudah jatuh tertimpa tangga pula.* You fall off the ladder and then the ladder falls on you.

"Go up there slowly with your hands up so he will see it is not a police officer coming. Ask what he wants and come back to tell us. If you try to join his side, this will go very badly for you. Do you understand?"

Happy nodded vigorously that he understood and they unlocked the handcuffs. "We will be watching you the whole time. We have guns and we have used them before." The officer uttered the last line with a stare that communicated he wasn't joking. He then punched a number into Happy's cell phone and handed it back to him. Then he asked for Happy's number and entered that into his own phone. "So far he has asked for three things—a cellphone, breakfast, and a flashlight. Here is your cell phone back. I've put my number into it if he wants to call us. Tell him that breakfast and the flashlight are on the way if he can be reasonable, and please let him know that surrender is the only way out of this."

Happy loosened up his arms and looked up toward the mouth of the cave. This was not going to be easy, but he had no choice now.

≈≈◻≈≈

Agung and Dina started to approach the policeman in charge of the back perimeter. Not only was he holding her hand, which was becoming normal, but had also placed his free arm around Dina's shoulder for extra emotional support. They had debated some more about who would do the talking, and Dina said that it didn't really matter at this point. They had to help Happy no matter who was their spokesperson. Agung thought it did matter and he volunteered to go first. If she disagreed with how he was handling it, she was to give his hand a squeeze as a silent cue and not say anything out loud in front of the police. He didn't want it to look like they had something to hide. After seeing how the police had treated Happy, Agung knew that the officer would slap those handcuffs on at the first sign of suspicion.

The officer turned from watching the scene unfolding up on the hill and seemed perturbed to be interrupted by two civilians. "I told you to stay down."

"Yes, I know, officer. We just wanted to see if we could help."

"No, you can't. Now go back behind the cars. I can't guarantee your safety here. The man in the cave has a gun."

They both responded with the appropriate shocked expressions and Agung counter-offered, "We know this area well and I have been in that cave many times. Maybe I can give you some information that you need?" Dina gave his hand a quick squeeze which he assumed meant he was a pathetic liar. That was true but he wanted to stay in charge so he kept playing the part of the helpful bystander, telling the officer that he grew up in this village and would be glad to assist with the schematics of the cave and the layout of the surrounding trails.

"Well, I was born and raised here too, and I've never seen you. What school did you go to?"

Uh oh. Another squeeze from Dina. The officer appeared to be about the same age as Agung and he realized the more he talked the more he would have to dig out of a hole of lies. He sputtered, trying in vain to think of the name of his alma mater, and Dina cut in. "What my boyfriend means is that we have been in that cave many times." She shot the officer a knowing, mischievous look. "He grew up not too far from here but my uncle lives right here in this village, Pak Umroh."

Either the image of a couple smooching in the cave or the name of a neighbor threw the officer off the trail. "Oh yeah, I know Pak Umroh. A good man. You are his niece?"

"Yes," she confirmed, then rattled on about Pak Umroh and coming to visit him as a little girl and the officer seemed quickly bored by the narrative. He glanced back to the action behind him, where there was a new development. All three of them looked up to see Happy struggling his way gingerly up the trail toward the cave with a cell phone balled up in his hand. What was he doing?

Dina squeezed Agung's hand again and he didn't know if that was a protest or a question. He squeezed back, not really knowing how he answered.

"I'm sorry, but I need to pay attention to what is happening here," the officer said, drawing his weapon. "Thank you for your offer to help us but please stay back and stay down." He trotted back to the clump of officers starting to stake out positions on the side of the hill and behind trees and didn't bother looking back to see if Agung and Dina had obeyed him.

They crouched down right where they were to watch. "Oh, poor Happy," Dina was saying to herself.

CHAPTER TWENTY-THREE

Stephen stood at attention when Mustafal stomped back into the back area of the cave. From the faint illumination of the cell phone light, he could see Mustafal's face grimaced into a tight, anxious expression. He was either feeling scared enough to do something foolish, or foolish enough to do something scary.

"You follow me," he said curtly with his gun pointed toward the pair and then turned and walked back toward the front of the cave. Stephen helped Donri to his feet and they started to follow.

Stephen thought this would be an excellent opportunity for a surprise attack. Just jump him while his devious mind was distracted, rip the gun from his hand and pin him to the ground. But it felt easier to watch a scene like that in a movie than to actually do it in real life. They dutifully followed until Mustafal stooped at the lookout spot near the entrance of the cave and motioned for his captives to walk in front of him, with the gun aimed at their backs to make sure they obeyed.

They did. Apparently he wanted them to move toward the cave's bright opening, but Stephen wasn't sure why. Maybe this was surrender and he was letting them go, just like that?

Mustafal grunted something from behind and Donri said it was a directive to place their hands up. Stephen did so while it took a couple of seconds for his eyes to adjust to the morning light and survey the scene before him. He counted several officers looking up from the trail and bushes, many with their weapons drawn. A lone figure was coming up the trail to them but he wasn't dressed in a policeman's uniform. When the man struggled a few more steps up the trail, Stephen saw that it

261

was Happy. What was he doing here, with the police behind him? It didn't make sense. He hoped beyond hope that the docile man was coming up to talk some sense into his ringleader.

Stephen felt exceedingly vulnerable with guns now pointed at him from both directions. His hands stayed straight up and stone still to show the officers in front of him and the madman behind him that he was just a neutral human shield in this showdown. Donri was also keeping his hands up and Stephen noticed them shaking, either from fear, weariness, or just old age.

When Happy finally planted his feet on the level spot just in front of the cave, he shot his hands up too, a cellphone clutched tightly in one of them. All three of them were reaching for the sky, an odd and awkward scene, and Stephen couldn't figure out who was in charge or what they were supposed to be doing now.

When Happy's face came into Mustafal's view, a barrage of Indonesian broke forth as Mustafal castigated his sidekick. Shuddering, Stephen dared not turn back and imagined Mustafal's harsh face contorting while he rebuked Happy, his hands possibly shaking the gun in anger with his finger twitching dangerously close to that trigger.

Donri wasn't translating, which was fine with Stephen, as he didn't want to attract any more attention in the middle of the tense standoff. Finally, Mustafal yelled out in English, "Everyone in here, now!"

Donri was the first to back up, slowly, and Stephen followed, while the police force watched the scene with rapt attention and aimed guns.

Stephen got a few steps backwards and crouched down, just next to Donri and too close to the argument between Happy and Mustafal. It was long and furious, Happy answering softly back to Mustafal's verbal rampage. They were all out of the gun sights of the police but Stephen kept his eye on Mustafal's weapon, now at his side but every now and then used in gestures to punctuate his points in the debate.

As the argument continued, Donri and Stephen took the opportunity to scoot a few paces back without being noticed. Donri whispered that the heated discussion centered on the issue of Mustafal not thinking the police believed he was serious. Happy kept countering that the police did think he was serious and that's why they were offering him a deal. Happy's plea was for his leader to let everyone go, come out and surrender. That way he wouldn't spend the rest of his life in prison. Mustafal countered that surrender would not help them meet any of their goals.

Stephen felt the frustration rising in him again, of being out of control for so long and having to wait for this terrorist to decide his fate. He desperately wanted to get back to his family and his life and be in control again, far away from the brute force of one lunatic.

The cell phone rang in Happy's still clutched hand and he answered it, listened for a few seconds and then tried to give it to Mustafal who refused to speak into it. Happy spoke softly into the phone and then hung up with a downcast expression on his face. What would the police do when Mustafal kept delaying? Were they patient like the police in American movies, negotiating for hours if need be? Stephen also felt flustered that he was continually ignorant about the rules of the game on this playing field.

As the argument dragged on, one that Mustafal seemed to be winning, Stephen stood and started pacing farther back toward the back of the cave. Still no one really noticed what he was doing. Donri was resting with his back against the wall in the cave's midsection, closer to the conversation and leaning toward it to eavesdrop.

Stephen thought about his options. He wondered about his worried wife and missed his kids. He tried praying again. He glanced back at Donri who seemed so calm and admired the old man's courage. It wasn't a Zen-like detachment from life's circumstances; it was more of a hope that a stronger power was at play, one that would get them all through this.

Mustafal and Happy didn't seem to tire in their argument over their own options, and Stephen decided to use the opportunity to verbally express his appreciation toward Donri. He stooped down and Donri stopped trying to overhear the other conversation, turning his attention toward Stephen.

"You know, Donri, something I have learned from you is that I need to be more fearless. You are so calm through all of this."

"Thanks, Stephen. But it's really not about me. Did you ever hear the story of Jesus when a big storm..."

Stephen didn't feel like another Sunday school lesson right then and tried to cut him off by going more personal.

"I look at you and see courage, and I look at me and see a pathetic man playing hide and go seek."

Donri started to ask a question, probably about what "hide and go seek" meant or maybe a counterpoint, but Stephen plowed on. He wanted to get this out. "You were right earlier. I've been hiding in this cave. I've been hiding on my job. I've been hiding from my kids. I've been hiding from my wife. And I've been hiding from God."

"Yes, you have."

The honest, sharp words jabbed him. He thought the seasoned pastor would offer some comfort when hearing his heartfelt confession. Stephen probably had never said something so gut honest out loud before, yet the old man dug the knife in deeper. That's what he sometimes felt from Leah, not rewarded for his rare displays of vulnerability but instead counter attacked. The old familiar emotional tug pulled on him to recoil, to take his ball and go home. But before he could quickly and deftly change the subject, Donri looked at him softly in the morning light streaming through the cave's entrance. "It's the last one you need to work on first, if you ask me," he said softly.

Stephen recalled what he had just said, "You mean, about hiding from God?"

"Yes, that's the one. That is the only thing that will give you the strength to come out of hiding."

"Is that how you seem to live without fear?"

"You could say that. It's like when King David said with God's help he could scale a wall."

"Well, I guess I need God's help to scale this wall then."

Donri didn't say anything but only smiled. Stephen thought the old man must have been delighted that all his sermonizing was finally getting through. A few moments of silence ticked by while Stephen felt a resolve rising up in him.

"I do want to come out of hiding. I do want to be more passionate."

"Yes, that good," Donri's smile spreading wider. "But if I may offer a suggestion."

"Sure, shoot." Stephen quickly realized it was a poor figure of speech considering the circumstances. "I mean, please continue. I think you were starting to talk about this earlier before Mustafal interrupted us."

"Yes," answered Donri, looking pleased that he had the floor. "When people are looking for passion they go on some adventure and then find it empty after a while. They are looking for a larger story to live in, but you won't find it there either."

"That's what I'm trying to do, I guess, find that larger story for my life. I really want more passion in my life and I read a book on the way here encouraging people to be more adventurous."

Donri cut him off. "That will never work!" He slapped his hand on his knee as if it were a pulpit. "You can't just be more adventurous. It's not like that because it's not about the story itself, but about the author of the story. He is the author and perfecter of your faith and the only way to know what that story is to know Him personally."

The words were going through Stephen's mind and he thought to himself that this was good stuff, like he had climbed a mountain and was getting ancient wisdom from an Asian elder at the summit, and no longer deep inside a darkened cave. These were the core questions of life. What does it mean to be truly alive? Could he just lift himself out of his life stupor from sheer will power and become someone more alive? He knew himself enough to know that he wasn't strong enough to lift himself by his own bootstraps. He wanted to add passion to his life, like you would buy a new set of stylish clothes and feel better about yourself. Feelings like that were so fleeting and lasted as long as New Year's resolutions. He was so tired of his own small story and ready for a change, but Donri was saying it was more than that. It seemed to be more about engagement with God than just a self-powered personality adjustment.

The volume of Mustafal and Happy's debate increased and Donri shifted his attention to listening in again. Stephen stood back up to pace and think. He felt disgusted with himself for retreating constantly and remembered item number three from his Personalized Action Plan: fight a good fight. He wanted more than anything freedom from his petty fears, freedom toward living again, with his family and in all areas of his life, unshackled from the familiar fear of being found and becoming known. Now he realized in the deepest part of who he was that it wasn't enough, and that he needed God's strength to fight that good fight. He knew he would have to engage with God personally, and couldn't ask Donri to pray for him again. That would be too easy. He needed to do this himself.

God, I admit I'm scared but I ask You to give me courage. I want to stop living in my own little story full of fears and start living in Your story for my life.

Donri turned back to him, probably to translate the latest round of heated exchange between their captor and negotiator, and Stephen suddenly felt a desire to say something wise, too, to balance out the discussion with his own input. "Have you ever heard the expression, 'It's always darkest before dawn?'"

"No, I haven't…what does it mean?"

"It means that we go through the toughest times before there is a breakthrough."

"I see…what does that mean to you?"

"That's what I'm asking myself."

Donri nodded his head approvingly, seeming to like questions as answers. Stephen smiled too.

"What are you smiling at, if I may ask?"

"Well, I thought I would be thinking of a Bible verse or something, but I guess I don't have any of those in my database yet. It's a song by a band you've probably never heard of called Twisted Sister from the 80's. My brother used to listen to them. It's called 'We're Not Gonna Take It,' and the lyrics are simple. They sing a line over and over, 'We're not going to take it anymore.'"

Donri laughed at that. "Twisted Sister?"

"Yeah, strange band and kind of a teenage rebellion song, but I love the beat, and I think I will make it my new theme song."

Donri laughed again. It was probably his most humorous and unique altar call song to date, Stephen thought.

"So you're saying we're not going to take it anymore," Donri exclaimed. "We should come out of hiding together and face our enemy?"

"Well, I don't know about that." The look of feisty confidence in Donri's eyes suddenly frightened Stephen. He was still getting his spiritual underpinnings and didn't want things to move too fast. "It's more of an attitude."

"No, you're right. It's time to face our enemies. Stand up to them. We're not going to take it anymore. Let's come out of hiding!"

Maybe having a new convert was giving the old preacher a surge of crazy energy. "Now don't do anything foolish, Donri." The argument between Mustafal and Happy was burning just fine without any more wood on the fire.

Donri took a few steps toward the melee. "Are you crazy?" Stephen called out after him.

Donri stopped, turned and smiled. "Yes. I think I am!"

≈≈▫≈≈

The long argument between Mustafal and Happy came to an abrupt end, with Mustafal decisively winning. No, he wasn't going to talk to the police using Happy's cellphone. The cops could probably tape it and then use the recording against him later in court. He didn't care about breakfast or a flashlight now. He would do this on his terms and use Happy as their only intermediary. His little cousin tried to refuse that role as he didn't want to be going up and down a rocky trail between Mustafal who intimidated him, and the police who could throw him into jail. There were also those guns aimed at him from either direction the whole while, Happy noted. Mustafal tried to assure him that they still had the upper hand, with two aces in the hole, and if they played their cards right they could still put the squeeze on the factory and get some concessions for their downtrodden and exploited co-workers. The biggest bargaining chip, Mr. Carlton Easley, was still on their side of the table and the police would do anything to avoid bringing shame on Indonesia with another international incident.

Happy said they had nabbed the wrong guy and the captive inside the cave was named Stephen Cranton. Mustafal scoffed at his naiveté at believing a conniving foreigner's lies. As Happy cast his gaze down in defeat, the old man approached to say something and Mustafal turned to hear what it was. The *bule* was still cowering nearby behind him.

"Go back to your master," Mustafal barked at Donri in an insulting form of Javanese. The old man was undaunted and wanted to have his say. But Mustafal showed that he was still in charge by pushing him backwards, spinning him around and flinging him on the ground next to his quivering co-hostage. He went down like a rag doll. The *bule* jumped up to try to catch the old man but missed, then tried to help him to his feet. Watching the scene made him hate Carlton Easley more than ever. There was the condescending white man helping the poor, feeble Indonesian man to his feet. *That's what's wrong with this country—Indonesians always thinking they need a hand up or a hand out from outsiders.*

Not only did the man represent everything unjust about a world of haves versus have-nots, but now because of him Mustafal would probably spend the rest of his life in jail. He pushed the thoughts of consequences aside as he did when he first had laid eyes on the white exploiter at the airport, and steeled his resolve to follow through on his one last play.

What really burned him was that the old man started laughing. Actually started laughing. What could be so funny? Did the two of them have some sort of inside joke? *So you don't think I'm serious?*

"Stop laughing," Mustafal commanded his prisoners in English. He scolded the old fool again in the bottom basement level of Javanese. With quick, jerky movements, he stepped behind Donri and wrapped his arm around his chest while pointing the gun at Carlton. "Move," he shouted in Indonesian. "We are going to the opening of the cave so the police can have another little look." Happy's spirited protest was ignored and the clump was shoved slowly toward the mouth of the cave.

When his prisoners stepped into the morning light, they shot their hands up. Mustafal's eyes again adjusted to the brightness and he scanned the scene down below. He saw a few gleaming guns aiming at him from the bushes and he knew one false move would result in a bullet to his head or one of theirs. Pressing the barrel of his gun hard against Donri's temple, he started shouting at them to stand down or he would shoot.

"Happy," he hissed sideways without taking his eyes off the stakeout positions, "go and tell them about our demands which if met will result in the safe release of Carlton Easley."

"Stephen Cranton," Happy answered back.

"Go," he shouted louder and angrier. "And if they try anything, I will kill the old man first to show them we are serious."

Happy didn't answer back but started to navigate his way down the rocky trail. All eyes were on him as Mustafal surveyed the entire scene before him, scanning from the beach all the way across to the back perimeter to count how many cops were out there.

He noticed a couple squatting down by the police cars and squinted to get a better look. The man had his arm around a young lady who had her head turned down so he couldn't make out her face, but the man looked familiar. A closer look revealed...Agung. It was Agung? What was his prisoner doing here? He was supposed to be back at the hostage house being watched by Dina. Had he escaped too?

Then the girl turned her face in his direction. No, it couldn't be. But it was her—he could make out her beautiful face plainly. Not only was she consorting with their former prisoner, but Agung had the audacity to have his arm around her shoulder and it even looked like they were holding hands. This was the girl he was going to marry! So everyone had turned on him—Happy and now his beloved Dina. Even Allah apparently.

A rage flooded his body and he felt like turning the gun on the cheating couple and unloading a few rounds. Instead he squeezed Donri's neck in a tighter choke hold.

"Listen," he yelled out, definitely getting everyone's full attention, including Happy who looked up at him from the trail below. "You don't think I'm serious but I will show you how serious I am!" he bellowed in Indonesian.

He clicked the safety off on his gun and pressed the barrel into Donri's temple. The old man winced with pain and closed his eyes.

"You will see!" Mustafal shouted to one and all.

≈≈□≈≈

Johanna arrived at the consulate an hour before it officially opened on Friday. After she got caught up on a few to-do's neglected from the previous day, she did one more internet search on Carlton Easley and Stephen Cranton, still finding nothing of significance. She then sent off a text message to the consulate general to ask if she could have 15 minutes of his time this morning for a brief meeting. A quick conversation with him would be at least one proactive step of precaution, in case there were a larger plot brewing.

In their cordial yet to-the-point meeting, Johanna gave the seasoned governmental veteran a rundown of her meeting with Carlton Easley from the day before, the kidnapping reference from Bambang and the gist of the email from Leah Cranton. She was curious to see if there was any connection between these two men and the recent chatter of an imminent attack, something maybe they should pass along to the embassy in Jakarta. He said he didn't believe half of what he heard from security briefings based on informants willing to sell information about their radical friends for the right price. It was his job to take things like this seriously and he gave her the phone number of one of his police contacts. If there were something to all this, the next steps would be for them to send out security warning emails and then organize a meeting of all U.S. citizens to wake them out of their secure slumber. It would take some time to organize a meeting that most could attend, so he asked to be kept posted as things developed.

The consular general also cautioned against going to the media at this early stage. Even if through that medium they could get the word of caution out more quickly to American citizens, it would be too easily spun that the heartless U.S. embassy was playing political games and giving Indonesia a bad reputation. There would be follow-up quotes from Indonesian police captains saying that they haven't heard of any kidnapping threats, casting the blame on the U.S. State

Department as overreacting and not sensitive to Indonesian's delicate economy.

On the way back to her desk Johanna stopped by the small consular library and picked up an alternate morning newspaper, *Surya*, which focused more on sensational crimes than high-concept news. She scanned it for any articles about missing foreigners or hit-and-run's but found nothing. No news from Pandaan either. Johanna felt uneasy and antsy, wanting to do something, but not knowing exactly what. Then the imagined face of Leah Cranton popped into her mind. Instead of waiting for this worried wife to find her way out of the airport and to the consulate in the complex traffic, maybe Johanna could at least meet her at the airport this morning. She checked the Cathay Pacific website to see when the flight from Hong Kong arrived in Surabaya. One more hour. Maybe she was getting ahead of herself, and it was definitely not required protocol, but it would surely beat another day of processing visas and passports.

She got permission from the consulate general and then called her driver, requesting to be taken to the airport immediately. He gave a quiet answer that Johanna couldn't quite make out but she was sure it was a yes, probably something like he would be waiting for her in the parking lot. He was extremely polite, bland but friendly, and didn't say much unless he was directly asked a question. Most Indonesians she had encountered were like him, gentle and polite, and it was hard for her to imagine any of them enticed into harming, kidnapping or killing innocent people.

As she gathered up her things from her desk to leave, Johanna remembered that Leah wouldn't be expecting to be picked up at the airport. She pulled out a permanent marker out of her desk drawer and scribbled in large letters on a piece of printer paper, "WELCOME LEAH CRANTON."

≈≈☐≈≈

After a surprisingly good night's sleep in the half-rate hotel, Carlton Easley felt the old fight back inside him. He wolfed down a greasy plate of fried rice in the smoky restaurant just off the lobby and mentally retraced his steps for the last two days that tangled him in this third world nightmare. Today would be a day of retribution and there were several issues to sort through in order for that to happen. The first issue was why he wasn't picked up by the company driver at the sweltering Surabaya airport. That misstep had caused him so much personal misery, and someone would have to pay for that. Then there was group coercion by the villagers, mistreatment by an elderly store owner, wrongful imprisonment by the police department and finally police extortion to pay a hospital bill. Justice would be meted out even if his only target could be mismanagement at the factory. Someone had to pay. Someone always does.

The waitress brought the bill and he scribbled out his room number. Just a few more minutes to go before Bambang would arrive, take care of the hotel bill and drive him to the factory. Carlton turned and looked at the other men eating breakfast, many of them wearing some type of green government uniforms and smoking *Firdaus* cigarettes. They ignored his stares and kept chatting and laughing amongst themselves. Indonesian tax payers would pick up the tab of these government workers staying in this hotel, he assumed. For all his troubles someone would pick up Carlton's tab, too.

CHAPTER TWENTY-FOUR

Stephen's hands stayed up as he pivoted his body sideways to take in the tense scene. Mustafal was about to shoot kindly Donri, right in the head and right then. The snarling man yelled out something loudly in Indonesian and Stephen could only assume it was a threat that he was about to pull that trigger.

No. No. No. We're not gonna take it anymore.

With a startling scream, Stephen lunged for the arm that was carrying the gun, clenching his hand around Mustafal's wrist and yanking it up and away from Donri's head. Mustafal yelled back, spun halfway around backwards and landed an elbow hard into Stephen's face. Blood spurted out of Stephen's nose but he held on to the wrist that Mustafal was trying to wrestle free. Donri jerked back in surprise and watched the melee with a gaped-open mouth.

The two men struggled over the hand with the gun, scuffling and grunting and landing knees and elbows into each other. Stephen could hear the sounds of Happy shouting below and the police running toward the fight. If he could just keep the gun out of Mustafal's control until the police jumped in, he could endure whatever pain Mustafal inflicted in the meantime.

In the scuffle, Stephen lost some traction on the ground slippery with gravel and his own blood. He fell down backwards but with the gun still in his possession. The back of his head hit the ground hard and darkened his vision momentarily. He looked up to see Mustafal bearing down on him with those evil eyes, then glancing down the trail toward the police who were fast approaching. This was the crazed man's last play.

Mustafal spat something else in Indonesian, bent over and forcefully grabbed the gun out of Stephen's awkwardly bent arm, flipped it around and pointed it back at Stephen. He flashed a menacing grin to celebrate that he now had the upper hand, but Stephen could see over his shoulder Donri rushing him.

The next scene unfolded for Stephen in movie-like slow motion. The police were now yelling and almost upon the scene, and Donri himself shouted as he pounced upon a shocked Mustafal. The gun wobbled in his hands but he still held on to it. Stephen could only watch as Mustafal turned to fling off his older and weaker assailant. Donri held on to his waist with a death grip and it looked like he was trying to push him off the ledge to the rocks below.

Screaming and scuffling. The police were cresting the top of the trail with their guns out. Mustafal was getting closer to the edge but now he had his gun pointed at the top of Donri's bent down head. He was about to pull that trigger and end the old man's life.

No. No. No. Stephen scooted forward on his back and heaved up enough on his arms to give a clumsy, lunging kick to Mustafal's legs. It cut him down but Donri was still gripping on tight. For a millisecond before they went over the edge, Mustafal looked into Stephen's face with a look of both horror and disgust. From his position Stephen couldn't see Donri's expression as both men tumbled down off to the side of the trail. Stephen screamed and then heard the gun go off in a sickening thud sound.

No. No. No.

Stephen struggled up to his feet and the police were shouting and ducking for cover when they heard the gunfire. Happy screamed out, too. Stephen got to the ledge and looked down, seeing both men in a tangle on top of a pile of large sharp rocks. Neither man was moving. The police who were at the bottom of the rocky trail came upon the scene first with their weapons still drawn.

Stephen found himself praying as he looked down while blood kept oozing out of his nose. *Please, God, help Donri. Help him just get up.*

There was a movement in the pile and one of the officers turned Mustafal's body over. Even from his high vantage point Stephen could see a wince of pain in Mustafal's sweaty face so he knew he couldn't be dead or unconscious. Two policemen lifted his limp body off the rocks and he was groaning but definitely alive. It was the man underneath that Stephen was most worried about. Stephen could see the gun had fallen into a crag of the rocks. Did it fire into Donri on the way down? There appeared to be no major blood on his chest or head but he still wasn't moving.

Happy cut through the underbrush off the trail and ran toward the scene at full gallop, yelling all the way. The normally submissive man looked angrier than Stephen had seen him yet. The sudden movement jolted Stephen into realizing that he, too, could get a closer look at the scene and check on Donri now that there were no more guns pointing at him.

Stephen quickly stepped down the rocky path as he pinched his nose with one hand to try to make the bleeding stop. His feet were still shoeless and the descent was painful. By the time he made it down and across to the site of the fall, which looked like a much longer drop from the lower vantage point, there were a half dozen police at the scene. One of them was tapping lightly on Donri's face to get a response but there was none.

Stephen rushed closer, ignoring a policeman who was ordering something at him, and knelt down over Donri's still body. The policeman seemed perturbed at the interruption but got back to checking for a pulse and listening for breathing. Still nothing.

The policeman started to lift Donri's head off the rocks by himself and Stephen shouted, "Don't move him. He may have a head or neck injury and you could paralyze him if you move him without a stretcher. Wait for the paramedics to come." He realized his vocabulary was going too high but he couldn't quickly think of a simpler way to explain it.

The policeman nodded as if he understood Stephen's first aid advice and called one of his partners over. Then, before Stephen could stop it, he watched in dismay as two police man quickly lifted Donri and heaved him over the rock pile, potentially paralyzing in him in the process. They laid him on a flat spot on the sand and Stephen could still see no obvious gun wounds but there was blood on the hands of the policeman who was holding Donri's head. Still no movement of breathing.

The other policeman felt the back of Donri's head and called Stephen over to feel it too. It was an enormous and bloody bump, probably where Donri's head slammed on the rocks first. The way they landed may have ended Donri's life and saved Mustafal's. It wasn't fair.

Stephen immediately started to ask himself if this were his fault and he replayed the scene in his mind. If he hadn't lunged at Mustafal, the madman would have surely shot Donri, right?

Still no pulse, no breathing, nothing. Stephen didn't want to admit it but the truth was too heavy now to push back. Donri was gone.

"Sorry, mister," one of the policemen said. "You friend die."

He might have broken down and started crying right there, but Stephen still felt so angry at Mustafal and the injustice of it to do anything but fume. He looked over and saw the murderer was coming to. Or was Stephen the murderer? *No, I was just trying to help. I was trying to save his life.* The awkward scissor kick scene replayed in his mind again with both men going over the ledge and Mustafal's last desperate look of defeat. He wished he could have seen Donri's face too. Was it a look of victory? They had defeated their foe together.

The officer who made the crude pronouncement of death closed Donri's glassy eyes with his hand and whistled to his partner to help remove the body. Stephen watched as the two men carried Pak Donri away to one of the squad cars. Would they wait for a hearse or just cart him away, crunched in the back seat of a squad car? So undignified.

I didn't even get the chance to say thank you. A flood of emotion suddenly unleashed inside Stephen and washed over him as if it had come crashing from the ocean. He would never be able to talk to the kind old sage again, and never get to introduce him to Leah. He just stood upright, sobbing and momentarily forgetting about the police and all the people watching him. After the ordeal he had gone through, he thought it permissible to let his tears freely flow. The deep sense of loss was overlaid with a heavy pall of guilt, as Stephen knew that he was in part responsible for Donri's death.

The police entourage looked on undecidedly. After a few moments and with no one trying to comfort him, Stephen finally tried to recover himself. He patted his face and wiped his wet and blood-crusted nose on his dirty sleeve. This was followed by an apology to the official onlookers and a question about if any of them knew how to get in touch with Donri's family. There was no ready answer and Stephen surmised that was due to a language barrier more than a lack of care.

Another officer approached, apparently to get a statement from Stephen, but his English was extremely limited and it was torture for Stephen to try to understand the intent of his questions. Stephen could tell it was awkward for the questioner, too, because the man kept smiling bashfully over his bad grammar.

"May I wash off in the ocean?" Stephen asked slowly and politely. He just wanted to get away from the questioning and all the activity now swarming like a bee hive around the scene of the crime. He could see Happy also being questioned and getting handcuffed again. Agung and Dina were even there. How did they get there? No matter, he just wanted to get away from the bewildering chaos for a few minutes to clear his overwhelmed mind and mourn his brave friend.

The officer didn't seem to understand the request and Stephen pointed to his filthy feet and bruised face and made a pantomime of washing off his arms and legs in the ocean, using sand as a prop. The officer got it and nodded his permission. "*Sebentar aja, ya, mister?*"

"Yeah, yeah. I just wash in the ocean for a few minutes."

The officer watched him trot off toward the water and called out something else after him. Stephen didn't look back but plunged his aching body in the cold water, clothes and all. Gentle waves slapped over his still aching face and the sudden plunge felt invigorating, waking his body and soul in an instant. The undercurrent was surprisingly strong and he let it tug at his feet for a few moments until he turned over and floated on his back, with his face toward the free horizon. Pink threads streaked across the dawn sky.

He felt like swimming all the way to the beautiful and beckoning horizon and away from what awaited him on the shore. More questions. More misunderstandings. More hassle and time away from his family. Yet now he was so tranquil and the only sounds he could hear where the thrush of crashing waves. From this distance there was not even the slightest squawk of a police walkie-talkie. He took in the peace and pleasure for a few more minutes and mouthed a prayer out loud of gratitude for Pak Donri's help and sacrifice.

Then he flipped over and starting swimming back to the shore, helped along by strong waves back to the reality of police matters. Muffled voices became stronger, and he looked up to see two policemen were calling to him on the water's edge, apparently making sure their main witness wouldn't swim away back to America.

The next few hours went by in a blur. Stephen was questioned again at the scene of the crime, but still no adequate translator could be found. He saw Dina, Happy and Agung all being stuffed together in the back of one squad car before he could speak to any of them or ask them any questions. How was Agung holding up? How would Happy be handled? Would Dina be given some leniency for helping Stephen or did the police even know that yet? Where was Mustafal anyway? He wasn't sure of anything but hopefully it would all be untangled soon. The important thing is that the terrorist threat had been neutralized. Stephen was escorted to another squad car by himself and placed in the back seat. Fine with him. He needed time to decompress and rest in the long car ride which he hoped would take them all back to Surabaya. He didn't have any contact info for Donri and therefore no way to contact his family. The police probably already retrieved Donri's wallet which Mustafal had tossed out the night before and would surely figure all that out. Stephen really just wanted to express his gratitude to Donri's surviving family members and let them all know that their loved one died a hero.

He looked passively out the window and felt thankful when they passed the familiar street where he had made his escape from the hostage house. So they weren't going to take him back to that painful memory and poke him with more hard questions to understand. As long as Mustafal was in custody somewhere, he was relieved. *Just get me back to my family.*

The windy roads were leading him over mountain ridges and through dense jungle forests, past tiny villages and through towns back to civilization. They had to be nearing Surabaya but he was still too emotionally exhausted to fire off any inquiries to the officers in the front seat who were consumed in their own conversation. This must be a pretty exciting day for them, he thought. It was okay with Stephen as he enjoyed being ignored and didn't have the stomach to be tumbled around in any more confusion. Just silence and the ride and time to think.

≈≈▢≈≈

As the Cathay Pacific flight from Hong Kong started its descent toward the Surabaya airport, Leah Cranton was awakened by a directive to put her seat back in the full upright position. The subsequent bumpy touch down jostled her weary and jet-lagging body, yet her first emotion upon landing in Indonesia was gratefulness for a safe arrival. Ever since Stephen's planned trip here she had been noticing news stories of recent plane crashes in Indonesia.

That didn't help her nerves about his trip, of course, and that was before he had gone missing. She steeled her emotions with courageous self-talk, reminding herself Stephen was somewhere on this island and still in one piece.

How surreal, she felt, for her first time overseas to become a search and rescue mission for her missing husband. Priority one would be to find him and then further down the list she would try to locate him emotionally. Her angry thoughts about his lack of emotional connection were starting to be eclipsed by concerns for his physical safety. For now she tried to focus her thoughts on logical explanations of his disappearance, and forced out of her mind thoughts of kidnappings or death. A perfectly reasonable explanation would make sense out of his incomprehensible no-show at the Surabaya branch office. After that she would let him have it, that is, if he didn't try to win her heart back first.

Once she descended the stairs toward immigration and baggage claim, an immigration officer informed her in broken English that she would need to go back upstairs to apply for a visa on demand. She wasn't sure what that was—she thought she would be able to walk into the country as a tourist. She found it only meant she had to fork over $25 and fill out a form. She did the quick paperwork for the temporary visa, pulled out the cash, got the stamp in her passport, and presented it all back with a smile to the immigration officer on the first floor. He didn't return the smile but said without looking up, "Have nice time in Indonesia."

"I'll try," she said as she squeezed through the aisle between the immigration booths and on toward baggage claim. She quickly found her one large black suitcase on the conveyer belt, yanked out its collapsible handle, wrapped her large carry-on bag around it, waved off a porter who wanted to help her, and meandered toward the exit. She was stopped and asked to put the bag flat through a security screening check and wished she had hired the porter after all. It strained her back to heave the baggage on the conveyer belt, but if she hired the man she wouldn't know how much to tip him, and she didn't have any Indonesian *rupiah* yet. She was quickly realizing how helpless she was in this strange land, not knowing the language or customs, and she had no one there to meet or depend on. She was all alone as usual.

Two customs officers were standing at the end of the security machine and watched her as she waited for the bag to come through. The larger, burly one asked her in a friendly way, "Where do you go in Indonesia?"

"I am going to find my husband," she said with a polite yet terse smile. The bag appeared and she lifted it in one swift stroke as she pulled the handle and set it on the floor at the same time. She was ready to roll.

"He lucky man have beautiful woman like you." The man's eyebrows bobbed up and down.

She nodded without dignifying the flirt, walking off briskly yet still able to hear the other officer laughing at his partner's audacity. Not looking back, Leah resolved to find the man who didn't know how lucky he was.

She stepped through the exit doors and was greeted by the heat. Masses of people swirled about and she wished she had someone to help her navigate through this chaos. Crowds of people were pushing forward against a metal gate. Noises of people calling to other passengers bombarded her senses. She looked over the heads for the sign of a taxi stand or an ATM or something that would put her in control and out of this mob. Several men were calling out "taxi" or "Hello, miss, where you want to go?" One called her mister. She stepped around them, wanting to find an official-looking taxi stand.

Leah walked along the metal gate and toward the opening of the outside corridor where she would have to force herself through the throng. She picked up speed and tried to look like she knew where she was going.

"Leah Cranton?" a woman's voice called as she passed. Disoriented, she turned and saw a white woman holding a sign with her name written in large letters. She looked and re-looked at her, blinked hard and was sure she didn't recognize the professionally-dressed lady. She almost didn't want to acknowledge that it was her, feeling a slight twinge of apprehension. Was this the official first phase of some somber new reality?

People were bumping her from behind, trying to squeeze through the same opening. "Uh, yes, hello," she finally admitted. "I'm Leah Cranton."

"Oh good!" the woman beamed cheerfully. She had a kind face. The two of them ducked out of the way of the other passengers scrambling for their taxis or drivers. She folded the paper under her arm and then stuck out a hand for an introduction. "My name is Johanna Grazen. I am the liaison officer for the U.S. Consulate in Surabaya. I got your email last night."

Leah felt like crying, both for relief of having someone on her side and for the sobriety that it made Stephen's disappearance seem much more real. An official representative of the U.S. government was meeting her at the airport. This must have been how young wives felt during the Vietnam War when Western Union telegram men arrived at their houses officially informing them that they were now widows. Was Stephen dead? The governmental greeter was smiling and seemed too relieved to be delivering that kind of news.

She returned the handshake and Johanna took up her bag to roll it along. "I hope I am not worrying you too much by being here. I just thought it would be better to meet you at the airport and we can work on finding your husband together."

"Have you heard anything from him?" she asked, trying to clear the emotion out of her throat.

"I'm afraid not, but we have some leads. I have been checking with the local police and I'm expecting to hear back from one of our contacts there any minute now."

"What do you think could have happened to him?"

"We're not sure," Johanna responded, but by her slight hesitation Leah could tell that her host was hedging on something.

"I've come all this way. You can tell me, please."

"Well, I was just wondering if there is any connection between your husband's disappearance and an American man who was involved in a hit-and-run incident around the same time."

"Why would there be? I don't understand." Leah's didn't mean to sound so challenging, but it blurted out in her pent-up stress.

Johanna's eyes and tone softened and she pointed toward the parking lot. "Let's walk to my car and we can talk about it on the way to the consulate. My driver will take us there first. I'll let you know everything I know and we can try to put all our information together."

"Okay. I, uh, really appreciate your help. I just feel so overwhelmed that my husband is officially missing."

"Yes, that's understandable. Let's talk through all the information, sort it out and I'm sure we can find him." The two of them clipped along to the parking lot with Johanna leading the way.

"I'm pretty sure he is not running away," Leah nervously offered. "He's not that kind of guy. Our marriage is fine and he loves our kids."

Johanna looked like she didn't know quite how to respond to the defense of Stephen's character and instead focused her attention on helping Leah lift her heavy rolling suitcase over a curb.

Why am I blabbering like this? Get ahold of yourself.

From a waiting bay Johanna waved and got the attention of her driver who was leaning against the hatchback of a fancy black car in the parking lot and smoking a cigarette. A text message beeped through and Johanna checked her phone and then looked up at Leah with a bright face. "Your husband has been found and he is safe," she exclaimed.

"Wh...what happened?" Leah responded, trying to get oriented before she celebrated.

"Let me ask. They probably wanted to send that through to me before they texted in all the follow up details."

Before Johanna could type in a follow-up question her phone beeped again and she read the message aloud. "It says he is on the way to being questioned by the police at a cigarette company in Pandaan." Johanna frowned before Leah could even formulate another question. "That's weird. That was the same factory where the American citizen I visited yesterday was supposed to visit before the hit-and-run incident I was telling you about."

"Questioned by the police? Does that mean he did something wrong?"

"I don't know," Johanna said and squinted up into the morning sun when she saw her driver approaching. "But my guess is there is some kind of connection." The driver jumped out, flicked out his cigarette, placed Leah's suitcase in the back and politely opened the door for her.

Leah felt grateful that she had been picked up and had help to get out of this disorienting airport. Yet her main emotion was worry. She had a thousand questions and they would have to be asked one by one, requiring her to control her tender emotions. She told herself the main thing was that Stephen had been found.

CHAPTER TWENTY-FIVE

The policeman in the front passenger seat finally spoke up and said something in English but Stephen couldn't quite understand it. Then the officer started pointing to the side of the road. Stephen looked and could see a grey, ash-covered mountain, with what looked like white clouds hovering at the top. Were those just clouds or volcanic steam? The mysterious and majestic mountain sat guard over lush green rice fields, with a few huts on wooden stilts perched in every field, either rice harvesting stations or maybe for napping farmers. The beautiful scene took him out of his anxious thoughts momentarily, beckoning him to grow in affection for a country that so far had traumatized him. Maybe he could take the whole family here for a unique vacation experience one day. Or at least a get-away for him and Leah.

Speaking again, the policeman pointed out the window and Stephen could now see from his uplifted angle that the man wasn't pointing at peaceful tropical scenery but at a large red and green billboard on the side of the road boasting *Firdaus Rokok*. So they wanted to take him back to the factory that he had desperately tried to get away from at the start of his misadventure.

"No, no. I need to go back to Surabaya, back to my office. I need to call my family, call my wife and tell her I am all right," Stephen pleaded. "No factory."

The officer just smiled back, either deflecting the protest or not having a clue what Stephen just said.

"Surabaya," Stephen finally demanded.

"We go here first," the driving officer interjected, "then Surabaya."

"But I need to call my family."

"You may use phone factory."

Maddening. Whatever Stephen said would not get him to where he wanted to go. He felt caught up in a strong current again, still powerless to steer, almost like a victim once more. But this time he would be more demanding of his law-abiding kidnappers.

"Can you notify the family of the man at the cave, Pak Donri, the man who helped me? I would like to speak to them."

"Yes, yes," the shotgun riding officer answered, probably not understanding. The driving officer wasn't helping to translate either as he was focused on slowing down the car and pulling into a large gated driveway off the main busy road. A large granite *Firdaus Rokok* sign welcomed them. Security guards stepped out of a post and greeted the officers, looking slightly concerned. Permission to enter was immediately granted and the car slowly moved ahead through the long curved driveway. Both sides of the scenic road were boarded by humongous billboard murals extolling the virtues of *Firdaus Rokok*. There were attractive people happily smoking, colorful art bursting in the backgrounds, and futuristic looking scenes of blissful beings all being led to paradise. It was such a serene contrast to the chaos of buzzing motorcycles, puttering trucks, the occasional ox-drawn cart and thousands of shack-like food stalls on crude highway shoulders they had zipped by for the last three hours. Stephen felt like he had entered the magical emerald city of Oz, and like the lion, he had already received a heart of courage from his adventure and didn't need a new one. He now just wanted to be granted a phone call home by this kingdom's ruling wizard.

The police car pulled right up into a VIP parking spot in front of the factory and the door was opened for Stephen by the shotgun riding officer who smiled and nodded at him. Stephen stepped out and saw other police cars in the parking lot. He wondered if Agung, Mustafal, Dina and Happy were already here, too, or if they were being questioned somewhere else. It seemed like a lot of police protection for just him. He looked toward the main entrance which was surrounded by lush green plants and bright tropical flower arrangements. So far this place from the front looked more like a country club than a sweat shop. A hanging banner next to the front door welcomed Carlton Easley in large letters. *Well, here I am at last.*

≈≈▫≈≈

In the back middle seat of their police car, with Happy on one side of him and Dina on the other, Agung strategized to himself. There was plenty of time to think as the police said they were taking them all back to the *Firdaus Rokok* factory in Pandaan. It was the place of employment for all three suspects, a good gathering spot for the full police inquiry where all the players would be assembled under heavy police security and all the facts would be sorted out.

Agung held the sweaty hand of Dina who was looking at the window in deep thought. Happy was quiet too. The two reluctant partners in crime dared not speak to each other as so much had already been blabbed out by Happy back at the beach. Not only that, but there was also the treasure trove of evidence from the text messages on Happy's cell phone. They surely didn't want to further incriminate themselves by talking details within earshot of the two policemen in the front seat. All passengers bumped along together in silence.

Agung hadn't done anything wrong, of course, so he felt no threat of personal consequences. He was just concerned for his seatmates, especially for the feisty and pretty one he had grown quite fond of in the last 48 hours. He looked over at Dina, her worried face watching the trees go by and her long black hair glistening in the streaming sun. He felt like putting his arm around her to comfort her but that would be way too public and inappropriate, so the hidden handholding would have to suffice. He also wanted the police to go easy on Happy, who had already confessed his involvement to them and cooperated with the police when they forced him to be their go-between with Mustafal.

Mustafal was riding in a separate car, handcuffed, probably raging about something loudly or silently plotting his next sinister move. The dominant ringleader was spiteful enough to make sure both of his partners went down in flames for his masterminded crime. Would he be charged for the murder of the old man that was with Mr. Stephen? Or would the police rule that a freak accident? Agung dreaded looking into Mustafal's cold eyes again, especially when he caught sight of his fiancée snuggling up next to Agung. Would Mustafal in a jealous rage suddenly lunge at him across a table, even in handcuffs, maybe head butt him or bite him? Agung knew him to be very rash and capable of violence and he shuddered at the imagined scene. Hopefully the police would question them separately and not herd them all together in one room.

Now that Agung knew Mustafal's real motivations for the kidnapping, he could at least sympathize as he was also very versed in the economic injustices of Indonesia. Yet Mustafal had gone way too far to right those wrongs. Agung would do anything he could to protect his new girlfriend from any more wrongs by her ex-boyfriend. She shouldn't have gone along with him in the first place, true, but she had learned from her experience and she would have a wiser partner at her side now.

Then there was Mr. Stephen. He knew his new friend would be all right and soon be reunited with his family. He hoped that they could become overseas friends, maybe exchange email addresses and keep in touch. Perhaps Agung could visit him in the United States one day or Stephen could come back to Indonesia with his family and visit his hometown of Sidoarjo. One day they could swap stories and laugh about their adventure together.

This moment was no laughing matter, however. People's fates were at stake and his new girlfriend could possibly be flushed down the Indonesian justice system. He would do everything in his power to protect her, short of outright lying, even if it meant bending the truth a little toward her favor. Or maybe he could try a diversionary tactic, eclipsing Mustafal's fierce verbiage with something outlandish?

Agung felt slightly superior that he could do whatever he wanted in the questioning. He was the powerbroker here, not Mustafal or anyone else. He would probably be the best English speaker there, he surmised, and surely would be called on to translate. He imagined himself seated at the middle of every negotiating table if a foreigner was involved, and he could skew the answer to any question in whatever way he liked. It felt great to no longer be a victim. He gave Dina's hand a celebratory squeeze and she looked up at him.

She squeezed back tightly as the police car pulled off the main busy road of Pandaan and pulled into the long driveway toward the cigarette factory.

≈≈□≈≈

The two officers opened the main entrance door for Stephen and they were soon greeted by a mousy little Indonesian man who chattered away at them in a very animated fashion. He had a couple of silent sidekicks behind him who didn't say anything, making it clear that the little guy was in charge. The man finally broke from the police conversation and struck out his hand to Stephen.

"Hello sir. My name is Mr. Bambang. It's nice to meet your acquaintance."

Stephen shook back. *Bambang?* Stephen still remembered the name from the note he received in Carlton Easley's car outside the airport on Wednesday. Stephen's silly little spontaneous stunt would soon be exposed in the light of persistent questions and cross checking. He suddenly felt more embarrassed by that than his disheveled, bruised and shoeless appearance. Could he get out of this and back to his family scathed with just a little personal shame, or would there be formal charges against him for wrongful impersonation? The thought of further delay in Indonesia made his empty stomach turn a somersault. Hopefully they would go easy on him after all he had been through.

"Right this way," said Bambang. "Everyone has assembled in a break room our employees use. It is large enough for all of us to be seated and for the police to ask their questions."

Just like that? Everyone? Would Stephen have to face Mustafal again so quickly? Anger toward Mustafal still boiled inside him for what he had done to Donri. He wanted him to pay for that, yet at the same time Stephen also felt guilty for his clumsy karate move that helped send Donri over the ledge to his death. He wasn't emotionally ready to encounter the man who kidnapped him and caused him so much physical and psychological pain.

Bambang led the entourage down a long corridor. They passed glass-encased offices which must have been for the managers and then through double doors to the large factory floor. It was a massive room where hundreds of workers were sitting in rows of neatly aligned work stations, furiously attacking the reams of paper, boxes of tobacco and cutting machines in front of them. Cigarette boxes were being stuffed at lightning speed. The floor was littered with leftover cigarette paper and strong-smelling tobacco. Stairs on the sides led up to more offices and perches where supervisors kept watch. Stephen took it all in as many of the workers looked up and noticed the visitors, some of them pointing and a few laughing aloud.

Bambang then led them around the periphery of the factory floor while the workers continued to gawk. The entourage entered a large break room, with vending machines on the sides and two large folding tables pulled together in the middle. Rickety folding chairs and wooden benches lined the makeshift conference table and at the head of it sat an intense-looking balding man with a dominant nose, two officers flanking him on either side. *Must be Carlton Easley.* He was sitting on a lopsided swivel chair, the best seat in the house.

Stephen nodded his greeting and the large man didn't smile back. He looked irritated at Bambang and ignored Stephen, then growled with a decidedly Texas twang, "Well, it's about time. Do you know how long we have been waiting for you here, Mr. Bambang?"

Bambang politely nodded to show the comment registered but kept his attention on Stephen. "Normally, we would have a meeting of this importance in our conference room. But I was afraid it was too small. We can all meet in here today, but I'm afraid it does not have AC. Just fan."

Carlton seemed miffed that he was being ignored. "Mr. Bambang, you should be afraid."

Bambang looked over at him but seemed unsure of the direct rebuke or how to respond. Stephen was caught off guard by it, too, and he tried to diffuse the tension by introducing himself. "Hello," he said, walking over with an outstretched arm. "You must be Carlton Easley. My name is Stephen Cranton."

Carlton eyed him suspiciously and lifted his arm for a reluctant handshake. "Are you from the embassy?"

"No, I'm not. I'm an American citizen visiting Indonesia too."

"Well, okay then. May I ask why you are here, Stephen, and how do you know me?"

The simple questions stopped Stephen, as he again considered potential legal issues for himself. Thankfully Bambang broke in before he could formulate an answer. "The police say they would like to take a statement by everyone involved in the crimes," Bambang announced, looking back and forth between his two American guests and the two police officers.

The crimes. Was there more than one? Was identity theft in Indonesia considered a crime? Surely they were talking about the kidnapping and some other unknown infraction.

A commotion got all five men's attention at the doorway. Two police officers, holding Mustafal by each arm, shoved him into the room. A cardboard sign was draped around his neck that read, *"Terdakwa,"* which Stephen assumed was the equivalent of bad guy suspect. After being pushed inside, he looked around to get his bearings and his eyesight trained on Stephen. Angry words exploded from his mouth and he tried to lunge toward his former captive, but the officers held him back. One of them slapped him on the back of the head and Stephen could see that he was handcuffed from behind. He kept up his rant and the other officers loudly barked at him, shutting him up and stuffing him into a chair.

The sudden entrance was unsettling for Stephen, who felt an abject fear mixed with intense anger toward this man who had taken Donri's life. Carlton started spouting off questions but Stephen ignored him. He only stared back at Mustafal who was sitting and fuming in one of the folding chairs. There was an officer on either side, and the one officer at the head of the table, who must be a captain, gave the other policemen orders in Indonesian. He looked like he would be the one in charge of this meeting, or at least co-charge.

The other officers started responding to their captain in Indonesian. Stephen focused his attention back and forth into the faces of Mustafal and Carlton, two people who had made his life totally miserable since he arrived. Mustafal, when he wasn't looking down to the floor, would pop his head up and glare at Stephen. Was there a possibility he still thought Stephen was Carlton, his intended target? Either Mustafal was sincere back at the hostage house when he claimed he couldn't find Stephen's identity documents, or more likely, his outburst here was just play-acting in front of his partners.

Another commotion at the doorway and Stephen looked up to see Agung walk in the room with Dina and Happy trailing behind and under police escort. "Agung!" Stephen shouted and jolted up, running over to his fellow kidnapped friend and hugging him. The sudden burst of movement made the police officers jumpy, and one of them started to draw his weapon. The captain ordered him to put it down. Agung seemed awkward accepting the hug but Stephen didn't mind, wanting to show his enthusiastic appreciation.

Mustafal stood and flew into another rage when he saw his partners walk into the room, and Stephen noticed that Dina and Agung were sitting snuggly together. The police man standing above Mustafal gave him a hard yank on the handcuffs and shoved him back down into his chair. He kept ranting and his guard scowled something that shut him up again.

Why cram all these dynamite sticks together inside one tight powder keg? Stephen was baffled by the investigation process.

The police captain in charge said something to Carlton in what sounded like English. It obviously wasn't understood and Carlton leaned forward to hear it again. Agung let go of Dina's hand, who was now sitting down under the shadow of her own police guard, and moved forward to confer with the captain. All eyes were on him except Mustafal's who kept boring holes with his eyes into Dina. She didn't return the unblinking stare but fiddled with her hands. She wasn't handcuffed, at least not yet, and Stephen wondered if she would be considered a witness or a suspect. He would help her if he could as she had supplied him with the secret key that led to his freedom. That courageous act may have saved his life.

Whatever Agung whispered to the dour-looking captain seemed to please him. He suddenly smiled and scooted his chair over to make room for Agung at the head of the table. Another officer placed a folding chair for Agung between the captain and Carlton. Stephen realized that Agung the kidnapping victim had just been promoted to official translator.

"Hello, ladies and gentlemen, I am pleased to meet your acquaintance. My name is Pak Agung but you may call me Agung." Stephen quickly glanced around the table and noticed that he and Carlton were the only native English speakers. It charmed him that affable Agung was warming up for a formal speech as if he were sitting before a large crowd. "I will serve as today's translator."

Carlton looked either annoyed or bored as the police captain made some opening remarks, dutifully translated by Agung. He asked for patience in today's questioning as they wanted to have a full accounting of everything that had transpired over the last three days. Thoroughness was a must.

"I understand we need to be thorough," Carlton broke in, "but we can we also be quick?"

Agung translated the request to the captain who stuck to his guns, answering back that the investigation would have to be completely thorough.

"You know what," Carlton shot back. "I have had it to here with police investigations in this town."

"You have had it to here?" Agung asked.

"It's just an expression," Stephen offered to help out. "He means he is sick and tired."

"You feel sick now, sir?" Bambang asked Carlton with concern.

Carlton was obviously exasperated at another round of translation. He snorted and looked like he was going to try to keep his big mouth muzzled.

Mustafal's hateful stare didn't let up, but Dina kept her attention focused at the head of the table, toward her apparently new boyfriend.

"We will start with you, Mr. Stephen," Agung translated for the captain. "What exactly happened when you arrived in

Indonesia?" The inevitable question caught Stephen off guard. Just like that he was called to the center of the spotlight and was forced to decide how much truth he would reveal. Carlton Easley perked up at the question, looking like a bulldog ready to attack. Stephen looked through the doorway as he thought about his answer. Factory workers at their work stations were craning their necks to get a better peek at the odd assortment of visitors, including three of their co-workers.

He cleared his parched throat and began. "I arrived in Indonesia on Wednesday morning on a business trip. I got into the wrong car at the airport, the one meant for you." Stephen nodded toward Carlton. The police officers' interest was piqued by the opening statement, and all of them turned their full attention toward Stephen except for the one who was standing guard over the erratic Mustafal.

"That doesn't make any sense," Carlton interjected. "Why would you do that?"

"That's not the important thing. But if you will hear what happened next, you might be thankful."

"Go ahead," Carlton conceded. "We're all listening."

"Soon after that I was kidnapped by this man," Stephen said, motioning toward Mustafal. After the statement was translated, the accused nodded his head up and down heartily in agreement. "He of course thought I was you," Stephen said, nodding back to Carlton. "He was helped by two people who went along at first. But they soon saw how wrong their actions were and both of them tried to help me escape."

The first part of his confession wasn't all that forthcoming and the second part wasn't 100 percent true, but Stephen sensed all along that Happy had been bullied into the plan by his intimidating older cousin. Stephen would be forgiving toward an unwilling accomplice, but he wanted Mustafal to be locked away in jail for a long time.

"This still doesn't make any sense," Carlton said over the confusing noise of the sentences being translated. He shot a suspicious glance at Happy and Dina, seeming like he wanted to rip into them with more questions, but a bigger issue pushed that line of questioning aside. "Why would these people want to kidnap me?" he demanded.

A female factory worker tiptoed in with a tray of plastic water cups. It was placed one by one before the visitors and Stephen starting slurping his through the tiny straw before anyone gave the go-ahead. He remembered from Dina that might be considered inappropriate but he really didn't care about offending anyone's cultural delicacies at this point. Carlton slammed his down quickly too, and Bambang gave permission for everyone else to partake. The manager then clapped his hands together once and said something to his employee who had brought in the water cups. It was so hot and stuffy in the room and Stephen desperately hoped that she were being sent out for more.

"That is the interesting part," Stephen said to get back to his narrative and still trying to think of a way out. "Do you believe in fate?"

"No," Carlton said flatly. "What's your point?"

"Well, I think I was almost meant to be kidnapped."

"What?" Carlton chuckled, and then smiled broadly to himself. "Well, I guess better you than me." He continued to laugh heartily at his own remark but no one joined him as they didn't understand it. Agung had stopped translating all the back and forth sparring between Stephen and Carlton.

"Yes, it is fortunate for you, Carlton. My impersonating you saved you from being kidnapped, but the experience in a strange way saved me."

"Go on," Carlton allowed. It was clear he had wrestled the reins of leadership away from both the police captain and Bambang, but they both seemed content to let him run the opening part of the meeting which was being dominated by English.

"I escaped from this man," Stephen said while pointing to Mustafal, "with the help of these two." He motioned to Dina and Happy still sitting tight together on the bench. "I ran to a place called China Cave on a beach and met a man named Pak Donri who helped me, too."

The facts of the case being recounted jumpstarted Agung into translating again. Stephen had to slow down after each sentence to let him catch up and felt thankful for the extra time that allowed him to think of what he would say next. As he waited between sentences he looked through the doorway into the faces of the cigarette workers straining to hear what was going on inside their break room. An idea started to percolate in his mind of a diversionary tactic, but he would need to discuss it with his translating friend first.

Stephen sprinkled in a few more facts about Donri, about how Mustafal found them in the cave and how he treated them inside. "I couldn't believe he got me the second time. Like I said, maybe I was meant to be kidnapped."

"Yes, maybe you were," Carlton interjected, smiling to himself again. He was the only one in the room finding humor in Stephen's traumatic experience. His smug superiority was annoying, but it strengthened Stephen's resolve to follow through with his half-baked idea. He would just need to figure out a way to confer with Agung in private before he tried it out.

"As I said, better you than me," Carlton said with the same grinning and condescending demeanor.

That's it. I am going to put this jerk into his place.

CHAPTER TWENTY-SIX

Leah dug her hands into the crevice of the back seat to find the seatbelt buckle holder and had to struggle to pull it out. Apparently no one sat back here very often. Her host, Johanna, was in the front seat, sometimes chatting with her driver in Indonesian and sometimes turning back to Leah to offer some information about the mountains and countryside they were driving past. There were no new updates and Leah could tell Johanna was just trying to help keep her guest's worried mind preoccupied. At first it unnerved her when Johanna would turn her head from what Leah's mind was telling her was the driver's side of the front seat to say something. *Keep your eyes on the road!* She would then remember that the sides were switched but couldn't keep herself from looking at the driver in the other seat to make doubly sure.

What had happened to Stephen and why was he being held by the police? It didn't make sense. He goes missing in Indonesia for three days and then turns up at a cigarette factory? Did he have some sort of psychotic break down that caused him to break the law? Stephen wasn't the kind of guy to do something out of character very often, if at all. There was either a misunderstanding with the other American citizen who was involved with the hit-and-run incident, or the man she was about to encounter was not the man she knew.

Her stomach fluttered to the rhythm of the bumps in the road as the car traveled toward the *Firdaus Rokok* factory. Johanna told her how the cigarette company helped sustain the economy of this small town. The only important fact to her was that her husband might be inside it, and was in some sort of police trouble. Johanna also related more about the other American that she had checked on this week, a visiting supervisor from the mother company of this large factory. There had to be some connection, and Johanna assured her that all the pieces would come together soon. She was sure that Stephen was all right. Easy for her to say.

After a while Johanna took the hint from Leah's minimal responses and stopped trying to chat. Leah felt too tense for small talk and looked out the window blankly at the beautiful scenery and maddening traffic. She didn't want distraction— she wanted news.

After almost an hour into their journey from Surabaya toward Pandaan, Johanna's cell phone chirped and she answered it. After a brief conversation in Indonesian, she turned to the back seat with an apprehensive expression to translate.

"Your husband is being questioned by the police at the cigarette factory, not as a suspect but as a victim. I don't know how to say this, but it seems that he was kidnapped here for the last two days."

Kidnapped. The word shot furiously through Leah's mind and she suddenly felt dizzy.

"He's okay now, they said, and we will be there in a few minutes. You can check on him yourself but they said he is safe and unharmed. He is cooperating with the police in their investigation."

The tears started to well up along with a hundred questions. As she placed her hands over her face and began to cry, Johanna ordered that the car be pulled over. She got into the back seat with Leah and put her arm around her while the tears flowed.

Leah appreciated the comfort but more than anything she just wanted to see Stephen for herself and hold him, offering him comfort after his ordeal.

Now that she realized she could have lost him, she experienced long dormant emotions of appreciation and affection for him, feelings that she hadn't felt in a long time.

"Sorry to cry like that," Leah said as she composed herself and wiped the tears with her fingertips. "When will we arrive at the cigarette factory?"

Johanna withdrew her arm from around Leah's shoulder. "No need to apologize. About fifteen more minutes."

That wasn't fast enough for Leah, but the important thing was that Stephen was now safe. Those questions would be answered in due time. Stephen was safe.

As they rode along, the relief that he had been found was followed by an afterthought of apprehension. She remembered something she read about what happened in the wake of the 9-11 terrorists, how a lot of troubled couples across the country withdrew their applications for divorce from court dockets. Government clerks all over the country were bewildered and had never seen anything like it. Their irreconcilable conflicts seemed so trivial in light of the nation's mourning. Then a few months passed and the breaking up got back on track. Would she and Stephen's marriage make it over the long haul after they got through this crisis? Or would this just be a temporary relief for his well-being followed by the inevitable split-up a few months later? *Get a hold of yourself girl—you are getting way ahead of yourself.*

They finally pulled off the main road in Pandaan and down the long driveway toward the large factory. Ahead of them they could see a police car full of officers pulling into a parking space to the side of the large building. Maybe these were the officers that Johanna was in contact with earlier. Why so many? Was Stephen still being held hostage inside, and Johanna somehow didn't get the full message? If they were organizing as some sort of swat team, they were taking their sweet time doing so. Leah could see them casually get out of their cars, stretching, and stomping out their cigarettes. She feared that the police weren't taking this seriously enough, but then again it made her feel relieved that maybe there was nothing going on inside that needed to be taken seriously.

"Just hang in there, Leah. I'm sure we will get all of this straightened out," Johanna said as they walked together toward the front doors. A few factory workers reporting for their shifts eyed the group. Leah imagined they didn't see foreigners very often by the way they stared.

She smiled back to be polite but fretted inside. She just wanted more than anything to see Stephen for herself and make sure he was all right. They could save their marriage later. First she had to have her husband back.

≈≈▢≈≈

"I'm so sorry; may I go to the restroom?" Stephen asked, not really knowing whom he should request permission from. Was it Bambang the factory manager, the neutral police captain or Carlton who seemed to be in charge of the meeting?

Agung translated the request to the captain who granted the request and Stephen stood. "Agung, could you step out here for a minute. I want to ask you something, too." Another request put to the captain and permission was once again granted.

The two men walked along the perimeter of the factory floor, and the workers looked intrigued at seeing some of the players leave the break room. The whispering started in clusters and some of them took long looks at both men, paying special attention to Stephen's shoeless appearance.

"How may I help you, Mr. Stephen?" Agung asked with eagerness.

"I'm glad you finally know my name, Agung," Stephen said with a wide smile. "I'm sorry I lied to you on Wednesday."

"Yes, I'm still confused about that."

"It's a long story but I want to make it right."

"What do you mean make it right?"

"Well, I can see that you like Dina. I can also see why—she is not only pretty but very brave. You know, she gave me the key that helped me escape. That took a lot of courage to go against Mustafal and to help me."

Agung smiled bashfully. "Yes I know she is very brave. She told me about the key." They came to the double doors that led from the large factory floor to the corridor that led to the managers' offices. Stephen felt thankful that it was just two of them in the long hallway out of audible range of so many ears. Who knew if some of the factory workers could understand English and would report back to their bosses the plan that Stephen was hatching in process?

"I would like to help you keep her."

"What do you mean, Mr. Stephen?"

"Well, we know the police might put her in jail for her role in our kidnapping, maybe Happy too. We need to do something in the way we answer these questions to help them both."

Agung frowned while he thought. "What do you suggest we do?"

They made it to the restroom but Stephen didn't really need to go, still feeling dehydrated. His only drinks so far in the day were two small plastic cups of water, one back at the scene of the crime and the one during the questioning. He washed his hands and splashed cold water in his face and it did feel refreshing. Then he turned back to Agung.

"Are you familiar with the term, 'game change'?"

Agung thought for a minute, looking down the hallway. "I know the definition of those words but not the meaning together."

"Okay, how about 'lost in translation'?"

"Yes, I think so. But I still don't get what you mean."

"Sorry. Let me explain."

≈≈◻≈≈

"What's taking them so long?" Carlton huffed and Bambang just shrugged his shoulders in reply. No one else seemed frustrated with the delay, which irritated Carlton even more. The police seemed content to just wait around, plenty of time to waste.

He had killed enough time in Indonesia, almost killing him in the process, and he could only wait for so long to get back to his life. The passive captain obviously was no leader, so Carlton decided to at least try to make something happen to get the process moving again.

"Bambang, could you go out and find Stephen and our translator and tell them we're waiting? We need to get through this police investigation quickly because I would like to go back to my hotel room. Have you heard any word from the travel agent about getting my flight moved ahead?"

"Why yes, I will go check on them now." Bambang jumped up and exited the room. Carlton noticed that Bambang didn't even respond to the second question, which meant he probably hadn't even called the travel agent yet to get Carlton's ticket moved up two days. *Unbelievable.* All the more reason for the so-called manager to lose his job, which Carlton would see to once he got out of Indonesia alive.

Without anyone left in the room who could speak decent English, Carlton waited in the awkward silence with a hard scowl on this face. He looked into the faces of the waiting policeman, victims and perpetrators and studied the terrorist who had planned to kidnap him. The man—Carlton had forgotten his name—stared right back.

At least there is someone in this country with backbone.

≈≈◻≈≈

Stephen ran through his sketchy plan as Agung asked lots of questions, sometimes looking over his shoulder down the hallway to make sure no one was listening.

"Mr. Stephen, I like your plan because I do want to keep Dina out of trouble, but do you think this 'lost in translation' will work?"

"I'm not sure," Stephen admitted, looking into Agung's kind face and seeing a mixture of emotions. He was sure his friend felt torn between doing the expected thing and the risky one. Stephen could definitely relate to those feelings, having done the expected thing his whole life until Chaz Wilton, Chopper and Om Donri showed up. It made Stephen ponder his own Personalized Action Plan. Do something spontaneous. Check. Take a risk. Check. Fight a good fight. Check. Still to go were to protect the underdog and love without fear.

The more Stephen talked through their strategy, the more excited he felt about it, even euphoric. Maybe it was delirium from post-traumatic stress disorder or he was just feeling giddy from being released from captivity. Whatever it was, it felt great to feel totally alive.

The noise of the double doors opening at the end of the hall caused both men to look up and see Bambang walking toward them.

"We need to get back to the meeting now, Mr. Stephen," Agung said, looking even more nervous now. It was show time.

Stephen agreed and started walking down the corridor toward their official escort. Then another sound pulled his attention, his name being called in a soft, familiar recognizable voice as if it were coming from a dream. Maybe he was really delirious because it almost sounded like Leah's voice.

"Stephen?"

He turned. *It can't be.* The unmistakable smile, the soft features, the long brown hair and dazzling brown eyes, the walk and carry of the person that he could recognize a block away. The love of his life just waltzing through the door as if she belonged here in Indonesia.

He tried to call her name but the emotions choked out the words in his throat. *Leah, I can't believe it's you.*

Calling out his name she ran to him, leaving behind a professionally dressed lady that she had walked in with. The two of them embraced more tightly than Stephen could ever remember. The Western lady turned away to give them some privacy, but Agung and Bambang were watching the show wide-eyed. Stephen wasn't worried about what anyone else thought of the tearful reunion. He pulled away just enough to look into her eyes. She was so beautiful. And she was here.

"Excuse me," Bambang finally interjected. "I'm so sorry to interrupt but may we go back to the investigation now? People are waiting for us."

The request was ignored. "I was so worried that I lost you," Leah sniffled with her head still buried in his chest.

"I was so worried that I would never see you again," Stephen answered, pulling back his head again so he could get another look into her face, which was smeared from her crying. He was beaming a bright smile through his own tears.

"Are you okay? Were you hurt? How did you get here?" she asked, dabbing the tears from her eyes with her fingers and straightening out her blouse.

"I need to ask you the same thing," he said, pulling her back toward him.

"I guess we have a lot of talking to do," she said, looking up and wiping the tears from his face.

"We do," he said, gazing at her again deeply and so grateful to have her in his arms that he offered a silent prayer of thanks to God. She was the most wonderful creature he had ever seen in his life and he would never let her go again.

CHAPTER TWENTY-SEVEN

The meeting was re-adjourned, with all players seated around the two pulled-together folding tables. There were enough policemen in the break room to stand guard over each invited guest, victim and/or suspect.

Agung took his seat again between Carlton and the police captain, Bambang was perched at the corner of the table closest to Carlton, and Mustafal with the *"terdakwa"* sign still hanging around his neck continued to glare at Dina and Happy from across the table. Johanna Grazen made introductions and seated herself, and Leah and Stephen held hands tightly and caught up in whispered tones.

With even more English speakers in the room, the captain seemed even in less control of the meeting. He kept writing notes to himself while Carlton charged ahead. "If we could, let's try to answer the questions as quickly as possible that need to be asked in the group, and then later the police can take one-on-one statements or do individual interrogations on their own." Agung attempted to translate the convoluted sentence to the Indonesian speakers but Stephen could tell he was having trouble.

Mustafal butted in, saying something calmly in Indonesian at first but then toward the end getting more animated. Agung looked reluctant to translate whatever he was trying to communicate and Bambang jumped in to help. "He says he wants to make a full confession about what he did with his two partners."

"Before we hear from my kidnapper Mustafal, I would like to make a full statement," said Stephen, suddenly not feeling as confident as he did in the hallway. Agung enthusiastically translated. Mustafal attempted to talk over him but his police guard gripped his shoulder tightly, indicating that the foreigner would go first.

The captain responded and Agung translated: "Yes, please go on."

Stephen kept his attention on the emotional center of gravity in the room, Carlton Easley. "My understanding is that you had quite an ordeal getting here, Mr. Easley." Carlton looked like he was about to respond with another grunt of disapproval, but then he suddenly nodded and smiled, seemingly pleased that someone finally empathized with him. Maybe the big old grumpy guy just needed some comfort.

While Agung translated for the Indonesian speakers, Stephen prayed under his breath. He asked God for both help and mercy for what he was about to do. "I'm afraid I owe you an apology, sir. I owe everyone here an apology, my poor wife most of all." Leah squeezed his hand and was watching him very attentively. Everyone was waiting for an explanation and the only sound was the chattering of factory workers just outside the door and the rolling and chopping sounds of cigarettes being made. The floor was his.

He rose from the bench and walked around to the head of the table next to the captain. The sudden movement made the two standing officers jittery. He felt like a lawyer making his opening statement to a fully attentive and engaged jury.

"I'm afraid I have made a real mess of things," he began. "I have a lot of apologizing to do, both to the people inside this room and the people outside."

"The people outside?" Carlton grumbled. "There are more people involved in this?"

A few English speaking people chuckled. "I can explain everything, if you can be patient." Carlton didn't look like he could but Stephen continued. "This is a strange request, but I would like to ask my friend Agung to stand in the doorway and translate my explanation loud enough so that those of us inside and those outside can hear my full story. As I said I owe them an apology too."

"I don't understand," Carlton interrupted. "What would you possibly need to say to them? Is that who you mean by the people outside? The workers here?"

"Again, Carlton...Mr. Carlton, I beg your patience. All that will be made clear." Carlton looked to Bambang to see if he had any objections and there were none. Both of them looked too fascinated by what Stephen was about to say to bemoan the loss of working time from their employees.

Agung rose, stepped over the bench and walked to stand in the threshold of the doorway separating the break room and the factory floor. He yelled out a word that must have meant to pay attention and it worked very well. The factory workers who heard him immediately lost interest in their cigarette rolling and their eyes were riveted on the man getting their attention from the doorway of the break room. As the ones closer to him got up from their work stations to walk closer to Agung, a mass movement rippled throughout the large room and within seconds hundreds were jammed around the doorway outside. The rolling and chopping and chattering noises were all stilled, making the factory eerily quiet.

As the moment transpired, Stephen felt like he was watching it all on a movie screen. *Is this really happening?* There he was standing in front of a bewildered and breathless audience, with the most important person in his life at the corner of the table and the man who could probably ruin him at the head of it. He would clip through this quickly and hope that Agung would stick to the sketchy plan, which was still in need of much improvisation.

"On Wednesday morning I arrived here in Indonesia on a business trip. I was supposed to conduct training for the International Courier Services company in Surabaya but I never made it there."

Agung translated first to the seated guest inside the break room, then slightly stepped into the crowd and translated toward them with a great force of volume.

"This is going to take too long," Carlton said impatiently. "Can we get some double translation going? Maybe someone here fluent in English could translate for us and leave your translator out there for the workers."

"Sounds good to me," Stephen said.

"My Indonesian isn't that great but I think it could get the job done," Johanna offered.

"Great," Carlton said. "You are our translator."

Agung stepped deeper into the factory crowd but still within ear shot of Stephen. The workers were packed around him now and looked like they were greatly enjoying the diversion.

Stephen continued. "While at the airport I got into the wrong car."

"You already told us that," Carlton interjected. "Can you come to your point more quickly?"

"Yes, but I didn't tell you why. It wasn't a mistake. This is something I am not proud of, but I got into your car on purpose." As the sentence was translated Stephen could see from the corner of his eye many of the puzzled workers try to get a look at him through the doorway. The facial expressions of the Indonesians inside the break room had also turned to puzzlement.

Carlton leaned in. "What? Why would you do something like that?"

"Honestly sir, I don't really know. For a brief insane moment I wanted to be more spontaneous, tired of living in a box you could say. I wanted to do something that would be totally unexpected. I'm not usually like that though."

Before Agung could finish translating, Carlton shook his head slowly and said flatly, "Stealing my car is not spontaneous, Stephen. That's a crime."

"I know, I know," Stephen said, looking at the police officers. They were engrossed in the narrative and didn't look like they were about to jump up and arrest him. Leah continued to stare at her husband with the same bewildered expression. "I sincerely apologize."

Agung translated the exchange at full volume outside and Johanna struggled through her translation inside. The doubling of the voices made it hard for the Indonesian speakers inside to catch it all and they leaned forward to hear Johanna better. Bambang helped with a word here and there when she couldn't think of it.

"I'll let it go and I won't press charges," Carlton finally responded. "After all, it kept me from getting kidnapped." He looked like he was trying to suppress another laugh to himself.

"Yes, it did," Stephen said with a forced smile. *That is mighty gracious of you.*

"Can you please proceed," Carlton asked, taking a quick peek at the clock on the wall followed by a survey of the people inside and outside the room. "Even people who are on the clock are listening so please proceed."

Johanna seemed to be unsure whether to translate this private conversation but Agung was broadcasting it full blast to the workers.

"Yes, I will. After this man Mustafal kidnapped me, many Indonesians tried to help me, and one even lost his life doing so."

After the last statement was translated to both inside and outside spectators, the place got even quieter. Stephen realized that Leah hadn't known yet someone had died on his behalf and it was a lot to process. She looked up at him through reddened eyes and tried to smile. Even Carlton was speechless for a few seconds then finally stammered, "I'm, uh, sorry to hear that."

"Yes, me too. He was a hero and taught me much. His name was Pak Donri and I would like to make sure that his surviving family knows the honorable circumstances of his death and my deep appreciation for his sacrifice."

The translation followed and the captain jotted some more notes down. Stephen paused to gather his thoughts and looked up to Agung still standing in the doorframe and waiting for the next statement. Stephen nodded toward him with a slight and knowing smile.

"And so, Mr. Easley, you know the character of the Indonesian people, as I do now. You know how friendly and helpful they are, how hospitable and hard working. As I said they are even willing to give their lives." He walked slowly to the doorway closer to Agung.

"Well, I don't know about all that," Carlton cut in, "but I am sorry to hear of your friend's death." Stephen could tell from the cadence of Agung and Johanna's voices superimposing over his own that Carlton's response wasn't translated. One person in the factory crowd shouted something that sounded like an "Amen" and others echoed a chorus of approval. Stephen turned and smiled at them and he thought he could hear a few lightly applauding.

"These are good people, Mr. Easley. They would only do something extreme if they felt pushed into it. Only if their conditions were so bad, and they were so stepped on for so many years, so trapped, like a volcano that holds its breath for years and finally one day...boom!" He shouted out the last word as a thundering sound effect.

"I have no idea where you are going with this. Maybe it's post-traumatic stress disorder or something but you aren't really making sense. I can appreciate that you have gone through a lot but please come to your point more quickly."

All eyes around the table quickly darted back to Stephen after the interruption. "My point is that you see this too, Mr. Carlton. From what I gather you are a reasonable man, and you have come to learn what kind of conditions these people are in."

The translation sailed out to the crowd and the murmur of approval grew louder.

"This is quite enough." Carlton started to rise. "I have no idea what you're talking about." The swivel chair squeaked and leaned over to its weak side. "I don't know if you're some kind of liberal nut here, but we've got bigger fish to fry."

Johanna looked unsure if she should offer all of this to the break room listeners and timidly started into her translation. Agung had no such inhibitions and was translating in full volume to the animated crowd. They responded with a burst of applause and loud shouts.

"What are you telling these people?" Carlton stood and demanded of Agung, who couldn't see him from his vantage point or hear him from all the whooping and hollering. "You are translating wrong. Stop it right now."

As Agung kept translating and his statements were met by an eruption of more ecstatic shouts and rowdy applause and gleeful hollering outside. Carlton's loud objections were drowned out by the raucous joy.

Stephen looked through the doorway into the faces of the simple factory workers, slapping each other on the back and smiling widely. A tear streamed down the face of one elderly woman and she hugged a toothless co-worker. The workers crammed around the door and looked into the break room. A couple of the workers in the front of the crowd ducked and entered, looking unsure of themselves at first, and walked over to Bambang and shook his hand. Then they reached out to shake Carlton's hand but he balled his fists and wouldn't return the gesture. He looked furious. The two workers' initial actions punctured an unseen boundary, opening a floodgate into the break room and filling it with dozens more factory workers. The small room was stuffed full of laughing and congratulating workers, all wanting to have some warm words with Carlton. A policeman stood and blew his whistle.

"What is going on here?" Carlton shouted over the din toward Stephen. "What did he just tell them?"

"I think just what you said." Stephen cut through the crowd to get closer to Carlton. "But I'm not exactly sure how the translation went. Something may have been lost."

"Ask him what he said," Carlton demanded, still dodging the people trying to shake his hand.

Bambang tugged Carlton's sleeve from behind. "The workers say you will give them raises and better working conditions like shorter shifts and guarantee workers' rights."

"What was that?" he demanded, still getting nudged from behind by well-wishers.

Stephen stifled a grin he was careful to keep out of Carlton's line of sight. By this time all the seated guests were up on their feet, and bracing themselves against the impact of the celebratory crowd pressing in.

"Get these people out of here," Carlton commanded Bambang. "We need to talk and finish this investigation."

"Today they already have a long lunch break because of Friday prayers," Stephen heard Bambang tell Carlton with a loud yet somehow still polite voice. "Should I let them go to their Friday prayers earlier?"

"Yes, yes, just get them out of here."

Bambang made the announcement and a louder chorus of cheers went up. Before they began filing out of the room all of them wanted a farewell handshake with Carlton Easley. "They are asking permission to leave," Bambang explained to him.

"Yes, I see that. Just get them out of here."

It took several minutes for the room to clear. Everyone was taken aback by the hurricane of humanity that stormed into the room, and were all standing with hushed silence in its aftermath.

Finally, Bambang broke the stunned silence. "Mr. Carlton, they say thank you and they will offer special prayers for you today. Normally many of them do not go to mosque to pray, just go home to rest. But all of them say they will go to mosque today to thank God and to pray for you and thank God for you."

Carlton didn't look like he appreciated the extra intercessions and thanksgivings he would be receiving today. He sat back down in his swivel chair, defeated, tired and breathing heavily. A few followed his example to seat themselves, but most of them remained standing, looking like they wanted to leave but not sure if the meeting was officially over.

"What did you tell them?" Carlton said softly to Agung without looking at him.

"I just told them what I hear, sir, that bigger wage we try and then you say after that you say like shorter shift."

Stephen could see Carlton rewinding the tape in his mind. His face snarled up into a disgusted grimace and half-shouted, "You know I didn't say any of that. You lied to them. Why would you do that?"

"Oh, sorry sir," Agung said meekly. "I say wrong."

Bambang surveyed the damage on Carlton's face. "Should I call them back in and say there has been a mistranslation?" he asked his supervisor cautiously.

"No, just get me to the hotel," he breathed out barely audibly. "I need a change and a shower before I can deal with any more of this."

Carlton slowly shuffled out of the room by himself. The fight was gone out of him just like that. He didn't say anything to anyone around the table, half of them sitting and half of them still standing. Bambang followed him out of the room, calling out questions and apologies after him. No one was sure what to do or who was in charge in the leadership vacuum that Carlton had left behind.

The police captain, getting looks from his fellow officers, yelled something after the exiting pair. Stephen assumed it was a reminder that Carlton's own personal investigation wasn't finished yet. But he didn't follow them out of the room nor did any of his fellow officers. Instead he took his place in the swivel chair at the head of the table. With the domineering bulldog gone, everyone except Mustafal looked more relaxed.

Agung sat back down beside Dina and held hands. Stephen held Leah's hand again and squeezed it slightly. He hoped she wasn't too upset over his spontaneous identity theft. Johanna was looking at the officer and waiting for him to begin the questions, and seemed to be the one who would be doing the translating, as obviously Agung could no longer be trusted with the task. The captain looked unsure how to start and Johanna said something in Indonesian, maybe another offer to translate.

The officer nodded yes and Johanna rose from her place and sat herself in Agung's former spot. Instead of directly launching into more questioning, the captain conferred first with Johanna in a low whisper. Stephen looked around the table while they talked. Mustafal was glancing over at Agung and Dina sitting together and looking perturbed, like he might lunge at them again if it weren't for his cuffs. There were a lot of charges against him, not only murder but also kidnapping and stealing a car. Hopefully he would take the blame for all of it and the police would let Dina and Happy go. The remaining officers were keeping their eyes on him. Stephen thought of Donri. The old man would have surely enjoyed that last scene, but may not have approved of the shady scheme that he and Agung had hatched. *But I bet he would have at least laughed.*

Finally, Johanna made the announcement, "The police would like to release the Americans here and put them under the care of the U.S. Consulate. I will take Stephen and Leah back to our Surabaya office for debriefing and for your statements. They have some questions about the death of the elderly man they want answered. The officers will take all the Indonesians back to the police station for a full investigation of the kidnapping."

"I'm sorry," Stephen broke in, trying to make his request sound as polite has possible. "Could we take Dina, Agung, and Happy along with us to Surabaya too?"

Johanna conferred again with the captain. "The police captain wants to know why," she translated back to Stephen.

"Well, the way I see it these three Indonesians are heroes. I want to make sure we have the full chance to thank them.

The police can focus their initial investigation on Mustafal, and then later the three heroes can make their statements. Let them focus on the bad guy first and let us at least take our heroes to lunch first." Stephen counted to himself that he had used the word "heroes" three times in his explanation and he hoped the identity would stick.

Johanna translated and the captain cracked a smile. "Yes, okay mister," he said directly to Stephen and both men smiled.

"Is there enough room in your car, Johanna?"

"I think so," she said, silently calculating. "There is a saying here about how many Indonesians can you squeeze into a car. The answer is always one more." She chuckled at her own joke when no one else did. She then recovered with a nervous cough and said, "I think we can all fit if you don't mind squeezing."

"I don't mind squeezing," Leah announced. Stephen liked that.

The meeting was officially adjourned and the police escorted Mustafal out of the room first. Johanna led the happily reunited couple and the three newly named heroes— Agung, Happy and Dina—to the parking lot. There Agung said he really appreciated the offer to lunch but his family was on the way to pick him up at the factory.

"They have been very worried about me and want to see me as soon as possible."

"I totally understand that," Stephen said while patting Agung on the shoulder. "But do you think maybe they could join us for lunch too? I would like to thank them and apologize to them."

Agung thought about the request for a second, looked down at his cell phone which the police must have already returned to him, and Dina walked over to confer. Her soft words showed he didn't need much convincing and he texted his family the change of plans.

"Thanks, Agung. I still feel bad for getting you mixed up in this and would like to meet your family."

"We too have an expression in Indonesian about mixing, Mr. Stephen. It's called *campur tangan* and it means 'to mix the hand,' like a painter mixing his hand in the paint. It can have a positive or negative meaning, but for me this *campur tangan* has been positive."

"Well, I'm glad you think it has been positive," Stephen laughed. "Thanks for mixing your hand in my paint."

Agung smiled at the expressed gratitude and looked back to Dina, saying something in Indonesian. Stephen could pick out the *campur tangan* word and he assumed he was thanking her for the same sentiment.

The factory parking lot was emptying out. Workers were starting up their motorcycles, excited about their upcoming raises and off to enjoy an extra-long lunch break. There was an air of celebration. The ones following through on their promise would head toward a local mosque to thank Allah for Carlton Easley's generous heart. The police car fired up its engine and sirens. Mustafal did not look up as he was being driven away. Carlton was already gone, presumably to his longed-for hotel, and Bambang was probably right behind him, apologizing. Stephen felt amazingly great—free and unburdened for the first time in three days, maybe years. He kept on holding Leah's hand, even as all six of them plus the driver packed into Johanna's official-looking government car and they were all whisked away back to Surabaya.

CHAPTER TWENTY-EIGHT

Stephen thoroughly enjoyed the late lunch celebration at a trendy steak restaurant in Surabaya, even though he felt rather embarrassed walking in with his shredded, socked feet and unkempt appearance.

It was a large crowd to seat—Leah, Agung, Dina, Happy, Johanna, and himself, along with a half dozen of Agung's relatives. Stephen hoped the U.S. State Department would pick up the tab.

Johanna and Agung sat toward the middle and helped translate to both sides of the table. The food was great and the conversation rich, each person taking a turn to tell his or her side of the story from the last few days. Stephen recounted the story of escaping from the hostage house thanks to Dina's hidden key and running like a madman through the village. Agung's relatives really got a kick out of that. He also relished telling the tale of Donri's bravery.

"I wish you could have met him," he said privately to Leah. "He had a real impact on my life and helped me to see how I have been hiding for far too long." Leah seemed to not know how to respond to that, either delighted just to have him back or not sure exactly who he was.

As they were waiting for the check, the people who had email addresses exchanged them. Johanna said she would get Stephen's full statement back at the consulate and then turn it into the police afterwards. He said yes on the condition that they stop at a shoe store on the way there. She glanced down at his feet and readily agreed. She also let Agung, Happy and Dina know that the police were allowing them to go home and get rested before coming in to the police station the next day to give their full statements. They were elated.

In the restaurant's parking lot, with traffic roaring by, Johanna texted her driver to bring the car around while Stephen started bidding his farewells to Agung, Happy and Dina. He hugged them all tightly and warmly and they weakly and awkwardly hugged him back. "They must not be huggers in this society," Leah whispered to her husband.

"I could tell, but I just felt like hugging them," he answered back in the same hushed tone. "They really are my heroes. Well, two of them are kidnappers turned heroes, I guess."

"We've got a lot of catching up to do," she said.

"Yes we do. And I want to tell you more about Om Donri. He really got me thinking."

"I'd love to hear all about him."

"I'll give you the full story. I would like to track him down and go to his funeral. I assume it will be tomorrow."

"Of course," said Leah, stroking his back.

Agung pardoned himself into their conversation for one last personal goodbye. Stephen promised to stay in touch and expressed his heartfelt thanks, apologizing again for getting him into the whole mess.

"No need to apologize, Mr. Stephen. Because of the mess I meet Dina," he said, turning to his blushing new girlfriend. "I thank you."

"And I thank you for all your help in translating, especially to the factory workers during my speech."

Agung grinned with a mischievous twinkle in his brown eyes. *Campur tangan.*

Agung's family handled the transportation arrangements to get the three heroes home. They doubled and tripled up on different motorcycles and Happy looked back to cast one last goodbye. He kept smiling and waving until they were out of sight.

"So Stephen," Leah said playfully. "That is your real name, right? Where to now?"

~~▢~~

Stephen, now sporting a pair of new tennis shoes, placed his first call late Friday afternoon from the U.S. Consulate to the International Courier Services office in Surabaya. He explained that he had been kidnapped, but had now been released, and that everything was all right. His wife had come from America to find him and they were reunited. They were shocked to hear the news but glad he was okay. He apologized for not being able to do the training on this trip and for the inconvenience this may have caused their company. Be assured, Stephen told them, another trainer from the U.S. headquarters would be dispatched shortly. That commitment would not be able to be fulfilled by him personally as he was being encouraged to undergo post-traumatic shock therapy. They fully understood and wished him well. He omitted to tell them that right after a friend's funeral, the post-traumatic shock therapy would be taking place at a five-star hotel alone with his wife in Bali.

His second call was to Fiona's house to talk to Randall and Tristan. Leah objected at first, reminding him that it was still too early there and they were probably sleeping. Stephen said he couldn't wait—he had to hear their little voices. A groggy-sounding Fiona answered the phone and after a few minutes put two sleepy kids on the phone. Stephen put the call on speaker phone from Johanna's office and both parents delighted to hear their children's voices and personalities coming through loud and clear. Stephen told them that Daddy would come home next week and that he and Mommy were having a good time and would bring them back some cool presents from Indonesia. The kids each mumbled their thanks and he wiped away a tear of gratitude. Leah got on the phone and thanked Fiona again for watching the kids, got a few details about their little lives away from Mommy, and hinted that she and Stephen were going to be fine.

Right after the call Johanna rushed into her office where Stephen and Leah were still chatting and catching up.

"You're not going to believe this, Stephen. Your wallet has been found!"

"Oh," he said surprised. "By Mustafal? How were you able to get it so fast?"

"No, by some con artist known as Dungaree Doug. He has other aliases and was going by the name Chopper here. They found four other wallets on him and caught him at a hotel on Mt. Bromo. Seems that local and international police have been after him for a while."

"Wow. I thought Mustafal had it." Stephen remembered the hard bump from Chopper at the airport and the spilled contents of his travel pouch.

"I guess things aren't always what they seem."

Leah jumped in. "You got that right. I hardly recognize my husband here. Are you sure this is Stephen Cranton?"

"We could fingerprint him if you'd like, ma'am," Johanna offered in a funny, police voice.

Stephen laughed.

"I guess I'll trust that he's the one."

Acknowledgments

It's embarrassing for me to admit how long it took to get this book from silly idea to published project (nine years if you must know).

But I am so grateful for the many friends who helped me throughout the creative journey, editing various versions on both sides of the Pacific. Thanks so much to Paul Richardson, Stephanie Myers, Sarah Williams, Rhonda Pope, Deborah Wittig, Peter Nevland, Paula Berinstein, Michael V. Carlisle, Courtney Wyrtzen, Tim Stewart, Ben Taylor, Dave Thomas, Russell Grigsby, Deb Ploskonka, Meredith Perry, Linda Perry, Jay Hall, Ed McGuckin, Kim Ramsey, Russell Rankin, Jennifer Korstad, Erik Korstad, Cindy Moore, Linda Lopez and Susan Sills. My sincere apologies for anyone I'm forgetting (nine years is a long time). Also thanks so much to Hilary Combs for designing the cover.

And finally, last but not least, overflowing thanks to my high school sweetheart and beautiful bride Stephanie—for her graciousness, patience with me and enduring love.

About the Author

Mike O'Quin Jr. served as missionary in Indonesia for nearly 14 years. He and his family fell in love with the Indonesian people and thoroughly enjoyed their own Javanese adventure. He thought the island would make a colorful backdrop for a story of a man finding his heart.

He and his family now live in Austin, Texas, where he serves on staff with a local church called Hope in the City.

You can find Mike on Twitter, @mikeoquin, and follow him along by reading his blog and listening to his podcasts at www.FaithActivators.com.

41415313R00187

Made in the USA
Charleston, SC
30 April 2015